# Inherited

Bernadette Y. Connor

BEE-CON
BOOKS

PUBLISHED BY BEE-CON BOOKS
P. O. BOX 27708, Philadelphia, PA 19118

This novel is a work of fiction. Any reference to real people, events, establishments, organizations, or locales are intended only to give the fiction a sense of authenticity. Any resemblance to actual persons, living or dead, organizations, institutions or locales is purely coincidental.



ISBN 0-9715838-4-6

Library of Congress Control Number: 2005900099


Printed in the United States of America
First Edition

2 5 4 - 4 9 5 4

# Acknowledgements

I thank God for once again allowing this servant to deliver another work of fiction to those who enjoy a good read as a respite from life's daily grind.

To my army of angels, I extend infinite thanks and blessings from the well of my soul. This project has arrived to my readers because you were there for me when I needed you. A special thanks goes out to Patricia Johnson for demanding that this book be my next to be published.

To my technical contributors; Blanche Patterson-Day for her endless hours of preparing promotional material, Paul Stallings for the graphics, Lisa Cross, web-mistress from Cross The Net, for an outstanding web presence and Ronald G. Patterson for his work with the Ebooks.

To my faithful readers, your ceaseless dedication gives me the drive to continue. As long as you're in my corner, I'll answer the bell.

## DEDICATED

**TO THE GREAT MEN WHO CREATED MY VISION OF MANHOOD**

Beverley Mosley (“Gran’daddy”)
John Moody (“Gran’pop”)
The man who became a father for the first time at thirty-four
who insisted he was too young to be called “Daddy”
Richard O. Smith (“Richard”)
Willie C. Smith (“Uncle Bill”)

## *CHAPTER ONE*

In the muted lighting of the bedroom, Derrick leaned back on the cool, thick, brass rails of his headboard and watched Cassandra dress. Derrick was thoroughly mesmerized by the sight of her taut, voluptuous body's fluid motion. Her smooth, deep copper skin teased the lights by casting shadows in the most provocative places. Cassandra had somehow evolved the simple act of dressing into a carefully choreographed dance of sensuality; the way she flicked her hair, or gave a seductive glance over her shoulder as she lovingly stroked her stocking covered leg. Soft jazz from the stereo served as her accompaniment.

Inwardly, Derrick wrestled with his rule of never dating a woman more than three times. He truly enjoyed Cassandra's company. If only she had not uttered one of the many bachelor-threatening latch phrases, “I love you,” Derrick might have dared to extend her stay in his life. The mere thought of belonging to any one woman made Derrick uncomfortable. After all, there were so many beautiful women to choose from. How could a man simply select one and never be attracted to any of the others ever again? How? In Derrick's estimation, it could not be done without acupuncture, hypnosis, or a witch doctor's long-winded, incomprehensible chanting and a good dusting.

The telephone rang as Cassandra sat in Derrick's wing chair pretending to comb her hair. Derrick knew she wouldn't comb it with abandon because three quarters of those heavily highlighted, shoulder-length locks were masterfully weaved. Derrick never answered the ringing telephone. As a matter of fact, he acted as if he never heard it.

Turning to the café-au-lait Adonis of her dreams, Cassandra smiled sweetly and asked, "Are you going to answer that?"

The coolest of casual smiles caressed Derrick's full, intricately sculptured lips when he responded, "If I answer, I'll be distracted."

"Distracted from what?"

"You."

Cassandra gave a nonchalant wave and said, "Please, Derrick. You just don't want me to know, for a fact, that you're seeing other women. In case you think I haven't noticed you never answer any of my questions, I have."

Feigning his trademark ignorance, Derrick asked innocently, "What questions?"

Standing and smoothing the tantalizingly form-fitting dress over her luscious body, Cassandra asked sarcastically, "Why don't I see you more often? Why haven't you returned my calls this week? Where have you been?"

Derrick bit his bottom lip briefly, folded his hands in his naked lap and replied, "I didn't answer those questions because I knew I didn't have an answer that would satisfy you."

"What kind of crap are you trying to peddle now, Derrick?"

"If I say to you I have work to do, I was visiting my mother, or I like to spend time alone; what would your response be?"

With crisp confidence, Cassandra responded, "Bullshit."

"Exactly as I thought, sweetheart. I have options. Waste a lot of time defending my bullshit arguing with you, or allowing you to form your own opinions and enjoying the time I spend with you. I prefer the latter."

Cassandra slowly strolled over to the bed. Like a predatory lioness, she draped herself over the length of Derrick's nude body and licked his lips. He didn't move. She purred, "While your reasoning escapes me, I must admit I prefer the latter, too." The long, hot kiss that followed threatened to rekindle the earlier fire of the night. Of course, Derrick had no complaints. After all, he was at home and had absolutely no place to go. It was Saturday. Cassandra could stay as long as she wanted and Derrick was willing to play any game she thought of.

Eventually, Cassandra pulled her mouth away from Derrick's and gave his lip a promising nibble. With a great sigh, she said, "I wish I could stay, sweetheart, but I've got to serve the good citizens of our fair city early in the morning. I'm the relief dispatcher this weekend. Would you like to take me to brunch afterwards? We could spend the rest of the day together."

Derrick meant it when he said, "I would love to." He also meant it when he added, "But I can't."

Sullenly, Cassandra asked, "Why not, Derrick Dawes?"

"Sunday is always a busy day for me, Cassandra. I have to get ready for the work week and visit my parents."

"I could hang out while you get ready for the work week and go with you to visit your parents."

"I don't think so, Cassandra. Not tomorrow. Maybe some other day."

Frustrated tears burned Cassandra's eyes when she asked with agitation, "Why not?"

This was the part of relationships Derrick despised. The never-ending string of "whys." If he could find a woman who never asked why, he would marry her in a flash.

Still Derrick didn't want to hurt Cassandra's feelings, and God knows he didn't want her to start crying. Weeping women put knots in his stomach. So he took the conversation to a place where he thought he might be able to get out of it rationally.

"Do you really think our relationship is strong enough to drag families into it already, Cassandra?"

Blinking once, Cassandra answered emphatically, "Yes. I would take you to meet my family right this minute."

Never caught off guard on this subject, Derrick asked in succession, "What would you tell them about me, Cassandra? What's my occupation? Where do I work? How do you know? What are my likes? Dislikes? What's my favorite food? Color?"

Stuttering, she replied, "You didn't ask me any of those questions last night, or two weeks ago. Why are you asking them now?"

Smiling comfortably, Derrick said, "Because you're trying to make this into something more than it is. We're still in the enjoying each other's company stage of the game. I don't know the answers to many of those questions about you either."

Seething, Cassandra asked, "Are you saying this is purely a sex thing for you?"

"No. But I am saying we haven't progressed beyond that point yet. We've been to dinner three times. Slept together three times. How many conversations have we shared? Honestly? What pertinent questions have you asked me? What's transpired between us that points toward family meetings? Before taking a woman home to my mother, I'd like to know a little more than what she prefers sexually, Cassandra. And honestly, that's the gist of what I know about you."

Without another comment, Cassandra snapped her purse closed and strolled out of the room. Derrick got up, slid into his teal and navy terry cloth robe, picked up his keys and followed her. She had already descended the stairs and was standing at the door. Derrick knew the dead bolt was the only thing keeping her there.

As he approached, Derrick said softly, "I really don't want you to go away upset, Cassandra. You have your way of looking at things and I have mine. Maybe we should discuss them."

Unemotionally, Cassandra responded, "If you want to discuss life, Derrick, surf the net. If you want to live life, give me a call. Good night."

She stepped away from the door, clearing the way for him to unlock it. Tilting his head in resignation, Derrick found the door key and put it in the lock. He hesitated momentarily. Holding onto Cassandra crossed his mind again. His attraction to her was slightly more than physical and he knew it. Cassandra's conversations lacked disciplined structure, but there was something endearing about her empty and breathless chatter. The very traits that made Cassandra delightful company had condemned the relationship. She had slept with Derrick without knowing anything about him. There was no intelligent, in-depth suspicious female inquisition. Derrick knew that Cassandra would have just as readily accepted him telling her he was the American Ambassador to Saigon as she would have been to hear he was an electrical engineer. What he did for a living did not matter to her. Cassandra had chosen Derrick for the same reason he had chosen her—she simply liked what she saw.

Standing there looking down at this magnificently packaged vessel of unlimited, uninhibited pleasure made the greater part of Derrick shout, "Open the damn door! Now!" And, as always, Derrick listened to the greater part of himself. He opened the door and silently watched Cassandra walk out of his life, the way so many others had.

# *CHAPTER TWO*

The ringing telephone woke Derrick at seven o'clock on Sunday morning. Not in the mood for conversation yet, he let it ring. He would listen to the messages later. It was probably his mother or sister wanting to know what time he would be there for dinner anyway.

No matter what, Derrick always felt women were crowding him. His father often said, "If you let them, women will smother you to death."

Derrick sat on the side of the bed and ran his hand over his coarse, short black hair. He looked at the telephone, considered calling Cassandra and trying to patch things up, thought about next week's chorus of whys and ditched the idea. Instead, he hoisted himself from the bed, slipped into baggy gray jogging shorts, a green cotton tee shirt and headed for the basement. An hour of rowing and running would clear his head.

By ten, Derrick was showered, shaved, fed and in the process of making his bed. The telephone rang again. He moved to answer it and decided against it. Derrick resumed what he was doing, relaxed and read the newspaper until noon.

Derrick loved spending time alone in his new two-bedroom townhouse. There was a fireplace in the living room, master bedroom and the basement recreation room. Two gleaming black and white tile bathrooms upstairs. Solid white powder rooms on the first floor and lower level. A midnight blue and silver kitchen, with an abundance of morning sunshine. Plush purple carpeting in every other room; his very own laundry room, parking space and private entrance. What more could a man ask for?

After years in an apartment and hotels on the road, the peace and quiet of his townhouse made it worth every penny he was paying. Derrick could have afforded a home years ago, but he couldn't persuade himself it was worth the extra expense. The day he came home and found he had no appliances or clothes drove him to the decision.

A little after noon, Derrick felt he had lounged enough. He would listen to his messages before dressing and heading for his parents' home for dinner. There were the usual harem messages left by extremely creative women with varying distinctive and alluring styles. Karen, Tyra, Khalia, Shawna and Cassandra—each wanting to know when he would be calling, or seeing them again. Cassandra had reconsidered her position on their stalemate and now thought it worth discussing.

Derrick smiled when his sister's tiny voice pleaded with him to come to dinner. A Sunday without her two big brothers would throw Deandra into a pouting fit for the entire day. Derrick knew her next call was to their eldest brother, David. Being born when they were fifteen and sixteen made Deandra feel like an only child most of the time—never on Sunday though. David and Derrick showed up for her with sports injuries, contagious diseases and hangovers.

A frown of confusion claimed Derrick's handsome face as he listened to the final three messages. The first message said, "Hello, Mr. Dawes, this is Mrs. Monet, calling from Metropolitan Hospital. I don't mean to alarm you, but your wife left her room sometime before dawn this morning. The staff seems to think she may have left the hospital. She was fine the last time they checked her vitals, so I wouldn't be concerned about her health. Please give us a call if she's at home, her release forms were not signed by the doctor. She wasn't scheduled to leave until tomorrow.

"Oh, and don't forget to bring your medical information when you come in. Mrs. Dawes didn't have it with her when she was admitted. The emergency circumstances forced us to admit her without it."

Derrick stared at the answering machine as if it had somehow become possessed. He waited for it to emanate a bright green glow and pulsate. It didn't. Instead, it beeped and that strange woman's voice began her second bizarre message.

"Hello, Mr. Dawes. This is Metropolitan Hospital calling again. If we do not hear from you or your wife before five this evening, we will be forced to bring Social

Services into this situation. Ask for Mrs. Monet when you call or come in."

Talking out loud to himself, Derrick asked the answering machine, "Metropolitan Hospital? Social Services? My wife? What the hell are you talking about?"

The third and final message sounded both angry and impatient. It made absolutely no sense to Derrick. The origin had to lie in someone's idea of a joke was his guess.

"Mr. Dawes, this is Mrs. Monet, calling from Metropolitan Hospital again. I sincerely hope you and your wife don't intend to do what I think you are. If so, there are appropriate forms to be filled out; agencies to be contacted. I implore you to do this the correct way. Otherwise, they will float in limbo for years. This can present you with astronomical legal ramifications, and I'm sure I don't have to speak on the scope of the devastating emotional damages. Please call me before five, 555-9438 extension 512. I hate being a part of these things."

Knowing this had to be a joke, or a clerical mix-up and feeling he should speak up to let this Mrs. Monet off the hook, Derrick dialed the number. He didn't have long to wait for Mrs. Monet's frustrated and breathless voice to come on the line. There was no greeting from the woman. She dove right into pleading the instant Derrick identified himself.

"Mr. Dawes, please don't abandon your babies this way. You will be sorry for the rest of your life. I don't know why your wife walked out of here without them, but this is not the way to resolve anything. If she was uninsured, we have other remedies."

Still undisturbed by this obviously mistaken revelation, Derrick said calmly, "Mrs. Monet, I have absolutely no idea what you're talking about. I don't have a wife or any babies. There must be another Derrick Dawes."

Hearing paper shuffle, Derrick waited for her response. Seeming uncertain for the first time, Mrs. Monet asked, "Are you the Derrick Dawes who lives at 347 Comly Court?"

Smiling and unperturbed, Derrick said, "Yes, I am. But, I don't have a wife. And before you ask, I don't have a pregnant girlfriend either."

"You have someone, Mr. Dawes. Your name is on the birth certificates of a set of twin girls born early yesterday morning. Their mother's name is listed as Paula Dawes. Her maiden name was Anderson."

Feeling genuine irritation slowly crawl up his abdomen, Derrick snapped, "Look, Miss. I don't know any Paula Dawes or Anderson. I don't have a wife, and I definitely don't have any twins. Girls or boys."

"I think you should at least come down here and take a look at these babies before you go through the entire denial routine, Mr. Dawes."

This time, Derrick did yell, "They're not mine! I don't have to come down and look at them!"

Completely out of patience, Mrs. Monet said sharply, "Okay, Mr. Dawes. If you won't cooperate with me, perhaps the police will have better luck."

"The police?! I've already told you there's been some mistake! They are not my babies!" Derrick screeched in shocked disbelief.

Obviously searching for some form of calm rationale, Mrs. Monet said sternly, "Fine, Mr. Dawes. They're not your babies, but if you're not here by five I will be calling the authorities. It is against the law to abandon newborn babies, and like it or not, all roads lead to you, Mr. Dawes. You will answer to someone regarding these infants."

Straining for composure, Derrick asked, "If I come down there, look at the babies and tell you they're not mine, what then?"

"I won't lie to you. No matter what you do, there will be problems. The babies are too young to establish paternity through DNA. You will have to sign all of the forms to turn them over to an adoption agency or the State. Answer all of the questions. Twenty years from now, these girls will come looking for their parents and they're going to find you, Mr. Dawes. If what you say is true, that young lady has dropped a bomb on you."

"Mrs. Monet, I'm telling you, I have no idea what you're talking about. I don't know a soul who would pull a stunt of this caliber. Can't you look in the directory and see if there's another Derrick Dawes to pick on? Or, are you sure there's no way out of this for me?"

Sighing heavily, Mrs. Monet said, "No. If you sign anything, you're acknowledging paternity. If you don't sign anything, you're going to be charged with abandonment until paternity is established. Of course, you can fight the charge. It will take months, perhaps years, to undo and cost a fortune in attorney and court fees. If the tests show they really are yours, you'll do a little time in jail, pay a hefty fine and all of the medical bills. In the meantime, the babies go into foster care. Not necessarily together."

Cradling his head with his free hand, Derrick moaned, "Jesus."

Sounding sympathetic for the first time, Mrs. Monet said, "Come down, Mr. Dawes. Let's try to handle this with some dignity. Two little lives are dangling in the wind."

Hoping with all of his heart that this was an elaborate prank pulled by his brother, one of his fraternity brothers, or a demented co-worker, Derrick nodded his head slowly and said, "Yeah. Okay. I'll be there in about an hour."

Derrick pressed the release button and dialed his parents' number immediately. It rang a few times before David answered. David knew the moment he heard his younger brother's stunned greeting, something was wrong. His questions began immediately.

"What's up, Dude?"

"I need you and Mom to meet me at Metropolitan, David."

"Why? What's wrong? Are you sick or hurt? You want me to come over there to get you?"

"No. I just want you to bring Mom down to the hospital and meet me in the lobby. Tell her to bring some baby pictures or something."

Astounded by Derrick's strange request, David asked, "Baby pictures? What does she need those for? What about Dad? Do you want me to bring him too?"

"No, David! Just Mom and the pictures."

"Okay. You've got it. We'll be there in about thirty minutes. You sure you don't want to tell me what's going on before we get there?"

"You wouldn't believe me if I told you. I don't believe it myself. See you down there."

When Derrick replaced the telephone this time, he told himself, "Stay calm, guy. They will have found their error by the time you get there. They have to. No one would really dump a set of twins on anybody like you. What would she think you would do with them? You don't know dick about babies. You've never taken care of anyone, except yourself. Not even a dog.

"Somebody's going to be waiting for you in that lobby, laughing his ass off. It has to be a joke. They're going to get a real charge out of the fact that you called your mother.

Don't worry about that though, because it won't matter when you put your fist in his jaw anyway."

Still mumbling reassurances to himself, Derrick dressed in tan khakis, a white dress shirt and loafers. He took his time. Looking disheveled would give them the impression he was nervous, possibly guilty of something. He climbed into his red Nissan 300 and drove to the hospital. Carefully.

# *CHAPTER THREE*

The first people Derrick saw as he entered the lobby of Metropolitan Hospital were David and Sonya Dawes. His brother, who many thought was Derrick's twin, sat watching their mother pace back and forth nervously; her long and shapely legs still attracting the admiring stares of much younger men. Sonya Dawes was dressed in the beautiful paisley and navy dress David had given her for her birthday, along with the navy blue leather purse and heels Derrick gave her. Sonya's full head of thick, black hair, with an impressive gray streak artistically caressing her forehead and make-up were done to perfection. She remained a strikingly beautiful woman at the age of fifty-five.

Sonya spotted her six-foot-five inch, two-hundred-and-twenty pound baby boy immediately. She raced to meet him halfway. Her eyes and hands busily examined Derrick's face, neck, arms and chest, as she asked urgently, "What's wrong with you?"

"I'm fine, Mom. Really."

Not believing him, Sonya continued her own examination while asking impatiently, "What are we doing here then, Derrick?"

Taking his mother's hands into his own to calm her, Derrick directed her over to where David stood. David and Sonya stared at Derrick with raw fear in their eyes. He hated having to tell them that someone was obviously playing a bad joke on him, but he had to. If this wasn't a joke, he needed their support.

Swallowing hard and licking his lips, Derrick said, "Mom, I got a call from this hospital this morning. They said my wife had left the hospital."

Interrupting immediately, Sonya yelled, "What wife?! If you brought me down here to tell me you married somebody without telling me, Derrick, you brought me to the right place! I'll crack your skull and pay the bill!"

Shaking his head pathetically, Derrick said, "I wish it were something that simple, Mom. This woman who said she was my wife gave birth to a set of twins yesterday."

Impatiently interrupting again, Sonya asked with what sounded like mounting hysteria to Derrick, "What did she do?! Stick you with the bill?! Are you taking up a collection?!! What, Derrick?!! What?!!!"

Again, a heart-sickened Derrick said, "I wish it were something that simple, Mom. She left the babies, and no matter what I do, I'm stuck with them because my name is on their birth certificates."

David and Sonya looked at each other with identical stunned and confused expressions. Shaking his head in absolute denial, David threw his hands up and said, "So what. She left her babies here. What's that got to do with you?"

"Are you listening to me, David? They think the woman was my wife. They think those are my babies. She put my name on their birth certificates. If I don't take them, they're going to call the police and charge me with abandonment. If I sign them away to be adopted, I'm acknowledging paternity. They're not mine. Can't be."

Sonya's lips were moving, but no sound came out. David said sarcastically, "Let them charge you! We'll fight it in court! Come on! Let's get it over with! We'll post your bail and deal with them later. I can call Roger right now, if you want me to."

Speaking in a conspiratorial tone, Derrick said, "I want to see what's going on first. Maybe they'll see where the error is and we can forget the entire thing."

Finally finding her voice, Sonya whispered, "Are you sure they're not your babies, Derrick?"

"As sure as I can be, Mom. I don't know any Paula. That's the mother's name."

Finding her maternal voice, Sonya chanted, "You know this is happening because you and your idiot brother never listen to me. I've told you both a million times not to take loose women home. The minute they see you've got two dollars to rub together, they pull stunts like this. If you say those aren't your babies, I don't want to go see any stray's litter. Let's get out of here. Call Roger, David."

Adamantly, Derrick said, "Mom, I'm not leaving this hospital until I know exactly what's going on. I would prefer it if you two went up there with me. If you don't want to, I'll go alone."

"You're not going anywhere by yourself! You'll probably be stuck with every baby in the nursery! I'll look at them and tell you if they're your babies or not. If they are, you will not be abandoning them, Derrick. No son of mine will ever do anything like that as long as I have a little sense about me. But, if they're not, the State can just start hunting down their sorry mama."

David asked, "Can't they stay here until DNA tests are done? I don't know if just looking at them will prove anything, Derrick. All new babies look alike. None of them really look like anybody."

Sonya hissed, "Typical male response. You have to look at babies with an abstract eye. They do look like somebody. If it looks like a Dawes, it is a Dawes, David. If not, we'll wait for blood tests. Since Derrick can't say with absolute conviction that these definitely are not his; and that is what he's saying by insisting we go up there and look at them, we will give them a look. If their mama shows up in the meantime, I'll kill her personally."

Taking a deep breath, Derrick said, "Okay, let's go up."

Under her breath, Sonya mumbled, "Sticking my child with two babies he don't know nothing about. I'll strangle that wench when I find her. This is what you get when you take up with a bunch of sorry women. Sleeping with men they don't know from Adam. No morals. Bet you won't take just any old thing that's offered to you anymore."

After asking the receptionist where they could find Mrs. Monet, the threesome took the elevator to the fourth floor. The moment the impersonal metal doors slid open, Mrs. Monet stepped forward extending her tiny, smooth, walnut colored hand to David and introduced herself.

David smiled at the pretty little woman with the short, tightly curled auburn hair and said, "Hello, Mrs. Monet. I'm David Dawes. This is my mother, Mrs. Sonya Dawes. And, this is my brother, Derrick."

After shaking Sonya's hand, Mrs. Monet smiled sympathetically up at the apparently shocked man she had spoken to on the telephone. Cradling Derrick's large, soft, yet obviously strong hand in hers, she said, "Relax, Mr. Dawes. I don't know exactly what has happened here, but I will help you in every way I can. Of course, I can not break the law."

Speaking barely above a whisper, Derrick said, "I wouldn't want you to do that, Mrs. Monet. And, I appreciate your help already, for some reason. I take it their mother hasn't returned."

Pursing her lips and shaking her head slowly, Mrs. Monet said solemnly, "No, she hasn't." Still holding onto Derrick's hand, she asked, "Would you like to talk about it, or see the babies first?"

Sonya answered for Derrick, "We would like to see the babies first. We need to get an idea of what we're talking about. These aren't sick babies, are they?"

"No, Ma'am. They're perfect."

"Better be. Derrick's not taking on the responsibility of any sick babies. I don't care who they belong to."

"Okay. If you'll walk down to room 410, I'll have the nurse bring them in so you can get a good look at them."

Sonya nodded and said, "Thank you."

Leading the way for her two towering, handsome sons, Sonya reached the room first. She put her purse down on the dresser, sat down on the edge of the bed and crossed her arms. No conversation was necessary until they saw the babies.

A few minutes later a nurse pushing one Plexiglas bassinet and pulling the other entered the room. Derrick noticed the names on them first. "Baby Girl Dawes No. 1" and "Baby Girl Dawes No. 2" were prominently displayed. The babies were wrapped so tightly with tiny pink skull caps pulled down over their heads that it was impossible to see them.

Without invitation, Sonya stepped right up and lifted Baby Girl Dawes No. 1 from her bassinet and laid her on the bed. Not liking the disturbance, the tiny face grimaced and fist clenched. Sonya opened the blanket and stared. The little agitated creature let out a cry when the cool air struck her body. Derrick and David tried to see from where they stood. Neither made a move in the baby's direction.

After examining the feet and hands of the baby, Sonya pulled her hat from her head. Big black, glossy ringlets circled the tiny pale face. She really let out a cry when the air penetrated her hair.

Sonya sighed, picked the baby up, sat on the side of the bed and said softly, "Okay, open your eyes. I want to see them."

The baby clutched at the air, flailed her arms and wailed with her eyes shut tight in response. As if a signal had gone up, the other baby joined her sister. However, the two crying baby girls had not distracted Sonya from her mission at all. But Derrick said nervously, "You're frightening them, Mom."

"No, I'm not, Derrick. She doesn't like the air. That's all. I want to see her eyes opened."

David asked timidly, "What do you think, Mom? Is she Derrick's?"

Stifling a hitch in her throat, Sonya said, "I won't pass judgment until I see her eyes. Give me those baby pictures out of my purse, David."

David moved toward his mother's purse. Derrick stared at the baby in his mother's arms. From where he stood, she looked like every other baby he had ever seen. There was only one thing that made him uncomfortable. The baby's hairline was exactly like his. A tiny, yet pronounced widow's peak shadowed the forehead.

Shoving his hands into his pockets, Derrick turned his back on his mother and the baby. He wondered, "How did I get into this mess? Who could I have slipped up with? I haven't had unprotected sex since I was a teenager. Nine months ago, I wouldn't have touched Mother Theresa without a condom. There's too much crap flying around for me. So, where did that baby come from? Who's her mother? Why didn't she tell me she was pregnant? What am I talking about? This is a mistake. Those are not my babies."

After a brief pause Derrick answered one of his own questions. "She knew I wouldn't have believed her. I'm looking at these babies and I don't believe it. What am I supposed to do now? I can't take care of two babies. I can't.

"What am I talking about here? Those are not my babies. Lots of people have widow's peaks. Hell, it could fall off in a week or two. Babies change every other day, don't they? I'll just sign whatever I have to. Maybe they'll get decent adoptive parents and never know today ever happened. If they look for me twenty years from now, I'll just explain it as best as I can."

Derrick's chin dropped to his chest when he thought, "If they're mine and I've already signed them away, I'll have to fight to get them back. If I lose, they'll grow up never knowing me, or my family. Probably hate my guts. What if they're the only children I ever have?

"I can't process this shit at all. I'm damned if I do, damned if I don't. I'm just going to have to hold onto One and Two until I know for sure they're not mine, or I find their mother."

David gave his mother the three tiny silver framed pictures she requested and moved toward the other crying baby. She seemed to be struggling inside the tightly bound blanket. Wanting to relieve her distress, David reached in and picked her up. The moment she rested in the fold of his warm, thickly muscled arm, her crying stopped. Then, something happened that made David gasp and hum in alarm—she opened her eyes.

Sonya asked, "What's the matter with you, boy?"

Stuttering, David said, "Mom. Mom. Mom. Look at her eyes. Look at them. Derrick, I think you have a problem."

Making his first tenuous step in their direction, Derrick asked in an unfamiliar paranoid pitch, "What? She does have two eyes, doesn't she, David?"

"You bet, she does . . . and both of them look exactly like yours."

David never acknowledged his likeness to his younger brother. As a matter of fact, they fought long, hard battles over the many comparisons all of their lives. Those were not just Derrick's big, bright, oval eyes with the slightest of exotic tilts he saw in the tiny face—they were his own. David knew those deep aquamarine eyes would turn to a soft caramel brown, like Derrick's, in no time at all.

Sonya said, "Bring her here, David. Let me see."

David walked over to his mother and lowered his ward for her inspection. If he hadn't known better, he would have said the baby looked as if she were inspecting Sonya, too. Getting his first good look at the baby his mother held, David said, "Hey, they're just alike. I mean really just alike."

Smiling at the staring baby girl in David's arms, Sonya said, "David. Sweetheart. They're twins. Obviously identical. And, those are your father's eyes. Take her hat off. I want to see if she's got my mother's peak, too."

Welded to the spot he stood in, Derrick's mind screamed, "Oh God, they are mine! What am I going to do now?!"

Sonya and David's banter wafted through Derrick's mind like a dream. He couldn't discern who was saying what anymore. Someone said, "They've got that double knot on their big toes like Derrick, too. Those are definitely his lips. I can't place that tiny nose though. Must be their mother's. It's cute."

Someone else said, "That must be their mother's hair, too. It's black like Derrick's but it's way too straight. Whoever their mother is, she must be awfully pretty. These babies are definitely the offspring of a pretty woman."

Sonya's distinct voice finally penetrated Derrick's fog, when she yelled, "Derrick! Derrick! Get over here and look at these babies! See if you can tell who their mother is. They look enough like you for me, but she's got some pretty strong genes showing through here, too."

Whining, Derrick said, "Mom, those can't be my babies. I haven't had unprotected sex with anyone in years. The similarities are probably coincidental. A week from now they'll be looking like Flava Flav."

Sonya asked seriously, "Who's that?"

Stifling a laugh, David said, "Ignore him, Mom. The Flav couldn't make babies like these in this life, or any of his next ten."

Mrs. Monet stood in the doorway, watching the Dawes family pour over the babies. She approved of the bonding of the grandmother and brother. However, she was concerned for the tall, elegantly handsome father. He looked as if he were going to fall over any minute now. Mrs. Monet could not control the smile on her face when she remembered her own husband possessing that same look of sickly stunned unease during the birth of their first child.

Observing Derrick's reaction to all of this, it was easy to see that he really did not know a thing about these babies. That was when Mrs. Monet decided she really would do anything she could to make the transition as easy for Derrick as possible. Inheriting a set of twins would be more than the average woman could handle. She didn't want to imagine how overwhelming it was for a single man. The babies could completely destroy any plans he may have for his future. God knows they would test the mettle of any woman he had any romantic designs on.

Mrs. Monet spoke to the gathering. She outlined all of the options open to Derrick. She made it abundantly clear that even after years of legal hassles the original birth certificates would still bear his name and the trail would always lead back to Derrick; and who their mother was meant absolutely nothing to the authorities, so they would not look for her. That would have to be done by Derrick.

Mrs. Monet's closing offer, specifically designed for Derrick's peace of mind was, "You hold onto the babies for three months, we'll do the DNA tests, get the results and move from there. I will not file anything with your name on it until we're sure. That way, you'll have a chance to consult a lawyer and take any appropriate measures available to you for your protection. I do, however, suggest you make payments to the hospital on the bill. If not, the entire thing will be brought to the attention of the administrator. That's the day it will be taken out of my hands."

Derrick responded in solemn defeat, "Okay. I don't have any idea what I'll do with them for three months, Mrs. Monet, but I'll take them. If they're not mine, I'll have to put them up for adoption. I can't keep them. I won't."

Sonya chimed in, "What are you talking about, Derrick? These are definitely your children. You think I don't know my own when I see them. Come over here and look at these baby pictures next to this baby. You can't miss the resemblances."

Derrick screamed at his mother, "You may recognize them, Mom, but I don't! Those babies could, and probably do, belong to anyone! They don't have to be mine! They could be David's!"

David laughed hysterically and said, "You're tripping now, partner. My name's not in this mix. Yours is. And if you don't lower your voice and watch your mouth, the first thing your daughters are going to see is Uncle David turning out Daddy's lights."

# *CHAPTER FOUR*

In the crowded hospital room, Mrs. Monet agreed to give Derrick twenty-four hours to prepare for the girls' homecoming, or the highly unlikely return of their mother. Sonya and David spent another hour adoring the babies and tried to persuade Derrick to come over and hold one of them. Derrick refused. He wouldn't even get close enough to get a good look. Derrick's mind was in an angry turmoil. He honestly felt that if he touched anything, he would wreck it.

Before leaving the hospital, Sonya phoned home to tell Deandra they had a few things to do before they came in. She didn't tell her daughter about the babies, that was Derrick's job. As it was their father, Ethan, would be mumbling under his breath about this for weeks to come. After all, Ethan had done everything he could to steer his sons away from permanent female attachments. Well, Derrick might not be attached to the mother of the babies, but he would definitely have to bond with those two little girls.

After three hours of shopping, Derrick could not believe his mother had actually spent twelve hundred of his hard earned dollars on baby things and came away saying, "That's enough to get you started. You can pick up things you need as you go along."

With at least two of everything loaded into David's jeep, there was no room for Sonya. She rode back to Derrick's house with him. Derrick had not rallied from his silent stupor. He was wrestling with the situation. Sprawled at the root of it all lay his fears.

In an attempt to pry some insight from her least talkative son, Sonya looked straight ahead at the road and asked, "What are you thinking, Derrick?"

With his father's great sigh, Derrick said, "I don't know, Mom. This is too surreal for me. I woke up this morning. Worked out. Ran through the park. Ate breakfast. Showered and read the paper. I did it all alone. Wasn't bothering a soul. Minding my own business. In a few short hours, my entire life has been flipped upside down and I don't even know who flipped it."

"Are you sure you don't know? Have you run all of the names through your mind, Derrick? Did any of your women friends say something a little melancholy that you might not have understood before she left?"

With an arrogant sniff, Derrick replied, "They all said something I didn't understand before they left."

"You didn't understand, or didn't want to understand?"

"Okay, I didn't want to understand any of them, Mom. I'm not ready for a committed relationship. No one believes you when you tell them that up front, so I stopped saying it years ago. God knows I'm not ready for fatherhood. What am I supposed to do with them, Mom?"

"What everybody else does, Derrick. Take care of them and love them. Cross bridges as you get to them and pray. Remember that. Pray a lot."

Derrick pleaded miserably, "Can't they stay with you, Mom? Please? I promise I'll come over every day."

Shaking her head adamantly, Sonya said, "No, sir. Those are your children. I've raised mine. I'll visit you every day."

"But, Mom, I don't know one thing about babies. I'll probably kill at least one of them before the first day ends. Babies need a lot of attention. They cry. Make messes. Please, Mom. Please take them."

"I will not take them. Granted, these babies will either make you or break you. I'm betting you can do it. I raised you. I know you can do it. May take a while for you to get the hang of it, but you will."

"What do I do with them when I go to work, Mom? I'm the chief engineer in the middle of a huge Southland job. I can't just drop it for a maternity leave."

"Look boy, I said I would help you. I'm not going to let you kill what looks like the only grandchildren I'm getting before I die. You will not bring any strangers in to take care of them either. Too many nuts out here for that kind of stuff. As you and your brother are so fond of saying, I've got your back, but I won't do your job, Derrick."

"All right, Mom. I'll do the best I can for the time being. But, I will not attach myself to those babies. If I find out three months from now they're not mine, they're going up for adoption."

"If they're not yours, I'll help you find a nice family for them. Since I already know they are, I'll see that they don't feel too unwelcome while their silly father gets his footing."

"No kid deserves a silly father."

"What are you talking about? That's the only kind anybody gets."

Derrick laughed at his mother's not-so-subtle jab at his father and said, "Well, if they have to be stuck with silly fathers, they should have a sane mother–any kind of a mother. How could she just walk away from two helpless babies, Mom?"

"I'm giving the nut the benefit of the doubt when I say, she thought this would be the best alternative for them."

Derrick's raised voice echoed in the tiny interior when he yelled, "The best alternative! Sticking a man with two babies with no warning!"

As the car’s speed accelerated with Derrick's voice, Sonya said, "Boy, if you don't slow down, those babies won't have a soul. Listen to me, Derrick. When women get pregnant, they're not always prepared for it either. Lord knows pregnancy wreaks havoc on a woman's mind. Since you don't know who she is, you don't know what her circumstances were. Just thank God she didn't do anything really stupid."

"What could have been more stupid than what she did, Mom?"

"She could have left them in the trash. Left them in a parking lot to be run over. Given them to abusive strangers. Sold them on the black market. Hell, Derrick, she could have taken them home and drowned them. Would any of those have made you feel any better?"

"Come on, Mom, she wouldn't have done any of those things. She couldn't be that crazy."

Looking at the handsome profile of her son with compassion, Sonya asked, "What part of the newspapers do you read, Derrick? Terrible things are done to babies every day. Just be glad she didn't take a notion to do any of them to your babies."

Mumbling again, Derrick asked, "Who says they're mine?"

As if reacting to her husband, Ethan, Sonya screamed, "I did!"

They rode the rest of the way in silence. Derrick knew when Sonya started screaming, there was no end to it. He also didn't want her to twist his ear the way she had done David's a month ago for giving her too much lip. With relentless brutality Sonya brought David to his knees for flippantly dismissing her opinion. She dared him to say it again. He didn't.

Parked in front of Derrick's beautiful townhouse, the three unloaded David's jeep. David and Derrick put the cans of formula and bottled water in the kitchen cabinets. Derrick examined the funnel and bottle-brushes. He thought about asking David what they were for and after thinking his brother didn't know anything about babies either, declined. Instead, they carried the many boxes of Pampers, undershirts, sleepers, blankets, bibs, towels, washcloths, a combination bathtub and changing table, and a seemingly endless supply of baby products up to the guest room.

Wondering where his mother had gotten to, Derrick called out for her. Sonya wasn't above snooping. Her reply came from Derrick's bedroom and he wasted no time getting in there.

With a totally mystified expression on his face, Derrick watched his mother work masterfully with things he had absolutely no idea what they were, or what purpose they served, and asked, "What are you doing?"

"Setting up their beds. What does it look like I'm doing? You'll need to bring some of those things in here, unless you plan on running in there every time you need something during the night."

Sonya heard all of Derrick's fears in the sound of his voice when he said, "They can't sleep in here, Mom. I'll take that stuff into the other room."

"So, you're going to run up and down the hall all night?"

"Run up and down the hall all night for what?"

"Babies don't sleep all night, Derrick. You'll have to feed them every three to four hours, day and night."

"What?! Jesus, Mom, I can't do this. Really. They can't sleep in my room. I never even liked sleeping in the room with David growing up."

Losing patience with Derrick, Sonya asked sarcastically, "Did you sleep with their mother in the room all night?"

Just as sarcastically, Derrick replied, "I don't know. I don't know who she was."

Putting her hands on her healthy hips, Sonya said, "If this situation wasn't so bizarre, I'd come over there and pull one of your smart lips off of your face, Derrick Dawes. I've heard the saying, 'Mama's baby, Daddy's maybe.' Only you would turn it around."

"I didn't turn it around."

"Whatever, Dear. Those babies have to sleep in here with you. Can't risk you not hearing them cry from the other room. Oh, by the way, you didn't get a monitor. You'll need one. Unless you're planning to carry them both to every room you're in."

"What?!"

"Stop screaming, 'what?!' and bring some of those things in here. I'll help you put them away. I have to get home. Ethan hasn't been fed. You know what a late meal does to him."

Derrick complied with his mother's wishes. He had every intention of taking it all out, as soon as he came back home. These babies were not wrecking his social life if he had anything to say about it. How could he spend any quality time with a lady with those two hanging out in his bedroom?

Standing in the doorway, with his arms crossed, David observed this battle between his brother and mother. He was basically happy Derrick was the one on the hot seat for a change. Derrick so seldom did anything wrong in their mother's eyes. The truth was, David was argumentative and Derrick simply accepted Sonya's word as gospel and let it be. Derrick hated arguments. They required speech. Loud speech.

But, David knew exactly what his brother was thinking. His sex life was unexpectedly being shut down on the whim of some crazy woman, and being enforced by another, their mother. While he thought the babies were pretty adorable, David couldn't imagine waking up tomorrow morning and finding two of them under his pillow either. His greatest domestic concession in thirty-one years was sharing his home with Hope, his girlfriend of three years.

David was certain Hope would start whining about them having a baby the moment she found out about Derrick. If not that, she would harp on getting married again. Either would keep David wide-awake. The repercussions of this could go on for months. Hell, years. Derrick had really stepped into a minefield this time. The only way out would be if they miraculously turned out not to be Derrick's babies. Or, their mother had a few nightmare-filled sleepless nights, changed her mind and returned in search of them.

It was after seven when the Dawes family sat down to Sunday dinner. Sonya, Derrick, and David decided to save the announcement until after they had all eaten. There was no need to further upset Ethan's appetite. After all, Sunday dinner being served after five was enough of an insult to the head of this household.

As Ethan prepared his plate from the bowls and platters on the table, he asked, "What took you all so long? Where were you anyway?"

Sonya, David, and Derrick ignored Ethan's questions. Everyone busied themselves with preparing their plates. Not accepting their silence, Ethan asked again, just a little louder, "What took you all so long? Where were you?"

Accepting the responsibility, Derrick said, "We'll tell you after dinner, Dad."

"Why? What's wrong?"

"Don't worry, we'll tell you."

"You'll tell me now, because I want to know now, Derrick."

Sonya chimed in, "Ethan, after dinner will be soon enough."

"For you maybe, Sonya. I want to hear it now."

Sonya and Derrick didn't bite. David shrugged his shoulders and said, "It's like this, Dad. Some woman had a set of twins yesterday. She put Derrick's name on their birth certificates and left the hospital. Just, up and left. Didn't take the babies with her. So, Derrick's stuck with them and you're a grandpa. Congratulations."

Giving David an empty stare, Ethan gave a sigh of dismissal and said, "Okay, David got that great wad of nonsense off of his chest. Anyone else want to make an offering?"

Concentrating on his dinner, Derrick said, "It wasn't nonsense, Dad. That's really what happened."

Deandra leaped up from her seat and screeched, "We've really got a brand new set of twins, Derrick?! What are they?! Take me to see them! Did you see them already, Mom?! Are they cute?! What are we naming them?!"

Annoyed by Deandra's reaction, Ethan snapped irritably, "Sit down, Dee! Eat your dinner! Your brothers are both pulling your leg. There are no babies. We'll just wait until after we've eaten to hear the truth."

Whenever Ethan didn't want to hear something Sonya, David, Derrick and Deandra spoke soundlessly to each other.

Looking at her mother, Deandra silently mouthed, "Are they telling the truth?"

Sonya nodded slowly.

Deandra could barely contain herself. She mouthed, "Did you see them?"

Sonya nodded slowly.

"Are they beautiful, Mom?"

Sonya nodded slowly.

Before she could ask another question, Ethan snapped, "Stop doing that, Deandra! Eat your dinner!"

Deandra did as she was told. She ate as fast as she could. There were just too many questions needing answers. Her father could stifle his for as long as he wanted. She had no intentions of following suit.

Everyone else ate at their normal pace. Their conversation consisted of one irrelevant question asked and answered after another. With the last forkful swallowed, Deandra asked, "Who's their mother, Derrick?"

"I haven't got a clue, Squirt."

"What do you mean, you haven't got a clue? How many girlfriends do you have?"

"Quite a few."

"Okay. So, which one's been missing long enough to have babies you don't know about?"

Sonya chimed, "Now, that's a good question."

Mumbling again, Derrick said, "Quite a few."

Ethan put his elbows on the table, rested his chin in his hands and said, "This had all better be a joke. You see, I know neither one of you is stupid enough to be tricked into making babies. You can't make me believe you trusted a woman's word on contraception. And, you can't be so trusting as to touch any of them without protection. You could be dying as we speak."

Derrick said miserably, "I didn't do any of those things and it looks like it happened anyway, Dad. What am I supposed to do now?"

"If you did what you were supposed to be doing, those are not your babies. Stay out of it."

Sonya said adamantly, "I saw those babies, Ethan. They belong to Derrick. I guess that proves that no system is foolproof. Your chauvinistic rhetoric backfired."

"You saw the babies? What does that prove? Nothing. Don't believe anything until it's scientifically proven, Derrick. Lots of women get a kick out of putting the wrong man in debt for twenty years. Don't pay, you go to jail. They've always had the upper hand when it came to babies. Their word was law. Leave those creatures right where you found them until you know for certain. If she didn't care, why should you?"

Astonished, Sonya responded, "I can't believe I just fed the man who said that. Are you trying to tell me you can't look at the three children sitting at this table and tell that they're your offspring, Ethan? Did you need scientific test results? Besides, who knows what DNA really is? Have you ever met anyone who actually performs that special task? For all you know there is no such thing. They've decided a certain percentage is or isn't. Decided on their mood for the day. Flipped the damned blood vial and read the drips."

"There you go being ridiculous again, Sonya. These were born after I married you. I would have been reluctant under any other set of circumstances. Besides, if there were no such thing as DNA, someone would have found out and told it by now."

"What did marriage have to do with it? Wives lie about babies too, you know. Maybe you should have them tested now. It's never too late to find out if you've been snookered."

"Please, Sonya. This is something so far-fetched from anything you would have done; it's moot. You would never have walked away from any of them."

"And, if I had, would that have made them any the less yours? What would you have done with them, Ethan? Left them in the hospital? Would you have trusted your eyes, or waited thirty years for a stranger with a magical test to tell you?"

Waving Sonya a dismissal, Ethan looked at Derrick and said, "Don't believe any of it without proof. Leave them right where they are, Derrick. The moment you take them, you're stuck with them."

"It's too late, Dad. I'm already stuck with them. If I don't take them, it's off to jail I go. The only way I don't go to jail is if I sign them over to the State or an adoption agency. If I sign anything, I'm acknowledging paternity. I'll have to put them up for adoption or bring them home. They'll be in the system with God only knows what happening to them, and if they're mine, I'll catch hell trying to get them back." Derrick said and gave his father a dry smirk.

"So what?! At least you won't be stuck with them, if they're not yours!"

"And, if they're really mine, Dad?"

Out and out yelling, Ethan ranted, "Are they, or aren't they yours, Derrick?! If you don't know, we damned sure can't figure it out for you!"

Standing, Derrick said, "Well, I guess I have a dilemma, Dad. Because I can't swear on a stack of bibles that they're not mine. Like Mom said, accidents do happen. And, I'm just a victim of a hit and run. I never even saw the car coming."

Derrick headed for the den when his father said, "Oh, you saw the car all right. You were just hypnotized by the fine form and the slick paint job."

With Deandra on his heels pleading to be taken to the hospital to see the babies, Derrick tried to watch the football game. It wasn't until his mumbling father and laughing brother came into the room that he conceded. Anything was better than listening to those two.

On their way out, Sonya yelled from the kitchen, "Leave your credit card and I'll pick up the two car seats for you tomorrow. We'll have to pick the babies up in my car. Your back seat will never hold them."

Derrick mumbled, "Okay, Mom. Next you're going to want me to buy a new car."

He dropped his American Express card on the hallway table and slammed the front door just as Sonya hollered, "Unless you're planning on being a prisoner in your own home, you'll have to do that too, Derrick Dawes!"

# *CHAPTER FIVE*

With Deandra's excited, ridiculously high pitch squeals over the two gorgeous baby girls still ringing in his ears, Derrick drove home. This day had taken its toll on him. Derrick's normally active mind lay silent. Numbed, after exhausting every possible route out of this situation it could process for one day.

Inside his bedroom, he sat on the side of his bed and stared at the two bassinets. His mother had them completely prepared for the arrival of the babies. Identical white teddy bears, with dramatic female eyes, dressed in pearls and pink frilled dresses were her welcoming girlie gifts. They were propped at what Derrick could only assume was the foot of the tiny odd looking beds.

Derrick undressed and hung his things in the closet. Looking at the intricately arranged diapers, undershirts and nightgowns on the dresser made Derrick slowly shake his head in wonder again. This could not really be happening to him. It just couldn't.

Before closing his eyes, Derrick prayed, "Father, please let their mother come to her senses and be at that hospital tomorrow. I won't kill her. I won't even yell. I'll protect her from my mother with my last breath. I'll donate everything we bought today. Throw in anything else she needs. Pay child support until they're thirty, faithfully. Please. I can't do this. Don't make me. Please."

Just as Derrick was drifting off to sleep, the telephone rang. Hoping it was the babies' mother calling to plead with him to let her have them, he snapped the receiver from its cradle. Cassandra's sultry voice quickly burst that delusional bubble. Before she could get into the crux of her spiel, Derrick said with complete fatigue, "Cassandra, I simply cannot talk to you tonight. Please, forgive me. I'll call you in a few days. Just give me that long to get my bearings."

Tartly, Cassandra responded, "Fine, Derrick. Good night."

Derrick sighed deeply and hung up. He sank back onto the bed and allowed himself to float away. His dreams were filled with the horrors of wailing babies. Sick babies. Injured babies. Babies in burning buildings. When his alarm clock sounded at 6:30 the next morning, Derrick felt as if he had not slept at all.

Forcing his eyes open, the first things he saw were the two bassinets. He quickly closed them again, groaned, rolled over and pulled the cover over his head. Derrick moaned into the sheet, "Damn, I wasn't dreaming. Who did this to me? Why did they do this to me? I have never intentionally hurt anyone in my life. Okay, maybe David a few times, but never anyone else. My dating policy may be slightly disturbing to some, but most women don't want a committed relationship with an unwilling partner anyway. I'm doing them a favor by ending it before anyone gets hurt. If there was a problem, why didn't she come to me before doing something as reckless as this? So what if I balked about it. We could have handled this some other way."

Turning over, Derrick said, "She probably didn't believe in abortion. I don't either. I believe in birth control to the infinite degree. She didn't want them put up for adoption either. I understand that, too. There is nothing more pathetic than displaced people. David once said adopted children probably felt like pets. Having to learn a bunch of weird domestic habits from people they couldn't identify with. Feeling the love, but on a deeper level knowing nothing matches."

Rising to a sitting position, Derrick said, "Maybe she did the right thing. If she couldn't take care of them, and I'm the father, this is the best place for them. I still wish I had known a little in advance. More than that, I wish I knew who she was. Then again, maybe I don't. She could have been one of the many pains in the ass I've come across. Even though I'm not up to raising two little girls, fighting with a nut for twenty years or more, could have given me permanent brain damage. Jesus, why me?"

Giving up on his pointless mental meanderings, a lifeless Derrick Dawes showered, shaved, dressed and prepared himself for the bizarre day ahead. With great effort, Derrick funnel concentrated on his work. His usually critical eye enhanced. Finding more errors than normal and bringing them to the attention of the engineering group with a vicious red felt pen, Derrick destroyed weeks of work with that pen. Normally, he listed any necessary changes on a slip of paper and attached it to the intricately drawn schematics. Not today.

The group elected Tyson Medley to approach Derrick about the pen. He and Derrick were high school friends and fraternity brothers. Tyson was the least likely to be fired if Derrick was in a foul mood.

Bouncing into Derrick's office, Tyson, a short, rotund man, smiled and said cheerfully, "Hey, Big D. What's up?"

Never taking his eyes off of the schematic before him and gripping that red felt pen like it was a lethal weapon, Derrick said sharply, "Nothing, Tyson. What do you want?"

The tone of Derrick's voice alarmed Tyson. Big D only got hot under the collar when something was drastically wrong on a job. Anything short of drastic, he handled. Tyson had visions of their bonuses flying away.

Moving closer, to get a better look at his friend, Tyson said, "I want to know what's wrong with you. Don't bother saying nothing either. You're single-handedly sabotaging this project and not nicely. So, just tell me what's wrong and let's see if we can work something out. I don't know about you, but I want the bonus we're getting when this job is done."

"Do you really want to know, Tyson?"

"I asked, didn't I?"

Putting the pen down, spinning away from the easel and crossing his arms, Derrick said, "Some crazy woman put my name on the birth certificates of a set of twins and left them at the hospital. If I don't take them, I go to jail. Now, what can we work out, Tyson?"

Derrick watched all of the vibrant color and muscle tone vanish from Tyson's cherubic face. The powerfully built, little robust fellow actually looked as if he were going to faint. If it were possible for a human to liquefy, Derrick thought his friend would have done it right then.

Astonished, Tyson exclaimed, "You're shitting me, Derrick! Don't say stuff like that out loud! There will be a stampede of women doing it!"

"Well, stand aside, my brother, because the first horse has cleared the gate."

Gripping Derrick's desk, to steady himself, Tyson clicked off all the now familiar questions. "She can't really do that, can she, Derrick? I mean, can't they make her take them?"

"Not if they don't know who she is. The only legitimate name on anything is mine. Address and telephone number included, of course. Can't have them picking up the wrong guy. Go away, Tyson. I don't want to talk about this anymore."

Not to be shaken off that easily, Tyson asked, "What are you going to do?"

"I'll be baby-sitting for the next eighteen years. Now, go away."

"Before I go, tell me one thing. Are they your babies?"

Derrick gave a great shrug of his huge shoulders and spun back around.

Panic wiped away all vestiges of male-to-male protocol forcing Tyson to literally scream, "You mean you don't know?!"

From where he stood, all Tyson could see was Derrick's head swiveling from side-to-side solemnly.

"Pardon my language, Big D, but 'fuck that!' I wouldn't take those babies anywhere! They would turn eighteen in that nursery! Grow up to be candy stripers and literature ladies, or something! Not me! If a woman ever thinks she's going to pull a trick like that on me, you'll have to help me with my commissary, brother! Because I'll be busy as hell, trying to figure out how to trip the prison electrical system for my escape! Shit on that!!"

Derrick tried not to laugh at his excited little friend and lost. He did manage to say one more time, "Get out of my office, Tyson."

Backing out, Tyson chanted, "Don't do it, Big D. Don't do it. Call a lawyer, a priest, a rabbi, a preacher, your congressman—the senate. Call anybody. If you can't get absolution, opt for sanctuary. Just, don't do it."

Tyson's interruption succeeded in stopping Derrick from using the red pen, because it stopped Derrick from working. Derrick had completely forgotten his mission.

When asked by one of the other engineers what Derrick had said, Tyson responded, "Leave the man alone. Bother him and that red ink will be the least of your problems. Your red blood might be the next thing you see on your drawings. Leave him alone."

Derrick somehow made it through the day without firing any of his engineers. He may have lost a supplier, but that wasn't an insurmountable setback. Hell, there were hundreds of suppliers who would be happy to get the account. That guy was trying to unload some useless, substandard equipment for the backup generators. The first time they were cranked up, there would be an electrical fire hot enough to bring the entire structure down. Not on Derrick Dawes, he wouldn't.

At four o'clock Derrick pulled up in front of his mother's house. She had the car seats strapped into the back seat of her car. Before Derrick turned his ignition key, Sonya and Deandra came flying out the front door. They each carried large pink bags with happy little animals all over them. Derrick hoped his mother didn't think he would ever carry anything like that. There are limits, even in the outer limits.

They loaded the bags on the car seats, Deandra crawled in between them and Sonya got behind the wheel. Derrick stood in the driveway with his hands jammed in his pockets, admiring the architecture of his parents' split-level home. He lost himself in the serenity of the setting. Derrick wondered if they had chosen it for the seemingly never-ending, tree laden, rolling hills, or merely the accommodations.

Sonya disturbed Derrick's ponderings by yelling, "Get in this car, boy! That bird will be there the next time you visit!"

Looking around for the bird his mother was talking about, Derrick moved toward the car. They always assumed he was looking at birds when he looked out of the windows, or sat alone under a tree. Indeed, Derrick enjoyed the little tunes the birds sang, but their multi-colored bodies and infinitely different shaped bills never captivated his attention. Unfettered tranquility held Derrick's complete attention.

Securely strapped in his seat, Derrick sighed and said, "Okay, I'm ready."

Sonya backed out of the driveway and maneuvered her way to Metropolitan Hospital to pick up her granddaughters. She had looked forward to this day since David graduated from college eight years ago. She was actually beginning to believe the entire grandchildren responsibility would fall on Deandra. Of course, this fiasco wasn't exactly what she had in mind. But, she could live with it and heartily hoped that Derrick could, too.

The nurse brought the babies to room 410 for the final time. Sonya and Deandra skillfully stripped them down, changed diapers and dressed them for their ride home. Deandra chattered the entire time. Derrick sat on the windowsill and watched.

"Derrick, they've got tattoos on their hands and feet. I guess they did that for you. My friend told me they did that with her twin brothers. But they only did it to their feet."

"Are you implying I need extra help, Squirt?"

"Do you know which one is which, Derrick?"

"No. I haven't really met either one of them."

Holding the newly dressed baby girl up, for what Derrick assumed was his inspection, Deandra said, "Here then. Derrick, this is daughter number one."

Readjusting his balance on his hands, Derrick said, "I'll have plenty of time to get to know her, Deandra. You and Mom enjoy them for a while."

Sonya snapped from the other side of the room, "Take that baby, Derrick!"

The nurse's reappearance saved him. She said, "Mr. Dawes, before you leave, they need to see you in the office on the third floor. I have some instructions for the care of the girls' navel cords, an emergency pediatrician and a get acquainted package for you."

Derrick rose from the sill and mumbled, "That must be some package."

He left his mother and sister with the babies, returning a half hour later with a terrible scowl on his face. Not only were they forcing the babies on him, they stuck him with a bill that would have sent both of them to college for a year. That woman seemed gleeful as hell to tell Derrick, "You can't get the insurance company to pay for a non-existent spouse, or the birth of illegitimate offspring."

Sonya and Deandra each held a baby in their arms, with purses slung easily over their free shoulders. The two giant diaper bags lay on the bed. Derrick's glance traveled from the two bags to his mother and sister.

Finally, he asked painfully, "You two don't think I'm carrying those big pink bags, do you?"

In unison, Sonya and Deandra said, "Yes."

Shaking his head and waving both hands, Derrick said, "No way."

Confused by her brother's refusal, Deandra asked, "Why not? They're just diaper bags, Derrick."

Mumbling, Derrick said, "They're pink, Squirt. No self respecting brother carries pink bags."

Sonya yelled, "Derrick, either pick up those bags, or take that baby from your sister! If you think we're carrying everything, while you walk out empty handed, to protect some infantile chauvinistic characteristic your silly father created, you are crazy!"

With an agonized frown, Derrick weighed his choices. He decided he would rather be seen with the baby and held his arms out to take it. The way Deandra had her wrapped; Derrick couldn't see her. Unprepared for the wriggle and tiny whine, Derrick changed his mind almost immediately.

Deandra gave her brother a smirk and said, "She wouldn't do that if you held her like she was a baby, Derrick."

"How's that?"

"Like Mom's holding the other one. Just make sure you support her head."

Derrick looked at the way his mother had the baby propped up on her shoulder and tried to mimic it. The baby let out a disconcerting groan. In painfully slow motion, Derrick's head turned to see what the problem was. If there was a problem, it must have passed, because he didn't hear anymore complaints from his tiny bundle.

As they paraded through the halls of the hospital, Derrick wondered if the babies were the proper weight. He barely felt the baby on his shoulder. Derrick asked his mother about it after they were strapped into their car seats.

"They're fine, Derrick. As a matter of fact their weight is exceptional for twins."

"You don't think they'll get sick or anything, do you, Mom? I mean, not knowing anything about their mother could be a problem with their health, couldn't it?"

"It could, but we will think positive. Cross the bridges when you get there, Derrick. Deal with each fever and sniffle as it crops up."

"How will I know if they've got a fever?"

Deandra jumped in to answer that question and Sonya cut her off. The rectal thermometer lesson was more than Derrick was ready to handle. The boy hadn't changed his first Pamper, or fed his first bottle. Sonya knew to take it one step at a time with him. If Derrick was frightened, he would start whining about her taking the babies again. And, there was nothing in the world Sonya hated more than saying no to any of her children. Especially Derrick.

She said, "You'll get used to the feel of their normal body temperature in no time. When it changes, believe me, you'll know."

"Is that why you were always touching our foreheads and arms? You knew what our normal body temperature was?"

"Yes, Derrick. Thermometers weren't always as plentiful as they are these days."

Back at Derrick's house, Sonya and Deandra unloaded the babies and carried them up to his room. Knowing he had dodged this bullet as long as possible, Derrick followed. He sat at the foot of the bed and watched the entire unwrapping.

The babies seemed to be relieved to be out of all of the gear. Little arms and legs twitched as they peeked and frowned at the people who kept disturbing them. Derrick wondered if they were already communicating with each other. Every time one made a humming sound the other repeated it.

Whatever they were doing, Derrick got his first really good look at them. They didn't even look the same as they had the night before. Not as wrinkled and exhausted looking. As a matter of fact, they were prettier today. Their hairlines and eyes hadn't changed though. Hoping he could cross-reference them, Derrick studied the little noses that definitely were not his. They didn't ring a bell, but they were terribly cute. His mother promised him their complexions would settle down soon. At the moment, they didn't look like two little black girls at all. They were sort of pink with brown trimming on their ears and fingers.

Deandra picked up a baby and said, "Okay, Derrick, you've already held daughter number one, now you have to hold daughter number two. Can't have either of them feeling neglected."

She placed the baby in Derrick's unprepared arms and walked away. Looking more like Frankenstein, than Deandra's big brother, Derrick stiffly handled the baby.

Daughter number two did not like Derrick's uncertainty one bit. She let out her version of a big fuss.

Right away, Derrick's eyes nervously searched out his mother and asked, "What's the matter with her?"

"She's sensing your fear, Derrick. The child won't break if you hold her. Just don't let her head go and you're safe."

"What'll happen if I let her head go?"

"The weight of her head will snap her neck."

With those great eyes stretched wide open, Derrick asked in rapid succession, "That's all I have to do to break her neck, Mom? That's it? Let her head go? Really?"

"Pretty much. Keep the back of their heads in the palm of your hand and everything will be just fine."

Derrick repeated, "Heads in the palm of my hand. Heads in the palm of my hand."

Holding onto her head, as instructed, Derrick laid the fold of his arm. She stopped crying and looked baby in the up at him. Then, she started making a sucking noise with her mouth.

Taking a guess at what that meant, Derrick asked, "Does that mean she's hungry, Mom?"

"It could. She's scheduled to be fed at six, and that's exactly ten minutes from now. We can feed them the bottles in the get acquainted package, change them and lay them down, while we prepare formulas for the rest of the night and in the morning. I'll be here by 7:30, so you won't be late for work. Deandra, give your brother a cloth diaper and a bottle."

Deandra moved to do as asked and whined, "Can I feed the other baby, Mom?"

"No. Let Derrick feed and change them. He has to learn how to do it. You'll get your opportunity to do it all before long. Don't worry."

Sonya made Derrick sit back on the bed. She laid daughter number one next to his leg, with her head away from his elbow. She told him the heat from his thigh would keep her quiet while he fed the other. It did. Number one laid there, looked up at Derrick and her sister and never made a sound.

After Derrick's timid attempt at burping the baby, his mother told him to place the diaper on his lap. He did. Then, she told him to lay the baby on it. He made a terrible face when she handed him the Pamper. She held one and demonstrated how it worked. The open box of wipes lay next to his other thigh. Derrick changed the diaper like a trooper. It was a little loose, but his mother deemed it satisfactory.

Relief flooded his body when Sonya took the baby from him and placed her in the bassinet. The tension returned when she said, "Okay. Now do the same thing with the other."

Derrick talked himself through the feeding, burping and changing of daughter number one. This diaper was a little snugger than the first. Unlike her sister, daughter number one fell asleep in the middle of her feeding. Sonya told Derrick to lay her down.

Without the blankets, they seemed extra tiny to Derrick, barely a handful for him. But, he held onto her head, laid her down and covered the tiny sleeping body.

Sonya looked proudly at Derrick and said, "Now, that wasn't so bad, was it?"

Derrick gave a non-committal shrug.

Sonya smiled and said, "Now, if those mats in their beds get wet, because Dad didn't make those diapers tight enough, you'll have to change them. The spares are in the other room. Let's move on to bottle washing and formula."

In a panic, Derrick asked, "Should we leave them up here alone, Mom?"

"Calm down. Deandra can stay up here with them, if it will make you feel better. I told you to buy that monitor."

"I'll pick one up tomorrow. Hey, Mom, we didn't warm those bottles before we fed them. They won't get sick, will they?"

"No, Derrick. Their milk is supposed to be room temperature. The warmer is for bottles you take out of the refrigerator. Don't ever give them anything cold. It will give them a stomach ache. And, boy will you be sorry. Come on, let's make formula."

Looking over his shoulder at the two bassinets, Derrick followed his mother to the kitchen. They washed, sterilized and filled the four ounce bottles with formula.

Every fifteen minutes, Derrick asked, "What time is their next feeding?"

Sonya told him over and over, "At ten, Derrick. We'll be leaving shortly thereafter. Your sister has school tomorrow."

Then, he wanted to know, "Will they know when it's time for them to eat during the night? Or, should I set the clock?"

"You can set the clock, if it makes you feel more secure. It may, or may not give you a few extra minutes to get down here to get bottles and start warming them. And, if they make a stink during the night, don't forget to wash their bottoms. These new mothers swear by those wipes. I don't. We don't know what all they put on those things. When you can, use soap and water, Derrick. Put a little Balmex on them after they're cleaned up."

With a gruesomely stupid expression, Derrick asked, "Will they be doing that tonight, Mom?"

"I don't know. They do it all of the time. Don't worry about it. Just handle it when it happens."

"We didn't buy any food for them. What will they eat during the day?"

Sonya's head dropped into her hands. Through them she said miserably, "Where were you when your sister was born? Brand new babies don't eat food, boy. They only drink milk. Water occasionally. You do the milk, I'll take care of the water."

"Will you be coming over on the weekends, Mom?"

"Maybe a few. Then, you're on your own. And, don't bring any of those trifling women you hang out with in here over my granddaughters either. In time, they'll tell me if you do."

Derrick was rescued from that discussion by the doorbell. His father, David, and David's girlfriend, Hope, came in. They went straight up to Derrick's room to see the babies. If Sonya only knew Ethan had picked them both up and inspected them, she would have screamed for the remainder of the night. He knew it, too. Deandra told him.

Without a word to anyone in the bedroom, Ethan left and headed for the kitchen. In there, he looked at Derrick and asked, "How could you not know those are your babies? You messed up somewhere, Derrick. I think you know where, too."

Angrily, Derrick snapped, "No, I don't. They can change, you know. I thought you were the one who said wait for the tests."

Waving his huge hand, Ethan said, "Run the test. I'm telling you, those are your kids. They look just like you and David, same facial expressions and all. Hey, maybe they're his."

Sarcastically Derrick offered, "Maybe they belong to one of your nephews."

Sonya interjected, "If that's so, how did they get my mother's hairline?"

"I don't know. Is your mother the only person you know with that hairline?"

"No, Derrick. David has it. My niece, Sandy, has it. My two nephews, Claude and Harold, have them. Oh, but we can't count them, can we? They're only twelve years old."

Laughing, Derrick asked, "Why not? I've heard stranger things."

Ethan said, "Sonya, what are we having for dinner? Your son seems to be missing the key combination here. Those babies have my father's eyes and your mother's hairline."

Before his mother could respond to the dinner question, Derrick said, "Maybe Sandy and one of your nephews made an oops, Dad."

Ethan calmly walked over, gave Derrick a sharp slap to the back of his head and said, "You made the oops! Sandy's husband would have noticed right away if she had unloaded a set of twins. So, don't go trying to turn this into one of those silly talk show topics."

Rubbing his head, Derrick said, "It already is, Dad."

## *CHAPTER SIX*

The first night with the babies only proved to be mildly disturbing for Derrick. Both infants were fed, bathed, changed and fast asleep when Derrick's family left at 10:30. After locking the front door, Derrick dashed back up to his room. For a reason he had not yet come to grips with, he did not want the babies left alone.

Finally, Derrick resumed his normal routine. He undressed, hung his clothes, turned on the radio, laid in bed and read the newspaper. The telephone rang at 11:00. Derrick snatched it up. The ringing made the babies go through a strange stretching and humming routine.

Without realizing it, Derrick whispered, "Hello."

The voice on the other end said, "Hello, Derrick? Why are you whispering?"

Recognizing the pleasant voice of his latest lady friend, Derrick said, "Yes, it's me, Khalia. I've got visitors tonight."

Surprised by this information, Khalia asked, "Visitors? Plural? More than one?"

Smiling at the thought of how that must have sounded, Derrick answered, "Yes. Plural. More than one. Two, to be exact. They're asleep. I'm babysitting."

Derrick could hear the humor in Khalia's voice when she said, "I didn't see you as the babysitting type, Derrick, and on a weeknight. You're quite the man, aren't you?"

"Believe me, this was thrust upon me. I've never babysat anything in my life."

Still in a humorous mood, Khalia asked, "How long will you have them?"

"I have no idea. May have them for the rest of my life."

Laughing, Khalia asked, "Did their parents dump them off and run away?"

"That's exactly what she did. Dumped them off and ran away."

"Very funny, Derrick. If you're trying to tell me our date for tomorrow is canceled, you could find something more appropriate to lie about."

Grabbing his head, Derrick said, "Oh, I'm sorry, Khalia. I completely forgot we were on for dinner tomorrow. Can I get a rain check? Please? I promise I'll make it up to you."

Confused, Khalia asked, "Are you serious, Derrick? You're not taking me out to dinner for real?"

"Really, Khalia. I can't. My mother's taking care of the babies during the day for me, and I can't ask her to extend her stay this early in the game. Once I get the hang of this, I'll be able to swing something, I'm sure."

"Are you, by any chance, the father of these children?"

"I don't think so. But, I could be wrong."

Indignantly, Khalia asked, "What the hell are you trying to pull here? Are you serious? You really have two children there? Where did they come from? Why do you have them?"

"It's a long, totally unbelievable story. I'll tell you about it when I see you."

"When you see me? You won't be seeing me. Derrick, I don't do babies under any circumstances."

A little defensive because of her reaction to the babies, Derrick said, "I didn't ask you to do anything with the babies. They're my responsibility. If you'd like to go out to dinner, see a show and have a drink with me, that's all you have to do."

"Right. First, it's dinner and dancing. Then, it's diapers and Disney World. Not me, Derrick."

"So, what you're saying is, as long as I have the babies, you're not interested. Right?"

"Right."

"Just remember you called it. Good night, Khalia."

Not waiting for her to say another word, Derrick hung up the telephone. Mumbling his anger, Derrick said, "Who does she think she is? Diapers and Disney World? I wouldn't let her change either of my babies' diapers. I wouldn't let her sit in the same room with them now if she begged. How dare she turn her nose up at One and Two? Well, that's it for her. Cassandra's prettier anyway."

Derrick fleetingly wondered how many of his female friends would be frightened off by the babies and drifted off to sleep. He completely forgot about setting the clock for the two o'clock feeding. Derrick didn't hear the twins doing their back and forth humming routine at one-thirty. He casually turned over when One let out her first tenuous cry at one-forty-five, and snapped to a sitting position when they both bellowed catlike wails.

Totally disoriented, Derrick looked around the room. For a few seconds, he couldn't imagine what that sound was, or where it was coming from. When the urgency of the cries escalated, Derrick remembered the babies. He looked at the clock. It was two-o-five and he had no idea how long they had been crying.

Jumping up, Derrick moved to the bassinets quickly. Both babies were completely absorbed in their crying—mouths wide open, wailing and gasping for air—arms and legs flailing angrily.

Panicking, Derrick picked up One. He cradled her on his shoulder, patted her back and tried to quiet her. It didn't work. With one screaming baby on his shoulder and the other throwing a matching fit in her bassinet, Derrick picked up the telephone and dialed his mother's number. It seemed to take Sonya forever to answer. She knew who it was by the background noise.

Derrick said in an excited rush, "Mom, I forgot to set the clock. They're both crying. I'm holding One and she won't stop crying. What do I do now?"

Calmly, Sonya said, "Lay her on your bed, Derrick. Pick up the other and lay her next to her sister. If being close to each other doesn't quiet them, you'll have to go get their bottles while they cry."

"You mean, leave them up here by themselves? They're crying, Mom!"

"I know they're crying, boy. I've got ears. Put those babies on that bed, like I said. Go get those bottles and feed them. After all, that is why they're crying, Derrick. Go on. They'll be fine."

Taking a deep breath, Derrick said, "I'll leave the telephone off the hook, while I'm downstairs. Stay on the line, Mom. Please."

While Sonya didn't quite understand what her being on the line would do, she agreed. Derrick laid the babies side by side on his bed. They didn't like it one bit and kept right on crying.

Gritting his teeth, Derrick dashed for the door and down the stairs. In the kitchen, he found the saucepan his mother told him to warm both bottles in quickly. He put water in it, turned the fire up high, retrieved two bottles from the refrigerator and put them into the pot. With that done, Derrick dashed back up the stairs, three at a time.

From the bedroom doorway it looked like the babies were fighting to Derrick. They cried angrily and hit each other with their frantically flying arms and feet. Not wanting them to hurt each other, Derrick separated them a little. That made them cry even louder. He shushed them, but they didn't listen.

Derrick ran back down the stairs. His mother had told him not to let the water boil. The milk would get too hot. He just wanted to knock the chill off. Hoping the milk was warm enough Derrick turned the eye off, snatched the two dripping wet bottles out of the pot and ran back up the stairs.

In his bedroom, with the two bottles in hand, Derrick looked down at the two screaming infants and couldn't decide which one to feed first. Dropping to his knees next to the bed, Derrick leaned on his elbows and put the nipples to their lips. Two took hers right away, sucked at it greedily and whimpered occasionally. One wasn't taking to being fed in this impersonal manner very well.

Derrick pleaded with her, "Aw c'mon, One. Stop crying and drink your milk. Please? I can't hold you and feed both of you at the same time. Please?"

A few drops of milk dripped into her mouth. Then, she seemed to realize what was going on. One closed her mouth around the nipple and the room filled with loud sucking noises and an occasional high-pitch hum from one or the other. Derrick wanted to weep with relief. He completely forgot he had left his mother on the telephone.

Two drank a little more than an ounce of milk and spit the nipple out. Now Derrick was faced with a brand new dilemma. She needed to be burped.

Remembering his mother, Derrick put Two's bottle down, picked up the telephone and asked, "How can I burp her and keep feeding her sister, Mom?"

All Derrick heard on the line was Sonya's soft snoring. He yelled, "Mom! Mom!" Both babies jumped. Two's bottom lip began to quiver. The resumption of crying rallied Sonya from a peaceful sleep. Derrick repeated his question.

Better than half asleep, Sonya said, "Put the diaper under her head, turn her on her side and pat her back, Derrick."

Derrick's long arms came in handy. He could actually reach the diaper draped on the bottom of the bassinet easily. Moving the crying baby back a little, he smoothed the diaper out, turned Two on her side and patted. Just as she let out a tiny burp, One pouted her nipple out. Without too much trouble, Derrick reversed the situation. Two was glad to get the bottle back and One quietly accepted the patting.

The fact that One didn't seem to drink as much milk as Two disturbed Derrick. He would ask his mother about that tomorrow. With both babies fed and changed, Derrick realized there was something different this time. Neither one was asleep. They seemed to be checking out their surroundings.

Waving his arms, Derrick said to them, "Okay, go back to sleep."

Two looked up at him and gave what appeared to be a smile. Then, she went back to looking around the room. They took turns humming.

Derrick picked up the telephone to ask his mother what to do now and heard her snoring again. Since the babies weren't crying, he decided to let her off the hook. He hung up the telephone, picked up One and sat down next to Two.

Holding her in his lap, Derrick said, "Okay, One. We've had enough excitement for one night. It's time to go to sleep. We'll be doing this all again way too soon."

One disregarded Derrick's speech and looked at Two like she'd never seen her before. Not knowing anything else to do, Derrick got up, laid One in her bassinet and covered her. He turned to Two and did likewise. Derrick set his clock for five-forty-five, lay back down and waited for the noise to begin again. It didn't. He fell asleep listening to the constant back and forth humming sound One and Two always made. Derrick had absolutely no idea when, or if, they ever fell asleep.

Six-thirty was Derrick's normal rising time. Most mornings, he put a half hour in on the rowing machine before he showered, dressed and ate breakfast. Occasionally, he even felt like running. All Derrick could say that morning was, "Boy, what a difference forty-five minutes makes when you've already been up in the middle of the night."

Derrick was prepared for One and Two this time. Those properly warmed bottles and Pampers were on his night table at exactly six o’clock. Derrick inspected the two sleeping babies. Neither stirred. Not wanting to disturb them before they were ready, Derrick lay back on the bed, folded his arms across his chest and drifted off to sleep.

At six-twenty, One's whining penetrated Derrick's fog. Not wanting a repeat of the earlier feeding failure, he jumped up and scooped the squirming baby up before she woke her sister. Studying One, as she struggled to get her eyes open, Derrick couldn't deny the fact that she resembled David. The way her forehead creased, as she frowned and yawned. The only difference was David didn't twitch.

One sucked happily on her bottle in Derrick's arms. She gripped his little finger and blinked slowly. Two hummed. One sighed and hummed without relinquishing the nipple. With only an ounce down, One pouted the bottle away. Not liking that, Derrick looked down at One and said, "You're going to have to start doing better than this. Two is going to be bigger and stronger than you. Right now, you're holding your own, but I'm telling you, being the runt is rough."

In reply, One gave him that same slow, sleepy smile Two had given him before. That's when Derrick noticed the first difference in the twins. One had more attitude than Two. It was the way she sort of smirked. As if she knew exactly what you were saying and thought it ridiculous. According to Sonya, that was the look Derrick always had. He never had to speak a word, his expression told the entire story.

With One fed, burped and changed, Derrick moved on to Two. She was awake, but she hadn't cried. Two made the identical faces and moves One made earlier and settled down with the bottle and drank enthusiastically. Like One, she too held onto Derrick's little finger. The only difference was, Two pulled it around as she drank and hummed.

Now Derrick had another problem. He didn't like the idea of leaving them in the bedroom while he showered and shaved. With a great deal of talking to himself, Derrick was sufficiently convinced he would hear them if he left the door open. Looking down at his tiny wards, Derrick asked, "Would you like it better if I left the two of you together on the big bed? That way, you can talk, or hum, and see each other. Or would you like to get back into your own beds?"

Since One and Two never took their eyes off of each other, Derrick assumed that meant they were happier together on the big bed. He moved them to the center of the king size bed and left the room. It took three times longer to go through his normal routine this morning. Every time Derrick thought one of the babies made an unfamiliar sound, he stuck his head out of the bathroom door. All he ever saw was the two of them touching each other accidentally. One had discovered Two's hair and found it fascinating. She held onto it.

One and Two drifted off to sleep watching Derrick get dressed. He gently pried Two's hair out of One's little fist and put them back into their bassinets. Derrick made his bed, sat in the chair, glanced at the sports section of yesterday's paper and waited for his mother's arrival.

At promptly seven-thirty, Sonya rang the bell. While the idea didn't thrill him, Derrick knew he would have to give his mother a key. The best case scenario Derrick could muster was, maybe this would all be over in a few months. One and Two's features could change, the tests could come back exonerating Derrick of any real responsibility and Sonya could stay at home. She wouldn't be critiquing his life up close and personally. Hadn't she already thrown the first stone, when she mentioned his bringing strange women around the babies?

To Derrick's surprise, his father accompanied Sonya. Ethan brushed past Derrick saying, "I want to see those babies in the daylight. Are they asleep?"

Feeling completely invaded now, Derrick said, "Yes, they are. Why?"

Ethan was halfway up the stairs when he said, "If you did what you were supposed to, there is no way they can be your babies, Derrick. I need to take another look. I'm not convinced."

Derrick wanted to remind him that wasn't what he had said the night before. But, he knew Ethan changed his mind constantly about everything. Sonya simply shook her head and asked if Derrick had eaten breakfast. He told her he couldn't leave the babies alone to make it. Sonya rolled her eyes, sighed and headed for the kitchen.

Derrick picked his newspaper up off of the walk-way and met his mother in the kitchen. He didn't like his father inspecting the babies while they slept, but at least they weren't up there by themselves.

Having another thought, Derrick asked, "Would you like me to bring the beds down, Mom?"

Never having spent much time in Derrick's house, Sonya had no idea what she would be doing all day. She said, "No, Derrick. Let me see how the day progresses. Did the girls make a mess I have to clean up, last night?"

Wanting to ask what kind of a mess, Derrick simply said, "No, Mom. They just screamed their heads off until I fed them. Then, they didn't want to go back to sleep."

"That was nothing. Wait until they get the hang of being awake, Derrick."

"Will it happen before they turn three months old?"

Not liking the sound of that question, Sonya said sharply, "Yes. But, what does three months have to do with anything?"

Raising his hand defensively, Derrick said, "Mom, please keep in mind that those babies have to go if they're not mine. I'm not cut out for sleepless nights."

Then Derrick said the one thing that would surely set Sonya's wheels spinning. "I've already had my first female defection because of them."

"What does that mean?"

"A young lady found out about the babies and gave me my walking papers. Said she didn't do diapers and Disney World."

With a distasteful twist to her face, Sonya sniffed and said snidely, "I can just imagine what she does do though."

"Aw c'mon, Mom. How is she supposed to feel? You're dating a single man who says he has no attachments. Suddenly, he has two brand new infants, with no rational explanation. If the tables were turned, I would pull up stakes and run too."

Sonya's yelling vibrated Derrick's brain. "That's what's wrong with young people! All any of you care about is yourselves! Your immediate gratification! Your inconvenience! This whole thing started in selfishness and it's going to end the same way, Derrick Dawes! Everybody passing babies around like they're ponies! You'll all be sorry! Mark my words!"

Derrick would gladly mark them as long as he didn't have to hear them anymore. Of course, he never expressed this thought to his mother. Instead, he said, "Okay, Mom. I'm sorry I brought it up."

Not assuaged by his apology, Sonya continued, "You all just keep looking at each other like pieces of meat! No more than tonight's dinner! Do you know where you find fresh meat, Derrick?!"

Knowing this was not going to be the answer Sonya sought, Derrick answered miserably, "The market?"

"No! The slaughterhouse! And, that's what you all have going! Killing and not caring! Too damn stupid to even know what you're doing! Eat your breakfast and get out of my face, Derrick Dawes!" Talking to herself out loud, Sonya chanted, "Everybody wants benefits with no babies. Kill it or dump it. Hell, kill it and dump it. That's why God took it out of man's hands. The planet would be deserted in no time, if He hadn't. Can't stop babies from being made with pills or plastic. Rubber don't stand a chance. Keep thinking you can push nature around to suit yourself."

Derrick had to stifle a laugh, when his mother said in a singsong fashion, "It's mind over matter. Too stupid to know that when God speaks, your mind don't matter. Spending a lot of time and money trying to match wits with the Master. Time and money that would be better spent housing, feeding, educating and loving. Idiots."

Leaning on the counter, holding her head, Sonya muttered, "And, I've been housing, feeding, educating and loving a group of them, too. I can't believe it. So much for mind over matter."

## *CHAPTER SEVEN*

Sonya and Ethan used up Derrick's listening quotient for the entire morning with their endless prattle. Derrick couldn't even face the radio, as he drove to work that morning. In the silence, Derrick's mind wandered back. To himself he posed the question, "Who was I seeing exactly nine months ago?"

That would have been winter. November, December or January. He had just moved into the brownstone. Only one person stood out in Derrick's mind. Angelique. They had dated each other exclusively at college, and she had surprised him with a Christmas Eve visit.

Derrick remembered having to break his date with Pamela. Boy, was she angry. It didn't matter. Prior to that night Derrick hadn't seen Angelique in four years. She went off to Denver and married a wonderful guy. At least that was what she said before they dove into their nuptials. Derrick knew marriage wasn't for him back then, too. But if he were ever going to marry anyone, it would have been Angelique. She knew Derrick as well as any quiet person can be known. She didn't press him for too much idle chatter and she was extremely affectionate. Quiet and affectionate were at the top of Derrick's desirability list.

Angelique had spent the night with Derrick and left for her parents' house early Christmas morning. She was a little distraught over having to break the news of her impending divorce to them. But off she went and Derrick hadn't heard from her since. He had called her office several times and left messages, but she never returned his calls. Derrick assumed her troubles were all she could handle at the time.

Derrick said out loud, "Okay, Pamela and Angelique go on the Mommy list. I haven't seen either one since then. Now, who else is there?"

As he pulled into his parking space, Derrick said, "Cynthia Wells. Spent New Year's Eve with her. I really liked Cynthia. She was easy to spend time with, too. Pouted occasionally, but didn't whine. And, she's got a tiny nose and a fair complexion. I wonder what happened with her. We only dated twice. Maybe I should give her a call."

The Mommy list grew as the day progressed. By three, Derrick could recall at least twelve women he had dated between November and January. Four of them he still ran into occasionally around town. None of them looked pregnant to him. Two had moved to Atlanta with their jobs in the spring. The rest he would have to get in touch with.

There was only one thing troubling Derrick. None of these women seemed to be the types who would inadvertently get pregnant. They all had the kinds of careers you had to strive and sacrifice for. Babies would impede their progress. Derrick couldn't imagine any of them taking the time out to deliver a kid; or God forbid, risk losing their fabulous figures without some guy making the kind of figures that would make it worth their while. Derrick refused to acknowledge fitting that bill either. Since he never made any offers, or hinted at one, he was completely disqualified. Derrick just didn't get it.

At four, Derrick walked through his front door. He was beginning to feel the effects of his broken nights' sleep. The last thing he needed was the great dinner his mother had obviously prepared. His house had never smelled so good and he was hungry. With a great meal under his belt Derrick would fall into the sleep of death and wouldn't hear babies crying, burglars, or a misguided demolition team on his roof. All Derrick desperately wanted was to simply take a nap.

Leaving his briefcase next to the front door, Derrick began to climb the stairs. His mother's call from the basement almost changed his mind. Before he responded, Derrick dashed up to his room and over to the bassinets. He breathed a deep sigh of relief when he didn't find the babies had been left up there alone and headed for the basement.

Sonya sat on the deep, heavily tufted, butter soft, burgundy leather sofa watching a soap opera on Derrick's big screen television. From the doorway, Derrick couldn't see the two tiny, sleeping forms, lying on the sofa next to her. Sonya had made comfortable blanketed pallets for them.

Derrick came into the recreation room asking, "Where are the babies, Mom?"

Absorbed in her soap opera, Sonya said, "Huh? Oh, they're right here."

"How were they today? Did they make any messes you had to clean up?"

Without taking her eyes off the screen, Sonya responded, "Several. The little greedy one puked. You're going to have to make sure she's on her stomach when you lay her down."

Alarmed, Derrick asked, "Why?"

"You don't want her throwing up on her back, Derrick. Could choke to death. Other than that, they were just fine."

Without knowing it, Sonya had just threatened Derrick with a totally sleepless night. How could he sleep knowing Two might choke to death? This was going to be tougher than Derrick thought.

Interrupting his thoughts, Sonya asked, "Did you remember to pick up the monitor?"

Slapping himself on the forehead and sighing miserably, Derrick said, "No. I came straight home. I'll do it tomorrow."

"They're going to need some of those little seats before to long too, Derrick. These babies won't be staying still like this very long. You don't want them falling off of anything."

"What kind of little seats, Mom?"

"I don't know what they call them. But, everyone has them. Don't forget to put a playpen on your list either. They can sleep in it down here. This sofa might make them too hot."

Sarcastically, Derrick said, "Expensive little devils, aren't they?"

Looking over at her son, who had taken a seat next to the sleeping babies, Sonya asked, "Are you ready to resume this morning's discussion?"

"No, Ma'am," Derrick said while holding both hands up in a gesture of surrender.

"Good. It's time for me to be getting home. If your father has to eat fast food again tonight, I'll have to move in here permanently. I do feel like Chinese though."

"What did you cook upstairs?"

"I just fried you some chicken, mashed a couple potatoes and opened a can of string beans. You have the emptiest kitchen I've ever seen, boy. You're going to have to do some shopping. Your days of eating out every night are over. I'll pick up enough to get you through the week later on tonight."

"Thanks, Mom. I don't know what I would be doing right now without you."

Giving Derrick a strange bittersweet smile, Sonya said, "And, it only took thirty years and a set of abandoned twins for me to hear one of you say that. You're more than welcome. Now, do you need me to help you get these two upstairs? Or, can you do it by yourself?"

Fascinated by the thought, Derrick asked, "Did you bring both of them down here at once, Mom?"

"Sure did. I'm too old to run up and down those stairs, sweetheart. Want me to show you how I did it?"

Anxiously, Derrick said, "No. They're too little for me to do any tricks with. They still feel like Slinkies to me."

"Slinkies? Never mind. Let's take them up."

Before Sonya left, she assured Derrick that there was nothing wrong with either baby. One ate what she wanted and Two ate what she wanted. Everything about them didn't have to be the same. Sonya wanted to ask Derrick when he was going to name the babies, but thought it better to give him a little more time to adjust. She also wanted to ask if he was making any progress on who their mother was, but she held her peace on that too.

That evening, Derrick did something he had never done before. He prepared his dinner, placed it on a tray and carried it up to his bedroom. Since it was after five and the twins were scheduled to be fed at six, the tray included two four ounce bottles of formula.

With the television's volume lowered, Derrick ate his dinner and struggled to stay awake. One and Two started humming and stretching at 6:10. Two gave the first cry. Derrick prepared his Pampers, wipes and cloth diapers for the ritual.

Feeling he had the situation under control, Derrick picked up Two. She felt squishier than he recalled. When Derrick turned her over on his arm, he saw why she felt squishier. Two had pooped up everything. Her sleeper was loaded. Thank God, Sonya had those pallets in their beds. It was a mess, too.

Looking down at the yawning, stretching baby, Derrick asked, "Now how am I supposed to clean you up and feed you before your sister starts making a racket?"

Two simply gave him a lopsided sleepy smile. Carrying his little squishy, slinky ward on one arm, Derrick went to the guest room. He collected a wash cloth, soap, Balmex and a clean pallet and arrived back in his bedroom in time for One to start crying in earnest. Afraid he would find the same situation with her, he focused on Two. After several trips to the bathroom, rinsing the washcloth in the bathtub and wiping down Two, Derrick knew he had set a new record for changing a poopie diaper. Glancing at the clock on his night table, it was six-twenty-two. Twelve minutes. Knowing he would have to shave quite a bit of that time off, Derrick still had no idea how. He could not make himself do anything with poopie apparel in the face bowl. That was where he brushed his teeth, washed his face and shaved. No place for poopie washcloths. Somehow, Derrick knew he would have to work the bathroom in the hall into his routine. For the moment, he made a delicate pile of the most disgusting apparel he had ever come across on a plastic trashcan liner and faced the more pressing issues.

In his bedroom, both babies were in a complete crying, gasping frenzy. That's when Derrick realized he had forgotten Two needed another undershirt and sleeper. Again, Derrick thanked God for his mother. There were extras on his dresser. As quickly as he could, Derrick dressed a screaming, totally uncooperative Two. He hurriedly retrieved the angry, red-faced, wailing One. Derrick was ecstatic when he found her unsoiled.

Laying the two babies side by side on his bed, Derrick got down on his knees and put the bottles to their lips. Two was angry, but she tried to suck the nipple between complaints and gasps. One wasn't having it. She refused to take the nipple. The miniscule ball of anger yelled with the drops of milk floating in her mouth until she choked. Little pools of rejected formula formed around her tiny neck.

Truly panicking, Derrick pulled the bottle from Two's mouth, picked up One and frantically patted her delicate back. The choking stopped, but One wasn't giving up the fit she was throwing. Angered by the withdrawal of her bottle, Two had joined in again. Derrick sat on the side of the bed, pleaded and coaxed One into taking her bottle. With One under control, he propped the bottle under his chin, balanced the baby on his chest and turned Two around on the bed with his other hand. When Derrick put the bottle near Two's lips this time, she quickly accepted it, gripped his little finger tightly and pulled it to and fro roughly.

In a matter of seconds, they were huffing, humming back and forth and loudly sucking at their bottles. Now Derrick knew why new mothers cried. If he could have faced himself in the morning, he would have done it too.

This baby stuff was nerve wrecking. He had no idea exactly when his head began to throb.

One angrily spat her nipple out first. The bottle slid down onto her stomach. Derrick waited for Two to relinquish hers. He didn't have long to wait. Thinking everything was back to normal, Derrick rose, laid One on her side next to her sister and started to pat both babies for a burp. Two gave up a good one almost immediately. One stiffened, opened her mouth soundlessly and began to twitch and kick furiously.

Just as One found sound, Derrick picked her up and started patting her back. She huffed, quieted and gave a burp after a few pats, too. The moment Derrick laid One down to give them the rest of their formula, she began to cry. When One cried, Two joined in. Resuming his original position, Derrick finished feeding them.

Still holding One, Derrick burped Two and turned her over onto her stomach. She whined and grunted miserably. He turned her onto her side and propped one of his pillows behind her back. She was agreeable with that.

Giving her the personal treatment she demanded, Derrick burped and changed One. Afterwards, he wanted to rinse those soiled things in his bathroom. Derrick didn't entertain the idea of leaving the babies alone for very long. After all, hadn't his mother said Two might throw up and choke to death. She wouldn't do it on his shift if Derrick had anything to say about it. He waited a half hour before he put them back into their bassinets.

At seven-thirty, everything in the Dawes household was in its proper place and all was well. Derrick reclined on the bed and pretended to watch television. His mind was in complete meltdown. Still dressed in suit pants and dress shirt, Derrick drifted off to sleep.

At eight-thirty, the doorbell startled Derrick. A delirious Derrick jumped up and headed down the stairs. He went to the kitchen, filled the saucepan with water and put it on the stove, turned to the refrigerator, retrieved two bottles and put them into the pot.

The doorbell rang for the second time before Derrick actually turned the stove on. Looking at his watch through bleary bloodshot eyes, Derrick said, "Eight-thirty. Jesus."

Without looking to see who was at the door, Derrick opened it. David stepped in with a frown and asked shortly, "What the hell took you so long?"

"I was asleep."

"You're not supposed to be asleep. Where are the babies?"

Smirking, Derrick said sarcastically, "They're asleep, too. What do you want, David?"

"I came by to see if you needed any help. Ready to throw the towel in yet?"

Blinking slowly, Derrick said, "The towels, wash cloths, sheets, pillowcases, blankets, drapes and the carpeting."

David laughed at his younger brother who stood eye to eye with him.

Only mildly irritated by his brother's laughter, Derrick said, "This is not funny, David. I've only been feeding them during the night, every four hours, for one night and I'm losing it already. Two made a monster mess all over and I had to clean up everything. Then, One wakes up and refuses to be quiet unless I hold her. I'm turning into a contortionist just feeding them."

Looking at his watch, David asked, "What time is their next feeding?"

"Ten o'clock."

"Okay. Next feeding's on me. You get some sleep."

"You don't know how to do it."

"Are you turning down my offer?"

Without hesitating, Derrick said, "No. Where's Hope?"

"At home, on the telephone with her mother. Telling her that if she doesn't at least get an engagement ring for Christmas, she's leaving me."

Interested, Derrick asked, "Is she going to get it?"

"You know how much I hate being threatened, Derrick. She won't get it one minute before December 26th. I might even let her pack her bags."

"But, you won't let her leave?"

"Hell, no. I'm tired of the treadmill. Besides, I could do a lot worse than Hope. It might take me another ten years to stop her from turning the heat up to ninety, but other than that, I have no real complaints with her."

# *CHAPTER EIGHT*

After turning the stove off and climbing the stairs, David fluffed Derrick's pillows and propped them the way he liked them and reclined on Derrick's bed. A brief search for the remote control satisfied David's need for entertainment. David's head shook slowly as he watched his obviously exhausted brother strip down to his briefs, fling his clothes onto a wing chair, drop onto the bed and fall fast asleep in one fluid motion. The babies had only been in the house one day and poor Derrick was brain damaged already. Derrick slept soundlessly for fifteen minutes, woke and groggily gave David five minutes of instructions on what to do with the babies when they woke. Just as suddenly as he woke, Derrick drifted off to sleep again for thirty minutes, woke up and gave David five more minutes of instruction. Derrick closed both of these sleeping sessions by saying, "Please watch Two, David. She's a puker. Don't let her choke to death. Please."

His poor demented brother was sound asleep when David fed and changed the babies. One and Two had to know something was different about the man feeding them. For openers, David was completely relaxed and talked the entire time. One started complaining first. David picked her up and asked, "Hey, are you hungry, kid?" One sucked at her hand loudly, in reply. With all of his preparatory instructions followed to the minute, David reached for the first bottle, sat and fed One without any trouble. He burped her twice and changed her.

Two still hadn't managed to do more than hum a few times. David laid One on the bed. The moment he turned away, she started to cry. David's eyebrows shot up when he asked, "What's your problem now, kid? I know the pins aren't sticking you. You don't have any."

One's wail shifted to a higher gear. David picked her up. One fretted a few moments and quieted in the warm, safe cavern of David's arm. The two studied each other's faces for a few minutes. Then, sounding exactly like Derrick the night before, David said, "I can't hold you and feed your sister. You have to lay down."

David laid her down again. Sounding like a car with a faulty ignition, One's wail finally caught on. Two joined her. Looking from one baby to the other, David said, "Oh, now I know why my poor brother is losing it. You're both ganging up on him at one time."

With both babies crying, Derrick never budged. David slid One close to his brother's huge sleeping body. As if the scent of Derrick hypnotized her, One stopped crying and studied him. Her tiny fist pummeled his lifeless arm. David mumbled, "Those itty bitty licks won't bother him, little girl. You'd better hope your Dad doesn't decide to turn over."

David fed, burped and changed Two. She seemed happier to see him than One had been. Two smiled at David's never ending chatter and sucked at the bottle happily. She kicked her feet while he changed her diaper. However, David noticed that the two babies sent up hums every so often, to ensure they weren't alone.

One fell asleep quickly with her little face buried in Derrick's massive arm. Two still kicked and nibbled at her fist. After putting One to bed, David laid Two next to Derrick. Her reaction to being near him mirrored One's. She hit him for a while and began to drift off to sleep. David thought it the most miraculous thing he had ever seen. Of course, he would never admit it. Seeing both babies' reaction of total contentment to

Derrick's nearness caused something to stir in David. A strange jealousy crept into his soul. He would never admit that either.

To be sure everything would remain sane, for his brother's sake, David hung around until after the eleven o'clock news went off. Then, he shook Derrick and told him to get up and lock the door. Feeling like he had too much to drink, Derrick dragged himself up to a sitting position and started asking questions.

David cut him off with, "They're fine, Derrick. Just lock the door and go back to sleep. Maybe you should set the clock first. You didn't even hear them when they cried earlier."

Stumbling down the stairs behind his brother, Derrick mumbled, "Okay. Thanks, Man. I owe you one."

"You owe me two. Keep up. Call ya' tomorrow."

Back in the bedroom, Derrick checked the babies. In his sleepy stupor, Derrick noticed something he would never be able to explain. Without being able to read their hands, he knew David had put the babies in the wrong beds. While this error mildly irritated Derrick, he was too tired to correct it. If they woke up now, he would break down and cry.

Setting the clock for one-forty-five, Derrick fell back into bed gladly. He felt a little better when the alarm woke him. Without too much trouble, he made it downstairs and prepared bottles. Even had enough time to dry them. Neither baby was awake when he returned. So, Derrick lay back down and closed his eyes.

This time, Two rose first. Derrick fed and changed the little good-natured baby. He even told her, "You are such a good girl. Can you tell me what's wrong with your sister?"

One woke with some fussing. She quieted the moment Derrick picked her up and ate without incident. One even drank as much as Two had. However, One fretted through the changing of her diaper and Two joined her. Derrick picked up One and scooped Two onto his lap. Both babies found that satisfactory.

Two dug her tiny sharp nails into Derrick's thigh. He flinched and said a little too loudly, "Hey, cut that out. I'll sit up with you guys all night. Make bottles. Change diapers. Hold you, if I have to. But, I will not tolerate any physical abuse."

As if they were waiting for him to say something else, both sets of eyes stared at Derrick. Two's little bottom lip began to quiver. Immediately, Derrick apologized, "I'm sorry, Two. You just can't stab a man who's doing his best."

Her tiny cry broke Derrick's heart. He pleaded, "I'm sorry, sweetheart. I didn't mean to scare you. Don't cry. Please."

With a great deal of patting and pleading, Two's cry turned to a whimper and she fell off to sleep. One seemed to be sleepy, but refused to close her eyes. She watched Derrick for another five minutes. Pulling One's bed closer, he laid her down. Still feeling guilty for hurting her feelings, Derrick held Two in his arms for a few minutes and stroked her big shiny black curls. When he laid her down, she grabbed his finger and pulled it a few times. Derrick felt like they had a truce.

Each feeding changed for the threesome, but they were getting used to each other. As the days progressed, Derrick handled the babies with less tension. One and Two felt it. He even began laying them on his bed and talking to them. They kicked, hummed and listened.

Derrick remembered the monitor on Wednesday. He remembered to get copies of his keys on Friday. Derrick decided David should have one too. He had dropped by twice that week to relieve him. Maybe he would make it a habit. Derrick certainly hoped so. He appreciated the break and the company.

On Friday, Derrick came home in a much better mood. He had never looked forward to any weekend like he looked forward to this one. He didn't know why. The babies would be his responsibility, for the most part, alone. But, he knew he could sleep whenever they did. If he could get one relief sitter, he might even get eight consecutive hours of sleep. Since dating was out, rest seemed an appropriate replacement desire.

Derrick found Sonya sitting at the kitchen table watching her soap opera. She had brought the tiny television from home with her that morning. Sonya told Derrick she expected him to buy one for his kitchen, if he expected her to stay there all day. He agreed. To keep his mother in his corner, he would put a television in every corner of every room in the house— gigantic ones, if necessary.

Derrick smelled food, but he didn't see any. As usual, he asked, "Where are the girls, Mom?"

Patting the monitor clipped to her dress pocket, she said, "They're upstairs. I had a time with One today, Derrick. You must be sitting up holding her all night."

Looking slightly guilty, Derrick said, "I only hold her if I'm feeding her, Mom. Just like you told me. She's fussier than Two. Wants more attention."

"Well, you can spoil them if you want to. You'll be a sorry camper. David told me she threw fits with him, too. He had to prop her up next to you to make her be quiet."

"He never told me that. I'll have to talk to One about that. She can't alienate my helpers."

"Your sister is going to die if you don't let her have them for a few hours this weekend. I told her she could sit with them while you went out to pick up their milk and Pampers tomorrow. If that's all right with you, make sure you tell her."

"That'll be fine, Mom."

"Did you call the doctor to make their first appointment? You don't want them falling behind in their shots."

Not liking the sound of the word shots, Derrick asked, "What shots? Shots for what, Mom?"

“They have to be immunized, Derrick."

Agitated by the thought of One and Two being hurt, Derrick said in a rush, "They're babies. Why do they have to stick them? Can't they give them drops or something? I'll pay for it."

Giving Derrick an incredulous stare, Sonya asked, "Do you think they only give needles to the poor and disenfranchised, as some type of peon torture? You can't buy their way out of this,

Derrick. They have to line up and get stuck in the booty, like everybody else, and you have to take them."

Just as Derrick was about to lodge a complaint, the doorbell rang. Derrick jammed his hands into his pockets angrily and went to answer it. He mumbled en route, "Torturing babies. They should be ashamed of themselves. I don't even like taking needles. Hell, they hurt."

Seeing his father's mixed gray hair through the glass in the door made Derrick's insides quiver. After a week like he'd been through, Ethan's abundant complaints and proclamations would not be well received. Derrick didn't really care whether his father thought the babies were his today or not.

Taking a deep bracing breath, Derrick opened the door. Ethan held a huge gift-wrapped package in his arms. While Derrick and David were a half-foot taller than Ethan, he was bulkier than either of them cared to be. The package he carried was obviously heavy, but he pushed Derrick aside as he brought it in.

Derrick turned and closed the door. Over his shoulder, Ethan said, "May as well leave it open, Derrick. The others are on their way in."

Flatly, Derrick asked, "What others?"

"Just leave the door open, Derrick. Maybe you want to go out there and help Deandra or David."

Before Derrick could ask, "Help them with what?" the doorbell rang again. Opening the door again, Derrick was greeted by his petite, golden brown, curly haired that was dyed blonde and cut short, little sister. Her eyes were similar to her brothers, but they slanted more and seemed divinely exotic on her delicate face. Deandra was dressed in regulation baggy gear, with three glittering earrings lining each earlobe. Deandra also carried a large gift-wrapped package that she refused to relinquish.

With all of the excited adoration a baby sister has for her favorite brother, Deandra gushed, "Hi, Derrick. You haven't killed either one of my nieces all week. I'm so proud of you. I knew you could do it."

Giving her a peck on top of her head, Derrick said, "Don't pass out any praises yet, Squirt. It's not getting any easier."

As Derrick and Deandra exchanged idle chatter, a literal parade of people entered Derrick's house bearing gifts. All of the people from his office, guys he and David played basketball, tennis and racquetball with. His mother's neighbors. His grandparents. He had no idea what they were doing. No one said anything more than, "Hi, Derrick." Everyone moved to the basement quickly.

David and Ethan made several trips. When Derrick asked if they needed his help, David said sarcastically, "Go check on the babies, Derrick. We've got this."

Derrick asked David's girlfriend, Hope, "What's going on?"

She shrugged her shoulders and said nothing.

He asked his father's mother, "Gran, what's going on?"

The tiny, gray haired and spectacled woman looked up at him and asked, "Where are my great grandbabies? I hear there's some room for doubt with them. I want to take a look now."

Pointing, Derrick said, "Upstairs."

Without answering Derrick's question, his grandmother brushed past him and started the slow ascent to his bedroom. He followed her. His grandfather followed him.

There was so much activity downstairs, no one heard the two crying babies upstairs. Derrick wanted to rush past his slow moving grandmother to get to them, but he dared not try it. So One and Two were extremely upset by the time Derrick reached them.

Talking to the two screaming infants, Derrick said, "Okay, girls, I'm here. Calm down."

Then it dawned on him he had no bottles for them. Turning to his grandparents, he asked, "Would you like to hold them while I get their bottles, Gran and Pop?"

They both nodded immediately. Derrick picked up Two and handed her to his grandfather. He gave One to his grandmother. One and Two fussed for a few moments, settled down and searched for their bottles with opened mouths. Derrick left before they started crying again. He was truly happy to find the two bottles already prepared on the kitchen table, and he felt his first twinge of jealousy when his grandparents held their hands out for the bottles, upon his return.

Taking his jacket off, Derrick relaxed and sat in the wing chair, observing the two old people with the babies. They compared them. Gran said to Derrick, "If these are not your babies, Derrick, they're David's, or one of your cousins. They're definitely Dawes babies. We don't have any twins, but these are Dawes babies, and that is Sonya's mother's hairline all right."

Pop asked, "Are you sure you don't know who their mother is? I can't believe she walked off and left them. Did you two have a fight or something you don't want to tell us?"

"No, sir. I don't know who she is. I've been contacting everybody it could have been with no luck. That's another reason why I don't think they're mine."

Upset with Derrick's admission that there were so many to choose from, Gran asked, "How many women are you talking about, Derrick? Don't you know being a slut can kill you these days?"

Smiling devilishly, Derrick said, "I know, Gran. I just can't seem to settle for one. There are so many beautiful women to choose from."

Never taking his eyes off of Two, Pop nodded enthusiastically and said, "Boy, do I know what you're saying. These girls today are something. Women have come a long way since I was a young man, Derrick. And, you get to see so much of them just walking down the street. I'd be dizzy if I had to choose now."

Gran said shortly, "Shut up, David. You and Ethan are the reason why David and Derrick act the way they do. And, you see what kind of trouble the boy's got into listening to you all too, don't you?"

"He ain't in no trouble, Tiny. Just got stuck with two babies. That girl may have done him a favor getting lost.

This way, he's got his children and can still sort until he finds what he really wants. Ain't nothing worse than being stuck with a woman you can't stand."

Angry in earnest now, Gran asked, "How would you know that, David? Are you saying you can't stand me?"

"Nope. Wouldn't have stayed around for over fifty years, if that was so. I've got friends, right this minute, who would rather go to the gas chamber, than be in the same room with their wives though. Only reason they're still there is because they waited too long to leave. Kick themselves every day for it."

"Who you talking about? That slimy Wilfred, or that drunk behind Mason?"

"None of your business, Tiny. Burp that baby. She ain't drinking no more."

Like always, One appeared to be listening to her great grandparent's back and forth banter. The infant was so engrossed in their conversation that she let the nipple fall from her mouth. When they stopped talking, One went back to drinking. After being burped, Two sucked leisurely and listened. She never let her nipple go until she was full.

Sonya appeared at the doorway, with two of the cutest little pink outfits in hand. Under the watchful eye of her mother-in-law, Sonya changed and dressed the babies for their coming out party. Derrick wasn't told a thing until he brought One's bassinet down to the crowded recreation room.

Tyson sauntered over to him and said sympathetically, "I'm so sorry to see this happen to a brother of your stature, Big D. You deserve better."

Grunting and then laughing at Tyson, Derrick asked, "What are you talking about now, Dude? I don't know what's happening. Who invited you here today? What did they say?"

Twisting his face, Tyson said sourly, "David called the office and gave us an open invitation to your baby shower, Big D. Before the night's over, some of your other frat brothers will be here. That ballplayer you play golf with will be here too. You're the first man I've ever known to have a baby shower. I didn't want to come see you being publicly humiliated, but the women in the office thought it was wonderful and I was stupid."

Derrick laughed again. Not at Tyson's remarks, this time at David. He wondered which one of the women dragged him into it. Derrick didn't have long to wait to get his answer. David came over with the other bassinet. When Derrick asked, David spat at him bitterly, "Your mother."

Derrick asked irritably, "Isn't this a little premature? Couldn't you all have waited until I knew those were definitely my babies?"

"Don't holler at me, Derrick. Mom says they're yours. Gran and Pop just cast their vote with her. The only hold out is Dad. And he flip-flops every other day. When Aunt Sylvia gets here and has her say, it will probably be unanimous. You try to get rid of those babies and they'll tar, feather and drag your sorry ass through every mall this side of the Mississippi."

Finishing for David, Derrick said, "Yeah, I know. And, they'll light my ass on the White House lawn as a finale."

"You know it. Mom's already had a fight with Aunt Sylvia about those babies. Aunt Sylvia says if you don't want them, she'll take them. Mom asked if she was insinuating you were irresponsible. Then, she says, 'Derrick will take care of his own children. We don't pass off our own. Thank you for the offer, Sylvia.'"

Giving Derrick's shoulder a sympathetic pat, David said, "Enjoy your baby shower, Li'l Brother."

Derrick gave it his best shot. By eight he was thoroughly exhausted. People were still showing up at nine. Sonya snatched Derrick's third beer out of his hand at ten. A totally surprised, uninvited and empty-handed Cassandra showed up at ten-fifteen. Sonya gave her a suspicious once over and said no more than a sour, "Hello."

All of the guys wanted to know how Derrick had arranged this. They thought this would be the next wave in the sexual revolution and they sort of liked it–offspring without a nagging, clinging, crying, perpetually complaining woman. In their eyes, the benefits far outweighed the sleepless nights and poopie Pampers. When they found out Derrick didn't even know who she was, they really loved the concept. Derrick's line brother, Gilmore, told him to accept his blessings gleefully and not to go looking for trouble. By the end of the night, even Tyson thought Big D was the man again.

Derrick opened gifts at ten-thirty. When he realized he wouldn't have to shop for One and Two for quite a while he accepted the good-natured ribbing with humor. Everyone had been extremely generous. Giving two of whatever they bought. There were a few duplicates, but Sonya would resolve those problems.

By midnight, everyone was partied out. One and Two slept off and on with all of the noise and tolerated being passed around. Everyone thought the babies were beautiful and belonged to Derrick. Sonya promised to return Saturday to clean up the mess. At twelve-thirty, Derrick locked the front door, for what he thought would be the last time that night.

Derrick roamed through the house turning off lights. The living room was his last stop. He was startled when Cassandra asked, "Is this why you rushed through our relationship and hustled me out of the picture, Derrick?"

## *CHAPTER NINE*

Not answering Cassandra's question, Derrick stood and stared at the beautiful, angry woman sitting on his living room sofa. Even wearing an oversized black sweater, Cassandra's ample breasts emphasized her mood. They rose, fell and quivered slightly over Cassandra's tightly crossed arms.

More weary than he could ever recall being, Derrick joined what he sincerely hoped was his one remaining guest. Derrick sat next to Cassandra. The keys he held in his hand rattled loudly in the now blessedly silent house.

Derrick had no idea how Cassandra would handle his situation. The truth was, he really didn't know very much about the woman at all. He knew he thoroughly enjoyed Cassandra on an intimate physical plane and with his three date rule already exercised with her, Derrick struggled with finalizing a clean break with Cassandra. So, he decided to try to explain as best as he could. If she could live with it, he would relax the rule long enough to get to know a little more about her.

Giving Cassandra a weak smile, Derrick said, "No, this is not the reason why I rushed through our relationship. I didn't hustle you out. As I recall it, you left because you didn't like my answers to your questions."

"And, you didn't bother trying to do anything about it. Said you were going to call me in a few days, the last time I spoke with you. A few are three in my world. What is it in yours, Derrick?"

"Look, this isn't the easiest situation to explain, Cassandra. Believe it, or not, the babies were literally dropped into my lap."

Interrupting Derrick, Cassandra asked angrily, "And, where is their mother?"

"I have no idea."

Dramatically rolling her magnificent dark brown eyes, Cassandra said, "Please, Derrick, don't lie. You and I both know she didn't just leave those babies on your doorstep and disappear into the fog-shrouded brush. It doesn't happen that way."

"No, she didn't leave them on the doorstep. She left them in the hospital, with my name, address and telephone number before she disappeared into the brush."

"Why didn't you call her and tell her to come get them? There are laws against abandoning newborns. The authorities would have forced her to take them."

"First of all, I don't know who she is. Second, the only name they have is mine. So, if any charges are brought, guess who will be wearing the cuffs?"

Holding a well-manicured hand up to stop him, Cassandra asked, "What do you mean you don't know who she is? Give me a break, Derrick. I know you don't think I'm a rocket scientist, but do you really think I'm buying this crap? You know who she is. You're protecting her for some reason."

"I'm not protecting anyone. I don't know who she is. Add this to the pile of things you can't believe. I can't swear those are my babies either, Cassandra. As you already know, I don't just sleep with anyone unprotected, haven't done it in years. So, when I say I don't know, I really don't. You take that any way you like. I'm simply trying to give it to you straight."

Moving away from Derrick, as if he had suddenly developed something contagious, Cassandra said loudly, "You don't know if they're your babies and you're having baby showers?! Derrick, I'll see you around. You've disrespected me on every imaginable level."

As she rose, Derrick grabbed her wrist and said rigidly, "I am not being disrespectful, Cassandra. I'm being honest. That's the way it is. I couldn't make up a story like this. If you think it's bizarre from your perspective, just imagine for one moment, how I feel. I didn't give that baby shower. That was my mother's idea. Do you really think I wanted all of my friends to know someone pulled a trick like this on me?"

Losing his temper for the first time since it all began, Derrick yelled at the top of his lungs, "Not only did she pull the nastiest trick she could think of! She got away with it! If I knew who she was, do you think I would allow myself to be publicly humiliated this way?! And, if she knows what's good for her, she'd better stay incognito! Now, if you think all I have to do is lie to you, move on, Cassandra! I don't need any more female nonsense right now! I've got babies to take care of!"

Cassandra hissed, "I'll be doing just that, Derrick. You see, I know Miss Mommy won't stay incognito. And you know who won't be dealing with you, or her? Me!"

"Fine. See ya."

Derrick relinquished Cassandra's arm and headed for the door. He unlocked it and flung it open. Cassandra tussled with her jacket and tears glistened in her eyes, as she opened her mouth to speak. Derrick's sneer froze the words in her throat. Without another sound, Cassandra left. Derrick slammed the door behind her.

After locking the door for the second time that night, Derrick leaned on it, sighed, dropped his head and massaged his temples. Needing silence more than air, Derrick sent up a silent prayer, "Please let One and Two sleep beyond their regularly scheduled feeding time."

Not only was Derrick's prayer not answered, One and Two woke fifteen minutes earlier and both refused to go back to sleep. Propped up on pillows, with One on his left shoulder and Two relaxing in the fold of his right arm, Derrick rocked and talked to them about his problems. He told them women were more trouble than they were worth. If either one of them ever did anything like this, he vehemently vowed he would give them a good spanking. They hummed their responses. Looking at the clock on his night table, it was four-ten when the girls gave up and allowed Derrick to lay them down for the night.

The telephone rang twice while Derrick tried to get the girls to sleep, but he didn't answer. The moment he heard Cassandra's voice, he turned down the volume on his answering machine. There was no way he would voluntarily listen to another chorus of, "You're not just a liar, Derrick . . . you're a big liar."

Six o'clock rolled around way too soon and Derrick found himself facing the same routine he had dealt with at two. At eight, he fell asleep again. At ten, the babies woke. His blonde-haired sister miraculously appeared at his bedroom door and volunteered to take them. If Derrick could have found the strength, he would have kissed all six of her studded and hoop earrings.

Without waking Derrick at noon, Sonya came into his bedroom, found his wallet and removed the cash necessary to purchase formula and Pampers. She and Deandra dressed One and Two, they packed the brand new twin stroller in the trunk of the car and with a baby and a diaper bag each, the two pulled off, heading for the supermarket and mall. They left Derrick a note on the kitchen counter. It simply said, "Gone shopping. Mom."

At two in the afternoon, Derrick struggled to a sitting position. Still feeling drugged, he wondered if this was the way it would always be. Derrick was definitely beginning to identify with what he always thought of as his mother's irrational bad moods. How spastic she would be for no discernible reason. He knew now that the years of broken sleep patterns had messed with her mind. At that moment, Derrick wanted to hurt someone, too. While anyone would do, he really wanted it to be the mother of One and Two.

Derrick threw on jogging pants and a sweatshirt. Shaving was out of the question. Derrick didn't trust his weary eyes. He settled for washing his face and brushing his teeth. He went down to find his family. Finding the note on the counter, he made coffee and drank it in silence. Knowing his mother and sister never returned from shopping before the sun went down, Derrick decided to get some exercise. He would eat later.

In the basement, Derrick saw how beautifully Sonya had displayed all of the shower gifts. He smirked at them and went into the small exercise room. After using the rowing machine for half an hour, the adrenalin rush spurred Derrick on to lift weights.

Derrick was so engrossed in what he was doing, and so accustomed to being alone, David's sudden appearance frightened him. Derrick recognized his brother one second before he threw the weight he was lifting across the room. This was why Derrick never wanted anyone to have his key. People would be sneaking up on him forever now.

In an unusually bitter tone, Derrick asked, "What do you want?"

Sarcastically, David said, "Hey, how ya doin', Derrick? See you've still got enough strength to lift a few."

"Very funny. What do you want?"

"I don't want anything, Mom. Roger wants to talk to you about the babies. I brought him over. He's upstairs in the kitchen."

Miserably, Derrick groaned, "Aw, David. I don't feel like talking. Roger can't do anything."

"You don't know that. If those are not your babies, shouldn't you know what your options are? Just talk to the man."

Reaching for his towel, Derrick dried his face, neck and chest. He glared angrily at David's back all of the way up the stairs and into the kitchen. Derrick mustered the most pleasant smile he could manage for Roger and shook his hand.

Looking into Derrick's weary eyes, Roger said, "They're getting to you, I see. Are you absolutely sure you don't know who their mother is, Derrick?"

Dropping into a chair, Derrick said, "Roger, if I knew who she was, I would never have taken those babies from that hospital. I've called everyone I dated at the end of last year and spoken to, or seen almost all of them. No one's owning up to the babies though."

"Were there any nameless, one night stands among them?"

Testily, Derrick snapped, "I don't do nameless, one night stands, Roger. That's David."

David put a finger up, as if to object to Derrick's charge. Then, with a guilty pout, he let it fall soundlessly.

Taking the spotlight off of David, Roger said, "Okay. That's not normal for you. But, we all have that one time we'd like to forget."

"There are things I'd like to forget, Roger. None of them were nameless though. Whoever she is, I know her and she knows me. It may be someone who just thought I would be a good guardian for her children. Who says I slept with her?"

Looking down at his shoe, Roger asked, "Would you like me to see what I can find out about her, Derrick?"

Without hesitating, Derrick asked, "Can you do it without bringing any of those children's agencies down on the babies? They're not going into any shelter or foster homes, Roger. Not before I know, for a fact, they're not mine anyway. I have to put that brick to bed first."

"If I approach the hospital to find out things like, if she came there for prenatal care, her blood type, or if she had any unique problems that would require further medical attention; it might do that. But those are the kinds of questions I need answers to in order to find her, Derrick."

David interjected, "Perhaps he could speak to Mrs. Monet, Derrick. She wouldn't tell. Maybe somebody can give up a decent description of her. That would be something to start with. She said she wanted to help you."

Wanting desperately to grab the string Roger was offering, Derrick's main concern held. He did not want any attention brought to the babies. His thoughts refused to be diverted from protecting One and Two.

Derrick looked Roger in the eyes and asked, "If I don't find out who she is, and the babies are mine, will she be able to show up and take them from me?"

"The way the courts think today, Derrick, she'll be able to do anything she wants. Of course, if that's not her real name on their birth certificates, she'll have to prove they're her children first. The best you could hope for is shared custody."

In a raised angry voice, Derrick said, "But she abandoned them, Roger! Won't that count for anything?!"

"Not if you're their real father. Leaving a child with its natural parent doesn't constitute abandonment in the eyes of the court. If that were so, there would be googobbles of men in prison for it right now. They only search them out for not supporting the child financially. Now, if you both walked away, they would charge whomever they could find. In this case, that's you."

With a twisted smirk, David said, "Now that really sucks. We can leave, if we pay. They can leave and to hell with it. We can come back and see the kid on the weekend. They can come back and we still get to see the kid on the weekend. Sounds like we get to pay for the short end of the stick, no matter what. Who said this was a man's world?"

Roger asked seriously, "Do you really want to find her, Derrick?"

Solemnly, Derrick answered, "I don't know."

"Let me ask you this then. If we find her, what do you want to happen? Are you willing to give the babies to a woman who could walk away from them? She could drop them on you anytime she wanted and walk again and again. Or, she could set up child support through the court that you'll pay, no matter where those babies are. No matter how they're taken care of. I don't have to tell you getting into the system is easy and getting out is a bitch, do I? Even if we tell them you have the children, they'll lock you up five times for non-payment before they correct the error."

Derrick's thumbs circled each other in his lap, as he sat thinking about Roger's question. David knew that meant he was giving serious thought to his next response. Whoever this woman was, she held Derrick firmly by his testicles. If he turned in either direction, it would hurt like hell.

Finally, Derrick said, "I don't want to look for her. Right now I'd just like to know if they're mine. If they are, we'll have to deal with her when, or if, she ever shows up. If they're not, I'll have you explore some adoption possibilities. Let her try to find them twenty years from now."

Roger asked, "Are you absolutely sure that's what you want to do?"

Looking Roger in the eye, Derrick said, "Yeah. I'll handle them until I know."

Looking at Derrick quizzically, Roger asked, "You really don't want to know who she is, Derrick?"

"Do I need to know who she is, Roger?"

"If she tries to take the babies five years from now, after she's got her life together, you might wish you had. For all you know she's watching everything you're doing. She'll be prepared when she fires the first shot, Derrick. Custody fighting is the most vicious fight you can get into. Worse even than divorce. They don't just throw dirt–they throw molten lava. Everybody's disfigured when it's over."

"Let her throw it then. If those are my children and she abandoned them, I'll put on an asbestos suit and go a few rounds with her. Leave the country with them, if I have to–just to give her a tiny taste of what it feels like to be left wanting and wondering. Let her cry on Oprah's shoulder fifteen years from now. I'm sure she'll be sympathetic to the poor, slobbering idiot. Telling the world how confused, frightened and alone she was. That leaving them was her only alternative, and how I stole her children."

Thoroughly understanding Derrick's bitterness, Roger let it go. He would get whatever information he could from the woman David had mentioned. Perhaps he could find the babies' mother and keep an eye on her for his friend. If the day ever came when he needed to know, Roger would have a step up on the young lady.

Derrick and David made breakfast at four in the afternoon. The three men were eating, sharing baby horror stories and laughing when Sonya, Deandra, One, and Two returned. One whined until Derrick held her. Then, she dropped off to sleep in his arms. Two sat in David's lap looking around. She too fell asleep the moment Derrick took her from him.

## *CHAPTER TEN*

In one month, Derrick had become a pretty good parent. Sonya didn't have to help him on Saturdays anymore. On his own, he could actually feed, bathe, dress and entertain both babies. Wash clothes, do a little house cleaning and get in at least one hour of exercise. He even allowed David to have his card games at his house on Friday nights. One and Two didn't seem to mind the noise and Derrick appreciated the company one night a week.

Of course, if Sonya and Deandra didn't do the shopping, cook and freeze his meals, Derrick would either starve to death or order out every night. Besides that, they saw that his clothes made it to the cleaners, ran the vacuum cleaner twice a week and saw that the girls got fresh air everyday. At the ripe old age of one month, One and Two probably knew more about the malls than Derrick.

There was one distinct difference in Derrick's life after the babies' arrival. The women. The ones who would have only looked at him longingly and silently before now spoke to him. They carried on over the babies first, asked all kinds of questions about them and gave Derrick more child-care and rearing advice than he cared to listen to. All of them said they loved seeing a father take an interest in babies so young. And, they all seemed genuinely pleased to find out the babies didn't have a mother at home. Derrick took a few telephone numbers, but called no one.

Other than an occasional futile argument with Cassandra, Derrick didn't speak to any women. He spoke to all of his suspects and got denials from each one. Some denied it more vehemently than others. Pamela went so far as to come to Derrick's office and show him her bare midriff. She screamed, "See! No stretch marks! Try again, Buddy!" Angelique thought it was the funniest thing she had ever heard, asked if there was anything she could do to help and told Derrick she had reconciled with her husband.

Accepting the fact that he was stuck with One and Two, Derrick gave up the Mommy search. Still, every woman who stared at One and Two too hard, Derrick noted them. He wouldn't put it past her to strike up a friendship with him to be close to the girls, without the responsibility of taking care of them, of course.

On Sonya's insistence, Derrick took the day off to take One and Two for their first physicals. She and Deandra made a big fuss about naming them, too. Derrick hadn't budged on that issue. He insisted he still saw them as One and Two. It didn't seem important, until Derrick took them to the pediatrician's office.

Using Sonya's car to transport One and Two, Derrick easily transferred them to their stroller and made his way into the medical building. He was glad the stroller had a pouch large enough to carry those two pink bags. Inside, Derrick was given two registration cards by the receptionist. He filled them out. In the last name slot, Derrick wrote, "Dawes." In the first name slot, Derrick wrote, "One and Two," respectively.

The receptionist smiled at Derrick, accepted the two cards and said, "If you'll have a seat, the nurse will be with you in a moment, Mr. Dawes."

Her eyes focused on the cards she held in her hand. Suddenly, the smile fell away from her pretty face and a frown replaced it. She gave Derrick's back the strangest look. Refusing to entangle herself in an argument with a client, the receptionist rose from her seat and carried the two cards into the back. When she returned to her desk, the receptionist stared at Derrick every chance she got.

Five minutes later, the nurse appeared in the doorway and said, "Dawes."

Derrick stood and followed her, pushing the carriage. She directed him to the third examination room. Inside, the nurse smiled and asked, "Will you need help undressing them, Mr. Dawes?"

Looking directly at the nurse, with his male mask of confusion in place, Derrick asked, "Why do they have to be undressed?"

The smile on the nurse's face vanished. Confused by Derrick's question, she asked, "Excuse me?"

Derrick repeated, "Why do they have to be undressed?"

In an extremely serious tone, she responded, "They have to be weighed, measured, examined and vaccinated, Mr. Dawes. We can't do that properly, if they're dressed. Don't worry, we do it to all of our patients."

Leery of this extremely attractive manila woman, with jet-black hair pulled back into a long, thick ponytail, and dressed from head to toe in white. Derrick asked in a whisper, "Are you going to hurt them?"

Batting back tears of laughter, she said, "The vaccination will be uncomfortable for them, Mr. Dawes, but it's unavoidable. If you would prefer leaving the room, the doctor and I will handle it."

"No! I'm not leaving them!" Derrick snapped so fast it made her jump.

Recovering quickly, she said calmly, "Okay, Mr. Dawes. Let's get them undressed then."

Derrick picked up a sleeping One and watched the nurse pick up Two. He laid One on the table next to Two. They undressed them down to their pampers. The cold air woke them. Both babies blinked and seemed agitated by the bright lighting of the room.

One shivered. Derrick picked her up and searched for their receiving blankets. He handed the nurse one of the blankets and said, "Would you wrap this around her, please? They're cold."

Smiling up at Derrick, the nurse said, "I most certainly will, Mr. Dawes. Wouldn't want them to come to the doctor's office to get sick."

Both babies were wrapped when the doctor arrived a few minutes later. He was an extremely personable man, five feet ten, or so. Thick, wavy blonde hair, cut short, startling blue eyes and the keenest nose Derrick had ever seen. The doctor looked as if he were an avid tennis player. He still had the remnants of a tan in October.

Dr. Kane extended his hand and smiled up at Derrick. Moving with stiffened apprehension, Derrick shook it. Dr. Kane asked, "I take it these are your first babies, Mr. Dawes?"

"Yes, they are."

As if these were the most natural of questions, Dr. Kane asked, "Why didn't their mother come in today? Were there any complications with the delivery?"

Unprepared for those questions, Derrick stammered his way through a variety of frustrated answers, "They don't have a mother. I mean, we're not together anymore. It's just me. There were no problems that I know of."

Incredulously, Dr. Kane asked, "Are you saying she left you and two brand new babies?"

"Yes."

"Is that why their names are One and Two, Mr. Dawes?"

"Uh, yeah. I haven't decided on real names yet."

Not wanting to delve any deeper too soon, Dr. Kane said cheerfully, "Okay, girls. Who's going first?"

Derrick didn't want either one to go first. Dr. Kane saw his indecision and suggested, "Maybe we should start with One, since she's the oldest, Mr. Dawes."

Reluctantly, Derrick handed One to the doctor. Derrick watched his every move like a hawk and approved of the way he handled One. Then, as Dr. Kane placed the stethoscope on One's tiny chest, Derrick thought he saw something under his nails. Without a moment's hesitation, Derrick snatched both of the doctor's hands away from the shivering baby. He carefully examined the nails. Derrick saw no dirt beneath the doctor's nails and turned the palms up. There was no dirt at all. Satisfied, Derrick let the doctor's hands go and nodded.

Obviously suspicious of Derrick's mental stability, Dr. Kane asked, "Are you sure?"

Derrick nodded.

One didn't care for any of the manipulations, but she didn't cry. The nurse handed Two over to Derrick and assisted the doctor. She weighed, measured and wrote on the chart while Dr. Kane looked into the baby's eyes and ears, listened to her chest and stomach, purposely tickled her feet and gauged her grip on his finger.

After removing One's diaper and checking for discolorations or rashes, Dr. Kane said, "You're doing a fine job, Mr. Dawes. She's not only beautiful she appears to be a picture of health and scrupulous loving care. Now, you do know I have to give them shots today?"

Derrick simply nodded.

Half smiling, Dr. Kane asked, "Are you going to try to rip my arm out of the socket, if she cries, Mr. Dawes?"

First, Derrick shrugged his shoulders. Then, he shook his head from side to side. Finally, he said, "I'll try not to. You just try not to make her scream too loud."

Looking at his nurse, Dr. Kane said, "Okay, Jocelyn. Let's see if we can do this, without making her scream too loud."

Handing Dr. Kane the capped hypodermic, Jocelyn positioned herself between Derrick and the examination table. If he made a move, she would block him long enough for the doctor to remove the needle, without injuring the baby. Still holding Two, Derrick easily saw what the doctor was doing to One over the nurse's head. Jocelyn couldn't help shaking her head and giving a tiny laugh, when the doctor stuck One's little thigh. Derrick's face contorted painfully, as he hissed loudly, closed his eyes and slowly sat.

The moment Derrick heard One's startled cry he stood. Jocelyn put both of her hands out to stop him. Derrick swept them down and her aside. All she could do was say in a rush, "Mr. Dawes, she's fine. Really, she is. Just let the doctor finish. I'll put her Pamper on and you can dress her while we look at Two. Okay?"

Shaken to the core by One's distress, Derrick snapped, "Are you sure?!"

Silently thanking God the baby only cried briefly, Jocelyn said, "I'm positive."

Seeing Derrick was relieved by Jocelyn's assurances, Dr. Kane stepped aside and allowed her to diaper the baby. He used the time settling his own rattled nerves. Dr. Kane knew that if Derrick thought he was hurting his baby, he was more than capable of doing quite a bit of damage to him and his office, before help could be summoned. The man looked like a professional football player. He wasn't too far off. Derrick had indeed played college football. It had paid for his education.

Jocelyn had her hands filled trying to get Derrick to trade babies with her. He was willing to accept One. He just wasn't too sure he wanted them to have Two. Jocelyn offered him the opportunity to wait outside the room again. Derrick looked at her as if she had suddenly spewed pools of green saliva. He said, "No way, lady. I'm not leaving her in here with you and Dr. Mengele."

"Will you sit, dress your baby and let us do our job, Mr. Dawes? It'll all be over much quicker."

Knowing it had to be done, Derrick sighed as if the weight of the world were on his shoulders. Shaking his head pitifully, he handed Two over and said, "Please try not to hurt her. She's not as tough as One."

Just as Jocelyn promised, it was over in no time. And, to everyone's surprise and relief, Two didn't even cry when she got her shot. Derrick happily dressed One as quickly as he could. He didn't want anyone to think of anything else to do to torture them. Jocelyn helped him by dressing Two.

Dr. Kane was pleased to report to Derrick, "Both babies are in excellent health. One weighs five pounds and fifteen ounces. Two cleared six pounds. They're strong and alert. Have perfect infant hearing and sight. Do you have any questions, Mr. Dawes?"

Still angry about the shots, Derrick said, "No. Yes. When will they start sleeping through the night?"

Trying desperately not to sound disrespectful, Dr. Kane replied, "When they're ready. No two babies do the same things. How often do they wake during the night?"

"They wake up every four hours, day and night."

Dr. Kane told Derrick they would break the pattern when they were ready again. The doctor shook Derrick's hand and said he looked forward to seeing them all next month. Then, he left the room.

Dressing Two, Jocelyn said, "My grandmother says babies only wake up because they're hungry. If you sprinkle a little rice cereal in their formula at night, they'll sleep longer."

Interested, Derrick asked, "Does it work?"

Smiling warmly, Jocelyn said, "I can't swear to it, because I haven't had any children to try it on. But, if Granny says it's so, she should know. She raised nine of us."

Derrick exclaimed, "Nine! Yeah, she knows. I'll try it."

Everything progressed smoothly. That is, until Jocelyn handed Derrick a bottle of liquid Tylenol and said, "If the babies experience any pain in their legs, or run a temperature, you can give them this. Follow the instructions. If it persists beyond tomorrow, give us a call."

Derrick asked angrily, "What the hell are you saying now, lady? Are you saying One and Two are going to get sick from those shots?"

"It's possible they'll run a temperature. Have an achy leg. That's about it."

"Why did you give it to them, then?! What's the matter with you people?! I bring you two well babies you make them sick and give them back to me! This isn't making any sense to me! Why can't you just give whatever to them by mouth?! If they're going to get sick anyway, why add injury to insult by cramping up their legs?!"

Not wanting to lose patience with the tall, exceptionally good looking single papa, Jocelyn held her hands out and said sternly, "Listen, Mr. Dawes. The shots will protect them from a lot of bad things you can't protect them from. Things that can and will make them a lot sicker than you would ever be able to handle. Possibly kill them. Isn't saving them from that worth a little fever and an ache?"

Taking the bottle of Tylenol from her hand, Derrick asked how much he had to give them and how often. Jocelyn wrote the instructions and their next appointment down, handed the paper to Derrick and said, "If you're not sure of anything, Mr. Dawes, please feel free to call. If it will make you feel any better, we'll call you before we leave this afternoon."

Glaring at Jocelyn like he wanted to break her neck, Derrick said, "Yeah, you do that. If they're sick when you call, you can just pick them up and fix them."

Really tired of fighting with Derrick, Jocelyn said, "Anything you say, Mr. Dawes."

Then, bending to see One and Two, she touched their cheeks, smiled and said sweetly, "See you girls next month, or later on this evening."

Pushing the stroller toward the door, Derrick mumbled, "Very funny."

Jocelyn remarked, "If you think that's funny, how about we won't treat them next month, if they don't have names?"

Derrick stopped at the door and asked, "Is that all I have to do to save them from this torture chamber you call a doctor's office?"

Sorry she had said it, Jocelyn said, "No, Mr. Dawes. We'll treat One and Two, without names, as long as we have to."

Derrick mumbled, "I thought so."

# *CHAPTER ELEVEN*

One and Two survived their first doctor's visit with Derrick, and they ate and slept in their usual patterns for the remainder of the afternoon. When Jocelyn, the pediatrician's nurse, called at six that evening, all was well. Sonya left Derrick and the babies around seven. One and Two seemed more irritable and difficult during their ten o'clock feeding.

At two in the morning, when Derrick touched them, both babies were burning up and had diarrhea. No one had said anything about diarrhea. Derrick considered calling his mother. Knowing she would say he was panicking unnecessarily, Derrick dismissed the idea. After cleaning them up, Derrick fed One and Two, gave them Tylenol and rubbed their legs with alcohol. That soothed Two, but One fidgeted and whined until after four-thirty. Derrick fell asleep with the fussy baby on his chest.

The clock rang at six. One whined when Derrick reached to turn it off. He rocked her gently until she fell asleep again and laid her in the bassinet. Knowing he had to go to the office today, Derrick was torn.

Those Southland people were scheduled to come into Derrick's office to discuss possible last minute changes. Derrick would have to assure them that their auxiliary power sources could handle all of their equipment during an emergency. Not knowing yet what all that included, Derrick could only hope the present design would be sufficient. If not, it was back to the drawing board.

Before showering and dressing, Derrick checked the sleeping infants. They still felt warm to his touch, and they were cranky as hell. He hated leaving them. What if they needed to go back to Mengele's office? Should he expect his mother to run there, too?

Accustomed to sleep deprivation now, Derrick made his way through his morning rituals. He darted down the stairs when he heard Sonya turning her key in the door. Derrick needed someone to tell him what to do. Go to work, or stay home.

Speaking with urgency, Derrick reported the night's turmoil to Sonya. Then, he asked, "Should I stay here, or go to work, Mom?"

Without so much as a blink, Sonya said, "Go to work, Derrick. They'll be fine. All babies run fevers after they get those shots. They get cranky, too. Relax. I'll call you if I think it's gone too far."

Rubbing his forehead, Derrick asked, "How will you know when it's gone too far, Mom?"

Taking his hand down, Sonya said, "Relax, Derrick. I'll know if my kittens need help. Trust me."

"What about the cereal thing, Mom?"

Producing the box from her bag, Sonya said, "Now that they're drinking almost eight ounces of milk, it should be all right to try it. I had to feed Deandra from a spoon before she was a month old. They don't recommend it, but the girl only slept two hours at a time. When you're not getting any sleep, you don't much care what they recommend. Don't think you're getting away with feeding them through a bottle either, Derrick. I don't like food in bottles. Makes big, fat, lazy babies. You'll feed them with a spoon."

Accepting Sonya's ruling, Derrick ate breakfast and left for the office. With an office filled with executives, Derrick excused himself and called the house every half hour. Tyson shook his head in disdain at Big D's behavior. His idol had finally fallen over the edge.

At eleven, the telephone rang at Derrick's house. Sure it was Derrick calling again and without waiting for him to speak, Sonya yelled, "They're fine!"

A woman's voice replied, "I'm certainly happy to hear that."

Feeling justifiably silly, Sonya said, "Oh, I'm sorry. I thought you were Derrick."

"No, I'm Dr. Kane's nurse, Jocelyn Avery. I wanted to check on One and Two while we had a break."

"I'm Mrs. Dawes, Jocelyn. The girls are fine. They've been running low temperatures. Cried about the pain in their legs and had a bout of diarrhea during the night. They've cooled off some since I bathed them. One's a little crankier than usual."

"That sounds pretty normal to me, Mrs. Dawes. I'm glad to hear you and your husband have put aside your differences. Those babies need both of you."

"The differences between me and my husband are too well entrenched to be put aside. Years of loving each other and the good Lord's grace keeps us on a pretty even keel though."

Knowing she was prying in a forbidden area, Jocelyn attempted to clean up by saying, "I'm sorry, Mrs. Dawes. Your husband was a bit of a handful in our office yesterday. When asked, he gave the impression that there was no Mrs. Dawes."

Laughing, Sonya said, "In Derrick's life, there isn't. I'm his mother. I take care of the babies while he works."

Pleased, without acknowledging why, Jocelyn responded, "Oh. Okay, then. Since everything's good, I'll see them next month."

With a second thought, Jocelyn couldn't help asking, "Mrs. Dawes, I know this isn't any of my business either, but when is your son going to name them?"

Laughing louder this time, Sonya said, "In Derrick's mind they've already got names."

"One and Two aren't names," Jocelyn offered apologetically.

"You call him and tell him that, Jocelyn. I'm running out of air on the subject. Derrick does exactly what he wants, when he wants. And, he's been more obstinate than usual, since he inherited the babies."

"Didn't he like the names their mother gave them?"

"All she gave them was him. No names, no nothing. That's a long ugly story."

Not caring for what she was hearing at all, Jocelyn asked, "Are you saying his wife left the two babies without bothering to name them?"

"Stop saying wife, honey. Derrick's not married. He's not even sure these are his babies. I think they are. They look like him. Of course, I could be wrong, but I doubt it. She left them at the hospital with his name. She didn't even leave a note. He's stuck with these little angels."

Stunned by Sonya's story, Jocelyn stammered when she said, "She did what? He doesn't know what? What kind of a mess is that? Why didn't he force her to take them? And, please don't tell me she threatened to put them up for adoption."

Undisturbed, Sonya said, "No, she didn't threaten him. He doesn't know who she is."

"He doesn't know who who is?"

"The babies' mother."

Laughing, Jocelyn said, "You're making this up, Mrs. Dawes. I'll stop asking questions now."

"I'm not making up anything, sweetheart. Just telling it like it is."

"Excuse me, but that's a lot to swallow. He takes such good care of them. I can't believe he doesn't think they're his."

"Truth be told, I don't know exactly what Derrick thinks. He's just a responsible, humane person. Been calling every few minutes checking on his girls, too. If they don't cool off and stop crying before he gets back home, he may come down there and wring Dr. Kane's neck."

Laughing hysterically, Jocelyn said, "I thought he was going to do that yesterday. If he has any questions when he comes in, tell him to call us."

Sucking her teeth in feigned disgust, Sonya said, "The other line's beeping. It's Derrick. I'll give him your message, Jocelyn. Thanks for calling. Good-bye."

Clicking over and without saying hello, Sonya shouted, "They're fine, Derrick!"

Not put off at all by her bellowing, Derrick responded, "Okay, Mom. I'll call later."

"I'm sure you will."

Derrick, One and Two survived the side effects of the tetanus shots without calling the doctor's office. As the month rolled on, things changed a little here and there. One and Two decided they didn't want to sleep and eat at the same times anymore. This meant Derrick was busy with one or the other all of the time. The only change Derrick appreciated was they slept six hours straight at night—together.

Even though their stencils were lightening, Derrick never confused One for Two, or vice versa. Physically, the babies were identical. The differences between them were subtle, but distinct to Derrick. It lay in their facial expressions, attitudes and behavior.

One was seldom satisfied if Derrick wasn't holding her. Two's life rolled along just fine as long as she could see or hear Derrick. Both babies tolerated their Grammy Sonya during the day, but after hearing Derrick's voice, Grammy Sonya could split whenever she felt like it.

Uncle David was interesting. He never gave them a chance to get all wound-up. Uncle David talked right through any of their complaints. If Derrick had to stay late at work, Uncle David was his pinch hitter. Derrick didn't appreciate the fact that David always shook the babies up. They puked every time. But, other than that, he was okay.

Aunt Dee made them cry all of the time messing with their hair and clothes every minute they were in her presence. Aunt Dee didn't get upset if they puked on themselves. That simply gave her another reason to dress them all over again. Aunt Dee also talked Grammy Sonya into taking them to the mall and getting their ears pierced without Derrick's permission. Needless to say, he was furious. Aunt Dee also made arrangements for their first portraits and Derrick appreciated that. They were beautiful.

Grampa Ethan must have seemed more like Derrick than anyone else to One and Two. Their reactions to him mirrored Derrick's. One reclined in his lap happily all day on Sundays. She kept her eyes on Derrick, though. Two giggled when Grampa Ethan spoke to her. She played with his face when he held her and laid her head on his shoulder in total contentment.

No matter who they were with, One and Two hummed periodically and waited for a response hum. If they didn't get it, then you saw what a real twin tantrum was. Nothing short of letting them touch each other ended it. When one or the other was asleep and didn't hear the hum, Derrick held their hands and guided the touch. This practice appeased them until they thought about the other again and sent up another signal.

In early November, Derrick spent a lot of time inspecting the wiring at the construction site. On occasion, the contractors substituted inferior materials. While they may look the same to a layman, they never fooled Derrick. There would be hell to pay if he found it, too. He had no problem informing other builders of the discrepancies. One contractor had to leave town to make a living afterwards.

Derrick didn't like the officials finding fault with his work and they very seldom did. That's why his group stayed in demand. The firm they worked for pretty much allowed Derrick's team their independence. They knew the day Derrick could afford his own firm they were going to lose him and at least five of the best electrical engineers in the business.

Derrick informed Clyde Majors, the president, that if they wanted him to work on the upcoming Crystal Towers project, he could only guarantee them twenty hours a week. When asked why, Derrick simply replied, "It's personal." They accepted his terms and his leave request for the month of December. If the initial architectural drawings were approved, Crystal Towers wouldn't start in earnest until the middle of January. And, even then, they only needed preliminary drawings that would change a hundred times before anyone agreed on anything.

The final touches were completed on the Southland building the Friday night before One and Two had to endure their second doctor's appointment. Since they didn't have to go until Monday, Derrick couldn't have been happier. He felt he could let his hair down just a tad.

To celebrate another job well done, all concerned parties went out for drinks afterwards. A pouting Cassandra joined them. So did David and Hope. Deandra was the official babysitter for the evening. Of course, Ethan stayed at Derrick's house with her. Sonya taught reading classes on Friday nights.

After three neat brandies, Derrick felt mellow. He only had an occasional harmless, flip remark regarding inheriting abandoned babies thrown his way. A few people wanted to know if the girls were old enough to have company, if Derrick would mind watching their kids because they had errands to run. Derrick smiled vacuously at such remarks and requests, but David asked how much they were paying.

Cassandra's conversation wasn't so lighthearted. Giving Derrick up for those babies didn't set well with her. More than anything, Cassandra wanted to know who their mother was and if she thought the babies would seal her fate with Derrick upon her return. It quickly became obvious to Cassandra that the babies meant a great deal to Derrick. He phoned home to check on them every thirty minutes without glancing at his watch.

Not having one maternal bone in her body didn't dissuade Cassandra. She hated admitting, even to herself, how much she had missed Derrick in those two months. While Cassandra wasn't looking for a husband and children, she was determined to forge a spot for herself in his life anyway. If babies absolutely positively came with Derrick, she'd learn to deal with the dribbling creatures.

Leaning her chin on Derrick's shoulder and gazing up into his sparkling caramel eyes, Cassandra asked in a sweet, breathless whisper, "What are your plans for the rest of the evening, Derrick?"

Looking at his watch, Derrick said, "I promised Squirt I would be home by ten. She has a class in the morning."

"On a Saturday?"

"Oboe lesson."

"Would you like me to come over tonight and help you with the babies?"

Flashing a gleaming set of perfect teeth, Derrick announced proudly, "I don't need any help with the babies. We get along just fine, Cassandra."

Stroking Derrick's earlobe with her finger, Cassandra said, "I'm really happy to hear that, Derrick. Perhaps, I could help you with something more personal."

"Now, that sounds interesting."

Giving Derrick's earlobe a warm, wet nibble, Cassandra asked, "Just interesting?"

Sighing deeply, Derrick blinked slowly and said, "Okay. It's the best offer I've had in a while. I just can't take you up on it tonight."

Moving away slightly and continuing to stroke Derrick's earlobe, Cassandra pouted and asked, "Why not? I know you're not worried about setting a bad example for two month old babies."

"That's not it at all, Cassandra."

Battling the agitation spurred by Derrick's rejection, Cassandra said tartly, "Well, tell me what it is, Derrick. I know you've missed my company after two months. I've sure as hell missed yours."

Looking down at her luscious red pouting lips, Derrick really hated having to say this, but he said, "Oh yes, I've definitely missed your company. I just don't want to start any bad habits with them, Cassandra. They're too hard to break. Before you start accusing and crying, let me say right now, there is no one else either."

The moment the last phrase passed his lips Derrick regretted it. Not because it would upset Cassandra. He never said there is no one else. It gave women the wrong idea. Now, Cassandra would automatically assume she was the only meal in town.

Truly aggravated, Cassandra asked bitterly, "So, what are you saying, Derrick? You're turning into a monk until the girls are adults?"

"No. I'm saying that if I can get my mother, brother, or sister to sit with the babies on a Saturday evening, I'll have to squeeze my extra-curricular activities into that time slot for a while."

"What am I supposed to do until you can arrange this mini- rendezvous, Derrick?"

"I can't tell you what to do, Cassandra. If I can make arrangements for tomorrow, or next Saturday, I'll let you know. We can take it one step at a time. Have dinner. See a show."

Finally, the tenuous reserve shield snapped and Cassandra screeched, "I don't want to have dinner, or see a show, Derrick! I need to spend some quality time with you! And, please don't act like you don't know what I mean!"

Smiling devilishly, Derrick said in his rich baritone voice, "Oh, sweetheart, I know exactly what you mean. If that's your preference, then I'll have to spend that time with you at your place. Mine is off limits for a while. That's all I'm saying."

Desperately wanting to believe Derrick's offer was genuine, Cassandra said, "Your brother and his girlfriend are sitting right over there. Go ask them about tomorrow right now, Derrick."

Knowing he would do anything to keep her from raising her voice again, Derrick threw his hands in the air and said, "Okay, Cassandra. If they say they have other plans, you'd better not throw any of your fits. I can't make anymore demands on my family. They've been too good to me through this."

Smiling and pouting prettily, Cassandra said, "I promise."

Derrick moseyed over to David and Hope's cubicle and asked if he could speak to David for a moment in private. Hope smiled demurely and nodded her consent. None of David's friends would have received such an amiable response.

David followed his brother to the back of the lounge. As soon as they stopped, David asked mischievously, "What's the matter, Li'l Brother? You need help with that exceptionally fine honey? It's women like her that keep me up at night wondering if I want to buy Hope's ring or not."

Ignoring David's sarcasm, Derrick asked, "What are you and Hope doing tomorrow?"

"I don't know. Hope gets her hair and nails done most Saturday afternoons. Since we're out tonight, she won't carry on too badly if I have other plans for the day. Why? What's up?"

"I need some free time."

"How much?"

Derrick and David both looked over at Cassandra and David answered his own question. "As much as you can get. Don't worry about a thing. I've got your back. Hope would love to spend the day with the babies anyway. She's already made a few remarks about you not trusting her with One and Two. Thinks it's because she's not a real Dawes. You want us at your house, or are you bringing them to mine?"

"I think Mom will find less fault if the babies stay in the house. You know she never wanted us dragged half asleep out into the night air."

"Yeah, that's why we stayed out in it so much when we got the opportunity."

David and Derrick both laughed. Boy, did they ever enjoy the night—especially at college. They agreed on two in the afternoon, until whenever. David wanted to be sure Derrick spent as much time with Cassandra as David would have liked to. While rushed romance served its purpose, it didn't offer as much fulfillment.

## *CHAPTER TWELVE*

Leaving the celebration, a slightly tipsy Derrick Dawes opened his front door at exactly ten o'clock that night and a baby's frantic wail greeted him. Looking at his watch, Derrick couldn't imagine why the girls were still awake. Up the stairs he went, as fast as he could go. In his bedroom, Derrick found Ethan rocking and talking soothingly to One. She wasn't responding to it at all. Deandra sat in the wing chair holding Two, who cried halfheartedly, the way she always did in sympathy with her sister.

Struggling with an approaching panic, Derrick asked, "What's the matter with her, Dad? Is she hungry? What time did you feed her? Did you give her cereal before you gave her milk?"

A mute Ethan Dawes rolled his eyes in exasperation at Derrick's questions, so Deandra answered, "We fed them at nine. Two fell asleep. One didn't seem sleepy, but Dad laid her down anyway. She's been hollering her head off ever since. Woke up poor Two. I think she's crying because she doesn't know what's going on either."

Moving toward his father and One, Derrick asked, "Is she running a temperature, Dad?"

Snidely, Ethan said, "No, she's not running a temperature. She's spoiled. Wants me to walk with her. You shouldn't have started that, Derrick. I don't walk babies. Neither does Sonya. If you want us to baby-sit, you'd better help her get her act together."

In One's defense, Derrick said, "Maybe something's hurting her, Dad."

Not verbally responding to Derrick's pitiful remark, Ethan stood. It only took One three seconds to realize she'd won. She stopped crying, looked up at Ethan and reached for his face.

Ethan walked over to Derrick and handed One over. She grinned and cooed her approval. Derrick returned her smile and said, "What are you doing, One? We can't run off the babysitters. You know I don't walk with you. Why are you making me look bad?"

Ethan mumbled, "Yeah. Right. You've been walking her. I can tell." Out loud Ethan said, "Let's go, Squirt. Give Two to her father or lay her down. She's not all out of whack like her sister."

Derrick muttered, "One's not out of whack either."

Ethan shook his head and said, "For your sake, I hope she's not. But, in any case, she's all yours now."

Derrick smiled weakly and said, "Thanks, Dad. Squirt. See you guys on Sunday."

Deandra asked, "Don't you want me to babysit tomorrow afternoon, Derrick?"

"No."

Getting up on her tiptoes and rubbing his head, Deandra said, "I think you should reconsider. You're seriously wolfing, Big Brother."

Stroking his own head, Derrick grinned idiotically and said, "Oh, but the ladies like me anyway, sweetheart."

"I bet they do. But, believe me, Derrick, you're way too sophisticated for the grungy look."

"I may stay this way until I go back to work in January."

Ethan said, "No, you're not. The first time that wooly hair of yours scratches one of the babies, you'll run to the barbershop."

Derrick gave his father a slightly intoxicated smirk and walked them to the door. Of course, he still had Madam One on his arm. Two's lonely cry forced their good-bye to be brief. Holding One at arms length, Derrick spoke to her on his way back up the stairs.

"I don't know what the name of this game is, but you'd better get a grip on it, Little Girl. I need them. My future will be extremely bleak, if they refuse to sit with you. I'm depending on you to behave yourself now."

Back in the bedroom, Derrick laid One on his bed. He turned to pick up Two. One's face contorted angrily immediately. She worked her legs furiously. Sound would surely follow any moment. Derrick called this her kick-start tantrum. Ignoring One momentarily, Derrick picked up Two. Her crying ceased and she smiled her pleasure at seeing him.

Returning Two's smile, Derrick said, "How's my good girl tonight? I know you're not going to join that trouble-making older sister of yours. Believe me, Two, it's not worth it. All that happens is you get a lot of somebody else's punishments. I know. I followed Uncle David to more licks and punishments than I care to remember."

Loving the sound of Derrick's voice, Two cooed and smiled. He gave her head a little kiss and stroked the beautiful curls. One's crying had elevated to impossible to ignore. Derrick sat on the bed and scooped her tantrum rigid body into his free arm. This didn't have its normal effect. One screamed and kicked as if nothing happened. To further test Ethan's theory Derrick stood. It took One five seconds to realize she'd won this round.

Refusing to give in to One's whim, Derrick sat down. Her bellowing resumed. If he gave her what she wanted, Ethan and Sonya would give him hell. Possibly abandon him. Derrick was determined not to begin any bad habits that would haunt him. To satisfy himself there was nothing wrong with either of them, Derrick put their changing pads on his bed, checked their Pampers and laid them down. One and Two cried and kicked for hours. Derrick couldn't believe the stamina and determination of the two tiny beauties.

His decision kept him up all night long. One and Two alternately wept and ate. Derrick undressed and crawled into bed, alone, at four-thirty. One realized she was asleep at six-fifteen and started the entire nightmare over again. At nine-thirty, Derrick's exhausted body and mind sank into a deep sleep. His date with Cassandra was the farthest thing from his mind. As a matter of fact, Derrick cursed all women to hell two seconds before darkness claimed him.

After a night of bizarre behavior, One and Two had totally disrupted their schedule. When David and Hope showed up at two o'clock, they were all still asleep. David called Derrick's name a few times and received no response. David crawled across the bed and shook his brother. Derrick's head popped up, saw who it was and dropped back onto the pillow.

Laughing, David said, "You don't look like a man on a mission to me. Have you forgotten about your date, Dude?"

Without lifting his face from the pillow, Derrick mumbled, "I'm not going. Any woman within ten feet of me today is in imminent danger."

"Why?"

"One and Two are experiencing some major mood swings. They want me to walk with them. If I do, Dad threatened not to ever baby-sit for me again. He also said Mom wouldn't like it either. If I don't walk with One, I'll never get another night's sleep. David, every time I think I can handle it, something changes. Man, I never knew anybody could cry that long about anything. When one of them went down for air, the other picked up the slack. It was awful. I'm surprised the police didn't knock on the door."

David laughed so hard he choked. Hope stuck her head in the door and asked, "What's so funny?"

David said quickly, "You'd better find a safe haven downstairs, Hope. Derrick's in a woman killing frame of mind."

Waving David's silly remark away Hope entered the room and asked, "What's the matter with you, Derrick? I thought you had the hots for Miss Wiggle-N-Weave."

Pointing at the bassinets, Derrick said, "The tears of those two put out the fire. If I go over there and Cassandra pouts one time, which I've never known her not to, I'll wring her neck. I can't go. I just have to face the fact that I can only deal with these two females in my life for a while."

"So, are you saying I've missed my nail appointment for no reason?"

Knowing Hope was getting ready to start complaining about forcing her to change her schedule for no reason, Derrick sighed and said miserably, "No, Hope. You and David can hang out here while I go get a haircut."

"That's not what I agreed to, but it's something. Get up and get out of here."

The moment Hope stopped speaking, Two's tiny head popped up. She didn't cry. She just looked around for a while and hummed. If One didn't answer her soon, the games would resume. She didn't. Derrick got up, went straight to the bathroom and closed the door. All he could hear was David's unrestrained laughter.

After his shower, Derrick avoided the guest room. If One and Two heard his voice, they would really give Hope a hard time. She was preparing them for baths. He only slowed up long enough to laugh at Hope and David's conflicting opinions on which baby was which. She refused to accept David's ability to tell them apart without seeing their stencils.

Derrick made and drank coffee in the kitchen alone and briefly wondered how he would handle being home with the babies for over a month. If they kept up the crying, Derrick would reconsider. Going to work might be his only respite, after all. Looking at his watch, Derrick knew it was time for him to call Cassandra and break the date. He dreaded even the thought of it. But, he walked over to the wall phone and dialed her number. The moment he heard her voice, Derrick wanted desperately to hang up. Instead, he said, "Hello, Cassandra."

Sounding as if she had just turned over in bed, Cassandra said, "Hello, Mr. Dawes. What time are you getting here? I thought you said David and Hope would be there at two."

Clearing his throat, Derrick said, "Yes, I know I did. I can't make it today, Cassandra. The babies are acting a little strange and I can't ask anyone else to deal with it."

Screaming, Cassandra asked, "What?!"

"Calm down. It's not the end of the world. Maybe another day."

"Another day?! It's today, or nothing, Derrick!"

Cassandra did not give Derrick an opportunity to say anything else. She hung up. Derrick shrugged his shoulders, thought he'd gotten off easy and left for the barbershop. Feeling slightly pent up, he decided to walk the seven blocks. He needed the fresh air and the exercise.

On this late fall Saturday afternoon Derrick didn't even mind the crowd at the barbershop. They were all men and testosterone-motivated-chatter flew all around him. It only occasionally touched Derrick and none of it was personal. Derrick flipped through the sports section of the newspaper and half listened. His turn in the chair came after more than an hours wait.

It was 6:00 when Derrick made his way back to the house. The sun had gone down and the temperature had followed suit. There was a quicker pace to Derrick's return trip. Standing at the corner near his house, Derrick saw Cassandra's car. In the cold crisp darkness he looked up at the miserable gray sky and uttered, "Why me? What have I done? Whatever it was, can I apologize for it now?"

Without an answer to any of his questions, Derrick closed the distance between sanity and insanity. Opening the front door, he heard David's never-ending conversation with One and Two coming from the kitchen. Derrick didn't see Hope and Cassandra until he actually entered the room.

If David's banter hadn't suddenly included him, Derrick would have wondered if anyone saw him standing near the doorway. Hope gave Derrick a tiny sympathetic shrug. Cassandra fumed and refused to acknowledge him at all. Intending to hang his coat, Derrick turned and left the kitchen.

Cassandra stormed into the foyer and stood directly behind him. Derrick felt her ominous presence and smelled her perfume. He wasn't crazy about the fragrance. When Derrick turned to face her, Cassandra hissed venomously, "I thought the babies were in some sort of crisis, Derrick."

Taking a deep breath, Derrick said, "I never said they were in a crisis. I said they were acting strange."

"They seem fine to me. If you didn't want to be bothered, all you had to do was say so."

"You're twisting things, as usual, Cassandra. The babies were in a bad mood last night. I didn't get any sleep. I was tired. I didn't know if they were going to carry the routine over into the day. I didn't want to burden David and Hope with two crying babies who refused to be satisfied."

Shifting her stance and placing both hands on her hips, Cassandra spat angrily, "If that was so, why did I find them sitting with the babies and you gone, when I got here?"

A tinge of anger touched Derrick's response when he said, "Because you weren't supposed to come here. I thought I explained that to you last night."

In shocked disbelief, Cassandra asked, "Are you asking me to leave?"

"I didn't ask you to come, so I shouldn't have to ask you to leave. You don't need my input to answer any of your questions anyway."

Derrick stepped around Cassandra and moved toward the kitchen. She was getting angrier by the second. Cassandra screamed in the foyer, "Don't you walk away from me, Derrick!"

Ignoring her, Derrick walked over to the table where David had One and Two sitting in their little carriers. One began her kick starting routine as soon as she saw Derrick. Two looked over, saw him and joined her sister. David blinked in confusion. The two infants had not given them a moment's trouble. The only thing David could fathom was this was their Daddy routine.

One and Two hit full blast in about ten seconds. Cassandra stood behind Derrick yelling, "I don't have to put up with a man who doesn't want to be bothered with me,

Derrick Dawes! You're not the only brother in town, you know! I could have been in the Bahamas this weekend with Ted! No! I sat around waiting for you to realize you missed me! You can just bet I won't be waiting anymore!"

There was so much noise in that kitchen, Derrick wanted to put his coat back on and run away. If this was what family life consisted of, he could live the remainder of his life without it. Deciding again to only deal with One and Two, Derrick picked the two carriers up and went upstairs. He left Cassandra's tantrum for David and Hope. The way Derrick saw it, since they had let her in, they could listen to her ranting threats.

The last thing Derrick heard was Hope saying in a consoling tone, "You do know the babies have to come first in Derrick's life, don't you, Cassandra? He would be less than anything anyone wanted, if he ran off to lay up with a woman and those babies were out of sorts. They could have been coming down with something. I understand where he's coming from. Why can't you?"

Not caring to hear Cassandra's response, Derrick took One and Two to his bedroom. The three were lying on his bed when David walked in. Each baby held a finger and gurgled up at Derrick. Derrick wasn't talking, just listening. David wondered if One and Two were trying to tell Derrick something he had done wrong.

Not looking away from One and Two, Derrick asked, "Is she still here?"

David sat on the foot of the bed and said, "Yes. Hope's trying to talk some sense to her. She doesn't own any reasoning skills, does she?"

Derrick smirked and said, "The really pretty ones never do, David. They were all adoring their reflections in a distant cloud when God passed out common sense."

"Hope has common sense, Derrick."

"Well, she's a rarity. If you know what's good for you, you'd better buy that ring and give it to her on December twenty-fourth."

"I don't know. I miss those days of irate women showing up at my front door. The screaming that runs on so long you can't concentrate. Dad says they melt your brain. You turn into a mindless zombie who does anything they say afterwards."

"Not if you don't listen, David. I can't listen to anyone who screams."

"What about Mom?"

"Okay. Mom, One and Two are as far as I'm bending the rule."

Rubbing his chin, David said, "You know you've still got enough time on the clock to spend a little with her if you want to. One and Two are only showing off for you and Dad, Derrick. They didn't do it to me and Hope."

If One and Two hadn't been holding onto Derrick's fingers so tight, he would have punched David for saying that. Glaring at his brother over his shoulder, Derrick said, "If I give in tonight, she'll throw an even worse fit the next time I can't go. I enjoy Cassandra's company, physically, David. It took a crisis to show me I can't deal with her psychologically. Let her go home. When the girls are a little older, I'll discuss it. If she's in the Bahamas with Ted, I'll just have to suck it up and live with it."

David noted Derrick hadn't said anything about the possibility of the babies not being there and said nothing. David really wanted One and Two to belong to Derrick. It was glaringly obvious Derrick hoped so too. Now, if only a good woman would come along, Derrick would have everything. That's what David wanted for his brother and himself. Everything.

## *CHAPTER THIRTEEN*

With a firm lesson on the demanding issues involved in child rearing freshly taught by Hope, Cassandra went up to Derrick's bedroom and offered an unenthusiastic apology. Derrick merely nodded acknowledgment and the flaccid exchange left Cassandra not knowing if it was accepted. Not another word to Cassandra passed Derrick's lips. At six-thirty David, Hope, and Cassandra walked to their cars together. Derrick locked his front door with a sigh of relief.

Now that the house was empty, with the exception of the now sleeping One and Two, Derrick realized he hadn't eaten a thing all day. He popped the veal dinner Sonya had prepared into the microwave and waited. The telephone rang, Derrick flinched and realized Cassandra could not possibly have gotten home yet. So, he answered it.

Timidly, Derrick said, "Hello."

Pamela, the office flasher, said, "Well, hello, Mr. Dawes. Did you ever find Mommie Dearest?"

Smiling, Derrick said, "No, Pamela, I have not. And, you didn't have to show me and half of the people in my office your abdomen."

"Couldn't have you wondering if I was lying, sweetheart. You want to tell me how you did the baby trick now? I know you didn't leave anything to chance with me."

Giving a tiny chuckle, Derrick said, "I didn't leave anything to chance with anyone, Pamela. I haven't got a clue who these babies belong to."

"You mean you don't know who the mother is, right? You know they're your babies though, right?"

"As a matter of fact, I don't know if they're my babies. My mother took one look at them and said they were. So, what could I say? When the law and your mother say they're yours, there's not much you can do without DNA."

"Have you had it done yet, Derrick?"

"It can't be done precisely before they're three months old. I'm Daddy Dearest until then."

"Are you saying you're turning them over to a shelter if they're not yours, Derrick?"

Sighing deeply, Derrick said, "I don't know, Pam. That's been the plan since I brought them home. But, the little things grow on you after a while. I've missed more nights of sleep than I can relay to you. I've been drooled and puked on. Cleaned messes I couldn't comprehend two months ago. And, they throw really loud unrelenting crying fits just for me. I feel so needed."

Pamela gushed and squealed, as only women do over infant reports, "Aw, that's so precious, Derrick. You're really getting into it. That's good. Maybe they'll stop you from flipping the page so often."

"What page?"

"The lady pages, Derrick. Everybody knows you only deal with women momentarily. You've dated the best this town has to offer and flipped the page on all of us. I knew you didn't want to get emotionally involved. But, you've finally run up on two little ladies you can't discard so easily. If their mother shows up, maybe you'll consider settling down."

Derrick threw his head back and howled with laughter. Catching his breath he said, "Can't settle down with a quadriplegic, Pam. That's what she'll be after I break her neck."

"You're not still angry with her, are you, Derrick? Not after she gave you those two little girls. I've heard they're adorable."

"They are adorable. And, yes, I am still angry. Will be for a very, very long time, too. You don't do things like this to a man and disappear."

"Why not? Women deal with men doing things like this to them everyday. We're expected to forgive and forget deeper stuff than being left to fend for ourselves with two infants."

"So, you're saying I'm paying for the dirty work of my entire gender?"

"Sort of. You can handle it though. Those babies couldn't have fallen into a safer lap than yours, Derrick. You're patient as hell when you want to be. Easy to deal with and you can afford them. You've got family to help when you need them, too. I couldn't say all of that about me. If I had a baby right this minute, it would be mine. All mine. My mother would pack her bags and move to another state before she sat with a baby I spat out."

"Whatever you say, Pam. I've got to get something to eat. I haven't had a thing all day. That's another of the many drawbacks of being a single Dad."

"What are the others?"

"Start anywhere. Whatever you can think of, I can't do it."

Pamela laughed and said smugly, "Certainly not everything, Derrick."

Derrick replied adamantly, "Everything, Pam. Everything. I either don't have time, my nerves are too raw to deal, or I'm too tired."

"Poor baby. Well, when you come up for air and need some company, give me a call. You can hide out over here for a change of scene."

"Thanks. I might do just that."

Sitting in the silent kitchen, Derrick ate his dinner and reflected on his conversation with Pamela. In the past two months, he had truly become attached to One and Two. The thought of giving them to anyone didn't flow through his mind the way it had originally. All he could think about was one or the other looking for him and not being there for them. Once they were in the system they could even be separated and Derrick wouldn't have a thing to say about it. No Derrick and no answering hum. That would surely warp them for the rest of their lives and they would not know exactly why. Could he really do that to One and Two, regardless of whether or not they were his flesh and blood?

One and Two slept peacefully through Saturday night. They seemed particularly exhausted after terrorizing Derrick all night Friday. One did not even fuss while Derrick held and fed Two. She lay on the bed, smacked her lips, hummed occasionally and played with Derrick's leg. He did not get upset when she scratched him with her little sharp nails either. If he raised his voice, Derrick knew it would upset Two. She was definitely the more sensitive of the pair.

Sonya insisted Two reminded her more of Derrick as a baby everyday. Two could be so solemn; she hated any sudden noises and was mesmerized by almost anything. The mobile on her crib held her attention raptly for long periods of time. Two cried with her sister every time and Derrick remembered crying when David got into trouble as children, too. That drove Ethan nuts and he would shout, "What are you crying for, Derrick?! I didn't hit you!"

Sonya couldn't put her finger on One. She vaguely reminded her of David at times and other times, Deandra. One was a busy body. The mobile frustrated her because she couldn't touch it. If One was on her stomach and only heard the music, that held her attention. She wanted your undivided attention all of the time, and there was something about Derrick and Ethan she adored. It had to be something innate, because there were never two people more different than those two, in Sonya's opinion. Both babies liked the soft jazz Derrick listened to at night and hated Deandra's rap music. Two got lost in the television Sonya loved so much and One tolerated it if Sonya held her.

After returning from his family's home on Sunday, Derrick laid the two sleeping infants in their bassinets. Preparing their things for the trip to the doctor's office the following morning occupied his mind. Before leaving his room, Derrick pushed the button on the stereo. The jazz they all slept to every night played. One and Two hummed back and forth once and never moved.

In the guest room, Derrick thought he heard crying. He hadn't brought the monitor with him, after all, he was only in the next room and both doors were wide open. If there was a cry, they must have changed their mind about it. Derrick didn't hear anything else.

Collecting duplicate changes of clothing for the babies and laying out undershirts, diapers, bibs and blankets busied Derrick's conscious thought until he heard an extremely stressful, piercing cry. He dropped what he was doing and hurried to his bedroom. One screamed hysterically. Derrick went directly to her. Out of the corner of his eye, he saw Two twitching violently. He was confused because she wasn't making any sound. Derrick quickly turned her over. Two was choking in a pool of vomit. He had no idea how long she had been struggling to breathe.

Mumbling prayers and curses under his breath, Derrick snatched Two up, started patting her back and raising her arms over her head, the way Sonya had showed him. Two gasped several times and let out a frightened cry. One cried frantically the entire time. If One had not alerted Derrick, Two would have choked to death.

Derrick carried Two into the bathroom and cleaned her up. He never noticed that One stopped crying when Two stopped choking and could cry for herself. One's head was up trying to see what Derrick and Two were doing. With a clean nightgown in hand, Derrick returned to his bed and changed Two. She started crying the moment Derrick laid her on his bed. Forcing him to sit and change her on his lap.

With Two's tiny body still on his lap, Derrick dialed David's telephone number. All David said was, "Hello." Derrick lit into him. "Don't you ever shake my babies up again! Two almost choked to death because of you and your nonsense! Do it again, and I'll kick your teeth in, David!"

Stuttering, David said, "Hey man, I'm sorry. Is she all right? I thought she was beyond that puking stage. I'm really sorry, Derrick. You know I wouldn't do anything to hurt them."

Spitting his words out through tightly clenched teeth, Derrick hissed, "You'd better not ever shake them up again, David! If One hadn't cried, Two would actually be dead now! I wasn't in the room with them! I didn't take the monitor into the guest room! They were asleep! I was only gone a few minutes!"

David didn't say anything else. The fear of something happening to Two had pushed Derrick into a dangerously unfamiliar zone. One David sensed instinctively Derrick would fight real hard to get out of. And, if anyone was in his way, they had better be ready, willing and able to battle masterfully.

After a long, uncomfortable silence, David asked softly, "Do you want me to come over, Derrick?"

"No!"

That one word set Two's crying into motion again. When Derrick slammed the telephone into its cradle, One jumped and started crying, too. Still angry, Derrick tried to quiet them. They didn't know what was wrong with him and they were frightened. One and Two jumped and cried off and on all night long. Derrick was so angry with David he didn't even care about not getting any sleep. If they had gone back to sleep, Derrick would have considered slipping over to David's house and popping him one good one anyway.

An exhausted and irritable Derrick Dawes was in rare form when he arrived at Dr. Kane's office the following morning. There was no greeting smile from the tall, muscular, handsome daddy. Hoping Derrick had given One and Two legitimate names, the receptionist was prepared to ask if he wanted to take another stab at filling out their registration cards. His no nonsense demeanor made her think twice about it.

After informing the nurse of their arrival, the receptionist spent the remainder of the wait stealing glances at the obviously angry Mr. Dawes. Only one of the babies was awake. She smacked her lips loudly and moved her hands around. The baby was trying to get a grip on something.

Other mothers and babies entered after Derrick. The nurse came out and called two of them while he sat and silently fumed. Derrick looked at his watch ten times in less than half an hour. Their appointment was at nine o'clock. It was now nine-forty-five. The receptionist noted this. She buzzed the nurse and relayed his pending impatient outbreak.

At ten o'clock, Derrick pulled a bottle and a bib from one of the diaper bags and began to feed the now fussing One. He didn't bother changing her diaper afterwards. They were only going to take it off again.

At ten-thirty, Derrick returned the happily playing One to her seat in the stroller, pulled another bottle and bib from the other diaper bag. Two's eyes were opened. She held her head up and grunted loudly. Derrick knew she was deciding if it was necessary to cry to get his attention. The last thing he wanted was for the two of them to do their tag team act.

Jocelyn Avery stuck her head out of the door at ten-forty and called, "Dawes." Without waiting for them, she let the door close behind her.

This further irritated Derrick. His scowl deepened. Two was only half finished her bottle. If he tried to take it away from her now, she would cry her heart out until he gave it back. As if the nurse hadn't called them, Derrick continued to feed Two. The receptionist turned her back to them several times because laughter overcame her.

Five minutes later, Jocelyn returned to the waiting room and said irritably, "Dawes."

Still holding Two's bottle to her sucking lips Derrick responded gruffly, "I heard you."

Vigorously waving her impatience, Jocelyn said sharply, "Well, come on, Mr. Dawes. We're behind schedule."

Derrick snapped bitterly, "No kidding. I've only been sitting here for nearly two hours. If this is the way it's going to be, why do you people give appointments?"

Skimming the surface of an apologetic tone, Jocelyn replied, "We do our very best, Mr. Dawes."

"Well, since you're behind schedule already, you can wait a few more minutes."

"If you don't come now, Mr. Dawes, I'll have to move on and squeeze you in when I can."

Giving Jocelyn the cruelest sneer she had ever encountered, Derrick said, "I wouldn't do that if I were you."

Truly uncomfortable with Derrick now, Jocelyn said, "Come back as soon as you're done, Mr. Dawes."

Everyone in the waiting room watched the exchange with great interest. However, no one said a word. They watched Jocelyn prance haughtily to the back and let the door close behind her again. They turned and watched Derrick give Two the final drops of formula in her bottle. Then, to their surprise, he placed Two on his shoulder and burped her. If anyone thought they were rushing Derrick Dawes after making him wait for nearly two hours they could just think again.

Placing Two in the stroller and packing her feeding material, Derrick stood slowly and pushed the stroller toward the door. The receptionist immediately rose from her seat to hold the door open for him. Derrick nodded his appreciation, but his facial expression never changed.

Inside the long hallway, Derrick looked into each of the rooms he passed for someone to tell him where to go. He was near the end when he saw Dr. Kane coming out of one. Dr. Kane gave Derrick his usual pleasant smile, extended his hand and said, "Hello, Mr. Dawes. How are you today?"

With more bass in his voice than necessary, Derrick shook the doctor's hand and said stiffly, "Hello, Dr. Kane. I've been better. Which one of these rooms do you want us in?"

"Let me ask Jocelyn. She runs this show. If I send you to the wrong room, I'll hear about mixing her up for the rest of the day."

Just then, Jocelyn stepped into the hallway. Seeing Derrick, she rolled her eyes at him and pointed at a door on the other end of the hallway. Wondering whom she thought she was displaying her insolence at like that, Derrick looked Jocelyn up and down slowly. Suddenly, his expression changed.

Quite sharply, Jocelyn asked, "Are you going to the room, Mr. Dawes? Or, are you going to stand there and try to give me a hard time for the rest of the day?"

With one eyebrow raised, Derrick smirked and said, "I'm not giving you a hard time yet, Miss whatever your name is."

Clenching her fists at her sides, Jocelyn closed her eyes. The long, loosely braided ponytail swung to emphasize her words, when she said in total frustration, "Just go to room three, Mr. Dawes. Start undressing the babies. We'll be there in a minute."

Giving Jocelyn one final look over, Derrick moved toward his assigned examination room. He thought, "She's not bad looking. Very attractive when she's angry. The flush does wonders for her complexion."

In the room, Derrick placed One on the table and started undressing her. One kicked and smiled at him. Derrick checked her Pamper. He didn't want to have to change a mess with an audience. She was only a little wet and could wait. Done with One, Derrick wrapped her in a receiving blanket and laid her back in the stroller. Of course, One kicked and fought with the blanket until it lay around her. Derrick had Two down to her socks, shoes and Pamper when Dr. Kane and Jocelyn entered the room together.

Dr. Kane said cheerfully, "Okay, One and Two, it's your turn. How have you been since I saw you last?"

Derrick answered for them, "Other than the temperatures, sore legs and diarrhea after those shots you gave them, they've been fine."

Never taking his eyes from the beautiful perfect baby in Derrick's grip, Dr. Kane said, "That's to be expected, Dad. Let's take another look at them. Who's going first?"

"One."

Smiling, Dr. Kane asked, "Which one is One?"

"She's in the stroller."

Turning to Jocelyn, Derrick asked, "Would you mind giving One to the doctor, Miss whatever your name is?"

Looking around emptily, Jocelyn asked tartly, "Are you referring to me, Mr. Dawes?"

"Yes, I am."

"Sure, I'll give One to the doctor for you. And, my name is Jocelyn Avery. Nurse Avery for you."

Oozing sarcasm, Derrick replied, "Thank you, Nurse Avery."

Mimicking his tone, Jocelyn asked, "Would you like to check to see if my hands are clean, Mr. Dawes?"

"Since you asked, I sure would, Nurse Avery."

Jocelyn held her hands out and turned them over. Derrick nodded his head slowly. Noting there was no wedding band, he finally said, "Very good."

Jocelyn sighed deeply, rolled her eyes, picked up One and placed her on the tiny scale at the foot of the examination table. Derrick watched Jocelyn's every move with Two nibbling on his hand. One caught sight of Jocelyn's swinging ponytail and happily tried to capture it. One actually touched it fleetingly as Jocelyn measured her. The baby's dimpled legs kicked with delighted enthusiasm.

Dr. Kane observed both Derrick and Jocelyn's behavior. He knew there were more than adverse reactions to an altered schedule passing between them. Since Jocelyn and Derrick were both single people, Dr. Kane saw no harm in their strange mating ritual.

With One's weighing and measuring completed, Jocelyn handed her over to Dr. Kane. Before accepting the baby, Dr. Kane held his hands out for Derrick's inspection. With his nodded approval, the doctor began his examination of the little, chubby, lightly browned beauty.

Jocelyn picked up One's chart and removed the pen from her breast pocket. Derrick's eyes wandered from Dr. Kane and One over to Jocelyn repeatedly. If Jocelyn noticed, she never gave any indication. Handing Dr. Kane the hypodermic of the month, Jocelyn looked at Derrick with a disgusted frown and said, "Please have a seat, Mr. Dawes."

Stubbornly, Derrick responded, "I don't want to sit down."

Again, Jocelyn rolled her eyes at Derrick and positioned herself between him and the doctor. Caught up in the warm intimate scent of Jocelyn and the view of the top of her head, Derrick jumped at the sound of One's startled, wounded cry. Two squealed, squirmed, and kicked along with her. Again, Derrick pushed Jocelyn aside and leaned over One.

As if she were reading from a script, Jocelyn said, "Please, Mr. Dawes. The baby has to have this shot and many, many others. Stand back and let the doctor do his job. He won't hurt her any more than he absolutely has to."

Dismissing Jocelyn's lifeless speech, Derrick handed Two over to her and picked up One. Cradling the wounded baby, Derrick cooed like a real Mom, "He's sorry, sweetheart. He didn't mean to hurt you." Then, like a real dad, threateningly growled at Dr. Kane, "You didn't mean it at all, did you, Doc?"

Playing along, Dr. Kane cooed back, "I most certainly did not mean it. Please forgive me."

Two quieted in Jocelyn's arms. She did not object to being weighed and measured. Two's fascination with Jocelyn's ponytail was exactly like One's. She watched its swinging motion, as if timing it. At exactly the right moment, Two caught the prized object and held onto it. Two massaged the thick braid and kicked excitedly.

"May I have that back, Miss Two?" Jocelyn asked, smiling.

Derrick looked up and said, "Give Nasty Nurse Avery her hair back, Two. That's not nice."

Leering at Derrick, Jocelyn pried her hair from Two's chubby fingers. Getting it away from Two, Jocelyn said, "Let Nasty Nurse Avery see if there's any hair left in your hand, Two. We don't want the ever diligent Daddy Dawes accusing me of soiling your hands."

"That's a good idea. One less side effect of this office, Two choking on hair after I get her home."

Dr. Kane disguised his laughter by pretending to cough into his hand. He thought Jocelyn and Derrick were a riot. The rapid, acidic, back and forth banter was amusing, original and strangely intimate.

When Two's regiment reached the point of Jocelyn standing between Derrick and the doctor, Derrick purposely stood closer to her. When Two let out the expected cry, Jocelyn stepped aside before Derrick could push her. On the verge of laughing, Derrick handed One to Jocelyn and picked up his now injured Two. Both babies cried as Jocelyn and Derrick rocked, stroked and spoke soothingly.

Dr. Kane observed the two briefly and gave Derrick the status of One and Two's progress. They couldn't have been more perfect. He said his farewells and started toward the door. Derrick stopped Dr. Kane in his tracks by saying, "Excuse me, but will you be performing the paternity test on the girls? Or, do I have to take them back to the hospital?"

A stunned Dr. Kane asked, "What paternity test?"

Derrick asked dumbly, "Is there more than one kind?"

"Well, no. But, why?"

"I need to know if these are my babies, Dr. Kane. Didn't anyone tell you anything about this? Didn't you speak to Mrs. Monet?"

Still in shock, Dr. Kane said, "No. Why do you feel the need to do this, Mr. Dawes?"

With both babies still crying, Derrick said, "There's the possibility they might not be my children. I'd like to be certain."

Giving Derrick a distasteful look for the first time, Dr. Kane said flatly, "They'll be three months old when you bring them in for their next checkup. I'll draw the blood, do the swabs and submit it to the lab then. It'll take about six weeks to get the results back."

Softly, Derrick said, "Thank you."

In silence, standing side-by-side, Derrick and Jocelyn redressed the babies, both of whom kept their eyes on Jocelyn's constantly moving hair. Jocelyn asked nonchalantly, "Do you still have the liquid Tylenol?"

Just as nonchalantly, Derrick responded, "Yes, I do. Are these shots going to make them sick, too?"

"They won't actually be sick. They'll experience similar side effects though."

Placing the bundled babies in the stroller, Derrick said, "I'll expect your call this evening then."

With a snap of her head, Jocelyn asked, "Who said I would be calling?"

"I can't believe a conscientious nurse like you would send two innocent babies off with an inexperienced single father after giving them medication with potentially life threatening side effects and not check on them."

Sighing and rolling her eyes, Jocelyn said, "Have a nice day, Mr. Dawes."

Pushing his stroller, Derrick said, "You too, Nurse Avery."

## *CHAPTER FOURTEEN*

Back at home, Derrick unpacked One and Two, brought their chairs down to the kitchen and positioned them in the middle of the table. He carefully strapped One and Two in and dialed his mother's telephone number. Sonya had to have an immediate report on her kittens.

After telling his mother everything she wanted to hear, Derrick asked, "Mom, do you think I'm making a mistake having the DNA test taken?"

"Only you can answer that, Derrick. If you can't see that those are your children, then do it. But, what happens if they're not? Are you honestly prepared to turn them over to the authorities?"

Looking at the two beautiful, gurgling and feisty kicking babies, Derrick said solemnly, "Honestly, I don't know if I could do that. But if I'm not their father their mother can waltz in and say, 'Thanks for babysitting.' Then she can just walk away with them and I'll never see them again, Mom."

"I thought you told me Roger said she could pretty much do that anyway." After a brief pause, Sonya added, "You do know the potential of your own pain is great in this situation, don't you, Derrick?"

Solemnly, Derrick responded, "Yeah."

"Now all you have to do is ask yourself how much of it you want to spill over onto One and Two. Then ask yourself how much you want to be personally responsible for."

"No matter what, I can't let her destroy their lives, Mom. If I turn them over and they're adopted, she might not be able to get them back. At the very least she'll have to prove beyond a doubt that she is capable of caring for the babies before the courts will rip them from the loving arms of their adoptive mother. Maybe she won't have the resources to fight with them year after year.

"With me, all she has to do is show up and say she's sorry. The judge will deliver an impassioned dress down, give her One and Two and tell her not to abandon them again. All he'll give me is a pitiful glance and a sigh. We won't get a fair fight."

"I don't believe that for one minute, Derrick. She's not walking off with my kittens without a fight. I don't care who she is, or what key she's weeping in. You have that test done, Derrick. If those babies are half yours, she'll have to share them with you. Don't leave them alone out there with her or anyone else. You're all they have. And, more important than that . . . all they know."

Done with his conversation, Derrick leaned on his elbows and stared at One and Two. Occasionally, one or the other stared back at him. To avoid the devastation of finding out they were not his, Derrick insisted he didn't see himself in them. He saw small resemblances to David, but even that could be coincidental. That was as close as he could get to himself. Derrick didn't see a genuine resemblance to any of the women he had dated either. These babies might be connected to him through the mind of someone who merely thought he was a nice guy. Someone who thought he had a nice car, for that matter. Who knew what their demented mother was thinking? All Derrick knew, for sure, was if she saw how beautiful they were at this very moment, she would demand them back.

At two months old, One and Two were almost the same soft shade of brown as Derrick. They had his hairline hidden beneath a mass of luxurious, black, silky smooth curls. Their big bright eyes were what Derrick called happy eyes that slanted up, and were almost, just not quite, caramel in color. Two little sculptured mouths with lips not too full, or too slim. One and Two had really long limbs. So long, they were quickly outgrowing the bassinets they slept in. And they were quite chubby.

Suddenly their button noses held Derrick's attention, and then his attention flowed back to their hair. He did know someone they resembled.

Derrick looked at his watch. It was two o'clock. That meant it was one in Denver. He got up from the table and went to the foyer closet to retrieve his briefcase. Finding his telephone book, Derrick flipped the pages to the number he wanted and dialed it. As he waited for someone to answer, Derrick held out his finger. Two grasped it and enthusiastically swung it back and forth.

Finally, someone said, "Gerhardt's Department Store. How may I help you?"

"Could you connect me with Angelique Thomas, please?"

"Hold a moment, please."

The person came back and said, "I'm sorry, Sir. We don't have an Angelique Thomas in this store."

"Oh, I'm sorry. Her name is Kelly now."

The response this time was a ringing. Another voice said, "Good afternoon, Mrs. Kelly's office. Mrs. Bean speaking."

Absorbed in Two's pleasure with his finger, Derrick said, "Mrs. Kelly, please. This is Derrick Dawes."

There was another pause before Angelique picked up the line and said cheerfully, "Hi, Derrick. How are you?"

"Hi, Angelique. I'm fine. I was wondering how you were."

"Oh, I'm fine. Working hard at everything. The last time I spoke to you, you were looking for the mother of some abandoned babies. Have you found her yet?"

"No."

"Do you still have the babies?"

"Yes. I've taken some time off. It's been a little rough trying to work and deal with two constantly changing infants, but we're hanging tough so far."

"That's good. If anyone can do it, you can."

"Why do you say that, Angelique?"

A noticeable pause came before Angelique said, "Well, because you have all of the ingredients necessary to be an awesome Daddy."

Continuing his baiting game, Derrick said nonchalantly, "That may, or may not be true. Anyway, I'll probably be relinquishing the position after the DNA tests are done."

"That may be best if you can't handle it full-time, Derrick. I bet you'll miss them though."

"Sure, I'll miss them. Maybe you and your husband would like to consider taking them off of my hands, if I have to give them up. I hate the idea of giving them to people I don't know."

"That would be nice. But, Aaron and I will be starting our own family next year. It's taken me a while to warm him up on the idea."

"Really? Is that why the two of you were having so many problems last year? I mean, him not wanting children?"

"Partially. We don't see eye-to-eye on a lot of issues, Derrick. I won't lie to you, Aaron and I don't have the type of relationship you and I had. We were good together, Derrick—similar lifestyles, goals and temperaments. Now, if you would have budged from your allegiance to bachelorhood, we may have still been together."

"Is that why you dropped these two babies off on me, Angelique?"

Shocked, Angelique yelled, "What?! This is the last time I'm telling you those are not my babies, Derrick! If they were, I have a husband a home and we both have excellent jobs! I would have kept them! You know I've always wanted children! Why are you insisting they're mine?!"

Not disturbed in the least by her yelling, Derrick said, "Because they resemble you more and more everyday, Angelique. Your nose. Your hair. Now that I think about it, they even have your chin.

"And, yes, you have all of those things. You also have an obsessed selfish husband—a husband who does not tolerate accidents, especially accidental births.

"Isn't it funny that One and Two were born exactly nine months after you dropped in to see me on Christmas Eve? Is that why you needed consolation from me that night and not your family, Angelique? Was that to make me think they may be mine? Or, did you suddenly find yourself pregnant afterwards? Which was it?"

"You're insane, Derrick Dawes! Obviously you're getting less sleep than you think! Those are not my babies! Is there anything else I can help you with?!"

"I only have one thing to say to you, Angelique. If you think you're coming back to get them, forget it. I'll fight you and win. One way or another."

Derrick hung up the telephone and dialed Roger's office. It took fifteen minutes to get him on the line. When Roger picked up, Derrick said, "I know who their mother is. I want you to check into it. Find out whatever you can and hold it. If it's her and things don't work out the way she's planning, she'll be back for them. She's always wanted children and she told me her husband didn't want any. I think that's why they wound up in my mailbox."

"You didn't tell her you knew it was her, did you, Derrick?"

"Yes, I did. It's someone I knew very well. If there were ever anyone I thought I could have worked with, it would have been her. She must have been desperate to do what she did."

"So are you saying there's no way you can be their father, Derrick?"

"The possibility is there, but it's so remote, I wouldn't bet on it. Didn't you say either way, it's better if I'm armed?"

"Yes."

"Well, do it."

Derrick gave Roger the information he knew about Angelique and the little he knew about Aaron Kelly. Roger told Derrick he hoped he hadn't stirred the pot prematurely and hung up.

Feeling he had accomplished something for the first time since the arrival of the twins, Derrick happily ate his lunch. One and Two reached for his sandwich and kicked out their frustrations. When they began to cry, he opened a jar of the applesauce Sonya said they could have. Derrick sat feeding them both from the same jar. It ran out in no time flat and he had to open another. That was followed by their usual eight ounces of milk. Full, One and Two drifted off to sleep in their chairs. Derrick turned on the new television he had bought to please his mother, leaned back in the high-back black leather kitchen chair, kicked off his shoes and watched a college basketball game on ESPN.

The doorbell rang at four-thirty. Derrick frowned and wondered who it could be. Everyone in his family had a key these days. Looking at his watch quickly, he mumbled, "It's too early for good old Uncle David. He never releases his staff before five."

Derrick went to the door and looked through the peephole. All he saw was the back of whoever it was. Then, he recognized the swinging ponytail. Opening the door in complete shock, Derrick asked sarcastically, "What are you doing here, Nurse Avery? The girls aren't due to get sick until after midnight."

Pointing her finger up and into Derrick's face with a great deal of hostility, Jocelyn spat angrily, "If you ever come into my office again and act like you did today, Mr. Dawes, I'll jab you with a hypodermic. I didn't know who to be more embarrassed for . . . you, or me. You're not the first person to have babies, you know. We had two very sick children who had to be admitted to the hospital this morning. I did not appreciate your callous impatience one bit. One day, that could be one of your babies."

With a feigned superior attitude, Derrick said, "Well, you should have explained that to me, and some of the others, this morning."

Poking him in the chest, Jocelyn snapped, "I'm telling you now! Be glad!"

Rubbing the poked spot Derrick tried not to laugh and said, "I guess I'm one of the lucky ones then."

Popping her neck and rolling her eyes, Jocelyn said, "Damn skippy, Dawes! Now, how are the babies?"

"If you promise not to poke me again, you can come in and see for yourself. They're on the kitchen table."

Twisting her face, Jocelyn asked, "The kitchen table?"

Grimacing, Derrick said, "Yeah, the kitchen table. What's wrong with that, Nurse Hatchet?"

"What did you call me?"

"Nurse Avery. I said they were on the kitchen table, Nurse Avery. They're not in any danger. You can come in, stop entertaining my neighbors and see for yourself."

Jocelyn turned around. Indeed, there were three people standing in front of Derrick's house staring at her. She couldn't see the neighbors looking out of their windows. If Jocelyn actually knew how many sets of eyes were on her, she would have melted right before them.

Mortified, Jocelyn stepped up and brushed past a grinning Derrick. In passing, she mumbled something about him constantly embarrassing her.

Inside, Derrick waved her toward the kitchen. One and Two's identical sleeping heads leaned at the exact same angle in the same direction.

Melting at the sight of them, Jocelyn gushed, "Aw, look at them. Making themselves comfortable anywhere dumb old Daddy puts them. Where else do you put them, Mr. Dawes? On the stove, while you warm their bottles? Or, to keep them safe, do you stack them on the refrigerator?"

Holding both hands up in mock surrender, Derrick said, "If you'll stop, Nurse Avery, I'll stop."

To Derrick's surprise, she said, "Okay. Let's move on. When are you going to name them?"

With eyebrows raised and a slightly pouting mouth, Derrick mumbled, "They have names."

"If you said they have names, why are you still calling them One and Two?"

Speaking a little louder, he said, "I like One and Two."

Sighing and shaking her head, Jocelyn asked, "What are their names, Mr. Dawes? Or, is it a secret?"

Mumbling again, Derrick replied, "Mia and Miranda."

"Do they know their names are Mia and Miranda?" Jocelyn whispered while pointing at the sleeping babies.

"No."

"When are you going to introduce them to themselves? The first day of school?"

"You don't understand what's going on here, Nurse Avery. I may not have the right to name them."

Stunned by his remark, Jocelyn asked, "Excuse me? Are you the one who stays up all night with them? Are you the one who comforts them? Are you the one who sees that they get their physicals and those God-awful shots? Are you the one who propped them up on the kitchen table just to have them in the same room with you to keep them safe from whatever, real or imagined?"

A deep frown creased Derrick's handsomely carved cafe au lait face when he answered, "Yeah. That would be me."

Jocelyn spun around, looked up the hall and said, "Well, I don't see anyone else around. If you haven't earned the right to name them, I can't imagine who has."

"If I name them and they're taken away from me, they'll not only have to adapt to a new environment, they'll have to learn who they are all over again."

Confused, Jocelyn asked, "Who they are? They're your daughters. Do you really think calling them One and Two will give them a head start in adapting to a foreign environment and strange people, Mr. Dawes? Honestly?"

"No. Would you like to give me your coat and have a seat, while you psychoanalyze me, Nurse Avery?"

"I won't be staying that long."

"Why? Your workday is done. Do you have anyplace to be, other than home alone? You are single, aren't you?"

Indignantly, Jocelyn chirped, "That's none of your business."

"Okay. I just thought that since we decided to stop taking cheap shots at each other, we could sit down and have a civil conversation. But, if I've overstepped my boundaries, please forgive me."

"No, I won't forgive you. You're always saying rude things to me. Now, you're asking rude questions."

"Exactly, which one was rude?"

Moving toward One and Two, Jocelyn said, "I'll just check the babies and be on my way."

Behind her back, Derrick silently mouthed, "So what."

Touching each one, she asked, "Did you give them the Tylenol?"

"No. You said to give it to them if they ran a temperature, or acted like their legs were bothering them. They haven't done any of that yet."

"When was the last time you checked them, Mr. Dawes?"

With frightened eyes lighting up his face, Derrick stammered, "I fed them about an hour ago. They were fine. Are you saying they're not now?"

"To save you the embarrassment, I won't say anything," Jocelyn said as she stood back and crossed her arms.

Taking what seemed to Jocelyn like one huge step, Derrick cleared the large distance between the doorway and the table. He touched One. She was burning up. He touched Two. She was just as hot.

Panicking, Derrick asked, "When did that happen? Do I wake them up to give them the Tylenol?"

Pulling her coat off and draping it over the chair, Jocelyn said, "Get the Tylenol and alcohol, Mr. Dawes."

Derrick dashed up the stairs. By the time he returned, Jocelyn had a sleeping One stripped down to her Pamper. Derrick handed her the Tylenol and sat the alcohol on the table. Without waking One, Jocelyn gave her the medicine, opened the alcohol and rubbed her down in it. Sitting One back in the chair and strapping her in, Jocelyn moved on to do the same with Two.

Done, she said, "I suggest you not give them milk right after they've had their shots. Try the Pedialyte. It may prevent the temperatures all together. If not, it will keep them down."

Nervously, Derrick asked, "What's that?"

"A clear liquid supplement. It's easier for them to digest. Doesn't upset the system. Whenever they're sick, give it to them instead of milk."

Looking at One and Two anxiously, Derrick asked, "Why didn't you put their clothes back on? Won't they catch cold?"

Closing her eyes, Jocelyn said, "Please sit down, Mr. Dawes. I'm getting a terrible pain in my neck looking up at you."

Derrick sat and waited for Jocelyn to answer his question. Eventually she said, "If you dress them now, it will take twice as long for their bodies to cool down. The little sleepers hold in all of the body heat."

"Can't we put their undershirts back on? They look so vulnerable like that."

"Get used to it, Mr. Dawes. They'll be in diapers a long time."

Irritably, Derrick said, "Stop calling me, Mr. Dawes. That's my father. I'm Derrick."

"Excuse me."

Derrick looked at the gorgeous manila woman with beautiful pitch-black hair and provocative dark brown eyes gracing her face. A keen nose gave her an authoritarian air. As David was so fond of saying, "Derrick would have to turn in his testicles if he didn't notice those lips." Jocelyn had one of the most sensuous mouth's Derrick had ever seen. Full, cinnamon, perpetually moist and pouting. They demanded attention, without intending to. He found it fascinating that

Jocelyn was so unbelievably attractive without a touch of make-up. An intriguingly subtle perfume was her only noticeable feminine concession.

Genuine amusement danced in his eyes as he asked, "Well, do I have to keep calling you Nurse Avery?"

"You most certainly do."

"Okay. Would you like something to drink, Nurse Avery? Coffee, tea, a soft drink?"

"I've had more than enough caffeine today. If you have orange, grape, or ginger-ale, I might be interested."

Standing to get it from the refrigerator, Derrick asked, "How long will One and Two have to be naked?"

Jocelyn started to say they weren't naked, but she knew that would only ring the bell for another round of biting remarks. Instead, she said, "Just until they cool off, Mr. Dawes."

Looking over his shoulder slowly, he said, "Derrick."

"Oh, I'm sorry. Derrick."

As Derrick pulled glasses from the cabinet, Jocelyn said, "I know all about your babies, Mr. Dawes. I mean Derrick."

Stopping with the glasses in mid-air, Derrick asked, "What do you know about my babies? Dr. Kane said he didn't know anything."

"He doesn't. I only know because I spoke with your mother the first time you brought the girls in. She told me you didn't know who their mother was. She also told me you weren't sure One and Two were your babies. I'd like to commend you. Not many men would have taken on the responsibility of two brand new infants. The uncertainty of their origin would have provided just enough of an excuse to avoid it like the plague."

Pouring the soft drinks into glasses, Derrick said, "Don't be so quick to commend me, Nurse Avery. When my choices were take them or go straight to jail, I buckled."

"If you wanted to fight, you would have only been there a few hours."

"Sure. And, in the meantime, they have my prints and my mug shot to show every victim in the city. One mistakenly identifies me and it will cost me a fortune to get out of God only knows what. No thank you. Do you know how many brothers are doing time for that right this very moment?"

"They can't keep your picture and prints if they find you innocent of the charges."

"What planet did you say you came from, Nurse Avery?"

"I came from this one. I just don't know much about the judicial system. Sorry."

"You're excused."

"I still think you're doing a wonderful thing, regardless of your motivation. No woman could take better care of these babies than you're doing."

"Wow! And, you say that, knowing I sit them on the kitchen table?"

"Oh, shut up. Today, everyone sits them on kitchen tables. These chairs allow parents to sit them in crazier places than this."

"Please don't tell me any baby horror stories. I lose enough sleep as it is."

Jocelyn laughed for the first time. Their conversation mellowed a bit after that. She asked Derrick all of the personal questions she could think of. Before the subject changed, Jocelyn knew what he did for a living, where he worked, his family background and even a few of his hopes and dreams.

At six, One and Two were still asleep. Derrick pulled two of his mother's frozen meals out and heated them in the microwave. He and Jocelyn ate and chatted friendly. Then, Derrick started drilling her for information. While this made her slightly uncomfortable, she answered his questions.

"Okay, Nurse Avery, I know you're a Registered Nurse. I know you work in Dr. Kane's office. Are you married, dating seriously, or single?"

"I guess I'm single."

"How does one guess they're single? Are you saying you're seeing someone, but you're not married? Or, are you saying you're married and in the process of or, recently divorced?"

Not believing the depth of Derrick's questions, Jocelyn answered, "None of the above. I am not in a relationship—remote or otherwise. I've been a widow for four and a half years."

Feeling a little stupid, Derrick said softly, "I'm sorry."

"Don't be. You couldn't have known if I didn't tell you."

"May I ask what happened?"

Giving Derrick a wan smile, Jocelyn said, "Of course, you can ask. Since you haven't attacked me in over an hour, I'll answer."

Taking a slow deliberate breath, Jocelyn began her story by saying, "Justine and I were high school sweethearts. His parents and my grandmother called us inseparable. My grandmother adored Justine's gusto, but my parents were not too happy about my attachment to him. According to my father, Justine couldn't be serious about anything but a bet. When we both enrolled at USC, they settled down and accepted the inevitable.

"We married the day after Justine completed the ROTC program. Anyway, Justine's dream was to become a pilot. All he ever talked about when we were growing up was taking off from the deck of an aircraft carrier. Well, he joined the Navy and breezed through Officer Candidate School and was well on his way to making his dream come true. It was the one thing Justine took seriously and worked like a demon to achieve.

"After officer's training, they assigned Justine to flight school at Miramar Naval Air Station in San Diego. I was lucky enough to find a position at the Children's Hospital after graduation and we moved into a beautiful tiny cottage apartment. Our plans for the future were all laid out in detail. If we lived frugally for five years, the world would be our oyster. It just didn't turn out that way."

Looking down at her hands as if the rest of the story were printed in her palms, Jocelyn continued slowly,

"Justine's first love was always speed, so you can imagine how in love he was with his Tom Cat. My competition was an airplane that went entirely too fast to take off from the deck of a ship if you asked me. But, no one asked me, and Justine happily took off from that deck, risking his life every time they ordered him to.

"During night practice maneuvers, Justine was goofing with the pilot of another plane. They were laughing about some trick they had played on another trainee. Justine wasn't concentrating on his landing. You know landing a plane on the deck of an aircraft carrier has to be done with absolute precision. The moment a pilot realizes he can't make it perfectly, they're trained to abort the landing, pull up and avoid the ship.

"Somehow, Justine was distracted beyond the point of no return. He hit the deck prematurely and missed the catapult. Fourteen other soldiers died with Justine that day and many more were horribly injured.

"Two days after his funeral, I miscarried. I never even knew I was pregnant. I can't tell you which loss hurt me more. For the longest time, I felt Justine had placed a bet with my entire life and lost and I would never forgive him for it. Afterwards, I needed to put as much distance between my self, California, and my past as I could. So, here I am."

Looking at One and Two, Derrick asked, "Isn't it a little hard for you working with so many babies?"

"No. I've wanted to be a pediatric nurse forever. Every baby I treat is a little bit mine, you know? Because I missed the opportunity to experience it completely, pregnant women disturb me some. That's why I prefer being outside the hospital. I only see an occasional pregnant mother."

Leaning on his elbows, Derrick asked, "Who are you dating now, Nurse Avery?"

Smiling, Jocelyn said, "Didn't I just say I'm not dating anyone?"

"Oh, did you? I'm sorry. I forgot. Did you tell me why?"

Shaking her head, Jocelyn answered, "I'm comfortable with my life right now. I go on a date here and there, but nothing worth mentioning."

While Derrick liked Jocelyn's response, it troubled him, so he asked, "Don't you get lonely?"

"Occasionally. I don't dwell on it too long though. One incorrect choice could throw my entire life into another tailspin. I'm more afraid of the spin."

Pointing at One and Two, Derrick said, "After this episode, I might be more afraid of the spin myself."

Turning the tables on Derrick, Jocelyn asked, "Do you get lonely?"

"Honestly. Before the babies, I never gave lonely a thought. I dated whenever I wanted company. Never saw too much of anyone. I enjoyed the simplicity of my life. Basically, Nurse Avery, I did as I pleased. Tried to be as inoffensive as possible as I traveled down the center of the road."

As if Derrick had spoken to her soul, Jocelyn responded from a deep, still segment of herself when she said, "Yeah, I know. Life won't let you get through it that simply though. No matter which path you take. No matter how well intentioned and disciplined you are. Eventually, you will be dragged into the fray."

## *CHAPTER FIFTEEN*

One and Two had cooled down considerably by the time Jocelyn prepared to leave Derrick's house. They were fed and fast asleep in their beds, as Derrick walked Jocelyn to her car. Of course, he had the monitor clipped to his pocket.

At Jocelyn's gleaming white Accord, she turned and said, "Thank you for a lovely evening, Mr. Dawes. I enjoyed the meal and the conversation."

Smiling, Derrick asked, "What are you talking about? We started off arguing. You took care of One and Two. I nuked you a dinner my mother prepared. We fed and changed One and Two. If you think that's a lovely evening, you're easier than you think, Nurse Avery."

Holding up a finger, Jocelyn added, "But we ended on a civilized note. For us, that was quite an accomplishment."

"I'll give you that one. I never thought the war would end between us. Since I'm on a sabbatical, maybe I could nuke you another meal sometime soon."

Smiling slyly and getting into the car, Jocelyn said, "Call me at the office when you're ready, Mr. Dawes."

"I'll do that, Nurse Avery. Good night."

"Good night."

Derrick watched the Accord pull into the street and walked back to the house. It was only the beginning of November and cold weather had settled in already. He made a mental note to prepare the fireplaces as soon as he got a free moment. A fire in the fireplace, a good book and a glass of red wine were heaven to Derrick. Music was optional. He couldn't hear the soothing random snap of the fire if it wasn't just right.

As far as Jocelyn was concerned, Derrick knew she would hear from him very soon. Not only was Derrick physically attracted to Nurse Hatchet she intrigued him. After being traumatized by the loss of her husband and child, she was actually beginning to stick her head out of the sand again. Derrick didn't get the impression Jocelyn even realized she was reaching out and touching someone. If asked, he knew she would deny it vehemently.

The telephone rang the moment Derrick locked the front door and he dove for it. The last thing Derrick wanted was One and Two screaming in his ear because they were disturbed.

After his rushed and breathless greeting, the caller said, "Well, hello stranger. Did I catch you at a bad moment?"

Not knowing whom he was speaking to, Derrick said, "No. I didn't want the telephone to wake the babies."

"What babies? Don't tell me you've gone and married someone and had children already."

"Who am I speaking to?"

"This is Cynthia. And, I'm wounded. You didn't recognize my voice."

Genuinely happy to hear from her, Derrick apologized immediately. "I'm sorry, Cynthia. These days, I don't recognize my own voice. Please don't hold it against me."

"Okay. Now, what babies?"

"The two someone left on my doorstep. That wouldn't have been you, would it?"

"Sorry. I'm not into leaving babies on doorsteps. But, you're just joking. Right?"

"No. Someone put my name on two birth certificates and split. You were one of my suspects. I haven't seen or spoken to you since New Year's Day, or was it the day after?"

"It was New Year's Day, Derrick, and I didn't know I had to report before I left. Besides, my telephone wasn't exactly ringing off the hook with your calls after New Year's."

Not wanting to get into explaining why he hadn't called, Derrick asked, "Where did you go?"

"The company sent me to Atlanta to teach some computer classes in February. I didn't get back here until the end of July. They tried to pull a whammy on me. Southern charm, balmy breezes and pecan trees are wonderful in small doses, I had to demand to be sent home when the drawl crept into my dreams."

"I can't believe you didn't enjoy Atlanta, Cynthia. It's beautiful, warm, and relatively peaceful."

"I hate bursting your bubble, Derrick, but when was the last time you were there?"

"It's only been a few years. I worked on the prelim's for the Olympic Village."

"Forget Atlanta, Derrick. It ain't the picture postcard town you think it is. Tell me more about your babies. Why did you keep them? Couldn't you just turn them over to the police, or one of those bleeding heart agencies?"

"Until I know if they're really mine, it was the simplest solution."

"Does that mean there's still a possibility you're giving them up?"

"Yes, that possibility is still open. I don't want to do it. They really grow on you. But, I'm not cut out for motherhood."

"If there's anything I can do to help, give me a call. I don't know much about babies, but I'll do whatever I can."

"Thanks, Cynthia. What took you so long to return my telephone call? I called you two months ago."

"Excuse me? I know you didn't expect me to jump for a man who slept with me on two of the biggest nights of the year and never called again until September. You're good, Derrick. Just not that good."

"Does that mean I can only call if I need a babysitter?"

"Not necessarily. I might get over your rejection after the guy I sleep with this New Year's Eve pulls a repeat performance. Then, I'll be angrier with him."

Derrick laughed. That's why he liked Cynthia. If any of this disturbed her, she wouldn't let anyone else know it.

They said their good nights and Derrick's mind cleared. He decided it was time to turn in. Upstairs, he looked at the sleeping babies and knew their bassinet days were coming to an end. Two actually had her foot propped up on the side. Neither one could stretch their arms out. They looked uncomfortable to Derrick.

As much as he wanted them out of his room in the beginning, Derrick was stunned by his own reluctance to see them go. If anything happened to them during the night in the other room, he would never forgive himself. More than anything, Derrick was surprised by how much he had grown to love the two little nuisances. As much as it was possible, Derrick felt they loved him too.

Exhausted, Derrick undressed and climbed into bed. The moment his head hit the pillow, he felt eyes on him. Through slits, Derrick peeked to see which one it was. Two strained to hold her tiny curly head above the rim of the bassinet. When Derrick didn't move in her direction, her bottom lip began to quiver. Derrick jumped up to get to Two before she woke her sister.

Speaking just above a whisper, Derrick said, "Okay, you win. What's the matter? Does your leg hurt? I know you're not hungry. You want some juice? Please don't start crying. Your old man can't take that tonight."

In response, Two rested her head on Derrick's bare chest and closed her eyes. When he moved, those eyes popped open. Realizing Two just wanted to be held, Derrick laid down with her on his chest. The two of them drifted off to sleep in no time. An hour later, he returned the sleeping baby to her bassinet. He fell into bed and covered his head.

The strangest thing happened to Derrick during the night. He dreamed vividly. Not only did he dream, he remembered who and what he dreamt about. Nasty Nurse Avery. Jocelyn.

In his dream, the events of his evening with Jocelyn repeated with subtle changes. Derrick didn't walk Jocelyn to her car and it didn't seem odd that One and Two's bassinets were not in the bedroom when Derrick entered.

Hearing water running in the shower, Derrick undressed and went into the bathroom. He slid the shower door open and in the steamy mist stood Jocelyn. There was only one thing wrong with the picture. Jocelyn was wearing her white uniform. As can only happen in dreams, they showered together anyway. Back in the bedroom, Jocelyn climbed into bed, still dressed in that damned uniform. Derrick had no idea what happened afterwards because, as people often do in dreams, Jocelyn disappeared.

This little episode stood out for Derrick, because he never remembered what he dreamed unless something truly disturbed him. He didn't think Jocelyn had done anything to disturb him. It would never occur to Derrick that Jocelyn's mere presence might have done it. No other woman had ever made that kind of an impression on him.

# *CHAPTER SIXTEEN*

A sudden high pitch screech woke Derrick at six the following morning. He shot straight up and looked around the dark bedroom. On the tail end of the screech he realized it was coming from One.

Half asleep, Derrick stumbled over to her bassinet and felt the heat emanating from One's body before he touched her. Not only was she extremely hot, One held her body rock rigid. Derrick picked her up and One's screech shifted gears as if he had hurt her. Tears streamed down One's tormented little red face.

Cradling the screaming baby to his chest, Derrick went downstairs to get the Tylenol, two bottles of juice, and the alcohol. One flailed her arms so frantically Derrick spilled more of the Tylenol from the infant dropper than he actually got into her. He tried coaxing her to drink the apple juice, but she screamed with the nipple dangling in her mouth until she choked.

Stripping off her undershirt, Derrick opened the alcohol and started rubbing her down. When he got to her leg, his mouth fell open. One's little leg was beet red, hotter than the rest of her body and swollen tight. Derrick rubbed it down with the alcohol and One seemed to respond to the cool manipulation of her leg.

Derrick picked One up and offered her the juice again. This time the tormented, delicate creature let out a sigh and a lone tear slid slowly into her hair, as she sucked at it. Looking at One suck and huff, Derrick heard Two's miserable whine. She probably had been whining the entire time, but with One screaming at the top of her lungs he never heard Two.

Knowing One wouldn't like it, Derrick laid her down and propped her bottle on his pillow. To his surprise, One was so exhausted, she didn't have the strength to complain. Before Derrick picked up Two, he dialed Dr. Kane's office.

Two's leg was nearly as swollen as One's. Derrick was livid when Dr. Kane's groggy night clerk answered. Derrick didn't say hello or good morning. He shouted, "This is Derrick Dawes! I have two babies with swollen legs and temperatures from the shots Dr. Kane gave them yesterday! I want to speak to him in ten minutes or less! My number is 554-3774!"

Without waiting for a response, Derrick hung up and turned his attention to the whimpering baby on his arm. He was in the midst of repeating his Tylenol, alcohol, and juice routine when the telephone rang five minutes later. Again, Derrick yelled. "Dr. Kane! What the hell did you do to One and Two?! They're burning up! Their legs are swollen and red! They scream if anything touches them!"

A sleepy woman's voice said, "Stop yelling before you have an embolism, Derrick. Babies have these kinds of reactions to immunization shots everyday. How hot are they?"

Still yelling, Derrick asked, "Who is this?! How am I supposed to know how hot they are?!"

"Take their temperatures, idiot!"

"Who is this?! I don't know how to take their temperature! Where is the doctor?!"

"Give them the Tylenol, rub them down in alcohol and give them something clear to drink. I'll be there in about thirty minutes."

Before Derrick could ask whom he was speaking to one more time, she hung up. Whoever she was, Derrick thought she had a lot of nerve calling him an idiot. He would set her straight as soon as she showed her face at his front door. Probably some intern the doctor had working as his flunky.

The doorbell rang a little before seven. Derrick went to answer it with a baby on each arm. All he could do was turn the key, step back and yell, "It's open!"

The doorknob turned and the door opened slowly. A woman wearing a heavy, navy blue, hooded parka came in. She turned to close the door and lock it. Derrick couldn't see her face. He waited for her to turn around. Before doing that, she swept the hood from her head, revealing thick black hair that filled the hood of her coat and flowed over. From where Derrick stood, he could see that it was all her hair. Momentarily impressed, Derrick forgot he was angry with this woman, whoever she was.

The face of the woman who stared up at Derrick said it all. One perfectly arched eyebrow danced dangerously high on her forehead. Pretty cinnamon, moist lips pressed together tightly. Her top lip curled up in the corner and nostrils flaring.

Derrick recognized the striking woman with the distorted features now. The missing ponytail had thrown him off. Jocelyn beat Derrick to the yelling this time.

"How dare you yell at people at six o'clock in the morning?! We can't help you if you're going to throw a tantrum every time the babies run a temperature, Mr. Dawes! And, why can't you take their temperatures?! They have idiot thermometers you only have to put under their arms now!"

Sniffing arrogantly at Jocelyn, Derrick said, "Well, I don't have one of those, Nurse Hatchet."

Seething, Jocelyn asked through clenched teeth, "What did you just call me?"

"My babies are sick. Are you going to look at them, or not?"

Taking her coat off and hanging it on the banister, Jocelyn took One from Derrick and asked, "Why didn't you get dressed, Mr. Dawes? I said I would be here in thirty minutes."

With a stupid expression on his face, Derrick said, "I've got on clean underwear. My mother said that's all that matters."

Rolling her eyes and speaking to One, Jocelyn asked, "What's the matter, sweetheart? Is loud, belligerent, nearly naked Daddy scaring you to death?" Turning to Derrick she asked, "Where would you like me to take a look at them, Mr. Dawes? Here, in the foyer?"

Losing patience with the attractive, smart mouth nurse, Derrick said sharply, "Upstairs, Nurse Avery."

In Derrick's bedroom, Jocelyn looked over both One and Two. They were beginning to cool off again. The immunization spot on their legs was still slightly inflamed. Jocelyn stood and excused herself. She ran out to her car and returned with two bottles. The smaller was liquid Benadryl, the larger, Pedialyte.

Jocelyn handed Derrick the Pedialyte and said, "Pour some of this into their bottles, please. And, put some pants on, for God's sake, Mr. Dawes!"

Derrick took his time putting his pants on, because he knew his near nudity made Nurse Hatchet uncomfortable. He watched Jocelyn lean over the babies lying on his bed and recalled his earlier dream. That's when he realized she wasn't wearing her uniform. She had on jeans, a bright red sweatshirt, white socks and loafers. Derrick couldn't decide which way he liked her best, so he dashed downstairs to do as instructed.

With two fresh bottles of Pedialyte in hand, Derrick returned to his bedroom. Leaning on her elbows, Jocelyn talked to the two flushed, weary looking babies. One and Two weakly reached for her dangling hair.

Jocelyn sat up and picked up One. She took one of the bottles from Derrick's hand and offered it to the baby. One sucked at it and continued to reach for Jocelyn's hair. Jocelyn nodded her head toward Two and said, "Would you mind giving Two the other bottle, Mr. Dawes?"

Again following instructions, Derrick had to admit he really enjoyed watching Jocelyn with the babies. They seemed to like her, too.

Jocelyn and Derrick sat side by side on his bed, each feeding a baby and neither saying a word. One spit her nipple out first. Jocelyn automatically flipped her hair back and put One on her shoulder to burp her. One drifted off to sleep with a fist-full of Jocelyn's hair.

As usual, Two didn't give up until there was nothing left in the bottle. Still holding the bottle, Derrick inspected her leg. He noticed it didn't seem as inflamed as it had earlier. Without looking at Jocelyn, Derrick asked, "Did you give them something to make their legs go down?"

"Just a little Benadryl. If it flares up again, I'll have to insist you take them into the emergency room. But, most of these reactions are minor."

Jocelyn laid One in her bassinet and asked, "Can you handle them from here?"

"I guess so. Can I offer you a cup of coffee?"

"You sure can. Is it made?"

"No. But, if you'll burp Two, I'll put it on for you."

Jocelyn held her hands out for the baby. Two's little eyes lit up at the prospect of getting into Jocelyn's hair. She could only pinch Derrick's bare skin, and she did that all of the time. Derrick sighed heavily, hoisted himself up and down the stairs to the kitchen. Jocelyn joined Derrick in the kitchen five minutes later with Two relaxed on her arm and the monitor clipped to her jean pocket. He pulled out a chair and poured coffee into two large mugs. Jocelyn sat and waited for Derrick's marvelous half naked service. She couldn't help noticing what a remarkably interesting male specimen he was. After all, she had seen him in nothing more than a pair of black briefs less than twenty minutes before. Jocelyn envied One and Two getting to see Derrick that way every day.

Neither Jocelyn nor Derrick said a word as they poured sugar and cream into their coffee. Two single-mindedly kept her eyes on Jocelyn's hair and as the silent minutes passed, Two's eyelids grew heavy and she finally nodded off.

Jocelyn smiled down at her and stroked the sleeping cheek with her finger. Suddenly, breaking the silence, Jocelyn said, "I can't believe you need a test to tell you these are your children. They look just like you."

"So I've heard. The test will only make it official."

"Have you heard anything from their mother yet?"

"Yes and no."

"What does that mean?"

"I've spoken to her, but she's still denying One and Two belong to her."

"Are you sure you're accusing the right woman, Derrick?"

"I think so. They kind of remind me of her sometimes. Other times, I can't imagine who they remind me of."

"How old is this woman?"

"She's twenty-nine. Why do you ask?"

"Because I can't imagine a grown woman doing anything like this. If I had to take a guess, she would have been much younger."

Giving Jocelyn a curious expression and tilting his head, Derrick asked, "Are you suggesting I may have committed a crime or something, Nurse Avery? Exactly how young would you have guessed her to be?"

Shrugging her shoulders, Jocelyn said, "I don't know. It's just the sort of thing a younger woman would do, that's all. They get frightened of the unknown and do all kinds of things. By the time we're twenty-nine, we know who the ghosts are and how to deal with them."

Changing the subject, Jocelyn asked, "Are you still considering giving them up if the test says they're not yours?"

"I don't want to talk about that this morning, Nurse Avery."

"Okay. What would you like to talk about this morning, Mr. Dawes?"

"Would you like to have dinner with me again this evening?"

"While that's a very nice request, I must decline. I have a date for this evening."

Looking puzzled, Derrick said, "I thought you said you weren't seeing anyone."

"I'm not seeing him. I'm having dinner with him."

"Why are you having dinner with him?"

"Because he asked nicely. Perhaps I'll stop by afterwards to see how One and Two are."

Derrick said sulkily, "Don't let us interrupt your evening, Nurse Avery."

moved toward the door. Out of Derrick's shadow, she another deep breath. The heat of his nearness seemed ke Jocelyn's breath away. She darted down the stairs and edly put her coat on. Jocelyn was fumbling with the key in loor, when Derrick made his slow descent down the stairs. actually looked at him with frightened eyes.

A frown of confusion covered Derrick's face when he d, "What's wrong with you?"

"Nothing. I can't seem to get this door unlocked."

"I'll unlock it for you. You don't have to be afraid. I ldn't dream of holding you here against your will. Your might show up and tear my house down."

"Shut up and open the door!" Jocelyn snapped.

Derrick clicked his bare heels together and said, "Yes, Ma'am."

Turning the key in the lock easily, Derrick opened the r. Without looking at him, Jocelyn left. She didn't like rush she felt from Derrick's nearness or the shock to her em merely bumping into him had caused. So far oved from being completely attracted to any man for so , Jocelyn was befuddled by her reaction to Derrick.

Jocelyn drove to her apartment building in a fog of fusion. She quickly showered, dressed in her uniform, ed her hair up into her trademark ponytail and made it to office ten minutes late. When Dr. Kane asked her how and Two were Jocelyn responded absentmindedly, ey had minor allergic reactions to the shots. I gave them tle Benadryl. They seemed fine when I left."

Dr. Kane said, "Good. How was Mr. Dawes? I heard he ed quite a ruckus this morning."

Through clenched teeth, Jocelyn said, "Mr. Dawes is a . He can't help it."

Giving Jocelyn a knowing smile, Dr. Kane said, "I'm e you're right."

Smiling, Jocelyn said, "I won't. An
call me Nurse Avery anymore, Derrick. I'v
your underwear. I think that trampled formal

Crossing his heavily muscled arn
smooth, hairless, chiseled chest, Derrick
so. It was an emergency situation."

"Now Daddy's pouting. He's quite
attitudes, isn't he?" Jocelyn asked, loo
sleeping infant. Giving a disgusted
satisfied glance, "I have to get to the off
how the babies are a little later. If they
again, call us before you take them to the

"Thanks. You have a nice day, Nu
genuinely hope you enjoy your dinner date

"Thank you, Derrick. Even if I can s
mean a word of it."

"I mean it. I hope you enjoy your din

"Okay. I'll take Two upstairs and lay her d

"You don't have to do that. I can take

"I'd like to see how One is doing, if yo

"I don't mind anything you do, Nurse A

Jocelyn struggled not to laugh at Der
was hilarious. Without saying anything
from the table and headed up the stairs wi
her down and touched One's brow. Both l
considerably. Their legs had lost that flam
Jocelyn couldn't resist bending to give bc
When she stood and took a step backwards,
the shirtless, barefoot Derrick Dawes. Withou
asked, "You shouldn't be doing that, should you

Inhaling deeply to clear her mind, Jocelyn a

"Kissing your patients."

"I shouldn't be arguing with their ha
either. Excuse me, Mr. Dawes."

Stepping around the big man in he
removed the monitor from her pants, place

# *CHAPTER SEVENTEEN*

Derrick's day unfolded relatively well. One and Two were in pretty good spirits after the early morning fiasco. As long as they didn't bump their legs, they ate, drank and played normally. Derrick opened their playpen in the kitchen and let them lay in it together. Reaching for each other always entertained them better than anything else. Fascination with their hands and feet came in second. Both babies could turn over, but Derrick couldn't understand how they moved forward without being able to crawl, however, they did it. Whichever way Derrick moved, eventually, they turned to find him.

Jocelyn's day unfolded relatively well, too. She kept calling all of the babies One and Two, but other than that, each patient survived. At noon, Jocelyn called to see how the real One and Two were feeling. Derrick told her they seemed fine to him. When he asked if she would be stopping by to check on them after her dinner date, Jocelyn gave him an unflinching, "No!"

Naturally, Derrick was surprised when Jocelyn called at five that evening. He had spent his day washing and folding clothes, feeding One and Two, and catching bits and pieces of college basketball games. Their conversation was short. For the most part, merely a repeat of the earlier call, without Derrick asking any questions about her date. He did ask when it would be all right to feed One and Two milk again. They were getting grumpy on the Pedialyte. Jocelyn told him it would be all right to feed them, if they hadn't heated up anymore since that morning.

Not wanting to push the envelope too soon, Derrick waited until eight to feed One and Two a little cereal and a bottle. Sonya had told him not to give them any fruit with it. All of those things together might overload their systems. One and Two fell asleep like two happy campers after Derrick wiped down their faces and hands.

It was only a little after nine and Derrick didn't feel like being cooped up in his bedroom. He clipped the monitor onto the waistband of his jogging pants and went down to the recreation room. He dropped down onto the plush burgundy leather sofa and flipped on the television. Before he could make head or tails of which college teams were playing football, his doorbell rang.

Just knowing it was Jocelyn, Derrick took his time getting there. A gentle breeze would have knocked him off of his feet if it had blown when he opened the door and saw Cassandra.

Making a mental note to always check before opening the door, Derrick forced a smile to his face and said, "Hi, Cassandra. What are you doing here?"

Whisking past him, Cassandra pulled off her coat and said, "Hi, Derrick. I was in the neighborhood and thought I'd stop by and say, 'Hi.'"

Without being invited to, Cassandra hung her coat in the hallway closet. She wore a bright red and rust silk wrap dress. It plunged down deeply at the neck and up at the hem. Rust colored three-inch heels accentuated Cassandra's already magnificent coffee legs. Any man with eyes would have appreciated seeing Cassandra in that dress. It said, "If you're really interested, come on over."

Derrick looked her up and down and felt none of the old spark. As attractive as she was, and as good as Derrick knew she could be, there was no pull. If asked, he would have simply said Cassandra had worn out her welcome.

Cassandra sauntered over to him, tugged on the front of his sweatshirt, gave him a warm, wet kiss and asked, "Aren't you going to offer me something to drink? A seat? Something?"

Snapping out of his stupor, Derrick said, "I'm sorry, Cassandra. I thought you were someone else. What would you like to drink?"

Biting her bottom lip provocatively, Cassandra said, "Now that's more like it. A glass of white wine would be nice."

Derrick went to the cabinet in the dining room and retrieved a bottle of zinfandel. At least he thought that was what Cassandra said she liked. Hell, it could have been someone else who said it. Derrick really didn't care. Derrick simply wanted Cassandra to disappear. Her presence irritated him.

Back in the living room, Derrick poured wine into the two glasses. He sat on the white brocade sofa next to Cassandra and handed her a glass. Cassandra asked one question after another. Suppressing his urge to yell, Derrick answered lifelessly.

"So, how are you making out with your wards, Derrick?"

"Fine."

"Has Mommie Dearest given you a call yet?"

"No."

Stroking his cheek with her perfumed finger, Cassandra asked, "Are you ready to change the house rules yet?"

"Not really."

Licking her bright red lips and resting the palm of her warm hand on his thigh, she asked, "Are you absolutely sure about that?"

Sighing, Derrick said, "Absolutely."

“Why haven’t you called me?” Cassandra asked with disappointment dancing in her sleepy eyes.

"I've been busy."

"That's not what David told me. He said you took a leave of absence. If you're going to be home all day, every day, it seems like you could find a few hours to spend with a friend. You can't be planning to sit here and play house all alone for more than a month, Derrick."

"I need the time, Cassandra. Taking care of two infants requires more than I thought. I appreciate every quiet moment these days."

Giving Derrick's thigh a gentle squeeze, Cassandra said, "I can be quiet, too. I thought you preferred a little noise."

Smiling his magnificent smile for the first time, Derrick said, "Oh, I know you know what I like, Cassandra. It's just not happening for me right now. That's all."

Rising from the sofa and lowering herself onto Derrick's lap, Cassandra cooed, "Oh, it won't take much to make it happen for you, Derrick. I can help, if I have to."

Inhaling her sharp, tangy perfume and getting a better view of her immaculately displayed cleavage, Derrick cleared his throat and said, "I don't need any help. I just haven't been in the mood for it. I know that's difficult for you to understand, Cassandra."

Giving Derrick a deep white wine kiss, Cassandra whispered, "It's not difficult for me to understand, Derrick. It's impossible for me to understand."

Cassandra gave Derrick one little kiss followed by another. She nibbled his bottom lip, licked it and slipped her sleek, wet tongue into his mouth. Without a thought, Derrick closed his eyes and responded to her manipulations.

First, his hand found Cassandra's perfectly rounded rear-end. He stroked and massaged it. Then, his other hand found her full, luscious breast. Dissatisfied with the feel of her silk dress, Derrick's hand wandered until it found itself inside Cassandra's dress.

Cassandra caressed Derrick with one hand and skillfully released her dress with the other. Derrick's kisses moved down her neck. His tongue did a warm, wet dance between her breasts. Before Cassandra could release her bra the doorbell rang. Derrick moaned loudly and dropped his head onto Cassandra's warm, heaving cleavage. She rested her head on the back of his and did likewise.

Cassandra whispered agonizingly into his neck, "Don't answer it, Derrick. Please?"

The doorbell ringing for the second time forced Derrick to say, "I have to. It'll wake the babies. It's probably their nurse anyway."

Cassandra's head popped up. She asked suspiciously, "What nurse makes house calls after nine, Derrick?"

Lifting and placing Cassandra on the sofa, as easily as he would a pillow, Derrick said, "Stay here. She just wants to check the babies. I'll be right back."

Looking through the peephole in the door this time, Derrick didn't see anyone. He opened the door and stuck his head out.

Hearing the jingle of keys and seeing the foyer light on the walk-way made Jocelyn turn around. She returned to the door. Before entering, Jocelyn looked at Derrick without saying a word. He had a stupid, guilty as hell expression on his face. Dismissing it, Jocelyn entered the foyer. The fragrance of heady perfume assaulted her. Jocelyn knew immediately that there was a woman in the house. Without fanfare, she asked, "How are the girls?"

Not looking at her, Derrick said, "They're fine. I fed them and put them to bed about an hour ago."

Thinking her presence annoyed him, Jocelyn asked, "Would you like me to check them before I go in for the evening?"

Closing the front door, Derrick said, "Sure."

He followed Jocelyn up the stairs. Derrick got his first look at Jocelyn's legs on the trip. They were the long, gracefully athletic, gorgeous legs of a dancer. Derrick could have strangled himself for falling into Cassandra's trap halfway up those stairs. If the trip up the stairs upset Derrick, the scene in the bedroom destroyed him.

Jocelyn walked over to the bassinets, removed her long black leather coat, dropped it onto Derrick's bed and lay her purse near the pillows. She wore a short black, form fitting dress, with a black and cream bolero jacket. Sheer black stockings gave her legs a shiny, veiled mysterious appearance. The black heels with the single cream stripe, not only flattered her exquisite legs they seemed to have been custom-made to match the outfit. If Jocelyn had been on the street in that outfit, guys would have been slamming their cars into each other.

Jocelyn's waist couldn't have been more than twenty-two inches tops, her firm, rounded hips thirty-four. To cap off Derrick's nightmare, Jocelyn's exquisite breasts were absolutely, positively a full, firm thirty-six. Reams of smooth, black hair cascaded onto her shoulders. One loose curl rested on the exposed top of her breast. That curl almost drove poor Derrick nuts. He wondered how she kept a figure like that shrouded so well.

When Jocelyn bent over the bassinets to get a good look at the babies' legs, Derrick got a mind-boggling look at her rear-end. If he thought Jocelyn would respond to him the way he wanted, he would have gone down those stairs and physically thrown Cassandra out the front door. As it was, he just wanted Cassandra to leave.

Still staring at Jocelyn's backside, Derrick asked, "How was your dinner date?"

Standing, Jocelyn said, "It was okay. How was yours?"

"I ate dinner alone."

Jocelyn looked at Derrick and laughed a little before she said, "Well, your dessert wears terrible perfume and you really should have wiped that lipstick off your face before answering the door."

Knowing he was caught red-handed, Derrick smiled and shrugged his shoulders innocently. Jocelyn picked up her coat and Derrick moved toward her quickly. Taking the coat from her hands, he held it open for her.

As she slid her arms into the sleeves, Derrick said, "You look awfully good to have only had an okay dinner date. I bet you wouldn't have worn that outfit to eat with me."

"You'll never know now, will you?"

"Please don't say you'll never have dinner with me, Nurse Avery. I mean, Jocelyn."

Smugly, Jocelyn said, "I don't do lines, Derrick. Long or short."

"What are you talking about? There is no line."

"Oh, yes there is. It starts with the woman who's in this house right this minute. I think I should be going before my presence upsets her."

"I don't care about her being upset. I'm upset right now. If she hadn't shown up unannounced, I probably could have talked you into staying and having a little dessert with me tonight."

Reaching up, Jocelyn wiped the lipstick from Derrick's mouth with her finger and said, "You've had enough dessert for one night, Derrick. I'll call to see how the girls are doing tomorrow. They're a little warm right now. But, it doesn't seem like anything to worry about. Their legs are still slightly swollen, too. Rub them down in the morning and massage them."

Pitifully, Derrick said, "Stay for a while longer, Jocelyn."

"What are you talking about now? You have company."

"I'll send her away."

"Not for me, you won't."

"Please, Jocelyn?"

"No."

Jocelyn moved toward the door and Derrick grabbed her hand. He held and stroked it with his thumb. Heat exploded in Jocelyn's mind. She fidgeted uncomfortably and said haltingly, "I have to go, Derrick. I'll call tomorrow."

Enclosing her tiny hand between his two extremely large ones, Derrick said softly, "Okay. Thanks for stopping by to check on my babies."

Gently extricating her hand from his, Jocelyn headed toward the stairs and Derrick followed. Something made Jocelyn stop mid-step, making Derrick bump into her. He had to grab her to keep her from falling. Following Jocelyn's astonished stare, Derrick saw Cassandra standing in the living room doorway. Her silk dress completely unwrapped. Blazing red panties and bra, and coffee colored flesh were dramatically revealed. Cassandra's face was twisted into a mask of disgusted accusations.

Still holding onto Jocelyn, an astonished Derrick stammered, "What are you doing, Cassandra?"

"Waiting for you to finish playing with the babies' nurse. You did say she was their nurse, didn't you?"

"Yes, I did. So, why are you standing there with your dress open?"

Rolling wide, expressive, brown eyes expertly, Cassandra spat sarcastically, "If she's really a nurse, she's seen more body than I'm showing."

Finally getting a handle on what was happening, Jocelyn turned to Derrick and said calmly, "I'll talk to you later, Mr. Dawes. You'd better take care of this."

Hating to let Jocelyn go with everything looking so very badly, Derrick knew it was best. He nodded slowly and said, "Okay."

Derrick stood at the door and watched Jocelyn get into her car. He didn't leave the door until the little Accord pulled off. Closing the door, Derrick didn't lock it. He turned to Cassandra and said, "Good night, Cassandra."

"What do you mean, good night, Cassandra?"

Adamantly, Derrick snapped, "I meant just what I said. You have embarrassed me for the very last time. Now, get your coat and get out."

"If she's just a nurse, why are you so embarrassed, Derrick? You had other plans for her tonight, didn't you?"

"So what if I did, Cassandra? What's it got to do with you? How many times do I have to tell you I'm not interested? I don't have time? I'm not in the mood? You had to keep pressing. Couldn't let me approach you. Couldn't give me the opportunity to decide what I wanted to do. It has to be your way and it has to be now. Well, I'm telling you straight out, Cassandra, I'm not interested."

Angrily snapping her dress closed, Cassandra mumbled, "You didn't say that before little Miss Nightingale showed up. I would have served the purpose just fine."

Derrick yelled, "There was no purpose to serve, until you started slobbering and climbing all over me! You wanted to see if you could seduce me into changing my mind! Well, you got your answer! Just leave, Cassandra!"

Retrieving her coat from the closet and tugging it on, Cassandra said, "I am leaving, Derrick. You can have your little nurse and your little babies. I'm done waiting for you."

"You have never waited for anybody in your life."

The cry of a baby over the monitor ended the back and forth dialogue and Derrick held the door open for Cassandra. He was angry and disgusted with himself. Derrick knew he wasn't interested in Cassandra when she walked in the door. But, what did he do? Let the dog in him take over. Women like Cassandra depend on the existence of the dog.

Running up the stairs, Derrick reprimanded himself over and over. In his bedroom, One and Two were both complaining. Derrick knew his yelling had wakened them. After turning down his comforter, Derrick picked up One and laid her on his bed. Then, he picked up Two. Derrick lay down, placed both babies on his chest and patted their backs. In a matter of minutes, both were asleep again.

Derrick laid the babies back in their beds and tried to begin over again. He went down to the living room, cleared the wine glasses and put the bottle in the refrigerator. Turning the light off in there, Derrick returned to the recreation room.

The television talked on and on as Derrick lay, not listening in the darkened room. The telephone rang and Derrick answered because he didn't want it waking the babies again. If it was Cassandra, he would hang up and block out her telephone number.

Derrick was shocked to hear Jocelyn's voice say, "I'm sorry to be bothering you again. I think I left my purse on your bed. Just put it up. I'll get it later. I hope your friend didn't find it there."

"No, she didn't find it. She left right after you. Are you sure you left it here? I went up to rock the babies back to sleep and I didn't see it."

"I'm pretty sure I did."

"Hold on, I'll check."

Derrick ran up both sets of stairs and found Jocelyn's tiny square black and cream purse, with a fine row of rhinestone accents, in the fold of his comforter. He put it on his dresser and returned to the recreation room.

Knowing Jocelyn had to return at least one more time comforted Derrick. He reclined on the sofa and spoke into the telephone with a victory smile on his face. "Yes, it's here. When will you be coming to get it?"

"Soon. My driver's license is in there."

"You could come tomorrow after work. That way you could stay for dinner."

"I don't think dinner is a good idea for us, Derrick."

"Why not? Because of Cassandra?"

"She's only part of the problem. I'm not ready for the kind of challenges I would encounter being friends with a man like you."

Not liking the sound of her answer, Derrick asked, "What challenges? What kind of a man do you think I am?"

Without hesitating, Jocelyn said, "The kind who has so many women in his life, he has babies he can't track."

"Ow! That hurt, Jocelyn."

"That's how the truth affects people. I'm not interested in being your next sexual conquest, Derrick. If I didn't care, I'd probably play with you. Since I do, it's best this way."

"Did I give you the impression that was how I looked at you? If I did, it was the wrong impression."

"Oh, really? How many times have you fed that line to the troops?"

"I've never said that to anyone. Believe it, or not. I'd really like to get to know you, Jocelyn. I don't know why though. So far, I know you're more than a handful, but the girls and I like you. All three of us can't be wrong."

"We'll see, Derrick."

"I'll accept that for now. Did you really wear that dress out to dinner with a guy, Jocelyn?"

"Yes, I did. Why?"

"And, he let you go right after the meal? No questions asked."

"He asked. I just didn't answer. It was none of his business."

"I would have made it my business."

"Like your girlfriend?"

"Very funny. Did you kiss him good night?"

Obviously agitated, Jocelyn said bitingly, "Why are you asking me these silly questions, Derrick? I don't have to ask if you kissed what's her name. You had her lipstick all over your face and neck. Reeked of her horrible perfume, too. Who opened her dress? You, or her?"

"Okay, okay. I won't ask anymore questions about your date." Then, Derrick mumbled, "Not now, anyway."

Jocelyn mumbled back, "I won't answer."

They both laughed at each other.

Before calling it a night, Derrick said, "Dinner's at seven."

"I'll think about it."

## *CHAPTER EIGHTEEN*

Early the following morning, Sonya's telephone rang. She had been up for over an hour getting Ethan fed and out the front door. He had his usual complaints about the world and she again regretted retiring from the school board. Sonya hated Derrick's staying home to take care of the babies, too, because they filled a big empty spot in her life. So Derrick's voice was a welcome relief, even if he wasn't calling to say he needed her to relieve him.

"Hi, Mom. What are you doing this morning?"

Sighing, Sonya replied, "Nothing much. I'm going to pretend to dust in a few minutes. You know I never cook on Wednesday nights. So, that's out. What are you doing this morning?"

"I would like to go shopping for something for dinner."

"Why? You have more than enough in the freezer, Derrick."

"I know. I invited someone over for dinner and I thought it would be nice to prepare something."

"Who did you invite over? I don't have to remind you about loose, low and no moral women again, do I?"

"No, you don't. I invited Jocelyn, the babies' nurse. She said she spoke with you on the telephone."

Sonya pondered that for a moment and said, "Oh, yeah. I remember her. Is that why she was so interested in your marital status?"

"I don't know. Was she interested?"

"Not overly, but definitely. She sounded like a very nice young woman. You're not planning on running her through that silly three date circus you and David are so fond of, are you, Derrick?"

Derrick had to laugh. Nothing slipped past Sonya. She knew the men in her life better than they knew themselves.

"No, Mom, Jocelyn's not for the circus circuit. I think I like her a little better than that."

"You think?"

"I think. She's a little argumentative. Says no a lot. Hasn't really meant it yet. But, she says it. She came out to check the babies personally at seven yesterday morning, and came again last night after her dinner date. She sort of ran into someone else here and got the wrong impression. I want to make a peace offering."

"Hold on. Did you say she came there yesterday morning and returned in the evening to check on the babies?"

"Yes. She called a few times during the day, too."

"She's better than merely interested. Who did she run into?"

"No one of consequence, Mom. She just did something really dumb. I think Jocelyn got the wrong indications from it."

"Stop beating around the bush. What did the heffa do?"

Clearing his throat loudly, Derrick said, "She stood in the doorway with her dress undone."

Sonya's eyes closed in horror at the thought. Very slowly she said, "Just tell me she had on underwear, Derrick."

His personal relief was audible in his gleeful response. "She had on very nice underwear, Mom. They were cherry red satin."

"If that Jocelyn comes to dinner with you after that, she needs her head examined. Can't she see you're up to your eyeballs in trash?"

"Mom! You're supposed to be on my side."

"I am. I'm on your side, telling you the truth. What do you want from me?"

"Your car. I can't take the babies in mine."

"It's too cold for you to drag those babies out. I'll come over and sit with them while you go to the store."

"You're on, Mom."

That was all Sonya wanted to hear anyway. She babysat with the girls for two hours, ran the vacuum cleaner, dusted and prepared the dinner Derrick bought. Derrick made lunch for them and tried to follow Sonya's soap operas. He didn't have the heart to tell his mother he thought they were the most ridiculous things he had ever seen.

David came in at five. Sonya and Derrick were playing video games in the recreation room. Hearing the commotion downstairs, David popped popcorn in the microwave, opened a can of beer and joined the group.

Derrick yelled at David twice in less than five minutes. Once for throwing One in the air. And, once for throwing Two in the air. The girls always appeared shaken by this, but they kicked in excitement every time they saw their uncle. David lay on the floor next to the playpen and played with them through the netting.

At 5:30, the doorbell rang. Sonya said it was time for her to be leaving, so she would answer it. Derrick and David played the video game. They yelled and called each other awful names. Sonya reminded them there were babies in the room from the stairs.

Looking through the window in Derrick's door, Sonya didn't recognize the woman, but she opened the door anyway. The two women stood looking at each other for a few moments. Finally, Sonya asked, "Are you Jocelyn?"

Jocelyn smiled and replied, "Yes. How did you know that?"

Pointing down at Jocelyn's white pants and shoes, Sonya said, "Your uniform. Come in. I'm Sonya Dawes, Derrick's mother. He's in the basement playing with his big brother. I'll walk you down, but I have to get home."

Softly, Jocelyn said, "Okay."

"Let me hang your coat while I'm here and we can go down."

Not intending to stay long enough to take her coat off, Jocelyn did so reluctantly. Noticing Jocelyn's unease, Sonya said, "Don't worry, there are no naked women in here today."

Jocelyn could not believe Derrick had told his mother about the night before. She wanted to disappear.

Derrick and David were shouting, pushing each other, laughing and trying to keep their eyes on the screen at the same time. One and Two kicked and squealed, as if they were playing, too. It was quite a scene.

David saw the white uniform out of the corner of his eye first. He stopped playing to get a better look at the woman wearing it. Derrick didn't know why David had stopped playing and he didn't care. He took full advantage of David's distraction.

At first, Jocelyn thought David was Derrick. She couldn't understand why he was looking at her like that. Suddenly, Derrick yelled, "That's it for you, Sucker!"

Sonya hollered, "Derrick! How many times do I have to remind you not to use bad language in front of those babies?! You have company, too!"

Still admiring his score on the screen, Derrick asked, "Who's company?"

David said, "She is. Why don't you introduce us? Then, you can go back to playing."

Derrick's head swiveled twice, from the screen to Jocelyn and from Jocelyn to his watch. Slightly nervous, he said, "It's early. I wasn't expecting you until seven."

Not wanting to say she had no intentions of staying for dinner in front of his family, Jocelyn smiled stiffly and said, "I came straight from the office. But, if I'm too early, I can always come back later."

Derrick stood and said, "No. Jocelyn, that's my mother, Mrs. Dawes. And, this is my brother, David. Mom, David, this is Jocelyn. She's One and Two's nurse."

Sonya said, "I already know who she is, Derrick. I'm leaving now. No foolishness. Goodnight."

David got up from the sofa, flashed his magnificent smile, extended his hand toward Jocelyn and said warmly, "Hello, Jocelyn. I'm not leaving."

Derrick said, "Oh, yes, you are."

From the stairs, Sonya said, "David, let's go."

Derrick grinned at his elder brother and said, "Thanks, Mom."

David smirked at Derrick, smiled at Jocelyn again and said, "Well, it was nice meeting you, Jocelyn. Maybe we'll meet again when my insecure brother feels better."

Defensively, Derrick snapped, "I'm not insecure. Get out, David."

"You're insecure and rude, Derrick. See ya."

David stopped long enough to give One and Two kisses. They started fussing when he didn't pick them up. Derrick wanted to run over and punch him in the head. However, he restrained himself. Jocelyn walked over and picked up One. That left Two. Derrick walked over and picked her up.

As soon as the front door closed, Jocelyn asked, "Why did you tell your mother about last night, Derrick?"

"She asked me."

"How did she know to ask?"

"Jocelyn, are we going to start off arguing every time we see each other?"

"No. Give me my purse and I'll be on my way. I didn't come to visit."

"What do you mean you didn't come to visit? You are going to have dinner with me, aren't you?"

"No."

"Why not?"

"I don't want to."

"Why not?"

"Look Derrick, you have more than enough women to play with. And, I don't intend to join the harem. I just want my purse. If you don't want to give it to me, I can go upstairs and get it myself."

Shrugging, Derrick said, "Okay. I'll get your purse."

With Two playing with his face all of the way, Derrick went up to his room and brought down Jocelyn's purse. He handed it to her and said nothing. Derrick laid Two down in the playpen and turned to take One from Jocelyn. She pulled the baby away from him.

Angrily, Derrick said, "Give her to me. You don't want anything to do with me and you can't leave with her."

"If I stay, will you get the wrong idea?"

Frowning, Derrick asked, "What idea is that?"

"That I'm applying for a harem position."

Rolling his eyes up into his head, Derrick said, "Believe me, I know you're not applying for a harem position. You want to tell me exactly what position you are applying for? Or, do I have to guess?"

"I'm not applying for any position."

Sighing, Derrick said, "Fine, Nurse Avery. Would you like something to drink? Or, are you ready to eat dinner?"

"A drink might be nice. I'll watch the babies while you get it."

Rolling his eyes up into his head again, Derrick mumbled, "Yeah, you do that, Nurse Hatchet."

Jocelyn's head snapped in Derrick's direction instantly. Heat waves emanated from her stare when she said sharply, "Stop calling me Nurse Hatchet!"

Derrick shrugged and left. When he returned, Jocelyn had both babies on her lap. She sat on the sofa staring at the noisy, colorful game on the screen. Derrick put the two glasses of wine on the table and asked if she would like to learn how to play. Jocelyn nodded.

They each held a baby on their laps as they played. It was almost eight when they left the recreation room. Derrick thought it would be best to feed One and Two before they tried to eat dinner. He fed One. Jocelyn fed Two. They sat quietly with babies and bottles.

One and Two fought sleep valiantly and lost. Derrick rose to take One up to bed and was surprised when Jocelyn followed him. She watched Derrick work with the two babies with rapt fascination. No one would have ever guessed this man knew absolutely nothing about babies before he inherited these two. There was no way he could give them up. Jocelyn saw the love in everything he did for them.

First, Derrick turned on the radio. Soft jazz caressed everything in the room. He headed for the bathroom and returned with wet washcloths, to wipe their faces and hands. Then, he changed their diapers effortlessly. Before leaving, he clipped the monitor onto his pants and waved Jocelyn out of the room.

Looking back at the bassinets longingly, Jocelyn brushed against Derrick and quickly excused herself on her way out. Derrick nodded, but said nothing.

Downstairs, Jocelyn automatically headed for the kitchen. Derrick took her hand and led her to the dining room. The gleaming glass dining room table was set with beautiful black china. One bold, gray stripe graced each piece. Black linen napkins circled by simple hand carved gray wooden holders lay at the top of each setting. Crystal and silverware reflected the chandelier lights. Derrick pulled out a large black chair with pinpoint charcoal dots and waited for Jocelyn to sit. Before leaving, Derrick poured Chablis into her glass.

Minutes later, Derrick returned with two fresh salads. Setting the two dishes down, Derrick shook out Jocelyn's napkin and laid it on her lap. She thanked him demurely. He nodded, but said nothing.

Halfway through the salad, Jocelyn broke the silence by saying, "You have a very nice home, Derrick."

Softly, Derrick said, "Thank you."

After waiting for him to say something else, Jocelyn asked, "Are you going to be quiet through the entire meal?"

Derrick nodded and said, "I think so. I don't want you misinterpreting anything I say."

"Since when have you cared how I interpret anything you say?"

"Since you made such a big deal about joining my harem."

"I only wanted you to understand. You can say anything you want, as long as you understand."

"So, what do we do with the obvious physical attraction we have for each other?"

Caught completely off guard by that question, Jocelyn sputtered, "What obvious physical attraction?"

Derrick smiled and said, "Forget I said anything, Jocelyn. I'll play your game for a while. Whatever it is."

Before Jocelyn could say anything else, Derrick rose from his seat and went back to the kitchen. She followed him. In the kitchen, with heavy mittens on his hands, Derrick removed two covered dishes from the warm oven. Jocelyn stood in the doorway and asked, "What game do you think I'm playing?"

"I don't know. Go sit down."

Frowning horribly, Jocelyn moved toward the dining room with Derrick following her. After seeing her all dressed up, he decided he hated that uniform. At the table again, Derrick asked, "What do I have to do to get you out of that uniform?"

Jocelyn screeched, "I beg your pardon?!"

"Not right this minute. I mean sometime in the near future."

"Who says you're ever getting me out of this uniform? You're a pig, Derrick Dawes."

"I am not. You looked like a million bucks last night. I want you to dress like that for me. At least once."

"Oh. You mean out of the uniform and dressed in something else?"

"Yeah. What did you think I meant?"

"Never mind."

Derrick knew exactly what she meant. He worded his request that way purposely. It was what he actually meant. He simply redressed it to fluster Jocelyn. The conversation came in dribbles after that exchange. They ate the baked flounder, broiled potatoes and broccoli in relative silence. Jocelyn offered to help Derrick with the dishes. He refused her offer.

At ten-thirty, Jocelyn said, "I hate eating and running, but I have work tomorrow. Dinner was delicious. Thank you for having me."

Derrick had just the right remark to set her feathers in the wind, but he settled for the standard, "You're very welcome, Jocelyn. Thank you for coming by to check on my babies again. Maybe you'll break down and just come by to see their father one day. Or, at least admit that's who you came to see."

Startled again, Jocelyn asked, "Did you just say their father?"

Unimpressed, Derrick said, "Yeah, that's what I said."

"You've never referred to yourself as their father, Derrick. You always say your babies or your girls."

"Okay, Sigmund, what does that mean?"

"I'm sure it means something. I don't know what though. And, I can use whatever excuse I want. If I prefer checking on the babies, that's what it'll be."

"So, when they spend a night at my mother's house, you'll use what excuse?"

Grinning, Jocelyn said sweetly, "None. I'll simply go over there."

Helping her into her coat, Derrick asked, "When are you going to give me your home number? I wouldn't dream of asking for your address."

"Why not? I may want to offer you a meal."

Not believing her, Derrick asked, "When?"

"When will the girls spend the night at your mother's house? Or would you prefer bringing them, too? They're more than welcome."

Disregarding her final remarks, Derrick said, "She wants them for the entire Thanksgiving weekend. I was going to ask if you would like to have dinner with us, over there, that day."

Smiling, Jocelyn said, "Oh, that's so sweet, Derrick. I would love to have Thanksgiving dinner with your family."

Honestly excited by Jocelyn's response, Derrick said, "Okay. Okay. What are you going to do with the rest of the Thanksgiving weekend? You don't have to work the Friday after, do you?"

"No. The office is closed. Would you like to have dinner at my apartment one evening during that weekend?"

"If you have room on your busy calendar for me, that would be very nice."

"No promises at this juncture, Derrick. That's a little more than two weeks away. If we're still behaving civil toward each other, I may be able to swing that."

"You didn't promise the time to the guy you went out with last night, did you, Jocelyn?"

Looking like he'd asked if she had paid October's electric bill for the Empire State Building, Jocelyn sucked her teeth and replied, "Naw. I didn't promise him anything."

"Are you sure?"

"What are you saying now, Derrick?"

"Nothing. I'm quitting while I'm ahead. Drive carefully. Do you have your driver's license?"

Derrick wanted to kiss Jocelyn good night so badly the desire caused tightness in his chest. He refused to give in to his selfishness and blow it all now. Derrick smiled warmly and opened the door.

Jocelyn gave him a pretty dimpled grin, rose up on her tiptoes and could only reach his chin. So, she kissed it and said, "Thanks again. I really enjoyed myself."

Before she could escape, Derrick slid his arm around her tiny waist, lifted her chin, bent down and kissed her lips lightly. Without pulling away, Derrick rubbed his nose against hers. When his mouth touched hers this time, Jocelyn's lips were slightly parted, warm and receptive. Still, Derrick restrained himself. He timidly tasted her tongue and lips. Derrick didn't know how to interpret the sudden hitch in her breathing though. So, he gave her a parting peck and stood up straight.

Jocelyn couldn't look Derrick in the eyes after that kiss. She held her blurred vision at Derrick's chest level, whispered good night again and dashed toward her car. Speaking loud enough for his voice to reach his sprinting dinner guest, Derrick told her to ring him when she got in.

Jocelyn continued her brisk step, breathed the cold night air deeply and nodded.

Derrick stood in the doorway and watched the white car pull out of its parking space and stop at the corner. It sat at the stop sign so long, Derrick thought about walking down to see if something was wrong. Eventually, it moved through the intersection. Derrick closed the door and congratulated himself. Progress was made.

# *CHAPTER NINETEEN*

Not hearing from Jocelyn on Thursday made Derrick a little uncomfortable. She didn't even call and pretend to check on One and Two. The only calls Derrick received were from Cynthia, Karen, and Cassandra.

Needless to say, the latter was wearying Derrick's patience. He wondered how he could have ever thought, even momentarily, that Cassandra might be worth giving a run at a legitimate relationship with. Dogged determination was her most prominent characteristic. Derrick didn't have to apologize for anything he said or did with Cassandra. She did it for him. Then, offered up the next serving.

No call came from Jocelyn on Friday either. For the first time, Derrick wondered if he had made a big mistake in kissing Jocelyn. But, hadn't she started it? Jocelyn confused and frustrated Derrick.

Attributing Jocelyn's sudden disinterest as a change of heart on her part, Derrick was glad David and his gang would be coming over to play cards that night. Taking care of babies all day put Derrick in a strange and unfamiliar frame of mind. After days and nights filled with interpreting cries, grunts, and groans there were times when Derrick couldn't process the English language. Without realizing he was doing it, Derrick associated all speech with the television or radio and wouldn't respond.

On Friday evening, David hadn't been inside his brother's house five minutes before he wanted to know all about Jocelyn. Derrick didn't want to talk about her. Right away David teased, "Uh oh, she's giving you a hard time."

Giving a little shrug, Derrick said, "Not really. Cassandra's giving me a hard time. She won't go away."

David touched Derrick's forehead and asked, "Are you sick or something? You don't want a woman like Cassandra to just go away."

"Yes, I do. She stripped for Jocelyn the other night. I don't need a woman like Cassandra in my life for any reason. You never know what she's going to do next."

David wore his first serious frown when he asked, "Were they both here at the same time? Why did she strip for Jocelyn, Derr?"

"To piss Jocelyn off, I guess. It worked. But, I thought she had gotten over it. We spent a very nice evening together on Wednesday. She even kissed me good night."

"So, what's the problem?"

"I haven't heard from her since, David."

Grinning from ear to ear, David said, "Stop worrying, Scout. She's giving you some serious thought. The longer she stays away, the harder she's thinking. You'll know which way it went before the weekend is over. Now, your problem with Cassandra could take on a life of its own and spiral out of control. Obsession does the strangest things."

Derrick asked, "Stranger than leaving a set of twins in my mailbox?"

Letting out a loud laugh, David sputtered, "Hell, no! That's tough to beat, Baby Brother!"

One and Two looked at Derrick and David and smiled. The infants didn't have a clue what they were talking about. All the babies knew was it made Derrick and Uncle David laugh and they liked that.

On Saturday morning Derrick had just taken the girls out of the bathtub, when the telephone rang. He picked up the cordless in the guest room and was pleasantly surprised to hear Jocelyn's voice. At least she didn't sound like gloom and doom.

"Hi, Derrick. What are you guys doing for lunch?"

"We're having our usual fruit and milk. What are you doing for lunch?"

"Thought I'd come over and hang out with you and the girls."

"Oh? Okay. The wreck room is always open for visitors on a Saturday afternoon."

"Need anything from the store?"

"No."

"See you in a little while then."

Done dressing One and Two, Derrick wanted to bathe and dress himself. He considered bringing up the playpen and opening it in his room. Then, he thought it might be a good time to baptize the girls in their cribs. Not wanting to frighten them, Derrick put both babies in one crib. He left them facing each other, to keep the fuss down. They didn't seem to mind at all.

After placing the monitor on the dresser and plugging it in, Derrick went to his room and prepared to shower and dress. He heard One and Two's usual grunts and squeals, as he got into the shower. Derrick took a peaceful, quick shower. After the night Two almost choked to death, leaving the babies unattended genuinely frightened him. Leisurely showers or baths were out of the question.

In the process of drying off, Derrick heard a blood-curdling scream from the monitor. Hurriedly, he wrapped the towel around his waist and ran to the guest room. One had a handful of Two's hair. Derrick saw how determined even tiny females were to hold onto whatever it was they wanted that morning. Two wailed in misery as he tried to pry her thick curls from her sister's fist without hurting her anymore.

Freeing Two, Derrick picked up the distraught baby. One immediately started crying. Pointing his finger at One, Derrick said, "You just be quiet, Mia. You're being a bad girl this morning. How would you like it if she pulled your hair?"

One looked up at Derrick, stopped crying and gave him a toothless grin. All he could do was sit on the chair with Two and groan. Accustomed to being alone with the two little girls, Derrick sat and talked to them for almost an hour. He had completely forgotten he hadn't finished dressing, or that he was expecting company.

The ringing doorbell snapped him back to reality fast enough. He grimaced and said, "Now look what you two made me do. Miss Jocelyn's going to think Daddy's a bona fide nut now."

With Two still in his arms and only wearing a towel, Derrick made it to the front door. One was in the crib complaining loudly about being left alone. Looking through the peephole, Derrick moaned and opened the door.

The smile on Jocelyn's face melted as she surveyed the nearly naked gorgeous giant. All she could think to say was, "I guess I caught you at a bad time again."

Waving and shrugging, Derrick asked, "What's in the bags?"

"Lunch."

"Okay. Put them down in the kitchen. Take Miranda up to the guest room. See what you can do with Mia and I'll get dressed."

Visibly shaken, Jocelyn said, "Yes, I'll take the babies. You get dressed."

Biting her lip, Jocelyn went to the kitchen and put the bags down on the counter. She pulled her coat off and Derrick pointed to the closet door. Jocelyn hung the coat and held her hands out for the baby in Derrick's arms. Handing over Two, Derrick nodded toward the stairs. Jocelyn went up to find the screaming One.

In his own bedroom, Derrick sat on the side of his bed and held his head for a few moments. All of a sudden, he felt like he needed a nap. Things were piling up on him. He had no idea how high the pile was until the telephone rang.

Picking it up reluctantly, Derrick said, "Hello."

He fell back on the bed and covered his face with his free hand when Cassandra said in a breathless and excited rush, "Derrick, I'm coming over there today. We need to sit down and discuss this seriously."

Derrick's mind screamed, "Oh, no the hell you won't be coming here!" His lips mouthed in a numb monotone, "We have absolutely nothing to discuss, Cassandra. Don't come. I'm not opening the door if you do. Enough is enough already."

On the verge of tears, Cassandra said, "How can you just dismiss our relationship like this, Derrick? I know you enjoyed my company. If you think I don't like children, you're wrong. I could get used to them."

"I don't want you to get used to them. I want you to leave me alone. This is stretching out a lot further than it should. Have you ever sought psychiatric help?"

In a low growl, Cassandra said, "I don't need any psychiatric help. And, if you think you're going to use me and throw me away like a piece of furniture, you'd better think again, Derrick Dawes. Every time you look up, I'm going to be in your face."

Unmoved by Cassandra's threat, Derrick asked, "Ever heard of the new stalking laws? If you're planning to be a nuisance to me, you'd better acquaint yourself with them. What you need to do is take that guy you were always throwing in my face up on his offer to take you to the Bahamas. You need a rest, Cassandra."

Derrick hung up the telephone. His head was beginning to throb. The knock on the door didn't help. Not moving, Derrick said, "Yeah?"

Jocelyn asked through the door, "Is it time for One and Two to eat? They're a little fussy."

Glancing at the clock, Derrick said, "Yes. I'll get their bottles."

He hoisted himself up from the bed and opened the door. Jocelyn's face twisted into a painful grimace. Physically withdrawing from Derrick's near nudity, Jocelyn said, "I thought you were getting dressed. Do you know how much of yourself I've seen in the last week? Hell, I've seen more of you and your girlfriend, than I've seen of any adult in years. What's with you people and clothes?"

Without waiting for his response, Jocelyn went back to the guest room. Derrick erupted in laughter. His life was getting stranger and stranger by the minute. To cap it off, David and Hope walked in while Derrick was warming the bottles.

Derrick looked at them and said, "Hi. Welcome to the nut farm."

Hope looked Derrick up and down and asked, "Why are you wearing a towel? Do you know what time it is? Those babies better be dressed. I'm telling Sonya if they're not."

Looking at David, Derrick said, "If one more woman threatens me today, I'm decking her. Call it what you will."

David grinned and said, "A man's gotta do what a man's gotta do."

One of the babies let out a holler. Derrick snatched the two bottles out of the pot, dried them off and dashed up the stairs. He left David and Hope looking after him.

A few minutes later, another baby let out a holler. Thinking he should volunteer to help his idiot brother, David climbed the stairs and followed the sound. He was surprised to find Jocelyn sitting in the chair feeding Two.

Smiling warmly, David said, "Hi, Jocelyn. Need some help?"

Letting her head fall back a little, Jocelyn muttered, "Please?"

Picking up One, David asked, "Where's Derrick?"

Sighing, Jocelyn said, "Getting dressed. At least, I hope he's getting dressed. He sure does run around without any clothes a lot."

"Yeah, he does do that. But, he's clean. Mom says clean goes a long way."

"I thought she said as long as your underwear were clean."

Nodding, David said, "Yes. She said that, too."

They both looked at each other and started laughing. Derrick's voice only made them laugh harder when he asked, "What's so funny?"

David answered, "You. You're dressed. He's dressed, Jocelyn. Now, aren't you proud of him?"

"Yes. I thought he'd never do it."

Hope came up behind Derrick and said, "Thank God, you put some clothes on. Boy, you sure do like showing everybody everything you have."

Derrick laughed and said, "You didn't see everything I have, Hope. I can show it all to you though. I'm clean, and that goes a long way."

Punching him in the arm, Hope said, "Not as far as you think."

Pushing past Derrick, Hope walked into the guest room and gave Jocelyn a strange look. David and Derrick knew she was wondering, "Now, this is not the same woman who was here the last time. Who is she?"

Only missing a beat, Hope smiled and said, "Hi, I'm Hope. And, you are?"

Putting Two on her shoulder to burp her, Jocelyn said, "I'm Jocelyn Avery."

David asked, "Hey, Jocelyn, are you still the babies' nurse? Or, are you Derrick's friend?"

"I'm still the babies' nurse," Jocelyn replied grinning.

Unsmiling, Derrick said, "Take that back right now, Jocelyn."

"Take what back? I am their nurse."

"Take it back."

Jocelyn looked at David and mumbled softly, "I'm Derrick's friend."

Hope said, "Well, I'm glad you took it back. He threatened to hit me downstairs. Do you know what's wrong with him today?"

"No, I don't. Maybe he'll tell us."

David, Jocelyn, and Hope stared at Derrick and waited for him to tell them what was wrong. He frowned and asked Jocelyn what she had brought for lunch. She told him cold cuts and condiments. David thought that sounded great. He handed One to Derrick, grabbed Hope by the hand and dragged her down the stairs saying, "We'll make lunch."

Alone in the room with Derrick and the babies, Jocelyn asked, "What is wrong with you today?"

"Who says anything is wrong with me? Maybe this is me."

"I don't think so. Who called on the telephone?"

"Why are you asking me that?"

"That's when you lost it, Derrick. You were only mildly disoriented before that."

Derrick's frown deepened when he said, "It was Cassandra. Yes, the naked woman from the other night. She is driving me nuts. The more I say I don't want to see her anymore, the more she insists I do."

Looking at One and Two, Jocelyn asked, "She's not their mother, is she?"

"Please, Jocelyn. No. I'd slit both wrists, tie a noose around my neck, stand on a chair and put a pistol in my mouth if she were."

"Wow, you really like her, don't you, Derrick?"

"Oh yes, Jocelyn. Can we go down and eat lunch now? I'm starving and I've got a headache."

The four adults ate lunch in the kitchen and went down to the recreation room. One and Two took naps while they shot pool and played video games. Jocelyn was a much better pool player than either David or Derrick and Hope loved it. They were so macho at times it made her want to gag and she boisterously rubbed in every defeat.

They made so much noise, it sounded like a house filled with out of control teenagers. One and Two joined them when they woke. Derrick glared at David viciously before he formulated the idea to throw the happy twins in the air. Hope laughed at David. So, when David was done tormenting One and Two, he threw Hope in the air. Quite accustomed to being treated like David's personal rag doll, Hope squealed.

Jocelyn looked over the pool table at Derrick and said seriously, "Don't you ever think about doing that to me."

Suppressing a laugh, Derrick said, "I would never do that to you."

A few minutes later, Jocelyn prepared to take her final shot of the game. Of course, she was winning. The eight ball dangled precariously over the lip of the side pocket. A gentle breeze would have knocked it in. Stepping up behind her silently, Derrick snatched the pool cue out of her hand and tossed it to David. Then, Derrick picked Jocelyn up effortlessly and held her over his head. She screamed for him to put her down. David yelled, "Throw her to me, I'll catch her!" Jocelyn's expression was one of sheer terror at the thought of being tossed across the room. Derrick laughed and put her down. Jocelyn punched him in the neck.

Rubbing his neck, Derrick laughed so hard he couldn't stand up straight. She pouted, pushed him and plopped down on the sofa. Jocelyn said, "You're just mad because I beat you again."

Unable to speak, Derrick nodded his head. Eventually, he sat next to her on the sofa and apologized profusely. Keeping him on the ropes for another fifteen minutes, Jocelyn accepted and the conversation moved on.

At eight, Derrick and Jocelyn went up to the kitchen to feed One and Two. David and Hope ordered pizza and beer. The women wanted to watch a movie after the babies were in bed. The men wanted to watch basketball. They flipped for it, and Hope and Jocelyn won. David insisted they go home after the pizza was gone. Hope didn't care because the same movie came on at their house, too.

In the recreation room, halfway through Bridges of Madison County, Derrick stretched out on the sofa, laid his head in Jocelyn's lap and fell asleep. He mumbled something about her waking him if Eastwood decided to punch or shoot anybody before it was over. She shook her head and watched the rest of the movie alone.

A little later, Derrick turned over and wrapped his arm around Jocelyn's hip. His face pressed against her stomach. Looking down at the sleeping man, Jocelyn let her mind wander. It prattled on and on about how handsome he was. What a lot of fun he was to be with. How responsible he was. How intelligent and sensitive he was. Then, her thoughts turned to the nearly naked Cassandra and what a big mistake it would be for Jocelyn to break her pristine record of abstinence with a known womanizer.

Jocelyn's new thoughts rebutted those thoughts with there was absolutely nothing about Derrick that reminded her of her late husband, Justine. Of all of Derrick's attributes, that was most important. Derrick didn't look or act like Justine. She didn't even feel the same way about him. The truth was, Jocelyn didn't know exactly how she felt about Derrick. All she could swear to was the warm, wonderful and totally secure way she felt in his company.

While Derrick was right about the attraction, the question of being able to trust him hounded her. Hope seemed awful happy with David. And, God knows Derrick and David were similar—at least, on the surface. Did Derrick only see Jocelyn as a possible helper with the babies? She answered that quick enough. "No." Derrick didn't need Jocelyn to help him with the babies. If he needed any help, his mother and brother would be here in a flash. Of course, he complained when they were sick, but who doesn't?

Derrick stirred. Jocelyn said, "Derrick, I think it's time for me to go home. You should go to bed."

Derrick mumbled, "What time is it?"

"Almost eleven."

"Is that all? Why do you want to go home so early?"

"You're asleep. Wouldn't you be more comfortable in your own bed?"

"Are you going with me?"

Incredulously, Jocelyn said, "I most certainly am not."

"Well then, I'm not going either."

Derrick stretched his thick neck and opened his eyes. He fixed the two caramel orbs on Jocelyn and said, "Since we can't go to bed together, can I at least have a kiss?"

"I can't reach your lips from here."

Grunting loudly, Derrick sat up and gave Jocelyn a little push. Jocelyn stood up. Derrick moved back on the sofa. She lay down in front of him and second-guessed herself right away. The touch of his body against hers that way caused a shivering, crawling sensation all over. Jocelyn's body desired Derrick's like it had no other man before him–not even Justine's. She tried desperately to tell herself deprivation was the cause of this phenomenon.

Derrick's moving to get his arm under her head, only made matters worse. When Jocelyn was where Derrick wanted her, he looked into her eyes. A frown of concern creased his normally smooth brow, when he realized he saw fear in her eyes. After waiting a few moments for Jocelyn to say something, Derrick asked, "What's wrong?"

Lying, Jocelyn replied shyly, "Nothing."

"Yes, there is. Just tell me. I'm really a bad guesser."

In a rush, Jocelyn said, "I don't think I'm ready for any of this, Derrick. I shouldn't be here."

"Can you tell me why you feel that way? Did I do something?"

"No. It's me. I built a wall around myself a long time ago and now I can't seem to scale it. No matter how badly I want to."

Derrick gave a little laugh and said, "Oh, I know a little about walls and fear. My mother has pushed me over more of them than I care to remember. She would say, 'Derrick, take your time climbing that wall. If you fall and don't die, get up and try it again. When you get to the top, straddle it, close your eyes and jump. If you wake up on the other side, you've done good. Standing around studying fear will only kill you slowly.'"

Looking at Dcrrick seriously, Jocelyn said, "I can't believe you were ever afraid of anything."

"Please, woman. I wanted to play football, but I was always afraid to hurt anyone. When my mother asked me what made me push David down a flight of stairs, I told her he had pissed me off. She told mc to imagine all of the other players were David. It worked. I won a four-year scholarship playing football. Whenever anyone upsets me, David crosses my mind. If they're still around afterwards, they're in trouble."

Jocelyn said pitifully, "Aw, and he's such a nice guy."

"That's because you didn't grow up with him. David's a pain in the ass, if there ever was one."

"Okay. I believe you. But no one wants to wait around for me to slowly scale the wall."

Without hesitation, Derrick said, "I might. If you stop beating me at pool."

Jocelyn smiled and asked, "For how long?"

"At least, until you throw yourself over the wall, get up and realize you're all right."

Jocelyn giggled and gave Derrick a pop on the head with her hand. He nuzzled her laughing mouth with his own. Eventually, Jocelyn stopped laughing, closed her eyes and accepted Derrick's tiny kisses. The longer he kissed her, the more relaxed she became. Each kiss grew longer, deeper and warmer. Finally, Derrick slid his hot, wet tongue into her mouth. Loving the texture and taste of it, Jocelyn melted.

The kiss and feeling the length of Derrick's hard body along her own caused Jocelyn to literally ache. His every move heightened the sensation. Derrick's embrace grew tighter and tighter, drawing Jocelyn closer and closer.

Jocelyn endured the ache of longing as long as she could. Feeling like she wanted to scream, Jocelyn started pushing away from Derrick. Pulling her face back and gasping loudly, Jocelyn whimpered, "Please stop, Derrick. Please?"

Relaxing his hold on her and running his hand down her hip, Derrick said, "Okay. It's okay."

Derrick gave Jocelyn a series of tiny kisses of reassurance, as he backed off. He stroked her body and hushed her whining. Into Derrick's neck, Jocelyn kept saying how sorry she was. Into her hair, he kept saying it was all right. Feeling luxuriously secure in Derrick's arms, Jocelyn drifted off to sleep. Loving the feel and smell of her, Derrick settled down and fell asleep, too.

Neither one of them knew anything else until One and Two's angry bellows came from the monitor at five o'clock in the morning. The babies had spent their first night in the guest room. Jocelyn had spent her first night with a man in years. And, Derrick hadn't jumped up for the screaming babies, for the first time since they were born.

Holding onto each other, Derrick and Jocelyn both groaned their disappointment at the prospect of having to separate. He gave her one last squeeze and they slowly unfolded. Derrick went to the kitchen to warm bottles and make coffee, and Jocelyn climbed the stairs to let One and Two know Daddy was coming.

## *CHAPTER TWENTY*

On Sunday morning, Derrick asked Jocelyn to join him at his parent's house for dinner. She refused, insisting Thanksgiving was plenty soon enough. A rejected Derrick fed One and Two while Jocelyn watched. Jocelyn helped Derrick bathe and dress the girls, and lay them down for a nap. Afterwards, they sat at the kitchen table staring at each other, each struggling with understanding where they stood with the other. They shared a solemn, yet somehow intimate cup of coffee.

Even though Jocelyn turned down his dinner request, Derrick felt a little better about things on Sunday morning. In his wildest dreams he had never thought she would have spent the night with him, on the sofa or anywhere else after Cassandra's one-woman show, and Derrick did have the Thanksgiving weekend to look forward to. He surely hoped he could hoist Jocelyn over that wall by then. He absolutely loved the way she felt in his arms all night. Derrick hadn't slept that well in years.

Jocelyn gave Derrick the briefest kiss good-bye and went home to do whatever she did all by herself. Derrick made and ate breakfast alone. Eventually wandering upstairs, he showered and dressed. Enjoying the silence, Derrick read thc newspaper and relaxed. He called his mother at noon to tell her he was ready to come over.

While waiting for Sonya, Derrick laid across his bed and fell asleep. He dreamed about Jocelyn. The way she smelled, felt and tasted. When the doorbell rang, Derrick was miserable again. He couldn't get Jocelyn to consummate the relationship in his dream either.

Derrick spent all of Sunday listening to David tell his Dad about Derrick's new flame. How beautiful she was, and how badly she had beaten Derrick at pool. David neglected to tell Ethan that Jocelyn had whipped him three times, too. But good old Hope reminded him.

If David asked once, he asked a thousand times, "Did Jocelyn spend the night, Derrick?"

Derrick never answered the question. Sonya wanted to know the answer to that question too, but she let David do the asking. Not having any objections to Jocelyn per se, Sonya worried about Derrick caring too much for her. Giving Derrick up to another woman had never been proposed before, and One and Two didn't count.

All Ethan wanted to know was, "Are you doing what you're supposed to be doing, Derrick? A set of twins should be more than enough to keep you busy for a while."

Deandra asked mischievously, "What's Derrick supposed to be doing, Daddy?"

Sonya answered sharply, "Mind your own business, Deandra!" Turning to Derrick she asked, "Are you sure Jocelyn's coming to Thanksgiving dinner?"

"I'm sure, Mom."

With a distasteful scowl, Sonya asked, "After the mess at your house the other night? Is she crazy?"

"I don't know, Mom. What do you think?"

Giving her favorite child a long, slow look over, Sonya responded, "Okay, she's not blind or crazy. Why isn't a pretty woman like Jocelyn married already, Derrick?"

"She's a widow, Mom. Her husband died in a military accident five years ago."

"Oh, I'm sorry to hear that. Does she have any children?"

"She was pregnant when he died, but she miscarried."

"Jesus, Derrick. Is that why she's got eyes for you? Because you come with two babies?"

"I don't think so, Mom. I think Jocelyn could find another man and have her own babies without much of a problem."

David interjected enthusiastically, "She sure could. All I can say is wait until you see her, Dad."

Sonya and Hope shouted in unison, "Oh, shut up, David!"

Waving his hand at them, David repeated, "Wait until you see her, Dad. Wait until Pop sees her."

Before he forgot to tell them, Derrick said, "Please don't bring up Jocelyn's husband or the baby when she gets here."

Ethan asked, "Why not? What if she changes her story for us? Then, you'd know she was a fraud."

Irritated by his father's suspicious mind, Derrick snapped, "She's not a fraud, Dad. She's been through enough. Being interrogated by you and Mom could send her over the edge."

"Well, you've never brought any woman home to dinner, Derrick. So, we know this one is different . . . at least to you. We won't just be looking out for you anyway. We've got two grandchildren to think about."

"Yeah, well, One and Two are my responsibilities, Dad. If I say Jocelyn's okay, she's okay."

"You're not saying she's okay, Derrick. You're saying she's pretty damned special."

"She is, Dad. Like David said. Wait until you see her."

Studying her empty plate, Sonya asked nonchalantly, "Are you planning to spend Thanksgiving weekend with her, Derrick?"

Irritated with his mother now, Derrick whined, "Mom?"

She snapped back, "Don't Mom me! I just asked a question! I thought maybe you had changed your mind about leaving One and Two with me for the weekend. Now that you've got a little extra professional help and all."

Sonya couldn't help laughing. She knew Derrick hadn't changed his mind. She knew Jocelyn meant a great deal to the man, and if she played her cards right, Jocelyn could have Sonya's favorite child eating out of the palm of her hand. Unlike David had done with Hope, Derrick wouldn't live with Jocelyn for three years before asking her to marry him either. Sonya could only pray Jocelyn was everything Derrick wanted her to be.

The remainder of November seemed to buzz by for Derrick. Because there is no such thing as a routine with a set of twins, Derrick honestly felt he had developed a real rapport with the babies. The twins continued to grow and change. They provided an occasional night of total sleepless excitement, and there was no doubt in Derrick's mind One and Two knew exactly who he was and what he was supposed to be doing. Taking care of them—feeding, bathing, changing, holding, rocking and talking to them.

Thanksgiving was upon them and it brought Derrick more anticipation than he had experienced since he was a teenager. Jocelyn had stopped by Derrick's home every day for over two weeks and he had held Jocelyn in his arms every evening. He kissed Jocelyn good night every night. But, she had not spent another night with Derrick on the sofa, nor had they even come close to moving beyond kissing and caressing.

As had become routine, Jocelyn ate dinner with Derrick on Monday and Tuesday before Thanksgiving. She always came straight from work. When she wasn't there by five-thirty on Wednesday, Derrick called her apartment. Jocelyn asked him, "Aren't you tired of looking at me? I'll be going to dinner with you tomorrow."

Derrick answered emphatically, "No, I'm not tired of looking at you. Get over here."

Jocelyn changed and showed up at his front door a half hour later. Derrick appreciated not seeing her in that uniform. She really looked cute in jeans. Even if Derrick couldn't see her figure in that oversized man's white dress shirt, he still preferred it to that white sack suit.

Derrick and Jocelyn ate dinner together, played with One and Two, fed them and put them to bed. Then, they cuddled on the sofa and watched television for the remainder of the evening. When Jocelyn mentioned going home, Derrick complained.

She asked, "What's getting into you? I have a home, too. I need to go there sometime."

Derrick's response to that was, "What night haven't you gone home, Jocelyn? Not counting the one night, weeks ago, that you accidentally fell asleep."

"Yes, I've gone home every night, Derrick, just in time to go to bed. There are other things I need to do at home. Dust. Wash clothes. Iron something. Soak in a tub. Wash my hair. Talk to a friend on the telephone."

Giving Jocelyn a serious stare, Derrick asked, "What friend?"

Rolling her eyes slowly, Jocelyn spat, "I have friends, too, Derrick."

"So, what's wrong with you staying here tonight? You can go home and get dressed in the morning."

"I will not. I will go home tonight, get up and get dressed in the morning, come back over here and go to your parent's house with you."

"Will you spend the night with me tomorrow night?"

"Maybe."

"With a fire in the fireplace? Upstairs?"

Jocelyn yelled, "Upstairs! Why upstairs?!"

"Because that's where I normally sleep."

"Oh. Maybe. I won't swear, Derrick."

At least she hadn't said no and Derrick took that as a promising sign. He cuddled, kissed and stroked Jocelyn's body until she said she couldn't take anymore and left for the night. Derrick noticed it was taking her longer and longer to get to that point everyday. If luck was on his side, she would be straddling the wall and be ready to jump by tomorrow night.

Jocelyn showed up at Derrick's front door early on Thanksgiving. She helped him pack One and Two's things for their weekend with their grandparents. Not wanting him to forget anything, Jocelyn had given him a list to check off. Of course, Derrick hadn't checked off anything. He kept everything in his head. Or, so he said.

Sonya and Deandra came in at two to get the babies. Derrick and Jocelyn would be coming over in his car behind them. Since he hadn't been working for over three weeks, Derrick's poor car was only driven on the infrequent market trips.

Deandra and Jocelyn went up to the guest room to get One and Two. In their absence, Sonya muttered to Derrick, "Did your sister tell you what she was going to do?"

Shaking his head in reply, Derrick asked, "What's she going to do, Mom?"

"She's done it already and I could kill her. If Ethan finds out, he will kill her."

Thinking there was a young man who needed to have his head realigned, Derrick asked, "What did she do, Mom?"

Sonya hissed through clenched teeth, "A tattoo."

Fighting the urge to smirk and wave off his mother's concerns, Derrick moaned, "A tattoo, Mom? That's not so bad."

Screaming, Sonya asked, "Have you heard what's being transmitted through tattoo needles lately, Derrick?!"

Wrapping his arms around his irate mother, Derrick cooed, "She'll be fine, Mom. Stop worrying so much. She hasn't done anything really detrimental yet."

Laying her head on Derrick's chest, Sonya pouted and said, "You just wait a while. Those two little girls are going to give you a serious dose of fear, Derrick Dawes. You can't raise children without it. You'll understand all of my petty fears one day."

"Oh, I know they will. But, let's have a nice day today, Mom. Squirt hasn't begun to act up and you know it. Her greatest sins so far are excessive shopping, excessive ear piercing and a tattoo. Cut her a little slack."

"Oh, that's what you think. She kissed that Haywood boy she goes to school with a few weeks ago. I had to pop her in the head about that, too. If I told Ethan half of things Deandra did, she wouldn't recognize a tree the next time she got out of the house."

"I wouldn't keep kissing from Dad too long, Mom. If anything else happens, you'll be in the doghouse with her. You know how Dad is. He blames you for everything we do. Then, when you keep it from him, he thinks you're protecting yourself."

"I don't care what Ethan thinks! He couldn't get a dried leaf to move on the energy of his thoughts. They're all recycled powerless Neanderthal thoughts. I'm worried about my child."

Kissing the top of his mother's head, Derrick said, "Squirt will be fine. She's your daughter. Remember that."

Jocelyn and Deandra came down the stairs with the two babies, chatting like old friends. Derrick looked Jocelyn over one more time. He loved the charcoal gray wool pantsuit she was wearing. The short fitted jacket, with what appeared to be zippers on both sides, flattered her figure without revealing any flesh. Stylish black leather boots added just the right touch. Her sleek hair flowed down over her shoulders today. The babies got a handful of it every chance they could. One actually managed to maneuver it into her mouth.

Derrick thought Sonya and Jocelyn never intended for One and Two to come back. David had taken the portable cribs over on Monday, and they made Derrick put almost everything else the babies owned into one car, or the other. He was glad to hear Sonya say she didn't need any formula, cereal, juice or fruit. At least Derrick could look in the cupboard and be reminded of his two little nuisances.

After much ado, they pulled away from Derrick's house and headed for the elder Dawes' residence. There were so many cars on the block that day, Derrick had to unload the car and park it near the corner. Jocelyn went into the house with his mother, sister and the babies. He thanked God she seemed comfortable with his immediate family, because Derrick's extended family could be more trying than Ethan any day.

Jocelyn wasn't the only new woman at Thanksgiving dinner this year. She was, however, the most attractive. Derrick enjoyed watching Jocelyn's irritated frown come and go swiftly when his male cousins barked at her. Derrick had to rescue Jocelyn from his father's mother, Gran, twice. Gran picked through Jocelyn's hair to see if it was a wig or weave, and she poked Jocelyn's breast to see if it was padded. Smacking Jocelyn's hips, Gran told her, "You need to eat a little more if you're planning on handling a Dawes man, Honey."

If Gran's act wasn't embarrassing enough, Derrick's Aunt Sylvia wanted to know exactly what race Jocelyn was—a complete breakdown. Pop ended that line of questioning by saying, "Whatever got together to make that girl did a damn good job. Leave her alone, Sylvia."

The only one who didn't have much to say about Jocelyn was Ethan. He stared at her every chance he got and frowned at David. Derrick had no idea what the two of them were transmitting back and forth. He found out after dinner.

Ethan trapped Derrick in the corner of the recreation room and asked, "What kind of problem are you having with that woman?"

"Who said I had a problem with her, Dad?"

"Your brother. He says you can't even get her to say she's your friend without threatening her. Is that true?"

"No. Well, sort of. She's not sure about starting a relationship with me. Thinks I want her to stand in a line."

Smirking irritably, Ethan said, "Get rid of the line now, Derrick. No more naked women meeting her at the front door. If she let you get away with it once, don't push your luck."

"There is no line, Dad. Hasn't been one since One and Two came. Just one nut who doesn't want to get lost."

"Get rid of the nut. Jocelyn's smart, damned good looking, works and loves your children. She keeps her eye on every woman who looks at you to long, too. She's been asking Hope and Deandra who they are. What are you two doing for the rest of the weekend?"

"I don't know, Dad."

"What do you mean, you don't know? Are you losing your mind? If you can find time to play with women who strip for company, you can figure out what to do with a real woman. Or, do I have to write it out for you?"

"I wish you and David would leave me alone, Dad. If Jocelyn wants to be in my life, she will be. If not, there's not a thing I can do about it. Now, what else?"

"Just do what you're supposed to be doing, while you're doing what you're supposed to be doing. On second thought, if you forget to do what you're supposed to be doing with her, I'll understand. Just try not to."

"Uh, right, Dad. Got it."

Derrick and Jocelyn were almost the last two to leave that night. They didn't want to leave before One and Two were asleep. But, the babies refused to fall asleep with all of the people stirring around them. At eleven-thirty, Derrick was saying his good nights.

Everything was fine, until Jocelyn bent to kiss the babies good night and said, "Mia and Miranda, behave yourselves for your grandparents."

Giving Jocelyn a strange icy stare, Sonya asked, "What did you just call them?"

All eyes and innocence, Jocelyn replied, "Mia and Miranda. Those are their real names."

Sonya snapped angrily, "Since when?!"

Derrick jumped in and said, "Mom, I haven't recorded their names yet. I just like those two."

"So, when were you going to tell me what you named them?!"

Deandra cooed, "Oh, Derrick, those are beautiful names. I love them. Gran'll love it, too."

Signaling Derrick to get out now behind Sonya, Ethan waved his hand toward the door feverishly. Derrick helped Jocelyn into her coat with Sonya glaring at him furiously. She was outdone. Derrick had told someone else the babies' names before he told her. Sonya wondered what else Jocelyn knew that she didn't.

Ready to go, Derrick gave Sonya a kiss on the cheek and said hurriedly, "I'll call you in the morning. Night, Mom."

Sonya asked sarcastically, "Are you sure you'll remember?"

Tilting his head, Derrick pleaded pitifully, "Mom?"

Sonya sucked her teeth and snapped, "Get out of here, Boy!" Still frowning, she said, "I hope you enjoyed yourself today, Jocelyn. I'm sure we'll see you for dinner again."

With an uncertain smile, Jocelyn said, "It was a very nice day, Mrs. Dawes. Dinner was delicious. I'm sorry if I've upset you though. I didn't know Derrick hadn't told you the babies' names. He acts like he's afraid to name them, but they should hear their real names from time to time."

"You're absolutely right. Now that I know what they are, I'll use them."

As Derrick and Jocelyn walked to the corner, he said, "Thanks for getting me into trouble, Big Mouth."

"You're more than welcome, Dummy."

In the car, Derrick and Jocelyn recounted the more bizarre moments of the day and laughed. The barking made her want to put someone's eye out and she thought Gran was checking her hair for lice. It never occurred to Jocelyn she wanted to know if it was real.

Back at Derrick's house, Jocelyn got out of his car and headed for her own. Panic stricken, Derrick asked much too loudly, "What are you doing? Where are you going?"

Smiling devilishly over her shoulder, Jocelyn said in a nonchalant whisper, "I'm going home."

Derrick dashed over, picked her up and threw her over his shoulder. Jocelyn squealed with laughter. He carried her into the house that way. Derrick didn't put her down until he had locked the front door and removed the key.

Jocelyn stood laughing at him. Derrick wasn't laughing, and after a few obviously hilarious moments had passed, he asked, "What's so funny?"

"I was only going to get my overnight bag out of the trunk."

"I don't believe you. Give me the key. I'll get it."

Digging in her purse, Jocelyn produced the keys. She handed them to Derrick and began unbuttoning her coat. He went out to Jocelyn's car, popped the trunk open and was genuinely surprised to see the small cream-colored leather bag. He wanted to open it to see just how long she planned to stay. But, if she only stayed tonight, he would be satisfied. Derrick knew that he could start begging for tomorrow night, tomorrow.

## *CHAPTER TWENTY-ONE*

Donning a cocky, self-assured stroll, Derrick moved from Jocelyn's car to the house. After hanging his coat in the closet, with Jocelyn's case in hand and without breaking his stride, he headed directly to his bedroom. Derrick stayed up there so long, Jocelyn followed. Not seeing him when she walked into the bedroom, Jocelyn called Derrick's name and jumped when he answered. Derrick's response came from close to the floor near the fireplace. Nervously, Jocelyn laughed and asked, "What are you doing?"

"What I said I was going to do. I'm starting a fire."

"Does that mean I have to sleep in here?"

Derrick sighed, looked over his shoulder and mumbled, "You can sleep on the roof if you want to."

"Is it warm up there?"

Without turning to look at her, Derrick asked, "Why don't you go downstairs, find a bottle of wine and some glasses?"

"Red or white?"

"I prefer red, but you get whatever you want."

Turning to leave, Jocelyn said, "Yes, sir."

When Jocelyn's foot touched the first step, Derrick mumbled, "Damn woman's going to drive me nuts."

With the fire started, Derrick turned the comforter down on the bed and went downstairs to turn the thermostat off. Jocelyn was fumbling around in the kitchen, so he went in to see if she needed his assistance. Next to the bottle of red wine and two goblets on the counter there was a small platter with cheese, crackers, and Dijon. After eating Sonya's Thanksgiving feast, Derrick couldn't believe food had crossed Jocelyn's mind.

While Jocelyn stood staring in the refrigerator, the telephone rang. Thinking it was his mother, Derrick answered in the kitchen.

Obviously happy to hear his voice, an excited Cassandra said, "Hi, Derrick. Did you spend the day with your family?"

Not lowering his voice, Derrick said in a hollow tone, "Hello, Cassandra. Yes, I did."

"Are the babies asleep?"

"I'm pretty sure they are."

"Want some company for a few hours? I'll be gone long before they wake up. I promise."

"No. Thanks for offering. Good night." Derrick spoke sharply and quickly hung up before Cassandra could make a counter offer.

Jocelyn's expression made Derrick want to shatter something. It said she was genuinely considering changing her mind. Derrick was surprised when Jocelyn said flatly, "Take the wine and glasses, Derrick. I'll take the platter."

Not wanting to further disturb anything, Derrick did as instructed. In the bedroom, they put everything on his night table. Derrick opened the wine and filled the glasses as Jocelyn sat on the bed pouting, with both her arms and legs crossed tightly.

With glasses in hand, Derrick sat next to her. Jocelyn took the glass offered, sipped the sweet, thick red wine and said stiffly, "Not bad. What did your girlfriend want?"

Hating the sound in Jocelyn's voice much more than the actual question, Derrick responded quickly, "She's not my girlfriend. She wanted to know if she could come over."

Choking on the sip of wine she was in the process of swallowing, Jocelyn coughed into her hand and asked, "Really? Does she offer often?"

"Every chance she gets."

"Really? When was the last time she was here?"

"You know the answer to that question, Jocelyn. She hasn't been here since, and you know that, too. You've been here every evening for weeks."

Full of suspicion, Jocelyn asked, "Are you sure? Maybe she stopped by for lunch. What time is it now? Perhaps she's been coming over after midnight."

"I'm sure. Are we going to argue about her tonight? Or, are we going to enjoy the rest of it?"

Jocelyn had no answer for that question. She merely rolled her eyes, gave a sassy sniff and sipped at her wine again. Derrick put his glass down, turned toward her and bent to kiss her pouting lips. Jocelyn didn't respond. Derrick took the glass from her hand and sat it next to his on the table. He put his hand on her tiny waist and kissed her again. There was only an inkling of a response from her.

Nuzzling noses, Derrick asked, "What's the matter now, sweetheart?"

In between Derrick's baby kisses, Jocelyn asked, "What does she want, Derrick?"

Determined not to be distracted, Derrick continued to nibble at Jocelyn's lips, as he responded, "What she wants doesn't matter to me, Jocelyn. I'm with who I want to be with right now."

"What about tomorrow and the next day?"

"What about them?"

"Who will you want to be with? How do I know I won't be the one on the telephone?"

Placing tiny, warm, wet kisses on Jocelyn's lips and chin, Derrick said with great sincerity, "Oh, you won't be on the telephone. You'll be right here in this room, if I get my way."

Feeling little tingling sensations erupting in the base of her stomach, Jocelyn asked, "Are you sure, Derrick?"

Barely moving his lips, Derrick said, "As sure as I can be about anything."

Letting the subject go, Jocelyn closed her eyes and returned Derrick's kisses. As their kisses deepened, Derrick unzipped Jocelyn's jacket, and she didn't object when he slid it off. With his hands, Derrick felt the smooth cool silk of Jocelyn's camisole. Not wanting to spook her, Derrick purposely didn't touch her breasts. More than anything, he wanted to look at the woman he was undressing, while undressing her.

With Derrick's mouth consuming hers, Jocelyn managed to mumble, "My boots, Derrick. Help me get my boots off. They're killing me."

Hating to relinquish her mouth, Derrick said, "Okay."

Jocelyn leaned back on the bed on her elbows as he got down on his knees in front of her. Derrick saw the beautiful black silk camisole clearly from that vantage point. How it carefully caressed Jocelyn's full, firm breasts and that she wasn't wearing a bra. Derrick loved the way the light from the fireplace played with the contrast of Jocelyn's skin and hair. The sparkle it gave those elegant chestnut brown eyes that were watching his every move.

It didn't take Derrick very long to get Jocelyn's boots and footies off. He massaged and inspected Jocelyn's feet and deemed them perfect in spite of the fact that one of her toes pointed at a strange angle. Still on his knees, Derrick moved between Jocelyn's legs. Before attempting to completely disrobe her, Derrick couldn't resist tasting her lips one more time. Jocelyn didn't make any frightened moves or gestures, so Derrick unzipped her slacks and began to slide them over her hips. His heart pounded with sheer joy, when Jocelyn lifted her hips, allowing him to remove them easily.

With Jocelyn's slacks in his hand, Derrick stood and got a really good look at her. She was, without a doubt, a golden goddess. Easily, one of the most beautiful women Derrick had ever seen. And, she still seemed relaxed.

Gathering Jocelyn's jacket with her slacks, Derrick turned and put them on the chair nearest the bed. He walked over to the stereo and pushed the button. Grover Washington's version of Feel The Fire drifted through the room.

Jocelyn reached for her glass of wine and took another sip. She didn't feel the confidence she tried so desperately to display. If Derrick only knew how frightened Jocelyn really was, he might want to reconsider what he was about to do.

Derrick didn't see Jocelyn jump when he sat down next to her and start taking his shoes and socks off. He never noticed how big her eyes got when he removed his shirt, and he definitely didn't see her wince when he stood and slid his pants off.

Even though Jocelyn had seen Derrick in varied states of undress before, somehow he seemed much more massive and formidable by firelight. While these features frightened Jocelyn, she had to admit that they were what attracted her to Derrick in the first place. He was the finest creature she had ever seen. He was also the most conscientious, caring, loving and patient man she had ever known. She truly believed she could trust him with her very life.

Jocelyn's mind screamed, "Are you crazy?! Look at him! You have never been with anyone like him in your life! You have bitten off a lot more than you can chew this time, Miss! Justine wasn't half the size of Derrick! This man is not a starter, or a re-starter kit!"

Derrick didn't hang his clothes in the closet. He put them on the chair with Jocelyn's. Noticing the tiny shudder Jocelyn gave, when he sat down next to her on the bed clad in nothing but his briefs, Derrick lightly touched her neck and asked, "What's wrong now, Jocelyn?"

Looking at him with tears standing in her glistening eyes, Jocelyn asked, "How upset would you be if I couldn't go through with this?"

Derrick shrugged his broad shoulders and said, "I don't know. Are you planning to back out?"

"I'm not planning it, Derrick. It's just sort of happening."

"What's sort of happening?"

"Fear."

"What are you so afraid of? You've been married, so I know you've slept with a man before."

"It's not the same. I mean, you're not the same."

"Of course, I'm not the same. I'm Derrick. He was Justine."

"I know that!"

"Well, if you know that, why won't you just relax and see what happens? I can't be that different. We both have the same parts, Jocelyn."

Grimacing sarcastically into her wine glass, Jocelyn mumbled, "I don't think so, Derrick."

Throwing his hands up and picking up his glass of wine, Derrick snapped in frustration, "Fine, Jocelyn. You don't have to do it. I don't know which one of us you're calling a freak, but I sure as hell hope it's not me."

A tear dangled dangerously on Jocelyn's lower lash, as she said adamantly, "I'm not calling anybody a freak. I just said the two of you were different. You're much bigger than he was. I can't even see around you."

Looking over his own shoulder, a baffled Derrick asked, "What do you want to see?"

Not believing he thought she meant that literally, Jocelyn said saucily, "Nothing, Derrick."

Derrick sat quietly and sipped his wine. Jocelyn sipped hers and slid back against the pillows. When his wine was gone, Derrick put the glass down, leaned back on Jocelyn's lap and closed his eyes. The feel of his warm, hard flesh on her bare legs caused another excited stirring in her stomach. She lightly touched Derrick's shoulder. He moved a little but said nothing. The crackle of the fire and the soft, soothing jazz dominated the room.

Five minutes later, Jocelyn felt really stupid. She knew she wanted Derrick. All of her wanted him. If she blew this because she was afraid to try, she would kick herself. Hell, like the man said, "It's not like I'm a virgin or anything. What can happen?" A tiny voice of foreboding said, "He could snap your little ass in half." Jocelyn giggled at herself.

Derrick's voice startled her when he asked, "What's so funny?"

Giving his shoulder a shove, Jocelyn said, "Nothing. Get up."

"Why?"

"So I can lay down with you."

Derrick hoisted himself up, poured himself another glass of wine and drank half of it. He had no idea what Jocelyn was doing now. This on and off was wearing him out.

Sighing deeply, Derrick laid down on his back, crossed his arms and closed his eyes. He felt Jocelyn's smooth, petite hand slide over his thickly muscled arm, but Derrick wasn't even considering attempting to interpret it. When that same little hand timidly slid down his stomach, Derrick issued a silent prayer, "God, please make her stop if she's not serious. Please."

Jocelyn leaned over Derrick and kissed him. Still refusing to bite, Derrick asked, "What are you doing, Jocelyn?"

"I'm kissing you, Derrick. What's the matter? You want me to stop?"

"If you're going to tell me to stop two minutes from now, yes, I do."

Mimicking his tone, Jocelyn said, "I'm not going to tell you to stop two minutes from now."

Derrick didn't budge until Jocelyn lowered her mouth onto his again. It was Derrick's turn to timidly return her kiss. Jocelyn accepted enthusiastically. Encouraged, Derrick moved and she didn't jump out of the bed. He turned to face her. Derrick's huge embrace squeezed the air out of Jocelyn, but she didn't complain. Jocelyn thought the feel of Derrick was mind-boggling with clothes on, but nearly nude, it made her brain slam against her skull and liquefy. If Jocelyn tilted her head, soupy gray matter would have spilled from her ear. She had never desired any man the way she had Derrick.

Derrick's hands skillfully wandered all over Jocelyn's body. Everything he touched bubbled past its boiling point. Jocelyn whimpered weakly and gasped for air from time to time. Other than that, she just gritted her teeth and enjoyed it all. Having his fill of touching silk, Derrick slid the camisole up and over Jocelyn's head. He flung it over his shoulder in the direction of the chair.

A man who genuinely preferred taking his time appreciating the beauty of a woman's body with his eyes, Derrick didn't want to spend too much time dallying with Jocelyn. She was capable of changing her mind at least ten more times before this was over. So, he only took enough time to get one good look at her gorgeous breasts before devouring one and gently massaging the other.

For Jocelyn, reawakened sensations recklessly crashed into brand new ones. Panicked passion elevated Jocelyn beyond all comprehension. Jocelyn gripped the back of Derrick's neck tightly and moaned, "Oh" in varying pitches over and over. Derrick's hand made its way down Jocelyn's smooth, taut stomach and found its way inside her panties. Jocelyn's eyes rolled back in their sockets. Her mouth fell open as her head bobbed backwards a few times. Jocelyn panted, gasped loudly and added, "God, please." to her, "Oh."

As Derrick shifted from one breast to the other, he slid Jocelyn's panties off. When his hand returned, there was no obstruction and his probing was stronger and deeper. It didn't take very long for Jocelyn to admit she couldn't process any more of the preliminaries. Feeling as if she was on the verge of exploding, Jocelyn whined, "Derrick, please just do it. Do it now."

Still enjoying what he was doing, a mildly disappointed Derrick asked incredulously, "Now?"

Breathlessly, Jocelyn screamed, "Now! Do it now or stop! I can't stand this anymore!"

The last thing he wanted to do was stop. Derrick flipped over, removed his briefs, retrieved a condom from the brass case on his night table and slid it on in what seemed like one fluid motion. Turning back to Jocelyn, Derrick asked, "Are you absolutely sure you're ready, sweetheart? I don't want you to be upset afterwards."

Sounding extremely angry, Jocelyn shouted, "I'm sure! Derrick, please! Just do it!"

He wasn't going to make her yell it again. Derrick knelt between Jocelyn's thighs and lifted them. She shut her eyes tight. As Derrick began his descent inside her, Jocelyn's eyes popped open. Unprepared for the depth and the breadth of him, Jocelyn's mouth popped open soundlessly. Her head pressed agonizingly into the pillow, her nails dug viciously into his chest and she wasn't breathing. There was no sound from her at all.

Realizing she wasn't breathing, Derrick stopped and panted with restrained passion,

"Jocelyn! Jocelyn! Are you all right?!"

It took a few seconds, but she nodded weakly. As Derrick began to move, Jocelyn's face contorted into a twin mask, reflecting both pain and pleasure. She met Derrick's initial thrusts tenuously and groaned loudly in response to the most tormenting perfect blend of physical agony and blissful ecstasy Jocelyn had ever experienced.

When Derrick felt she was acclimating herself, he added a little more energy and depth to his thrusts, Jocelyn gripped his sides so tightly, it hurt. That didn't deter Derrick. As a matter of fact, the sting of her sharp nails stimulated him. He closed his eyes, gritted his teeth and relinquished control of his body to his senses. Derrick knew instinctively they would take them both to places they had only dreamt of thus far.

Ten minutes into their lovemaking, Jocelyn's hair was soaking wet. In an undiluted harmonious heaven, she moaned Derrick's name over and over. She never said stop though. Jocelyn knew right then that she had never been made love to before. With Derrick, one orgasm followed another. He filled that cold, empty spot in Jocelyn with the most excruciatingly wonderful lovemaking she had ever known.

When Derrick gripped the small of Jocelyn's back and gave up his final deep thrusts, Jocelyn screamed in agony and was disappointed. She didn't want him to ever stop. He leaned on his elbows over her, kissed her gasping mouth and asked, "Are you all right, Jocelyn?"

Licking her lips, Jocelyn panted, "Why'd you stop, Derrick?"

With a twisted frown, Derrick asked in shocked disbelief, "What?"

Still breathing heavily, Jocelyn giggled and sighed with great satisfaction.

With his own satisfied smile, Derrick asked, "Oh, so you jumped off the wall and realized you survived?"

Shaking her head she said, "Nope."

"What then?"

"I jumped and realized I loved the sensation of falling."

"Not too much, I hope."

"Meaning?"

"You don't think you'll want to fall off of anyone else's wall, do you?"

"Not as long as this one's still standing, Derrick."

Giving her nose another quick peck, Derrick said, "As long as we understand each other."

When Derrick pulled away from her, Jocelyn winced in pain and said, "Oh God, we understand each other."

Jocelyn closed her long awaited lovemaking session curled up on Derrick's lap, sipping wine with him and listening to the crackle of the fire. During the night they explored each other's bodies extensively by firelight, making love more intimately two more times. When they fell asleep in each other's arms, the wine and cheese were gone. The fire burned low and they were both totally satiated and exhausted.

## *CHAPTER TWENTY-TWO*

Accustomed to being wakened by One and Two, Derrick stirred at six and again at eight on Friday morning. He listened for their cry, didn't hear it, tightened his grip on Jocelyn, buried his face in her hair and drifted off again.

Jocelyn squirmed under the pressure of Derrick's embrace and slid her hand down his back. It came to rest on his hip. Jocelyn readjusted the tilt of her face, burying it in his neck and never regained even a semblance of consciousness.

Derrick rallied around ten, looked down at the beautiful sleeping woman in his arms and grinned. Actually, she looked more like a little girl than a woman, volumes of black hair some frizzy and some straight lay everywhere. It was hard to believe it all connected to that one tiny head.

Half-heartedly, Derrick tried to wake Jocelyn and failed. He stroked her sleeping face with his finger, kissed her forehead, nose and lips. Derrick sighed with great satisfaction and extricated himself.

Feeling the exhilarating sting of cold air, Derrick carefully tucked the sheet, blanket and comforter around Jocelyn. He made a mental note to turn the heat back on as he dialed his mother's number and was told sarcastically by Sonya that Mia and Miranda were fine. Throwing on sweat pants, Derrick trotted downstairs to his workout room. He gave exercise a genuine thought and abandoned it. God knows he needed it after that Thanksgiving meal. Instead, Derrick returned to the bedroom, only to find Jocelyn just as he'd left her.

Derrick sat on the side of the bed and touched Jocelyn's nose with his finger. She swatted it and coughed. He called her name a few times before she frowned irritably and grumbled, "What?"

"Aren't you ready to get up yet?"

Wretchedly, Jocelyn grunted and said, "No."

"We could shower together, if you get up now."

"Don't want a shower. I need a bath. Hot. Aspirin. Coffee."

Feeling laughter bubbling, Derrick asked, "Why do you need all that? Are you sick? Does something hurt?"

Covering her head, Jocelyn moaned miserably, "Please, Derrick. Don't try to be funny. I feel awful. Everything I own is aching."

Honestly impressed with himself and feigning sympathy, Derrick asked, "Everything?"

Never seeing the satisfied expression on his face, Jocelyn muttered painfully, "Oh God, Derrick. Everything."

Stroking Jocelyn's hip, Derrick said, "I'll get you the coffee and aspirin. After I shower, I'll run your bath water. Hot. Okay?"

Jocelyn's blanketed head nodded slowly. Twenty minutes later, Derrick returned with coffee, juice and aspirin. He shook Jocelyn gently and tugged at the cover. She reluctantly stuck her head out. Attempting to sit up, Jocelyn yelped.

Derrick jumped. Truly shaken, he asked, "What's wrong?"

Running her fingers through her hair, Jocelyn exclaimed, "Jesus! Turn on the heat, Derrick! It's freezing in here! What's wrong with you?!"

Glad her complaint was only the cold, Derrick said, "Sorry, sweetheart. I meant to do that when I went down earlier. I'll do it now."

Derrick darted downstairs and turned on the heat. Back in the bedroom, he saw that Jocelyn had taken the aspirin, sipped at her juice and was now clinging to the hot coffee mug. She took a few sips of coffee and put it down. The last Derrick saw of her, she was sliding beneath the covers again.

Showered, shaved and wearing a towel, Derrick woke Jocelyn again. Her bath water was ready. Jocelyn lifted the cover and snatched it back immediately. She insisted it was still too cold for her to trek to the bathroom with nothing on. Derrick gave her his terry cloth robe and Jocelyn put it on under the cover.

Jocelyn didn't get an accurate assessment of how sore she really was until she tried to get out of bed, feeling like she had been run down by a fully loaded freight train. While being closely watched by Derrick, Jocelyn made her way to the bathroom.

A serious groan escaped Jocelyn's throat at the sight of herself in the full-length mirror on the bathroom wall. Turning toward the bathtub, Jocelyn was puzzled by the thick, billowing steam rising from the bath water. Never having seen that much steam emanate from anything, Jocelyn decided it best to test it first. Boy, was she glad she had. Upon closer inspection, Jocelyn found that the water was a mere degree or two shy of boiling. Jocelyn now knew for a fact, Derrick had no comprehension of what was too hot or too cold. She fleetingly wondered how Mia and Miranda had escaped being scalded to death.

Getting the water cool enough not to burn her skin, Jocelyn dropped the robe and climbed into the tub. She had just reclined when Derrick came in with another cup of coffee for her. Accepting it and expecting him to leave was as far as Jocelyn's mind wandered. She couldn't believe he had actually sat down, stretched his unbelievably long, magnificently muscled legs out and crossed his arms.

Sighing, Jocelyn asked, "Aren't you going to get dressed?"

"Sure. I'll do it when you do it."

Taken back, Jocelyn asked, "Do you intend to sit there and watch me bathe, Derrick?"

"Sure do. Wouldn't miss it for anything less than a fire. Are you feeling any better?"

Jocelyn snapped irritably, "I feel fine. You get out of here. I don't need you watching me."

"I'm not leaving, Jocelyn. Just drink your coffee, take your bath and forget I'm sitting here."

"How am I supposed to forget you're sitting there?! You're staring at me!" She screamed so loud, she had to grab the top of her aching head.

Laughing at her, Derrick said emphatically, "I'm not leaving. I've waited too long to get to see you without that hideous white outfit of yours. You don't happen to have one of them stashed in your little bag, do you?"

"If I had known how fond you were of them, I would have brought one."

"I know. That's why I never made a big deal of it. You hide pretty good in it. Keep wearing it."

"Why? If you find it so unflattering, why do you want me to keep wearing it?"

Derrick smiled and said, "I want everyone who ignored you before to keep doing it. And, put your hair back up in that ponytail, too."

Touching her hair, Jocelyn asked, "You don't like my hair either?"

Lying, Derrick said, "It looks just fine, Jocelyn. I like your hair in the ponytail."

"Anything else I need to know?"

"Yes."

"What?"

"Get rid of the guy you went out to dinner with."

"Oh, you've got a lot of nerve, Derrick, the man with more women than he knows what to do with whining over one little dinner date. You're the one with the half naked woman in your living room and lipstick all over your face. Let's not forget the telephone ringing the entire time you're being intimate with me, and I have to get rid of someone. Please."

Derrick laughed and said, "Okay, you got me on that one. Just get rid of him."

"I don't have to. I only had dinner with him twice."

Derrick's smile faded when he said, "Twice? You had dinner with him twice? Well, you have someone else to eat with now. Get rid of him, Jocelyn."

"I guess you think I belong to you now. Well, I don't. I just wanted to see if I could do it. And, I did."

Glinting at Jocelyn, Derrick asked with a touch of anger, "Why didn't you see if you could do it with him?"

Smiling wickedly, Jocelyn pointed one dripping wet finger at Derrick and said, "I didn't want to. I wanted to see if I could do it with you."

"Why?"

"None of your business."

"Get rid of him, Jocelyn."

"Not until you get rid of your harem, Derrick."

"What's his name? I'll get rid of him for you."

Sitting straight up in the tub, Jocelyn snapped, "Oh, no you won't."

Momentarily distracted by Jocelyn's wet breasts bobbing on top of the water, Derrick muttered, "Oh, yes I will."

Just as she asked him to get out again the telephone rang. Thoroughly disappointed, he rose slowly. Jocelyn watched Derrick's toweled rear-end leave the bathroom with great interest. It was one of his many outstanding assets. She smiled and settled into bathing.

Before Derrick returned to the bathroom the telephone rang three times. First, his father called.

"Derrick, Why do One and Two cry most of the night?"

"They don't cry, Dad. Where did they sleep?"

"One slept in Deandra's room. Two slept in here with me and your mother."

"That's why they cried, Dad. You can't separate them. They hum to each other. If they don't hear the hum, they look for each other. If they don't see each other, they cry."

"Okay. What did you do with Jocelyn last night?"

"What do you mean, what did I do with her?"

"Did she spend the night?"

Knowing this conversation could go on for days if he didn't answer the question, Derrick said, "Yes, Dad."

"Good. I knew David didn't know what he was talking about. Talk to you later."

The second call came as a complete surprise to Derrick. It was his grandfather. He asked the exact same questions his father had asked. When David called on the tail-end of Pop's call, Derrick was livid. He told David to stay out of his business and hung up the telephone.

To add to his disappointment, Derrick saw Jocelyn climbing out of the bathtub from the bedroom. He hustled to catch her dressing and for the entire time she applied lotion, perfumed and put her underwear on, Jocelyn frowned at Derrick. Looking at her hair in the mirror, she frowned and asked, "Do you have any shampoo?"

Startled she had said anything to him at all, Derrick answered numbly, "Yes. It's in the cabinet."

Searching for it, Jocelyn asked, "Feel like washing my hair?"

Sounding like a kid, Derrick responded with genuine excitement, "Who me? Yeah. Sure."

Having washed his share of female parts, this request was a first. Derrick washed Jocelyn's hair and enjoyed every moment of it. The manila woman with the pitch-black hair, had no idea what an erotic sight she made bending over the sink in her beautifully laced green bra and panties, or how much he enjoyed watching her dry, brush and maneuver the massive sleek black mane back into that God awful ponytail. There was no way Derrick was going to let Jocelyn get away from him today.

Both dressed in jogging apparel, went down to the kitchen and made lunch. As they washed dishes, Jocelyn started announcing her approaching departure. Unable to disguise his disappointment, Derrick said, "You are not going anywhere, Jocelyn."

Startled, she asked, "Why not?"

Grabbing her hand and dragging her down to the recreation room, Derrick said, "Because you're spending the day with me. Alone."

"But, we spent the night alone."

"So. Are you saying you're tired of me already?"

"No. I just thought you might be ready to spend some time alone. You don't get many days without the babies."

"That's right, Jocelyn. I don't. That's exactly why I should be able to spend my free time with whomever I want. That's you. So, sit down."

Sarcastically, she said, "Oh, it's still my turn. I thought there was a one-night rotation on the harem wheel. You'll have to let me take a glance at the harlot handbook. I know you've got a copy."

Derrick smirked at her and said, "If that's what you want to call it, Jocelyn."

The ringing telephone only made matters worse. It was Karen. She wanted to know if Derrick felt like going to a movie. A few minutes later, the telephone rang again. It was Doreen. She wanted to know if Derrick wanted to catch the Will Downing show at the Arcadia.

Lying back on the sofa, with her hands behind her head, Jocelyn wanted to know, "Derrick, do you have any male friends at all?"

"Believe it or not, I do. They just don't call as much."

He bent down and kissed her lips. Jocelyn said, "Nope, I don't believe it."

Pulling her up, lying on the sofa and pulling her back down with him, Derrick said, "You don't have to believe me. Just don't leave."

Before Jocelyn could respond, Derrick devoured her mouth. His hands roamed freely. One came to rest under her sweatshirt on her breast and the other massaged her hip.

After the long, passionate kiss, Jocelyn decided to pick up the discussion later. If Derrick was toying with her, she was too far in now to do anything about it. Other than the women, Jocelyn loved everything about the man.

Derrick picked up the remote and clicked on the television. Jocelyn snuggled down and they argued over what to watch. Derrick kept changing the station to see what the basketball scores were. Jocelyn grew weary of the fight and drifted off to sleep.

Upstairs, David came in and yelled for Derrick. Groaning, Derrick didn't respond. It didn't take long for David to hear the television and come down the stairs. Hope followed.

David asked, "Didn't you hear me calling you?"

"Yes, I heard you. Stop yelling, David."

In the darkened room, David didn't see Jocelyn's tiny body. She was wrapped in Derrick's arms. One leg between his, the other draped neatly over his thigh. Just as he was on the verge of raising his voice even more, David caught a glimpse of Jocelyn's ponytail. Grinning, as if he'd won the Super Bowl pool, David nudged Hope and said, "I told you she was still here. That's my brother."

Turning to Derrick, David lowered his voice considerably and asked, "Well, did she spend the night?"

"How many times do I have to tell you, Dad, and Pop that's none of your business?"

"Give me a break, Derrick. I know you didn't tell those old guys it was none of their business. If you had, Dad would be over here clubbing your head in with Pop's cane. Just tell me and I'll go away."

"I'm not telling you anything."

"Okay. I'm leaving. If she didn't stay last night, she'll have to stay tonight. It's snowing. If she's not out of here in the next hour or so, she may be here for days. Do you think you can get anything accomplished with her snowed in for days, Derrick?"

Hope said, "That's enough, David. If Derrick doesn't want to tell you she spent the night, he doesn't have to. I'm telling you she spent the night. Look at how she's sleeping. Couldn't sleep like that if she hadn't."

Hearing voices, Jocelyn muttered into Derrick's chest, "Who are you talking to now?"

Derrick snapped, "David and Hope."

Jocelyn turned her head and mumbled, "Hi, guys. What are you doing here?"

Derrick answered, "They came to see if you spent the night."

Surprised, Jocelyn asked, "Really?"

Hope replied, "Wild horses couldn't have kept David from here today, dear."

"Why?"

Derrick said, "Yes. Please tell us why."

Smiling devilishly, David responded, "No real reason. I just like keeping track of my little brother."

Jocelyn hummed and said, "Sounds like you're living vicariously through your little brother to me. Hey Hope, how long was the female line at David's house when you got there? Derrick's telephone rings constantly."

Hope screamed with laughter and said, "It was pretty long, Jocelyn. Just hang around and answer the telephone a few times. Most of them will go away."

"I don't know if I can do that. Besides, he may not be worth the wait."

David uttered angrily, "You slept with him last night. You know if he's worth the wait."

Leaning back and staring up at David, Jocelyn said, "He's not that good, David."

In defense of his brother, David shot back, "You're wrapped around him like he was pretty damned good."

Derrick said, "Okay. That's enough you two."

David, Hope, and Jocelyn laughed. David asked if Jocelyn really spent the night one more time. She and Derrick both hollered, "Yes!"

Throwing his hands up, David said, "Let's go, Hope. That's all they had to say to get rid of me in the first place. Saying he's not that good could make me spend the night giving him pointers."

Speaking with Derrick's hand over her mouth, Jocelyn mumbled, "He definitely doesn't need any pointers."

Grinning from ear to ear, David asked, "What did she say, Derrick?"

"Nothing. Goodbye, David and Hope."

Kissing Jocelyn's forehead, Derrick whispered, "If I move my hand, can you say goodbye and nothing else?"

Jocelyn blinked innocently and nodded.

Derrick lifted his hand. Jocelyn said sweetly, "Good-bye."

David and Hope left. Derrick kissed Jocelyn's lips lightly and said, "That was done very well, sweetheart."

Smiling demurely, Jocelyn said, "Thank you, dear. Did you call to see how the babies were?"

"Yes, I did. My father called to say they cried all night."

Concerned, Jocelyn asked, "Why? What was wrong with them?"

"Calm down. They separated them. Just because they sleep in different beds doesn't mean they can sleep in different rooms. They signal each other all of the time."

"Are you sure they're not crying because you're not there?"

"I'm sure."

Jocelyn stretched a little. The movement of her body made Derrick moan. She asked, "What's wrong now, Derrick?"

Stroking her hip slowly, Derrick said, "Wrong? Nothing. Absolutely nothing."

Jocelyn was shown in excruciating, sizzling detail what spending a day with Derrick alone entailed. Not believing her already battered body could handle it, Jocelyn actually protested once. But, with the right man pushing all the right buttons she flowed into the stream easily enough.

They spent the remainder of the weekend together. Jocelyn insisted they spend Saturday night at her apartment. After stopping at a gourmet seafood shop, Jocelyn made Derrick an unbelievably wonderful lobster dinner. Then, she persuaded Derrick to do something Sonya couldn't make any of her children do anymore; Jocelyn dragged Derrick to church on Sunday morning. They went to Derrick's parents' house afterwards and it was difficult to tell which one of them One and Two were happiest to see.

## *CHAPTER TWENTY-THREE*

The balance of the year saw the man who determined not to be part of any serious relationship deeply ingrained and sprouting roots in several. Occasionally complaining, but knowing he wouldn't trade any of the participants for anything in the world. Typical.

One and Two, as only Derrick referred to them anymore, were making valiant attempts at sitting up and getting their bearings. They knew exactly what they wanted and how to make Daddy give it to them. Others, like Gram and Jocelyn, took a little longer to catch on. But, the girls enjoyed their dedication and enthusiasm.

Jocelyn wallowed gloriously in her new life with the Dawes family. She had to remind Derrick she wasn't his wife often though. He felt Jocelyn should be at his house every day after work. She disagreed and stuck to her guns. However, if too many days passed without her, Derrick borrowed Sonya's car, and Derrick, One and Two showed up at Jocelyn's apartment and refused to leave unless she came home with them. The Dawes trio only had to try to spend one night at Jocelyn's apartment to change her mind. She found out the hard way that conditions had to be just right for One and Two to sleep.

After pleading with Derrick not to have the DNA tests done, Jocelyn refused to speak or sleep with him for a week after he insisted they be done anyway. She refused to believe he was still considering doing anything other than keeping Mia and Miranda. If he could give up those babies, she knew she didn't stand a chance in hell of holding his attention much longer. Jocelyn tried to hold Derrick at arm's length emotionally.

Derrick was intrinsically familiar with One and Two's every mood, whim, or desire. They never cried, because Derrick didn't give them a chance. If he came home without a treat for them, which seldom happened, he went back out to get one. Still, he insisted he might have to give them up.

He couldn't make Jocelyn understand that it wasn't a good idea for her to become too attached to One and Two either. Their mother could step in and take them anytime she wanted. There was nothing he could do to stop her. No precautions. No net. Sure, he loved those two little characters already. And, they loved him. They were even trying to call him at three months old. But, without a miracle, loving them would be his undoing.

The result of the DNA test took longer than anticipated. It arrived in March. Dr. Kane and Jocelyn hovered over Derrick as he dressed Two for her trip home and waited for him to read the highly anticipated conclusion. Derrick beamed on his two six month old beauties as if nothing was happening. Without opening the envelope, Derrick slid it into one of the dreaded pink diaper bags and left Dr. Kane's office.

Jocelyn visited Derrick later that evening and Sonya let her in. Loving Derrick, Mia and Miranda with an intense dedication, the two women had developed a reliable relationship. Sonya just wasn't sure if Derrick loved Jocelyn more than he loved her. Why it concerned her, she wasn't sure. After all, Jocelyn could do things for her son she couldn't, and Sonya was happy he had finally found one someone to do that for him. In the corner of her mind, Sonya vaguely remembered this scenario playing out before. If she had given it any thought, she would have remembered it playing out between Miranda 'Tiny' Dawes, Ethan and herself.

Seeing the expression of concern on Jocelyn's face, Sonya asked, "Is something wrong, Jocelyn?"

Hanging her jacket in the closet, Jocelyn said, "I don't know, Sonya. Did Derrick tell you the result of the DNA test?"

"No. Did he get it?"

"Today."

"Well, he's downstairs working on something. Let's go see what we can find out."

Sonya's foot hadn't cleared the final step when she asked, "What did those papers say, boy?"

Without looking at her, Derrick asked, "What papers, Mom?"

Jocelyn walked up behind him and wrapped her arms around his neck. Derrick automatically leaned his head back to receive her kiss. Jocelyn smiled and gave it to him. Holding Derrick's lip between her teeth, Jocelyn said, "You know what papers she's talking about, Derrick. Just tell us."

"I didn't open it, sweetheart."

Sonya said sharply, "Stop kissing and tell me why you didn't open it!"

Looking at his mother with all the sincerity of his soul beaming in his eyes, Derrick said, "I don't want to know what it says, Mom. It doesn't matter now. One and Two belong to me. It stays that way until the law knocks and says something different."

Sonya asked, "What did Roger say? I thought he filed some papers for you."

"He did, Mom, their birth certificates. He formally petitioned the court for custody on my behalf. The judge read the petition and signed it without too many questions. Mrs. Monet's input played a great part in that. None of it amounts to a hill of beans if their mother wants them back though. All she has to do is petition the court. The most I can demand is a DNA test from her. Roger says the judge may give her temporary or partial custody of them before the results are even in."

Astonished, Sonya said, "Definitely not before the results are in, Derrick. I can't believe that. That's even bleaker than I thought." Waving a dismissal for Mia and Miranda's wayward absentee mother and sucking her teeth, Sonya continued, "Aw, that girl won't show up. If she had enough nerve to leave them, she's got enough to stick to her decision. What do you think, Jocelyn?"

Looking at the two happy babies maneuvering their new walkers backwards, Jocelyn said, "It's anyone's guess, Sonya. I could never have left them. So, I can't imagine what she's thinking now." Tapping Derrick's shoulder, Jocelyn asked, "Have their legs been bothering them since you brought them home?"

"I don't think so. They're still going backwards, Jocelyn."

All of the females went upstairs to give Derrick a little peace and quiet to finish the drawing he was working on. Clyde Majors, Derrick's boss, had asked him to personally handle a Fortune 500 proposal. If they accepted it, Derrick would have to be in Denver for at least six weeks. That meant leaving One and Two for six weeks. That also meant leaving Jocelyn for six weeks. Needless to say, Derrick did not put forth his greatest effort.

Too bad Derrick's effortless work was better than most. His firm won the contract and he would be in Denver for the greater portion of the summer. The architects were slow and not as proficient as their employers thought. Most of the time Derrick wanted to strangle them. Two of them didn't know their lefts from their rights and couldn't independently count from one to ten consecutively.

Sonya insisted the twins stay at their house while Derrick was away. Jocelyn was welcome to come see them anytime she wanted, and indeed she stopped in every day like clockwork. Jocelyn's only real assignment from Derrick was to stay away from men, especially the guy who kept asking her to go out to dinner.

One and Two took their first real unassisted steps on August 14th and Derrick left for Denver on August 15th. He hated leaving those two. They came up with something new every day. At eleven months old, One and Two were as pretty as babies could be—adventurous, shy, manipulating, calculating and tormenting. They were inseparable, yet somehow independent. That frustrated Sonya and tickled Ethan. But, overall, they were good babies. At least Derrick thought they were. Before leaving, he promised to do everything he could to be home for their first birthday party, on September 10th.

Jocelyn spent the night with Derrick at his house the night before he was to leave. She couldn't believe how hard it was to know Derrick wouldn't be there at the end of every day. If not for the entire night, they always saw each other for a few hours. The thought of returning to her solitary life kept her in tears. They made love and clung to each other through the night. Neither slept.

All Derrick could think of as he held onto Jocelyn that night was, she had been the first woman he had forged a real relationship with since college. He loved almost everything about her. That stubborn streak, so like Sonya's, drove him nuts from time to time though. When Jocelyn decided she wanted to stay at home, she stayed. If Derrick didn't go to church on Sunday morning, she didn't go to his family's house for dinner. But, if she wasn't exactly who she was, he didn't think he could love her so much.

Derrick fully intended to ask Jocelyn to marry him when he returned from Denver. He wanted to wait until they had been together a year. If there were any real flaws, they would surely surface in a year. The fact that Jocelyn never let the telephone calls and occasional random visits from Derrick's old female friends cause unreasonable problems between them impressed him most. Cassandra's many visits only made Jocelyn shake her head. Pamela, Karen, and Cynthia all came to see the babies Derrick tried to say were theirs and Jocelyn took it all in stride. She never left them alone with him, but she didn't make a big deal out of it either.

That's why Derrick let his guard down. Jealousy wasn't one of Jocelyn's characteristics. She always said Derrick had ample opportunity to have any woman he wanted. If he decided he wanted someone else, all she asked was that he tell her. She wouldn't tolerate being strung along. It was unnecessarily cruel and demeaning.

Derrick had been in Denver for two weeks when he received his first call from Angelique. A call to his home office informed her of his whereabouts. Of course Angelique wanted to see him while he was in town. Derrick promised to save an evening for her and asked if her husband would be joining them. Somehow, Angelique didn't think that was a good idea. Not wanting to entertain any of Angelique's new whims, Derrick avoided meeting with her, and the last thing he wanted was to discuss One and Two with her.

By the fifth of September, Derrick had managed to persuade his team they could live without him for a few days. On the evening of the eighth, Derrick was doing everything to prepare himself for his trip home the following morning. In his hotel room, Derrick's telephone rang at eight. Thinking it was Jocelyn, Derrick answered quickly.

A familiar female voice, not Jocelyn's, said warmly, "Hello, Derrick. When are you going to find time to have dinner with me?"

Catching the voice immediately, Derrick answered impatiently, "When I get back, Angelique. I have to go home for Mia and Miranda's birthday."

"Is that what you named them? Mia and Miranda? Those are lovely names, Derrick. You should call them that more often. One and Two sound a little impersonal."

"They like One and Two. I'm the only one who still calls them that anyway."

"How long will you be at home?"

"Just for the weekend."

"That's nice. How did you manage to leave them this long anyway? Did you find them a great Nanny?"

"No. They're with my parents. Why are you asking me so many questions about One and Two? I didn't think you would be interested in them."

"If they're your children, Derrick, why wouldn't I be? I loved you very much at one time, and I have forgiven you your moments of bizarre thought. I know you loved me at one time, too, and I sincerely believe your fits were hopeful thinking. Has this past year erased all memories of me?"

"It hasn't erased a thing, Angelique."

Taking a deep cleansing breath, Angelique said, "Good. When we have dinner, perhaps we'll reminisce. Like the last Christmas Eve we spent together."

Not giving what she said any thought, Derrick said absentmindedly, "Sure, Angelique. But, I've got to finish packing now. I'll talk to you when I get back."

Hanging up, Derrick dialed Jocelyn's number. He knew she had called and gotten a busy signal. Eight o'clock every evening was their time, and Derrick didn't want anything to upset her now. He was looking forward to spending three great days at home and three breathtaking nights.

Jocelyn answered on the third ring. Immediately Derrick asked, "What took you so long?"

"Forgive me, oh exalted one. I was polishing my toenails on the other side of the room. Since you were talking to someone else when I called, I thought I would use the time beautifying myself for your return."

Laughing, Derrick asked, "Do you really think I'm going to be looking at your toenails when I get there?"

"You'd better. I don't do this every day."

"I'll look at them first and get them out of the way then. Okay?"

"Okay."

"I've missed you so much, Jocelyn. I can't wait to get home. Boy, am I glad One and Two weren't born another day later."

"I've missed you more, Derrick. I know I have."

"How do you know that?"

"Believe me, I know it. I feel lonely. I haven't felt lonely for years. My life's not the same without backing into you every two minutes."

Loving hearing every word she said, Derrick said, "I feel the same way, sweetheart. Maybe we should discuss changing things when I get home."

"Changing what things, Derrick?"

"Our living arrangements, for openers. I'm tired of you getting up and going home before the babies wake up in the morning."

"Well, that's the way it has to be. We're not married and I'm not their mother. You could want another woman in there one day. Do you want to have to explain what you're doing to Mia and Miranda? They're girls you know. They will do what they see."

Being facetious, Derrick said, "Yes, Sonya, I know. They're never seeing any woman but you, Jocelyn. I'm not letting you go anywhere."

"Is that the new chauvinistic version of a proposal, Derrick?"

"Could be. How did you like it?"

"That may have been good enough for Hope, but I'm not buying it."

"Oh, yeah. How are the wedding plans coming with them?"

"Fine, I guess. Derrick, did David mention that Hope was pregnant to you?"

"She's what?!"

"Pregnant. Three months, to be exact."

"No, he didn't. Does he know?"

"I don't know. Hope's beginning to think there's another woman in the picture. She's not very happy right now. So, that's probably why David hasn't mentioned it. I know your mother doesn't know."

"Oh well, David's a big boy. He knows what he's doing. If he doesn't, Ethan will remind him. Believe me. Did you see One and Two today?"

"Of course, I did. They ran to me and said, 'Hi, Dosh.' Then, they looked around and whined pathetically, 'Daddy.' I have to tell them every day, 'No Daddy.' They cry every day, Derrick. They miss you. Sonya says they really cry when David shows up."

Sadly, Derrick said, "I miss them, too. I'm considering taking another sabbatical in December, Jocelyn. Maybe the four of us can go somewhere. Or, maybe we can just stay at home together. All day, every day."

"Are you asking me to take a sabbatical too, Derrick?"

"Doesn't that sound good, Jocelyn? You know it does. We might want to make a baby of our own by then."

Really liking the sound of that, Jocelyn asked, "What are they doing to you out there? One minute, you're giving me an off-handed proposal. The next, you're proposing making babies."

"Well, we could practice making them."

"We do that anyway, Derrick."

"No, we don't. I mean we've never done it without . . . you know."

"What?"

"Protection. I'm ready to get rid of it, Jocelyn."

"Not without tests, you won't."

"Are you serious?"

"As a heart attack, sweetie."

"Can we get it done while I'm there? That way we'll be ready when this is over."

"If you say so. Dr. Kane's associate can do them, if you'd like. He loves drawing your blood. You're such a big chicken."

* * *

Ethan picked Derrick up at the airport the following day at two in the afternoon. He took him directly to the offices of Dr. Kane, pediatrician, and Dr. Willows, general practitioner. To see that Derrick actually had his preliminaries out of the way, Jocelyn volunteered to assist Dr. Willows with collecting Derrick's specimens. Squinting his eyes at Jocelyn, Derrick rolled up his sleeve and handed his arm over to the doctor. Derrick didn't flinch once while the blood was being drawn. However, he looked at the cup Jocelyn handed him with a peculiar expression.

Returning the cup, Derrick gave Jocelyn the warmest, wettest kiss filled with promise for the night to come. He winked at her and left the office. Dr. Willows' receptionist couldn't resist saying, "You go, girl. That brother is fine."

Grinning, Jocelyn said, "Uh huh. And, you don't even see the best of him."

"Bet you will tonight, though."

Saucily cocking her head to the side, Jocelyn winked her eye and said, "Try to stop me."

# *CHAPTER TWENTY-FOUR*

With all of the intellectual energy two one year olds can muster, One and Two tried to get the knobs off of Grammy Sonya's recreation room entertainment unit. Grammy Sonya wasn't paying them any attention because the soaps were on. She glanced at them every few minutes or so, and as long as the two tiny curly heads were nearby and not in imminent danger, she allowed them to do anything they wanted. Today's trick was pulling their headbands down around their necks. Sonya had fixed that by removing them earlier. One of them would have been choking the other with it by now, if she hadn't.

Neither Sonya, One or Two saw Derrick walk into the room. Two looked up and Derrick heard her say in perfect breathless baby talk, "Hi, Unkie Dabid."

Derrick stood there a little while longer with his hands in his pockets. Two looked up at him again, in all probability thinking that if the man standing in front of her was Uncle David the room would be much noisier. Two teetered over and looked straight up at Derrick. As if she had mastered the joke, Two hit Derrick's leg, gave him a great six tooth grin and screeched with excited adoration, "Daddy!"

Derrick picked her up, planted a big kiss on her forehead and said, "Hi, Two. How's Daddy's pumpkin?"

Laying her head on Derrick's shoulder, Two stroked his neck and purred, "Daddy."

Hearing Two, One finally became interested in who came in. The moment she saw Derrick, One knew exactly who he was. One toddled to Derrick as fast as her wobbling legs could carry her, afraid she would fall, he winced. With very little assistance, One climbed Derrick's leg. She never called his name; One simply clutched Derrick's neck tightly and would not relinquish it. That was the way Derrick spent the remainder of the afternoon. With his two girls attached to his neck.

Jocelyn came in and found them that way at five. David came in and found them that way at six. Sonya insisted it was the most pathetic sight she had ever witnessed. She only said that because One and Two refused to come to her, Ethan, or Deandra anymore. They wouldn't even get down for Derrick to use the bathroom. He had to wait.

Two announced Derrick to everyone. With her head still on his shoulder, she said lovingly, "Dosh. Daddy." "Aun' Dee. Daddy." "Unkie Dabid. Daddy." "One. Daddy."

They all smiled and said, "Yes, Mandie. Daddy."

One and Two made a mess of dinner on Derrick's lap and Jocelyn wiped them down several times before the meal ended. Looking for changes, Derrick watched Jocelyn's every move intensely. There were none that he could see, and he could see most of her in the pretty indigo blue tank top short set she wore. Every time Jocelyn moved, Derrick completely lost all powers of concentration. The topic of conversation got away from him several times. Derrick wanted to touch Jocelyn so badly that forcing himself not to made his arms ache.

No one sat around too long after dinner. The birthday party would be held in Sonya's yard the following afternoon at three. Sonya told Derrick he didn't have to come early to do anything, that they had everything under control. Seeing how Derrick literally drooled at the sight of Jocelyn, Sonya offered to keep the babies overnight, too. Derrick declined her offer. One and Two would go home with Daddy and Dosh.

Derrick couldn't help noticing how quiet David had been all evening. He made a mental note to pry into his elder brother's business during the birthday party. All Derrick could think about at that moment was getting One and Two to bed. Then, getting Jocelyn to bed.

At home, the foursome played on Derrick's bedroom floor until nine o'clock. One yawned, but she wouldn't close her eyes. Two lounged on Derrick's lap and fought sleep valiantly, also.

Looking at the three sets of caramel eyes, Jocelyn said, "Oh, Derrick, they've missed you so much they're afraid to go to sleep. You might disappear on them again. I hope you're not planning to make travel a big part of your life."

Smiling at Jocelyn weakly, Derrick said, "If I could get out of going back this time, I would. It was never my intention to travel for the company again. This should have been Tyson's gig. I've done all of the preliminary traveling for the past eight years. Now that I have a family, it doesn't interest me as much as it used to. I've already told Majors I won't be able to do it anymore."

Impressed, Jocelyn said, "Really? You just told him you wouldn't be able to do it anymore. And, he accepted that?"

Smirking, Derrick said, "Sweetheart, I really don't care if he accepts it. That's the way it's going to be. Look at my poor babies. They're frightened to death and I've only been away three weeks. I'll work in a stationary position for a lot less money, to keep from putting them through this. Hell, I'll start my own business. I'm planning to do it in a few years anyway."

"You are? You never told me that, Derrick. Won't that mean you'll have to put in more effort than you are now? Travel more?"

"Not if I assemble the right staff. I've been solicited to do it lots of times already. Still, independence costs. To get on top and stay there, costs a lot."

"So, how long do you think it's going to take you to do it?"

"Honestly, I could have done it three years ago, Jocelyn. I've become spoiled and complacent under Majors. Letting him do the part of the job I'm not at all crazy about."

"What part is that, Derrick?"

"Marketing. I'm not a real people person. I can do it, but not comfortably. There are times when the thought of people drives me nuts. Performing for their favors might be more than I can handle. That's why I want Tyson with me. He loves brown nosing for the elite. He's both technically and business savvy. Majors hasn't used a millimeter of Tyson's real skills. If David wanted to move with me, I'd go with him too. He has a Master's degree in Electrical Engineering and Design. Calls it his back-up vocation."

As if a light had been suddenly turned on, Jocelyn perked up and asked, "Didn't you find David quiet this evening, Derrick?"

"Yeah. He's into something he doesn't exactly know how to get out of. That's the only time David shuts up. You can bet a year's salary Sonya and Ethan noticed before you or I. They've grilled him mercilessly by now. I'll find out what it's all about tomorrow."

Looking at One and Two, Jocelyn spoke naturally when she said, "They're asleep, Derrick. You want me to take one of them?"

"Your choice, sweetheart."

Picking up One, Jocelyn stood and headed toward the guest room. Derrick followed with Two. They undressed them and laid both down. On his way out of the room, Derrick plugged in the monitor, turned on the radio and turned off the light. Soft music drifted through the darkened room. One and Two never stirred.

Wrapping his arms around Jocelyn's waist, Derrick mimicked her step back to his bedroom. Inside, he closed the door with his foot. Jocelyn asked playfully, "Am I staying or going?"

Derrick laughed and said, "If I have to answer that, David's not the only one who needs questioning."

With him massaging her ribs and nuzzling the top of her head, Jocelyn sighed deeply and said, "You don't have to ask me anything. As a matter of fact, you don't have to say anything else."

Needing no more conversation, Derrick turned Jocelyn around to face him. He lightly touched her lips with his, teased the tip of her nose with his tongue, slid his hands beneath her top and pulled it over her head. Derrick rested his forehead on Jocelyn's and admired her gorgeous breasts from that vantage point. Deeming them perfect, he moved on to her shorts.

Derrick kissed Jocelyn's body here and there, as he pulled the shorts down and away from her feet. She couldn't help giggling when he kissed his way back up, too. As he explored Jocelyn's mouth with his warm tongue, she unbuttoned his shirt, slid it off of his shoulders and enjoyed the feel of Derrick's smooth, hard, hairless chest. With one hand, Jocelyn expertly unfastened Derrick's belt and pants, and gave them a little push, knowing they would fall to the floor. They did.

Stepping out of his pants, Derrick closed the tiny space between them. He pulled Jocelyn into his embrace and kissed her passionately. She received and returned it with heated enthusiasm. If there was any doubt about either missing the other, that moment annihilated it.

In the midst of their re-acquaintance stroking, Jocelyn's bra disappeared. They stood straining to be closer to each other, rocking slowly and kissing. The excitement of it all forced a series of soft sighs from Jocelyn. When Derrick picked her up, laid her on the bed and slid his body on top of hers, she swallowed hard and hummed. The undivided attention he gave her breasts elicited tormented groans.

As Derrick stroked, massaged, kissed and probed Jocelyn's body with his hands and mouth, the pitch of her responses climbed. They were both intoxicated with nature's elixir and missing each other desperately gave it unbelievable potency. When Derrick entered Jocelyn, she gripped his sides viciously and bit his shoulder. They made love with complete abandon. However, unlike the first time they made love, Jocelyn was not the only one to come away feeling battered, bruised, and satisfied.

Miraculously, without waking One and Two, Derrick and Jocelyn made love several times during the night. They actually fell asleep after four in the morning. Two's tiny muffled cry of, "Daddy" woke Derrick at seven. Feeling like a drunk, Derrick clumsily pulled his pants on and stumbled down to their room. One and Two beamed at the sight of their slightly beat up looking father.

Pointing at Derrick's shoulder, Two said, "Boo boo, Daddy."

Unable to see what she meant, Derrick grunted. He was in the process of changing Two's diaper when Jocelyn stumbled into the room, wearing Derrick's white dress shirt. Her ponytail, a tangled frizzy mess, didn't even have any swing in it.

Incredibly excited, One yelled from her crib, "Dosh, Daddy! Dosh!"

With her arms extended for Jocelyn to pick her up, One stomped her feet. Jocelyn picked up the wide-awake, thrilled little girl. Every ache Jocelyn possessed screamed at that very moment. Sitting painfully, Jocelyn said weakly, "Happy Birthday, sweetheart."

One clapped her hands and started singing Happy Birthday. No one knew if she realized it was her own birthday or not. Two joined her sister in the song.

Finished changing Two, Derrick carried her downstairs to look for breakfast, without One protesting. Jocelyn quickly changed One's diaper, picked up the exceptionally tall and somewhat heavy baby, winced and staggered down the stairs with her. One sang the birthday song and played with Jocelyn's hair.

It looked like Sonya or David had brought over milk and bread. There was also a brand new box of cereal for the girls. Lots of microwave waffle and sausage breakfasts were stacked in the freezer for Derrick and Jocelyn. All Derrick had to do was make a pitcher of orange juice, start the coffee pot, pour milk over cereal and hope he kept it straight.

Strapping Two in her highchair wasn't easy. She didn't want Derrick to put her down at all. He promised he wasn't going anywhere and pleaded with her. Tearfully, Two allowed Derrick to seat her. Before he walked away, she kissed Derrick's shoulder and said, "Boo boo, Daddy."

Unable to decipher what his own brain was trying to tell him, Derrick nodded at Two. He moved through each task as if he were drowning in quicksand. Jocelyn and One were down and seated before Derrick finished opening the juice can. Jocelyn looked at him miserably and asked, "Do you need help, sweetheart?"

Without looking at her, Derrick nodded slowly.

Sidc by side, with One and Two watching them, Derrick and Jocelyn managed to put breakfast on the table for the babies, but neither one of them wanted anything to eat. They sat at the table drinking juice and coffee.

Jocelyn said, "We have to try to get them to take a nap, Derrick. They'll be irritable at the party this afternoon, if we don't."

Leaning on his elbow, staring at the woman he absolutely, positively adored, Derrick said, "If I don't take a nap, you'll really see a case of irritability at the party this afternoon."

Jocelyn laughed and said, "Oh, not you. You usually get up and run down to exercise after we've made love all night."

"We don't usually do it the way we did last night either."

"I know. What was wrong with you, Derrick? You acted like you were on a deserted island for years."

Laughing, Derrick said, "Oh, I acted like that. And, what were you stranded on?"

"My living room sofa, darling. Don't you know? I'm going to run home and get dressed. I'll be back in time to help you with the girls. Or, did your mother have something specific she wanted them to wear at her house?"

Rubbing his head, Derrick mumbled, "I don't know. Can you call her and find out, sweetheart?"

Picking up the telephone, Jocelyn made the call. Sonya did have outfits for the girls at her house. All she wanted Derrick and Jocelyn to do was bathe them. Knowing exactly what their rolls were, Jocelyn dressed and went home. She took the keys with her. Derrick, One, and Two laid on his bed and fell asleep.

Jocelyn returned at noon. One and Two sat happily baby babbling over their giant sleeping father. They both saw her at the same time and yelled cheerfully, "Hi, Dosh!"

Sliding down on the bed with them, Jocelyn smiled and said, "Hi, Mia and Mandie. I see Daddy's still asleep."

Pointing at Derrick, Two said, "Daddy. Sheep. Boo boo."

Frowning, Jocelyn asked, "Boo boo where, Mandie?"

With her chubby finger, Miranda poked Derrick's shoulder. He woke with an, "Ouch."

Jocelyn smiled and asked, "Did you know you have a boo boo, Derrick?"

Trying to fall asleep again, Derrick grumbled, "No. Yes. Two keeps pointing them out for me."

"Okay. What time do you plan on getting up?"

Sighing heavily, Derrick said, "Now."

Seeing his handsome face fall back into the mask of sleep, Jocelyn said sternly, "Get up now, Derrick. I'll start the girls for you. Get up, Derrick."

Checking to see where the babies were, Derrick shoved himself up to a sitting position. He asked, "Don't women ever sleep? The three of you just pester people all of the time. Poking and picking."

With an elegant brow raised, Jocelyn said smartly, "We sleep just as much as men, when we can. And, we can poke, pick and pester you as much as we like. We haven't seen you for three weeks."

Looking at his three girls solemnly, Derrick said, "I'm hungry."

Securely tucking One and Two under her arms, Jocelyn said, "I'm not. I ate breakfast at home."

"And, I thought you loved me."

Turning, with a provocative sway in her hips, Jocelyn said over her shoulder, "I do."

Moving down the hall to the bathroom, Jocelyn ran water in the bathtub, undressed the girls and asked, "Mia, who is she?"

Giggling, Mia said, "Two."

"No, sweetheart. That's Miranda."

Understanding what Jocelyn wanted her to say, One said, "Manda."

Jocelyn asked Two, who was already in the bathtub, "Who is she?"

Splashing water, without looking up, Two yelled, "One!"

Frustrated, Jocelyn put One into the tub and said, "Her name is Mia, Miranda."

Pointing at her sister, Two said, "Mia." Pointing at herself, she said, "Manda." Pointing at her sister again, she said, "One." Pointing at herself, she said, "Two." Pointing at Jocelyn, she said, "Dosh." Splashing water on everyone, she squealed, "Wadder!"

Trying to regain control of the situation, Jocelyn held Two's hands and said, "Yes. Water. Don't splash it."

Jocelyn gave up the battle when One started splashing water too. She bathed Two and washed her hair. Jocelyn always wondered what their mother looked like. She had to have had beautiful hair because the girls had thick, glossy, black hair. Not long yet, but promising. It curled anyway it wanted and dared you to try to braid or pull it into a ponytail. They also had the cutest little noses and tiny ears. Derrick's nose was broad and straight. His ears were average. Those were definitely his eyes and mouths, whether he opened the envelope or not.

Even though Derrick never mentioned her, Jocelyn knew their mother lived in Denver, too. She waited for

Derrick to say he had seen her. He hadn't yet. Jocelyn wondered if their mother could force her way back into Derrick's life by threatening to take the girls away from him. That thought remained the only distraction of what Jocelyn saw as a completely secure relationship. If Derrick was forced to choose between her and the babies, Jocelyn knew he would stay with his girls. Derrick would die without them. That's why Jocelyn loved him.

In his own bathroom, Derrick stepped into the hot shower and jumped out again. He examined his shoulder in the mirror. There were angry red bite marks on both of them. Derrick ran his hand down his side and felt tiny pricks in the skin. He said, "That woman's slightly cannibalistic, or she was damned glad to see me." Gritting his teeth, Derrick returned to the shower. He bathed, shaved and dressed in a red tee shirt, black shorts and sandals.

Derrick walked into the other bathroom and interrupted Jocelyn's thoughts. Two sat on her lap, as Jocelyn rinsed One's hair. Two bounced dangerously, the moment she saw him. Derrick picked her up, carried her into the bedroom and dressed her with Two singing the birthday song the entire time. Derrick wondered how long his mother had been drilling it into them.

They couldn't leave for the party before Derrick ate breakfast, so he had to share it with One and Two. They walked up to Derrick, he put a piece of waffle into their mouths and they wandered off to take pots out of the cabinet. When their mouths were empty, they returned to Derrick. Jocelyn watched the three with admiration, they co-existed so easily. The fact that they did it most of the time without speaking amazed her.

At Sonya's, Deandra dressed One and Two in their matching pink and green outfits. She put green headbands with big pink flowers on their heads and changed their earrings. The scuffle began when Deandra tried to get their sandals on. The twins hated having anything on their feet. They tolerated shoes and sneakers for short periods of time only and pulled them off every time. Occasionally losing a foot here and there. Derrick had to put the sandals on.

The yard was all decked out in pink and green. Streamers, balloons and a Barney pinata blew in the warm September breeze. The tables were set with the pink and green Barney theme. A huge white birthday cake sat on a table of its own, decorated with pink and green clowns that had, "Happy 1st Birthday Mia and Miranda" beautifully written in thick pink icing across its top. Beneath that in parenthesis, "(One and Two)."

Guests began to arrive promptly at three, because everyone in the family knew when Sonya said three, she meant it. All of One and Two's cousins came including Derrick's Aunt Sylvia and four of her grandchildren. Several of Sonya's neighbor's children walked over. Derrick was surprised to see some of his neighbors in attendance with their children. One and Two forgot all about Derrick in the excitement.

Adults, without children, arrived late—David and Hope, Derrick's boss Clyde Majors and his wife, Pop and Gran. Quite a few of the guys from the Friday night card parties showed up with their wives. Tyson came with Cynthia. They had been seeing each other quite a bit. Because her position required that she spend several months at a time in Atlanta, Cynthia made it perfectly clear that she and Tyson had no commitments. And, because he enjoyed the company of Big D's spicy castoff immensely, Tyson understood and accepted those terms. Their newfound relationship made them the perfect candidates for Mia and Miranda's godparents in Derrick's estimation, and they accepted the title and responsibilities happily.

When the adult attendance nearly matched that of the children, Derrick, David, and Ethan went into the house to get the ice chest. Ethan filled it with adult refreshments. In the kitchen, Ethan asked Derrick, "Has your brother told you what he's done now?"

Looking at David suspiciously, Derrick said, "No, Dad. What's he done now?"

"Got mixed up with one of your throwaways and can't get rid of her. Hope's catching on, too."

Puzzled, Derrick asked, "One of my throwaways? Who?"

David mumbled miserably, "You know who. Who couldn't you get rid of?"

Astonished and afraid to say her name, Derrick whispered, "No, David. Not Cassandra. Are you crazy? I've got a bank account saying Hope will know before it's all over, Dad. Cassandra's a little on the batty side."

Ethan asked, "Is that the woman who stripped for Jocelyn?"

Derrick nodded soundlessly.

Ethan looked at David and said, "You'd better tell Hope yourself, if you're planning on keeping her. If that woman tells her, Hope's out the front door and I don't blame her."

"I can't do that right now, Dad," David said, looking like he had just been told they found him on the doorstep.

"Why not?"

Truly agonized, David muttered, "Hope's pregnant."

Ethan screeched, "What?!" Ethan's hands went to the top of his head.

Leaning on the sink, Derrick rallied first and asked, "I know you've told Cassandra you don't want to see her anymore, David. Can you give me an idea what her response was?"

David answered flippantly, "Oh, she shows up at my office every day. If I refuse to see her there she shows up in front of my house, and I think she's already said something to Hope. Cassandra got real chummy with Hope after that day at your house, Derrick. They shop together occasionally. If we're not out of the house before ten, she joins us for lunch on Saturday afternoons."

Derrick looked his older brother in the eyes and said, "Listen to me, David. You tell Hope the truth now and stay away from Cassandra. She'll pull the I'm pregnant too routine on you next."

"She's not pregnant by me! I haven't touched her in months! She can't say that!" David bellowed near hysteria.

Ethan said, "She can say anything she wants, David! We're having a birthday party today for two little girls who couldn't be your brother's either! They look more and more like him every day! You should have married Hope last year and left that damned woman alone! If Sonya finds out, she's gonna preach you a sermon fit for your leaving, Boy! And, if Miranda 'Tiny' Dawes finds out, just climb in the box and make yourself comfortable! Me and Derrick'll slam the lid shut for you! Clean it up, David!"

Derrick said, "Point Cassandra in the direction of one of your buddies, David. She'll never leave you alone unless she replaces you. I was wondering who got her off my back. You never crossed my mind."

"I'm not pointing that lizard in anybody's direction. I'll have to tell Hope. She's just so happy about the baby, I hate doing this to her. What if she has a miscarriage? I'll never forgive myself." Slapping himself in the forehead, David whined pathetically, "I am such a fuck up!"

Ethan said smugly "Yeah. And, it's a good thing Hope already knows you're a fuck up."

Back in the yard, they found a clown had joined the festivities. One and Two enjoyed the colorful fellow from a distance. They didn't want him anywhere near them. Derrick had to paint their faces and hand them the balloons the clown made especially for them. One and Two sang, clapped and danced close to Derrick. If the clown looked as if he were coming in their direction, they frantically climbed Derrick's legs.

Everyone was having a great time. The men discussed the job Derrick was working on, and Clyde tried to persuade David to join the firm again. He turned him down flat. Reporting to anyone, for any reason, had always been a problem for David. That's why he was in the jam he was in with Cassandra, marriage meant having to report to Hope.

The women mingled with the children. Singing songs, refereeing altercations, cleaning and bandaging boo boos. One and Two would only allow Grammy Sonya or Jocelyn to take care of their boo boos. They ran from Aunt Dee all day. She kept repairing their outfits and hair. Ethan and Pop took turns videotaping the event.

Sonya fed all of her guests quite well. The children enjoyed their hot dogs, baked beans and potato salad. There were chips, pretzels and candy from the pinata ground into Ethan's normally pristine lawn. And, of course, there was that wonderful birthday cake and ice cream. The adults preferred the barbecue ribs, sausages, chicken, and pasta salad. Derrick ate like he had been to Siberia for a year and Cynthia teased Jocelyn about it. She said, "If boyfriend keeps eating like that, you're going to have a great big, fine, super wide brother on your hands, honey."

Jocelyn stole a glance at the handsomely thickening Ethan Dawes and said quickly, "That's enough, Derrick."

Cynthia and Hope screamed with laughter.

## *CHAPTER TWENTY-FIVE*

As dusk hovered over Sonya's yard, those remaining helped clean up. One and Two chased each other in circles and giggled. Both girls were completely entangled in the remnants of pink and green streamers. Most of their gifts had been taken into the house earlier. Thinking Derrick had forgotten birthday gifts, Jocelyn had bought extras. She should have known Derrick would never forget anything concerning One and Two. In fact, he had remembered how attached One and Two became to one of the children's Raggedy Ann dolls at an earlier birthday party, and Derrick was pleased with the excited reception One and Two gave their very own Raggedy Ann dolls. Unfortunately, like most children, now that One and Two had two dolls of their own, the dolls lay on the ground with their duplicate colorful smiles entertaining the sky.

With everything packed up and back in the garage, a few people sat out in the yard. Jocelyn didn't bother getting a chair. She sat on Derrick's thigh and jumped up with One and Two every few minutes.

Clyde Majors admired Jocelyn from his seat next to Derrick. Not giving a thought to good taste, Clyde asked, "Is Jocelyn their mother, Derrick?"

"No, she's not."

"Are you sure? They kind of look like her."

Feeling slightly uncomfortable, Derrick said, "I'm sure."

In the true Clyde fashion of never giving up a subject until it bleeds, he asked, "Have you figured out exactly who their mother is?"

Nervously digging in his ear, Derrick said, "Yes, I know exactly who their mother is."

"Did she come today?"

"No, Clyde, she didn't."

"Oh, that's right. You said she lives in Denver. Have you spoken to her since you've been out there?"

Wanting to slither inconspicuously beneath his chair, Derrick said, "She's called a few times, but we haven't talked about anything."

Angry that she had even bothered to call his good friend, Tyson asked, "What's she calling for, Big D?"

Derrick said, "Nothing. She hasn't really said anything. I haven't given her the opportunity," Derrick said, all the while smiling at Jocelyn.

Clyde interjected again, "If you don't give her an audience, Derrick, I think she'll make you regret it. You don't want to antagonize her, do you?"

Truly agitated by the conversation, Derrick snapped, "I'm not trying to antagonize anyone. I don't have to talk to her if I don't want to. Let's talk about something else please."

"May I ask one question on the subject, Derrick?" Cynthia asked, waving her hand excitedly.

Without responding, Derrick stared at Cynthia. She ignored it and asked, "Who is she? I mean, what's her name? What's her story?"

Derrick replied sarcastically, "Angelique Kelly. You don't know her. We went to college together, and I don't know what her story is. Can we let it go now?"

"I think you're making a *big mistake* not talking to her. Perhaps the two of you could work out an amicable arrangement without the courts. Angered, she's much more lethal." Clyde said with a heavy emphasis on big mistake.

Speaking for the first time in a long while, David said in a bitter tone, "If he sees her and says one thing she doesn't like he's making a mistake, too. And, if she's recording it, he'll hear it again. Let her roll a dead tape in court, Derrick. Playing games with crazy people is a losing proposition. No one knows the rules but a nut."

Unaccustomed to having anything less than the last word, Clyde offered, "I know you don't want to do anything to jeopardize your relationship with Jocelyn, Derrick. And, I can see why. She's not only quite a looker she's intelligent and loves your children. But, you think long and hard about not knowing the mind of your enemy."

Slyly darting his eyes in the direction of his wife, Clyde continued, "Sleep with them. Know them inside out. Pay particular attention to inconsistencies. Therein lies the answer to your dilemma."

Jocelyn frowned and spat sharply, "Derrick better not sleep with her. I don't care what's in her mind."

"Oh, he won't be doing it for the reasons you think. He'll be doing it to protect those two little girls the two of you love so much. Are they worth an infidelity or two to you, Jocelyn?" Clyde said, giving Jocelyn a knowing grin.

Knowing the answer was yes, Jocelyn refused to vocalize it. Rolling her eyes at Clyde and stomping off, Jocelyn went about bringing the wandering One and Two closer to the group. Her festive mood had been thoroughly trounced by the Angelique discussion.

Derrick muttered, "Now look what you've done, Clyde. I did not come home to argue with Jocelyn. Do you know any appropriate subjects for mixed couples? Who is the mother of your children is not one. I should refuse to go back to Denver. Jocelyn will never believe I haven't slept with Angelique now. Thanks. Why did you send me there in the first place? Tyson should be there."

Offended, Clyde said, "I didn't send you, Derrick. They requested you. If you didn't want to go, you could have told them Tyson would be there in your place."

"Can he go now?"

"Yes, I'm sure he could. I wouldn't recommend you do it though. Harold Savitch really admires your work, Derrick. If he thinks he's not getting you, he'll pull out and we both lose. You're due a hefty bonus on this assignment. And, if you're serious about taking off the entire month of December again this year, I think you should give it some serious thought."

Hoping the subject would end without any further input from him, Derrick didn't respond. He listened as they took turns giving their opinions on the subject. Everyone left shortly after.

The girls fought sleep again that night. Sonya wanted them to stay there, but Ethan didn't exactly look like he agreed with her. Jocelyn told Derrick, "I think we should take the babies home tonight."

Derrick asked, "Why? If Mom says they can stay, what's the problem? We'll be here for dinner tomorrow anyway."

Looking down at her feet, Jocelyn whispered, "I think your father wants to spend the night with his wife alone."

Frowning, Derrick said, "Don't be ridiculous, Jocelyn."

Stopping there, Derrick gave the situation some thought. If One and Two had been sleeping in Ethan and Sonya's bedroom the entire time he had been in Denver, that meant Ethan and Sonya had not had any privacy for a while. But, hadn't Sonya asked for them to stay? Maybe she didn't want to spend any time alone with Ethan these days. Maybe last night was enough for her. Visibly cringing, Derrick mumbled to himself, "Jesus. Those are your parents. How sick can you get? They don't do things like that anymore."

Speaking softly into Derrick's ear, Jocelyn said, "Oh, yes they do. And, they can't if they have those two in the room with them. We're taking them home."

Gathering his two, slightly incoherent midgets, Derrick headed for home. Sonya told Derrick she would be there for the girls by two and that she would bring dinner for Derrick and Jocelyn when she came. Then, they were given permission to forego Sunday dinner from Sonya. Ethan appeared satisfied with those arrangements and to see them go. He would deal with tomorrow, tomorrow. Tonight, he had his wife to himself. He never said a word to Derrick. He merely nodded and smiled.

During the ride home, the girls lost their fight with sleep. As Derrick parked the car, One and Two gave their familiar hums. They also slept through getting undressed and being put to bed. One was missing a sandal. Derrick could only hope his mother found it. Jocelyn and Derrick wiped cake crumbs and soured ice cream from the folds in their necks before leaving them.

In Derrick's bedroom, Jocelyn sat on the side of the bed. Her arms and legs were tightly crossed and there was an unfamiliar twist to her lips. A definite no nonsense smirk held her beautiful face in its grip.

Sighing deeply, Derrick sat next to her and waited. Even though Jocelyn had never given him the third degree about anything, or laid down any laws, he knew there was at least one law lurking behind that expression.

Quite a few minutes passed without Jocelyn saying anything. Derrick stroked her stiff neck lightly with his finger. Jocelyn gave a tiny flinch, but said nothing. Giving up, Derrick asked, "What's wrong, sweetheart?"

Not looking at him, she responded angrily, "You know what's wrong, Derrick. You didn't tell me Mia and Miranda's mother gave you a call. Nevertheless a few."

Knowing it wouldn't set well, but that it was the truth, Derrick said, "Her calls aren't important to me, Jocelyn. I'm not interested in anything she has to say."

"You should be interested. She can take Mia and Miranda away from you." Stopping and shifting her legs, Jocelyn looked as if she were concentrating on her knees when she asked, "Is the reason you don't want to talk to her strictly about the girls, Derrick? Or, are you afraid to talk because your own feelings may betray you?"

Lifting Jocelyn's chin until her eyes met his, Derrick asked, "Are you trying to insinuate I might be in love with this woman?"

Jocelyn blinked and nodded slowly.

"You're wrong. Those days are long gone. The only woman I'm in love with is sitting right here with me. And, she doesn't have a thing in the world to worry about."

Whining, Jocelyn asked, "Are you sure, Derrick? I really don't want to find out in a public way that I've been replaced for months."

Kissing her forehead lightly, Derrick whispered, "You're never being replaced. Didn't I just say I loved you?"

Smiling, Jocelyn said, "Yes, you did. And, I love you, too. That's why it's so important for me to know what's going on."

"Well, you know. Angelique called and I had nothing to say."

As Jocelyn prepared to ask if he was sure, Derrick lowered his lips to hers. She stopped mid-sentence and received the warm, wet kiss. The moment Derrick retreated, she asked, "Are you sure that's all that happened? Did you have dinner with her? Did she visit you at your hotel room? I know she asked about Mia and Miranda. So, what did you tell her?"

Unfolding Jocelyn's arms and tugging at her top, Derrick said, "I'm sure. No, we didn't have dinner. No, she didn't visit me at my hotel room. And, if she asked about One and Two, I don't recall. They're none of her business. The less she knows about them, the better. I may have mistakenly mentioned their names, but that was about it."

Letting Derrick remove her blouse, Jocelyn twisted to keep him away from her bra and said, "If you can't remember what she asked, you can't remember how to undress me."

Not really wanting to recall his conversation with Angelique, but wanting desperately to undress Jocelyn, Derrick gave his memory a polling. It took a few seconds for any of it to surface. Then, he said, "She wanted to know who the girls were staying with while I was away. I told her they were with my mother. And, that's all I remember."

His hand moved toward the clasp on Jocelyn's bra. She slapped it away and said, "Oh, so she doesn't know about me. Why didn't you tell her about me, Derrick?"

Rubbing his hand, Derrick pleaded, "Oh, come on, Jocelyn. I couldn't talk to her because I was packing to come home. Sweetheart, I'm not hiding anything from you."

Giving Derrick the evil eye, Jocelyn said, "You'd better not be. If I find out different, you can forget you ever knew me."

Reaching for Jocelyn's ponytail, Derrick wrapped it around his hand, pulled her face close to his and said, "I'm never forgetting I ever knew you, because I'm never letting you go."

Just as Jocelyn started to say, "If you're lying, you won't have to let . . . ," Derrick devoured her fussing lips. His hot, smooth tongue slid into her mouth. Derrick's free hand found the clasp on her bra and released it, and just as his mind-numbing kiss had stopped Jocelyn's speech, his molten caresses fused all of her thoughts together. Jocelyn couldn't remember what she was saying or how to say it when Derrick removed the rest of her little outfit. The remainder of the night was spent in a sea of splendor. No questions. No answers.

The ringing telephone woke Derrick at seven the following morning. When he moved to answer it, Jocelyn gave a tiny moan and moved closer to fill the space vacated by his arm. Blinking hard to focus his eyes, Derrick said groggily, "Hello."

A defeated and exhausted voice said, "She's packing."

Not recognizing the voice, Derrick asked, "Who's packing?"

"Hope."

## *CHAPTER TWENTY-SIX*

Unable to believe how David could have been so stupid, Derrick listened to David on the telephone for over half an hour. Cassandra was nothing more than a game for him, a game that got out of hand. The fact that Cassandra had played so many mind games with Hope only made everything worse. Cassandra had visited their home, went shopping with Hope, and suggested names for their baby. Leaving Hope humiliated and devastated.

Before walking out the front door, Hope had thrown the house keys down on the table and spat, "You can give these to Cassandra. And, tell the slut to stay out of my way too, David. This baby is the only thing keeping me from hunting her down and kicking an unconscious twitch in her ass."

David openly admitted having no idea what he would do without Hope. Never, in his entire life, had Derrick ever heard David sound so miserable. He listened to David recount the emotional night of confrontation, confessions, shock and finally, the ear piercing screams.

It seems, a somewhat intoxicated Cassandra greeted Hope and David at home after the twins' birthday party. When David suggested she go home and sleep it off, he ignited Cassandra. Never taking her eyes off of David, Cassandra gave an extremely loud verbal review of their relationship. David tried to stop her, but that only incited her to be more graphic. As it was, Hope and half the neighborhood knew what David and Cassandra had done, when and where.

Cassandra's blow-by-blow description of how they had done, what they had done, and her personal ratings of each activity, knocked the wind out of Hope. She hyperventilated and scared the living crap out of David. He carried Hope into the house and left a ranting, drunk woman on the lawn. If he could have strangled Cassandra and helped Hope at the same time, he would have been making his call to Derrick from the police precinct.

There was no apology for what he had done and David knew it. Hope wept, yelled at the top of her lungs, and packed. David didn't tell Derrick she had threatened to abort the baby, too.

Derrick didn't know what to say to him, and he didn't want to mention Cassandra's name in Jocelyn's presence. She may, or may not have been listening. Jocelyn knew Hope spent a lot of time with Cassandra, but she didn't hold it against her. If they were friends, it was okay with Jocelyn. Jocelyn never mentioned the stripping incident to Hope either. If she had, maybe Hope would have kept her defenses up with Cassandra.

One's tiny cry for Daddy forced Derrick to say hurriedly, "Don't worry, David. She'll come home. Give her a little time. That was a lot to hear and deal with at one time. There's a lot at stake for both of you. If you've learned anything, it may have been worth it."

Derrick went about his morning solemnly, commiserating with his brother. Derrick knew only too well how easy it was for a man to find himself in those kinds of jams. If women only understood that it was the nature of the beast to be a beast, everything would move along a lot smoother. Who was he fooling? Women didn't want beasts . . . they wanted men . . . men with morals. That's where the problem started and stopped. It was somehow easier for women to adopt morals than men. At least, Derrick thought so.

His mother never openly admired other men. Now Ethan, on the other hand, openly admired every woman he could but he never touched any of them. At least, none that

Sonya knew of. She would have broken his back while he slept if he had. Pop did it, too. He never did it in front of Gran though. She didn't take to it with any semblance of humor. Hadn't Derrick heard her say on many occasions, "If you want to see tomorrow, David, you'd better find something else to do with your eyes today." Pop would slowly divert his vision to a safer object.

Derrick thought about what Jocelyn had said the night before. She didn't care for men being men either. She was extremely self-assured and didn't have a jealous bone in her body. She just wasn't tolerating any nonsense. If Derrick wanted someone else, all Jocelyn asked was that he tell her first. Give her time to get out of the way. Jocelyn did not want any mud slung on her.

Sonya was just as solemn when she came for the girls. One look at his mother told Derrick she knew what had happened, too. Jocelyn helped Sonya put the food away and collect Mia and Miranda. The twins went along with the program, until they realized Derrick wasn't going with them. He hugged and kissed them repeatedly, promising he would see them soon, and to be good for Gram. One and Two screamed like Derrick had said he was never coming back.

Giving Derrick a look of disgust, Sonya picked up Mia and said, "Come on, sweetheart. You'll be wailing about one man or another all of your life."

Looking into his mother's angry eyes, Derrick asked, "Why are you telling her that, Mom?"

Sonya snapped bitterly, "Because she will, Derrick! It comes with the territory! Call us when you get back to Denver."

Jocelyn looked from Sonya's smoldering eyes to Derrick's pleading eyes. She didn't have a clue what was transpiring between them. Feeling it better to ask Derrick after Sonya left, Jocelyn held her question.

It took fifteen minutes to get the screaming and kicking babies securely strapped into their car seats. Derrick was a wreck by the time his mother pulled off. He stood on the sidewalk and looked up at the sky for a few minutes, hoping the rattled molecules of his mind would settle down. For the first time, he wondered if coming home was a good idea. What had his little visit produced? Suspicion from Jocelyn and two horribly disappointed and distraught babies.

Jocelyn stood in the doorway studying Derrick. Every time she thought she knew him, he did something else. She wondered what he was looking at the sky like that for. Looking up for herself, Jocelyn saw nothing but a beautiful early autumn sky. There were too few clouds to daydream on.

Taking a deep breath, Derrick turned and walked back to the house. Jocelyn stroked his back and asked, "What's wrong, Derrick?"

Listlessly, Derrick responded, "Hope left David this morning."

"Cassandra?"

"How did you know it was her?"

"I know women, sweetheart. I have a cousin who could be Cassandra's twin. She smiled in my face and slept with Justine. I know exactly how Hope feels. I should have packed up and left, too. But, I didn't."

Looking down at Jocelyn with an extremely serious expression on his face, Derrick asked, "Why not?"

"I loved him more than I hated her. Besides, she wanted me to leave to prove her point. That she was a better woman than me. Prettier, sexier and smarter."

"Does that mean Hope may come back?"

"No. Every woman handles situations like that differently. I know how much Hope loves David though. I know how much she was looking forward to marrying him, having his child, and building a real life. I also know he dragged his feet. He dragged them after he proposed. Kept dragging them after she told him she was pregnant. After the long wait, she has to hear about a fling he had with the village tramp? Contrary to popular belief, there's only so much a woman can take. Love has a long rope. It's just not endless."

"When you say it like that, it sounds so bad, Jocelyn."

"It is bad, Derrick. Real bad."

They spent the rest of the day together quietly. Derrick didn't want Jocelyn to move an arm's length away from him. He made her eat dinner sitting on his lap. Derrick memorized everything about Jocelyn. The feel, smell and taste of her. Her smile, smirk and grimace, the sound of her voice. Her laughter. There was more to it than knowing he was going back to Denver in the morning. Something had frightened him.

Jocelyn drove Derrick to the airport at six the following morning. They sat in the car staring at each other so long a policeman tapped on the window and threatened to give her a ticket. Derrick held Jocelyn's face in his hand and gave her a tender, loving kiss. The tears she had so gallantly held back all morning fell. Derrick wiped one away and kissed her cheek.

Luck was with Jocelyn that morning; there wasn't much traffic. If there had been, she would have surely hit someone. Tears blinded her for the remainder of the day. Jocelyn laughed at herself from time to time. She was worse than Mia and Miranda when it came to Derrick.

The days dragged on with Derrick calling Sonya every day to talk to One and Two. They cried the minute they heard his voice. Sonya asked Derrick to stop trying to talk to them until he came home. She reported what David had already told him. Derrick never told Sonya that David called him every day, too. Hope refused to talk to David about anything, and seeing him was out of the question. The only thing Sonya said that David had not was that Hope and the baby were both fine.

Derrick faithfully kept his eight o'clock appointments with Jocelyn. He let nothing and no one interrupt that call. Their conversations consisted of how much they missed each other, what progress Derrick was making toward coming home and the girls. The results of Jocelyn and Derrick's communicable diseases tests were back and cleared the way for Derrick to do what he had wanted to do for months. Jocelyn whined about birth control, and after deciding on the pill, she let Derrick know she hated it. That she was only doing this for him.

Derrick and Jocelyn avoided David and Hope's problems. The sound of Cassandra's name really irritated Jocelyn now, and Derrick did not like the tone of Jocelyn's voice when she wasn't happy. And since Angelique hadn't called, Derrick never mentioned her either. Derrick and Jocelyn ended every conversation with a long string of I love yous.

The project Derrick was working on fell behind schedule twice and rebounded both times. Derrick did not want to spend one extra day in Denver. The final week came and moved along with great promise. Derrick didn't dare breathe a word about the prospect of getting home a day early. He wouldn't have been able to handle Jocelyn's disappointment if it didn't happen. That's why Derrick couldn't wait to call Jocelyn from the office on that Wednesday to tell her he would be home the next day.

Jocelyn's first question was, "Why can't you leave tonight, Derrick?"

"I have a wrap meeting in the morning. Don't worry. This deal is done. My plane leaves at noon."

After work, the architectural design team invited Derrick to dinner and drinks. Since it was only four when they called it a day, Derrick accepted. He planned to be in his room packing by eight.

Derrick lost track of time and arrived at his hotel at nine o'clock. He hadn't been so lost that he forgot to call Jocelyn at eight from the restaurant telephone though. He told her where he was and that he would call her when he got back to his room. She told him to have a good time and to behave himself.

It was an extremely happy Derrick Dawes who strolled through the hotel lobby later that night. His job was well done and he was going home to all of the women he loved—big and little women.

Derrick pressed the button for the elevator and froze when he heard Angelique say, "How long did you think I would let you avoid me, Derrick? You know I'm not used to you not being glad to see me."

Hoping she was an apparition, a poltergeist, or some other ethereal malformation, Derrick turned his head toward her slowly. Shaking his head, Derrick said, "Go away, Angelique. Not now."

Frowning, Angelique asked angrily, "What do you mean, go away? I'm not going anywhere. You're going to talk to me tonight, Mr. Dawes. Don't make me announce to the world why either."

The elevator doors opened and Angelique followed Derrick onto it. He never glanced in her direction. Derrick already knew exactly what Angelique looked like. The walk to his room seemed longer than usual, with her dogging his trail.

There was a sharp pain growing over Derrick's right eye, as he moved down the long corridor. Common sense said not to take Angelique into his room. Talk to her in the lobby, at the bar. Derrick ignored it. He didn't want her making a scene in front of people.

Derrick opened the door and actually thought about slamming it in her face. He didn't do it though. He held it open for what he knew would be her extravagantly perfumed entrance. Angelique floated into the room as only she could.

Standing with her expensive camel colored all-weather coat untied, Angelique asked, "Are you going to help me get out of my coat, Derrick?"

"Did I help you get into your coat?"

"Oh, age is making us testy. You used to be such a gentleman, too."

"Age has nothing to do with it, Angelique. What do you want?"

Giving Derrick the bitterest smile he had ever seen, Angelique said, "I want to know all about our wonderful babies. Mia and Miranda. Right?"

Snow capped mountains seemed like a hot and hazy vacation spot compared to Derrick's demeanor when he asked, "What do you want to know about them?"

"Stop acting stupid, Derrick. Take my coat. Offer me a seat. A drink. You were the one who insisted those were my babies. I tried to tell you they weren't. I see you still don't believe me."

"No, I don't believe you."

Laughing at Derrick, Angelique said, "Okay. Since they're mine, I'd like to hear about them."

Angelique removed her own coat and tossed it on the sofa. She saw that Derrick had wine and brandy on his dresser. Without being offered, Angelique walked over and poured brandy into a glass. There was no ice. Angelique turned and asked, "Would you mind getting some ice?"

Not in the mood for any of this, Derrick flicked the key, picked up the ice chest and headed for the door. Angelique smiled at his back. She had to admit Derrick still had it. He could stimulate a woman's imagination while simply walking away from her. And Angelique had no intentions of letting him go home without spending at least one night with him. Now that she and Aaron had called it quits again, Angelique genuinely thought it possible to pick up the pieces with Derrick. Sitting on the bed, Angelique tested its firmness while thinking with a set of twins between them, what could stop her?

The photograph on Derrick's night table answered that question for Angelique. Not the one of the two adorable little girls, who really did resemble Angelique, but the only possible showstopper–the beautiful, smiling woman with thick, flowing black hair. Angelique was impressed. However, not discouraged.

A sullen Derrick returned with the ice and without offering any to Angelique, he placed the bucket on the table. Seeing Derrick's mood had further deteriorated since he left the room, Angelique didn't bother asking for ice. She rose gingerly from the bed, strolled over and dropped two of the cubes into her glass. Derrick simply stood in one spot watching her every move. After taking a leisurely sip of the now slightly chilled brandy, Angelique lightly touched

Derrick's elbow and asked, "Can we at least have a seat and pretend to be civilized, Derrick?"

"You've got a real knack for pretending, don't you, Angelique? You've pretended not to be pregnant with twins, delivering them, and that you did not leave them on me without notice for over a year now."

Smiling coolly, Angelique said, "Derrick, sweetheart, I never pretended to do any of those things. If I had ever been lucky enough to conceive a child of yours, those would have all been the furthest thoughts from my mind. Do you have any idea how much I loved you and still do?"

"I don't want to discuss this anymore tonight, Angelique. All you're going to do is deny One and Two. You can't see that I've grown to love those two little girls too much to listen to you disown them with the same ease you use slipping out of your dress."

Giving Derrick a vampish smile, Angelique said, "Oh, I know how much you enjoy a good floor show, Derrick. The dress coming off with style is as important to you as the few scant items left behind. I've got a brand new surprise for you tonight though, sweetheart."

Putting her drink down on the dresser, giving Derrick a wink and seductively licking her lips, Angelique released the tie of her jacket and let it fall from her shoulders. The butterscotch, burgundy and green linen jacket drifted to the floor after lightly brushing Angelique's firm, generous hips. Never allowing her eyes to stray from Derrick's, Angelique's hands danced toward the silver discs that rode up and down leisurely above her firm, heavy breasts and held her dress in place. She paused, as if listening to music, flicked the gleaming silver discs with her thumbs, threw her hands over her head, grinned wickedly and gave her hips a seductive wiggle. The butterscotch dress slid down her nude body, past flesh tone lace thigh stockings, and landing gingerly around her butterscotch high-heeled feet.

Derrick scanned Angelique's exquisite body with interest. As he surveyed her, Derrick asked himself, "Damn, is this the body of a woman who gave birth to a set of twins a year ago?" There were a few unfamiliar marks on her abdomen that had not been there the last time Derrick saw her. But, would that be the extent of the damage left from carrying a set of twins? Derrick had no idea.

Stepping out of her discarded dress, the nude, seductive stocking and high-heeled Angelique moved toward Derrick in tantalizing slow motion that perfectly displayed every sensuous muscle and contour of her body for his inspection. Standing close enough to nuzzle the base of his throat with her nose, Angelique lifted Derrick's hands and placed them on her hips. Not getting the anticipated response from him, she covered his hands with her own, slid them down her hips and manipulated his fingers. Angelique lightly ran her smooth tongue up his neck and nibbled his chin. She knew that the moisture of her tongue, combined with the heat of her breath on Derrick's skin was always one of his favorite turn-ons. Surely, life with a set of twins had not robbed him of his sexual senses.

Derrick closed his eyes and made a tentative movement toward Angelique. He toyed with the thought of playing along with this charade to deflect Angelique's focus away from One and Two. Derrick knew all Angelique really wanted was a physical relationship with him. The girls meant absolutely nothing to her. Glaring down at Angelique with pure hatred, Derrick spat, "Get out of here."

Undisturbed, Angelique continued to manipulate Derrick's stroking of her body for emphasis and whispered, "What do you mean, get out of here? We haven't discussed the children yet, Derrick. Throwing me out isn't a good idea. It certainly isn't worth losing Mia and Miranda over, is it?"

At the top of his lungs, Derrick shouted, "Yes, it is!"

Genuinely stunned, Angelique asked, "Really?"

"Really!"

"Are we discussing Mia and Miranda, or the woman in the photo, Derrick? Are you passing up a blissful trip down memory lane for your daughters, or your new woman? We both know you won't keep her after you've had her once or twice, so what's going on? You haven't kept a woman in your life since I left it. Last year, you were ecstatic about the possibility of rekindling the love that kept you ticking for four years. Come on, Derrick. If you don't take it personal, I promise I won't either. If we make another set of twins, I'll keep this set for myself." Angelique laughed at her little play on words and stroked Derrick's back.

"Just get out, Angelique. You've changed and so have I. Memory lane will dust over for you one day, too."

In a final attempt at arousal, Angelique gave her hips a provocative sway against Derrick's groin, moistened her lips and said, "No, it won't, Derrick. I'll blow the dust off of you every chance I get."

Giving Angelique a disgusted smirk, Derrick stepped out of her embrace, walked across the room and opened the door. He stood there holding it open until Angelique believed he was adamant about her leaving.

Not saying another word, Angelique sauntered over to her discarded outfit and redressed with the same ease she had undressed. Finishing her drink and picking up her coat, Angelique finally said, "For your sake, I certainly hope dust covers memory lane for me, Derrick. But, more than likely, I'll be seeing you soon—in court. Don't bother spending too much on a lawyer either; the judge is going to give Mia and Miranda to me anyway. Call me at home if you change your mind, sweetie."

## *CHAPTER TWENTY-SEVEN*

Derrick lay on the bed of his hotel room for the remainder of the night staring blindly at the ceiling. He didn't even bother undressing. Derrick's mind fluctuated from complete numbness to vibrating with a hailstorm of negative activity.

Angelique held his happiness in the palm of her hand and she knew it. Clyde Majors was right, perhaps Derrick should have given her a listen without the hostility. He should have slept with her if he had to and ran the risk of losing Jocelyn. It could have worked out. Maybe Jocelyn loved him more than she hated Angelique.

Now, Angelique walks in and takes the babies he has taken care of and grown to love. He gets to lie in darkness always wondering if they were screaming for him half the night, if they were refusing to eat or misbehaving out of frustration.

Angelique knows absolutely nothing about them. She wouldn't know that One and Two only sleep with the radio on. That Two refuses to eat or drink anything red. Would the rambunctious twins dilute Angelique's resolve when she had to bathe them after every meal? How would Angelique handle it? Would she be mean to them, or would she give them a chance to adjust? Angelique would bring them to Denver and Derrick would always be at the mercy of her word on how they were doing. And, most important of all, when would he get to see them?

The telephone in Derrick's hotel room rang through the night. Thinking it was Angelique, he never answered. The truth was both Angelique and Jocelyn were calling Derrick for different reasons. Angelique wanted to take another shot at persuading Derrick to see her that night. Anticipating his homecoming the next day, Jocelyn simply wanted to hear Derrick's voice before she fell asleep.

His not answering the telephone all night upset Jocelyn. She didn't understand what was going on. If Mia and Miranda's mother had cornered Derrick, the least of Jocelyn's fear was of him sleeping with her. His anger wouldn't allow that to happen. If a sexual rendezvous were all it would take to rid them of the problem, Jocelyn would have paid for the hotel room. But, a blind man could see that there was more to that relationship than that.

There were still aspects of Derrick's personality Jocelyn couldn't get a grip on. When things aggravated him, he closed himself in and everyone else out. She had seen this happen once when Sonya screamed at him for an hour after Derrick had left the basement door ajar and One took a terrible fall down the stairs. A trip to the hospital only revealed a deep bruise to her shoulder. What could have happened, combined with his mother's screaming, did something to Derrick. He wouldn't say a word to a soul for two days afterwards. That's also when Jocelyn saw how Derrick sat next to a ringing telephone and seemed not to even hear it.

Jocelyn was certain everything would be fine when a dozen peach roses were delivered to her at the office on Thursday. The note said, "Nothing happened. Absolutely nothing. I love you. Derrick." Not knowing exactly what he was trying to tell her, Jocelyn happily worked through the remainder of her day looking forward to finding Derrick at the end of it.

However, Jocelyn didn't know what to think when she didn't actually hear from Derrick at all on Thursday. Jocelyn called Sonya late in the evening and asked if he had made it home. Sonya said, "He sure did. I don't know what's happened, but he's in a foul mood, Jocelyn. Don't expect much from him right now. And, please don't take it personal. This is the real Derrick."

Derrick took his two happy little girls home and shut the three of them in. Because there were no groceries, they got up early on Friday and went shopping. The girls needed milk, juice and pull-ups. Derrick bought fruit and cookies for them, too. One and Two opened the packages as Derrick put them into the cart.

At home that weekend, the only telephone call Derrick made was to his lawyer. Derrick told Roger that Angelique had threatened to file for custody. Roger told Derrick there was nothing he could do before then, to just sit and wait for the Process Server. The Motions and Requests were all prepared, waiting to be dated and spirited over to the courthouse for filing.

There was no sitting around for Derrick with One and Two anymore. As a matter of fact, he could barely keep up with them. If they ever stopped calling his name every two minutes, he would never find them. They climbed over and crawled under everything. They put things in their mouths Derrick couldn't believe. Lint balls, mothballs, old dead bugs, handfuls of butter, detergent—you name it.

Flipping off the back of the sofa was quickly becoming a favorite game for the twins. Getting their hands on the remote control and pushing buttons was second on the Dawes' twin hit parade. Both One and Two had little knots on their heads because Derrick took his sneakers off in their presence and trying to maneuver those giant sneakers onto their tiny feet had caused them to fall into each other.

Mealtime presented unique problems because Onc and Two fed each other. They smeared food in their hair, noses and ears, and screamed like demons possessed if Derrick moved them too far away from each other to do these things easily. If Derrick dared sit close to them, they fed and smeared him, too. Having to wash them up before he could travel through the house with them to the bathroom, for a real bath, became commonplace.

One and Two had one redeeming quality—they still slept through the night. So what if they could climb out of their cribs now, so far they had only traveled to Derrick's bedroom. He woke with tiny fingers poking in his eyes, nose and ears most mornings, but the little wet baby kisses that accompanied the annoying attention made it all worthwhile.

Before he knew it, a month had passed and Derrick had not called Jocelyn. He sent her a single rose everyday with a note that always said, "Thinking of You. Love, Derrick."

Jocelyn stopped opening the roses after the second week. She wasn't dealing with Derrick's absence well. If he had kept it down to a few days, she would have settled. As it was, Jocelyn didn't know what to make of it. So, she cried about it, let it go and accepted a dinner date invitation.

Jocelyn spoke to Sonya every day for weeks. She visited Mia and Miranda at Sonya's house to avoid Derrick since he obviously did not want to see her. Of course, the two little girls were always happy to see Jocelyn. They showed her every boo boo they ever had in their lives and Jocelyn, with animated concern, stroked and kissed every one.

Sonya looked on the reunions fondly and asked, "Has Derrick called you yet?"

"No. I don't think he's going to."

"And, what about you?"

"What about me?"

"Come on, Jocelyn. You know what I mean. Are you re-evaluating your priorities, too?"

"No, Sonya. I've always known exactly how I felt about Derrick. I fell in love with him the first time he pushed me. I've analyzed our relationship from a million angles and found it flawless. But, if my presence in his life is causing some sort of conflict for him, I'll bow out. I've given it all a good cry and I'm moving on.

"Derrick can't keep a woman he shuts out. Not this one anyway. Be angry. I can handle it. Just let me in the room."

Sonya laughed a little and said, "The only other person I've ever known like Derrick was my mother. If anything upset her, she wouldn't say a word to anybody for days. It frustrated my father to no end. She slept on the sofa until she felt better and moved if he came anywhere near her. He tried to force a conversation out of her once and she carried on so bad he never did it again. Things were broken all over the house.

"Derrick's not prone to breaking things, but he can get a real click going with that yelling on occasion. I guess he got that from me. Ethan seldom yells. He smirks and mumbles. I could slap his face when he does that, too. I say all of this to say, everybody's got some quirkie behavior. What's yours?"

"Stubborn, I guess. At least, that's what my Grandma always said. I haven't spoken to my family in six years, none of them. They make me sick."

"You're not planning on putting Derrick on that list, are you?"

"Derrick's putting Derrick on that list, Sonya. I haven't seen, or heard from him in over a month and he's not making a move to do anything about it. I've called and left more messages than I'll ever admit to anyone, except you. I will not knock on the door and be left standing on the step, Sonya. If that happened, I know I'd never speak to Derrick again."

"Well, please don't knock. He'll come get you when he's ready."

"Who says I'll be there when he's ready?"

"Please, Jocelyn. I've had enough of you all and the leaving. Hope just came back. Says she only did it because she doesn't want to have the baby by herself. She couldn't care less about David. Well, you know my David. He could care less about why she came back, as long as she came back."

Smiling, Jocelyn said, "I know she went back. I asked Hope if she really wanted to leave enough space for that slimy Cassandra to slink through the other day. David's silly, but Hope loves him. And, she needs him. Raising children alone is no fun. I see too much of it in my office."

Sonya watched Jocelyn while she spoke and a smile bloomed on her face. Sonya had heard a touch of envy in Jocelyn's voice. She wanted her own children too, and she wanted Derrick to be their father. Jocelyn was disappointed with Derrick right now, but she would snap out of it if he played his cards right—and, soon.

Mia and Miranda stomped and screamed when Jocelyn left Sonya's house and it tore a hole in Jocelyn's heart. She hated doing that to them. Jocelyn cried too as she sat in the car, and into her hands she muttered, "Derrick Dawes, you make me sick."

If Jocelyn had not been crying, she would have seen Derrick pull up behind her. Instead, she pulled off. He saw her and that old demon ache of missing her returned. The last thing Derrick wanted was to hurt Jocelyn. If Angelique had her way Derrick knew he would not be any good for Jocelyn for a long while. She was better off without him.

In the house, One and Two ran to Derrick and wept their version of Jocelyn's name over and over. Sarcastically, Sonya said, "They want Jocelyn, Derrick. What are you going to do about it?"

Sighing, Derrick said, "Nothing I can do, Mom."

"What do you mean there's nothing you can do? Are you going to sit around pouting about something you really can't do a damn thing about until she's gone for good?"

Looking at his mother for the first time, Derrick asked urgently, "Did she say she was going somewhere for good, Mom?"

"Her exact words were, 'I gave it a good cry, let it go and I'm moving on.' Did you know Jocelyn hadn't spoken to her family in six years? If she can drop her mama like a hot potato, imagine what she can do for you."

Shrugging his huge shoulders, Derrick said, "Maybe she would be better off, Mom. I'm not very good company these days."

Screaming at the top of her lungs, Sonya said, "Well, you'd better hurry up and get in a better damned mood, Boy! You're about to let the mother of your children get away!"

Looking at One and Two pitifully, Derrick said, "I might not have any children in a little while, Mom."

"You listen to me, Derrick. As sickening as your father can be, there is one thing I know about him. If I need him, he's there. No matter what I have to face, he faces it with me. You have no right shutting Jocelyn out because you're afraid. That's when you really need her. If you lose Mia and Miranda, do you think that's the end of the world? No. You're losing Mia, Miranda and all of your other children, with a woman you love as much as she loves you. That's the end of your world, Fool."

Shaking his head, as if to clear it, Derrick stood and said, "Okay, Mom. We're going now. I'll call you in the morning."

Pulling on coats, Derrick gave Sonya's speech a little thought. Other children had never entered the equation before. Even if they had, they couldn't replace the two Derrick already had. One and Two belonged to Derrick. Just Derrick.

Deandra came in as Derrick was leaving. She got up on her tiptoes, gave her brother a kiss on the cheek and said, "You need a haircut, Derrick."

Returning her kiss, Derrick said, "You've got five holes in one ear, Squirt. You're turning into a pin cushion."

"Wait until I take Mia and Miranda to get their second holes."

Pointing his finger at his little blonde haired sister, Derrick said sternly, "I will break your neck if they ever get another hole in their ears. I let you get away with the first one. That's it, Squirt."

"Jocelyn's got two holes in her ears now. She went with me."

As if he had been stuck with something, Derrick twitched at the sound of Jocelyn's name. He said smugly, "You and Jocelyn can just punch all of the holes in your heads you want. Leave One and Two's in one piece until they can decide how many holes they want in their own heads."

"You're worse than Daddy, Derrick. You're never going to let them get anymore."

"Shut up, Squirt."

"No. Are you bringing Jocelyn to Thanksgiving dinner? I'm bringing somebody."

"Who are you bringing?"

"You'll meet him then. You didn't answer my question."

"Not going to either."

On that note Derrick picked up One and Two and left. At home, he fed them their dinner, played with his own and cleaned up. He took his two woman tag team down to the recreation room. They knocked over pool cues and stuck their fingers in the chalk. Then, they took turns pushing the reset button on the pinball machine, causing the bell to ring unceasingly. Derrick threatened to put them in the playpen about ten times. They ignored him.

At eight, Derrick picked up the telephone and called his mother. He asked if she could come over and watch One and Two for him for about an hour. Knowing exactly where he wanted to go, Sonya said she would be there in less than half an hour.

Derrick pulled up in front of Jocelyn's apartment building at a little after nine. Her car was parked at the curb. Derrick parked, reached for the door handle and was stopped by what transpired next.

A red Mazda pulled up next to Jocelyn's Honda and stopped. Jocelyn got out of it immediately. Then, the guy driving got out and followed her up the walkway.

Derrick sat in the car and watched the little exchange between them for a few minutes. He had every intention of allowing this guy to say goodnight and leave. When it appeared Jocelyn's friend was trying to move in for more than that, Derrick got out of his car. Jocelyn was so engrossed with her begging date she never noticed Derrick's approach.

Walking past the two on the dark walkway, Derrick stopped and leaned on the wall about two feet away from them. Derrick heard Jocelyn say, "No." and, "I don't think so." several times. However, she still had not noticed Derrick. Everything moved along at an extremely slow pace, until Jocelyn's date said, "Since I can't come up for a drink, maybe you'll give me a goodnight kiss."

Before Jocelyn could respond, Derrick said listlessly, "No, she won't be doing that either."

Both Jocelyn and her date looked around. Spotting the exceptionally large man leaning on the wall immediately, Jocelyn's date asked, "Do you know that guy?"

Again, Derrick answered, "You'd better believe she knows this guy. And it's time for you to go now. I'm tired of leaning on this wall, listening to you beg for something you're never getting."

Jocelyn snapped, "Derrick!"

"Yes, Jocelyn?"

"I don't believe you're hiding in shadows these days!"

"Not hiding, sweetheart. I walked right past you. You were so engrossed with his intense conversation you never noticed."

"Well, go home. I have company."

"I know that, Jocelyn. He's leaving though."

Jocelyn's date asked, "Who says I'm leaving?"

Walking toward them slowly, Derrick said calmly, "I did."

"It sounded like Jocelyn asked you to leave. This is her apartment building," Jocelyn’s date said, struggling to keep confidence in his voice.

Derrick's tone reflected a sudden change of attitude, when he asked, "Who asked you for a residential run down?"

"Derrick, please. Greg is my date. He has to leave when I tell him to. You can't just come over here getting rid of my company."

Glaring at Greg, Derrick said stiffly, "Well, you tell him it's time to go once more, Jocelyn. As long as the brother gets out of here, I don't care whose instructions he's following."

Stubbornly, Jocelyn snapped, "I will not!"

Taking the one step necessary to breathe down on Greg, Derrick said sharply, "Get the hell out of here right now! Don't make me tell you again!"

Greg didn't move. Two things held him in the spot. The first being, Greg hated people telling him what to do. The second was the fear that had frozen him. He knew the best he could hope for was being able to run faster than Derrick.

"You stop it right now, Derrick!" Jocelyn said squeezing between them.

Derrick moved Jocelyn aside with one hand, the way he had done so many times in Dr. Kane's office. Derrick's other hand went to Greg's throat so swiftly, all Jocelyn had time to do was scream, "Derrick, don't you hurt him!"

Greg tugged at Derrick's thick wrist and it didn't budge. As a matter of fact, the pressure from Derrick's thumb seemed to be constricting his breathing. Greg was no fool. He knew that if he took a swing at Derrick, the pressure on his windpipe would increase and he would black out in about five seconds. Besides that, Greg was only five feet ten inches tall. He couldn't reach Derrick from where he was standing.

Putting both hands up, Greg whispered, "I'm out, Brother."

As if a switch had been thrown, Derrick opened his hand.

Looking at Jocelyn, a deflated Greg asked, "Are you going to be all right?"

Jocelyn nodded and apologized softly. Greg turned and walked toward his car. Jocelyn moved as if she were going to follow him. Derrick's hand reached out and held onto her arm.

Mad as hell, Jocelyn spun around and shouted, "Who the hell do you think you are?! You don't come over here running off my friends because you feel like it, Derrick Dawes! Go home! You make me sick!"

Still holding onto Jocelyn, Derrick said, "Please stop screaming, Jocelyn. I hate screaming."

"Who gives a shit what you hate! You make me sick and you're still standing here!"

Derrick didn't respond. He picked Jocelyn up, threw her over his shoulder and headed toward his car. She ranted as loud as she could the entire time. Before he put her into the car, Derrick asked if she would mind refraining from screaming until they got to his house. The answer was obviously, "No!"

Jocelyn yelled and cursed Derrick from her walkway to his. If she had something to poke him with she would have done that, too. The last time Jocelyn hit Derrick with her hand it stung, so that was out of the question.

Jocelyn's colorful bellowing alerted Sonya that they were coming. What she actually heard was, "What are you supposed to be?! A caveman! Am I supposed to do anything you want now that you've clubbed the competition and dragged me off to your cave?! I hate you, Derrick Dawes!"

Inside, Derrick said, "Thanks, Mom. I'll talk to you in the morning."

Smiling at the fuming Jocelyn, Sonya asked, "Do you want me to take the girls with me? They'll never stay asleep with all of that screaming."

Turning to Sonya, Jocelyn snapped angrily, "I can't believe you're going along with Derrick's behavior, Sonya. He embarrassed me. He choked my date!"

Alarmed, Sonya asked, "Did you hurt the man, Derrick?"

"No, Mom. He wouldn't have gotten choked if he had listened to Jocelyn in the first place. The man begged for twenty minutes with her saying 'No'. I just stepped out to help her get rid of him."

Jocelyn asked, "Did I ask for your help?! I don't need your help getting rid of anyone! Besides, I haven't seen hide nor hair of you in months! What do you want now anyway?!"

Sonya sighed and said, "I'm going home now, you two. Don't wake up Mia and Miranda. You'll both be sorry if you do."

The moment Sonya closed the front door behind her Derrick reached for Jocelyn. She squealed, hit at his hands and backed up. Ignoring her protests, Derrick picked her up and threw her over his shoulder again. With Jocelyn yelling to be put down, Derrick picked up a bottle of Chianti and two glasses. To her surprise, he didn't carry her up the stairs. Instead, he took his noisy guest down to the recreation room.

Sitting on the sofa, Derrick poured two glasses of wine. He handed one to a very angry Jocelyn. Scowling, she took it and put it down on the table. As long as she didn't throw it, Derrick could live with it.

Taking a sip from his glass, Derrick smiled and asked, "How are you, Jocelyn?"

Rolling her eyes, Jocelyn said sarcastically, "I'm fine. Why did you drag me over here?"

"Because I wanted to talk to you."

"We could have said whatever right there on my sidewalk. You didn't have to be rude."

"You didn't really think I was going to let good old Greg beg until you gave in, did you?"

Indignantly, Jocelyn said, "I wasn't going to give in. That's none of your business anyway."

"It is my business, Jocelyn. Can't have my future wife kissing other men. Sorry."

"Please, Derrick. Take me home. I don't want to hear your nonsense tonight."

"Not nonsense, Jocelyn. Fact. You have every right to be angry with me. I shouldn't have shut you out. It's just that when my world's off kilter, I can't share the problem. I have to work on that. Did you get my flowers?"

"Every day. I don't want flowers from the man I love, in lieu of his presence."

Knowing explanation was his only way out of this stalemate, Derrick said solemnly, "The problem was Angelique, Jocelyn."

"Oh, I knew there was a woman in the picture. I just didn't know which one it was." The odd expression on Derrick's face told Jocelyn volumes about what had transpired between him and Angelique. Jocelyn abandoned her accusatory language and asked, "Have you been served with some sort of change of custody papers, Derrick?"

"Not yet. I'm hoping she was just blowing off steam. She doesn't want One and Two. You know I'm sorry, Jocelyn. Hurting you wasn't what I wanted at all, but if she takes the twins away from me, I knew I would not be an easy person to get along with. And, I'm used to handling things alone. Burying things in the silence."

"If she takes them, Derrick, she won't just be taking them from you. No matter what our living arrangements are."

Another strange expression fell on Derrick's face, as he tilted his head. He shook his head, closed his eyes and let it fall. Jocelyn finally heard what he had. Shuffling feet and tiny voices calling, "Daddy. Dosh."

Leaving a pouting Derrick, Jocelyn rose and climbed the basement stairs. In the hallway, near the kitchen, two little heads peered at her through the railings. Jocelyn asked, "How did you two get down here?"

Mia and Miranda's pace quickened when they saw it really was Jocelyn. Miranda's hands went up for Jocelyn to pick her up first. Immediately stroking Jocelyn's hair, Miranda laid her head on her shoulder. Mia climbed up and duplicated her sister's actions. The three went down to the recreation room. Derrick couldn't believe neither baby wanted him. They fell asleep on Jocelyn's lap, kicking Derrick occasionally.

The conversation between Jocelyn and Derrick mellowed over the sleeping twins. It only threatened to flare up again when Derrick asked if that was the first time Jocelyn had dated good old Greg. Jocelyn's menacing stare told Derrick to let it go. When he thought the weight of One and Two made her look uncomfortable, Derrick picked up One. He reached for Two, but Jocelyn insisted she could carry her. Not thinking she wanted to go upstairs, Derrick let Jocelyn do as she pleased.

With both babies back in bed, Derrick silently eased out of the room. Jocelyn wasn't in the hallway. Derrick went down to the basement looking for her. She wasn't down there either. Maybe he had passed her in the kitchen. Derrick turned off the television and lights. Upstairs, he looked in the kitchen. No Jocelyn. Knowing she wouldn't be in the living room, Derrick checked it anyway. No Jocelyn.

Running up the stairs, Derrick checked the girl's bathroom. No Jocelyn. There was only one room left, Derrick's bedroom. But, why would she go in there? She didn't seem to have forgiven him that much yet.

The door was only slightly ajar. Derrick pushed it with his finger. Muted lighting over the mantle reflected on the bed and music played softly. Derrick hadn't turned on either. That was a promising sign for anyone born after Psycho. However, Derrick remembered it vividly. He laughed at himself when he thought, "Is it Norman, or Norman's mama?"

Jocelyn wasn't in bed. But, she had to be in this room or the bathroom. There was no place else for her to be. Derrick sat on the bed and waited to see what her next move would be.

God was good. Jocelyn came out of the bathroom. The pretty aqua dress she had worn on her date was gone. Now, dressed in one of the many silk nightgowns Derrick had given her, Jocelyn's face was make-up free and her hair pinned up.

Walking toward Derrick slowly, Jocelyn said, "It's time to stop talking and go to bed, Derrick."

Incredulously, Derrick asked, "You mean all I had to do was kidnap you and apologize?"

"Oh, you've got a lot more apologizing to do, Dawes. The fight's not over yet. Just this round."

Pulling his sweatshirt over his head, Derrick mumbled, "Good thing I got there when I did. Good old Greg might have begged his way in after all."

With one hand on her hip and an eyebrow arched villainously, Jocelyn said shortly, "No, he wouldn't have either."

"Why not? He didn't look that bad to me, kind of on the short side. That's all. You know he would have served the purpose."

With head and hair bouncing, Jocelyn asked angrily, "Did you just say he would have served the purpose, Derrick?"

Knowing he had said too much already, Derrick shrugged and said, "No, sweetheart, I didn't." He had learned how to lie like that from Ethan and his grandfather.

"Yes, you did. Let's get one thing straight, before you make me get dressed and leave you sitting here looking stupid. I don't do serve the purpose—make do, desperate, or lonely. I'm only doing you because I love you. Now, watch your mouth."

With Jocelyn standing between his legs and his hands on her hips, Derrick said, "I'm sorry."

Nuzzling his nose with hers and lightly kissing his lips, Jocelyn asked softly, "Sorry for what? I thought you said you didn't say it."

# *CHAPTER TWENTY-EIGHT*

It was anyone's guess which one had missed the other more. Derrick and Jocelyn's lovemaking took on the appearance of a highly charged and perverted wrestling match, which included biting, pinching, scratching and lots of flipping. One minute, he's on top. Then, she's on top. The sounds of the night consisted of grunts, groans, moans, hisses, pants, and yelps. The bed was soaking wet on both sides an hour after they started.

At eight the next morning, Derrick and Jocelyn's nude, abused and satiated bodies lie completely entwined beneath the crumpled sheet. Tired of calling Daddy, One dangled over Derrick's lifeless body and called, "Dosh." Two toddled around to Jocelyn's side of the bed, climbed up and played in Jocelyn's hair and face. Two kissed Jocelyn and Derrick, pointed out their boo boo's and stroked their faces lovingly. The thump of One falling off the bed woke Jocelyn.

Nearly knocking Two on the floor, Jocelyn leaned up and looked over Derrick. Good thing One didn't cry because Jocelyn couldn't have gotten to her. Between Derrick's death grip and Miranda, Jocelyn was hopelessly locked in.

One got up and made it around the bed. It was her intention to climb up next to her sister and Jocelyn. However, the ringing telephone distracted her. One couldn't wait to pick it up. She pulled the entire telephone down on the floor. Speaking into the receiver breathlessly, One said, "Hi."

The caller said, "Hi. Mia?"

One answered, "Huh?"

"Where's Daddy, sweetheart?"

Pointing at Derrick with the telephone, One said, "Daddy sheep, Unkie Dabid."

Jocelyn reached for the telephone. One shook her head and said, "No, Dosh. Daddy."

Unable to turn over to face One, Jocelyn smiled over her shoulder and said, "I know it's for Daddy, Mia. Give me the telephone, sweetheart. I'll talk to Uncle David for Daddy."

That must have sounded reasonable to One, she handed Jocelyn the telephone and said, "'kay."

Into the slightly moist telephone, Jocelyn said, "Hello."

A smug David said, "Well, hello, Nasty Nurse Avery. I take it my brother is indisposed."

"Yes, he is. Can I help you with anything?"

"Do you two have any plans for this afternoon?"

"Not that I know of. Why?"

"Hope wants to come over. She hasn't seen Mia and Miranda for a whole week."

"I'm sure that will be fine, David."

Thinking he had heard an edge in her voice, David asked, "Are you upset with me about something, Jocelyn?"

Flatly, Jocelyn said, "Not really."

"What does that mean?"

"It means whatever I am with you, it really doesn't matter."

"I know I'm supposed to dismiss that, but I won't. Please tell me whatever it is, Jocelyn. I'd really like to know."

In one word, Jocelyn explained, "Cassandra."

"Okay. Is there anyone left on the planet who doesn't know about that?"

"I doubt it."

"Did Derrick tell you?"

"I told Derrick."

"How did you know before him?"

"It really doesn't matter, David. If you see her again, I think you should know that Hope won't overlook it a second time."

David was on the verge of asking what Jocelyn would do if Derrick saw Cassandra again. But, he already knew the answer to that. Besides, Derrick really wasn't interested in any other women anymore. Or, at least he made everyone around him believe that.

Jocelyn pried herself free from Derrick and begged Mia for her discarded nightgown. She couldn't believe Derrick had actually flicked it that far away. Mia dragged the silk gown. As she moved across the room, she stroked it and said, "Pretty, Dosh. Pretty."

Sitting up, with Miranda peeking at her bare back, Jocelyn laughed nervously and slid the gown over her head. It took some doing but Jocelyn managed to get the gown all of the way down before she eased from beneath the sheet. Miranda's interest moved to her sleeping father. Derrick never wore anything on top when he slept, so what he wore under the sheet didn't intrigue the inquisitive little girl. Why he wasn't getting up with them confused Miranda though.

Jocelyn went to the closet and got a robe with Mia following her every move. Miranda climbed back up on the bed and started picking at Derrick's face. He never responded to her probing or calling. Jocelyn picked her up and took Mia by the hand. The three went down to the kitchen.

Downstairs, Mia and Miranda watched Jocelyn as if they wanted to ask what she was doing. Jocelyn prepared Cream of Wheat for them. She started a pot of coffee, poured juice into their spouted Disney glasses and put them down. Mia and Miranda both looked toward the stairs. This picture wasn't making any sense to them. No one ever fed them breakfast but Daddy, with the exception being Grammy Sonya, of course.

Mia and Miranda sat and stared at the bowls in front of them. Jocelyn asked, "What's wrong? I know you both eat Cream of Wheat. I've seen Derrick make it for you before."

Looking at the stairs to see what they were looking at, Jocelyn realized they expected Derrick to come down, too.

Smiling, Jocelyn said, "Okay, Mia and Miranda. Eat your breakfast Daddy's sleeping. He'll be down soon."

They didn't get it until Jocelyn actually put the first spoonful into their mouths herself. Then, the games were on. Mia and Miranda ate what they wanted and tried to smear each other with the rest. Jocelyn didn't stand for that though. She wasn't as much fun to eat with as Daddy. He let them do anything they wanted with what was left.

Jocelyn only drank a cup of coffee. She wanted to wait for Derrick to eat breakfast. Maybe he would be up by the time she cleaned the girls up and dressed them. All Jocelyn knew for sure, was she was glad to be back. She knew she didn't want to be with good old Greg. If Derrick hadn't shown up soon, she may have considered it though. Being with Derrick had definitely shown her how lonely she had been since Justine died. But, there were things about Derrick that Jocelyn didn't think good old Greg, or anybody else, could duplicate. And, boy, would she have missed them.

With both girls dressed, Jocelyn, Mia and Miranda went back to Derrick's bedroom. He was still asleep. Jocelyn sat down on the bed and shook him. Derrick mumbled something incomprehensible. Jocelyn shook him again. He grabbed her hand and held it. He never opened his eyes though.

Mia came over to Jocelyn with a Barney tape in her hand. She pointed at the television. Jocelyn asked, "Do you want to see Barney?"

Both girls clapped, laughed and said with unbridled excitement, "Barney, Dosh. Barney."

Jocelyn put the tape into the VCR. Mia and Miranda climbed up on the bed and propped themselves up on Derrick to watch. Seeing how raptly the tape held their attention, Jocelyn decided to take this opportunity to shower. She locked the bedroom door, so they wouldn't escape and get into God only knew what. Maybe Derrick would wake up while she was in the shower.

With hot water beating down on her skin, Jocelyn felt the sting of every passion mark. Miranda had already shown her several boo boos. Jocelyn didn't dare dally because she had no idea how long a Barney tape was. Jocelyn was glad to see that Derrick hadn't moved any of her things. If he had, he would have had to explain why.

Lotioned and tying her robe, Jocelyn was visited in the bathroom by Miranda. She had another Barney tape in her hand. That meant the other one was over. Jocelyn put it on promptly and lay down on the bed next to Derrick. He had covered his head with the pillow. When Mia and Miranda started singing with Barney, Jocelyn knew why Derrick had covered his head with the pillow.

Two tapes later, Jocelyn was singing with them. None of it bothered Derrick. He slept through it all. Jocelyn brushed her hair and enjoyed Barney, Mia and Miranda. In the office Jocelyn never had the opportunity to observe the silly purple dinosaur. Jocelyn's favorite was Baby Bop though. Every time Baby Bop showed up, Jocelyn got excited too.

During the fourth Barney tape, Jocelyn tried to wake Derrick again. She called, pushed and pinched. Derrick grabbed at her hands and said, "Stop, One and Two. Daddy's sleeping."

Jocelyn said, "It's time for Daddy to get up, Derrick. We've been up for hours."

With his head still under the pillow, Derrick mumbled, "Jocelyn, is that you?"

"Yes, Derrick. Who did you think I was?"

"One and Two. I thought I had dreamt last night. You really were here."

"Yes, I was. Now, get up. I'm waiting for you to eat breakfast. I've fed the girls already."

"You did? Where are they?"

"At your feet watching Barney."

"Oh, well they're happy campers. They'll watch that goofy thing all day. I hate Barney, Jocelyn. I could do really mean things to him, if given an opportunity."

"Don't let Mia and Miranda hear you say that. Get up."

Derrick lifted the sheet and Jocelyn stopped him. She hustled Mia and Miranda out of the room. In a sleep-laden stupor, Derrick had no idea he was naked, but when Jocelyn stopped him, Derrick laid still long enough to drift off again.

In the kitchen, Jocelyn turned on the television for Mia and Miranda. They were not happy with Nickelodeon at all. They wanted Barney. Jocelyn gave them another cup of juice and started making breakfast for herself and Derrick. The twins ignored the television and played in the corner with the toys Derrick kept there for them.

A half hour later, David and Hope came in. Jocelyn hadn't seen Hope in over a month and was truly surprised at how big she was already. It was hard to believe she was only five months pregnant. There was an unmistakable sadness in Jocelyn's eyes as she greeted Hope that complete strangers could interpret. Mia and Miranda met David with their usual enthusiastic, "Hi, Unkie Dabid. Daddy sheep."

Holding a twin on each arm, David said, "Daddy can't still be sleeping at noon. I'll have to go wake him up right now."

Mia and Miranda nodded their heads in agreement. David put the girls down and headed up the stairs. Hope sat at the kitchen table and smiled at Jocelyn.

Jocelyn smiled back and asked, "What's so funny, Hope?"

"Oh, nothing. I'm just surprised to see you here."

"Yeah. Me too. Do you believe he interrupted my date last night? Choked him and dragged me over here?"

"No. That sounds more like something David would do than Derrick. Did the police come?"

"Jesus no, Hope. I would have died of embarrassment, if they had."

"David would have held out for them. He never half does anything."

Giving Hope a serious look, Jocelyn asked, "Are things going okay now?"

"It depends on what you call okay. I came back to torture him, Jocelyn, and to keep that slut out of my house. If I see her after I have this baby I'm planting both of these swollen feet in her ass."

Jocelyn laughed hysterically and said, "I'm truly anti-violence, Hope, but if you need me to hold her while you do it, give me a call."

Hope laughed and said, "You're on. How are things going with you two? I heard Derrick was in one of his black moods."

"We'll be fine, if Derrick learns not to lock me out, Hope. I'm not one to be ignored for long periods of time. I know he was upset and afraid about the babies. But, I didn't do it. And, she hasn't even done what she said."

"Do you really think she's going to do anything, Jocelyn? I don't. I don't think that woman wants anything to do with those babies. If she cared even a little, she would have come forward before now. I could not know what was happening to my baby. Even though I know David would take good care of it."

"Well, it's been over a month and he hasn't been served with any papers. She could have forged a decent set with crayons by now. I don't think she's going to do anything either."

"Do you think Derrick slept with her, Jocelyn? Maybe that's why there are no papers."

Giving that the briefest of thoughts, Jocelyn said bluntly, "No, I don't. I think he wanted to wring her neck and the frustration of not being able to do it pushed him over the edge. She wants to play games with him. What she doesn't understand is that Derrick won't play when it comes to Mia and Miranda."

Hope laughed and said, "Maybe I'll get to hold her while you plant both of your feet in her ass. I'm really tired of these sluts messing up our business."

"You just don't forget that they can't mess up our business unless David and Derrick allow them to. Don't go blaming it all on the women, Hope. Even if they are sluts and can't help it."

Jocelyn and Hope laughed so hard they had to hold onto each other. One and Two looked up at them and started to laugh too. David and Derrick were having an entirely different discussion upstairs. Derrick couldn't believe what his brother was proposing.

David walked into the bedroom. Derrick lay sleeping on his back with the pillow over his face. David yelled, "Damn it, Derrick, it's afternoon! Get up!"

Derrick popped straight up in bed. He frowned at David and asked, "Who let you in? Where's One and Two?"

"Downstairs with Jocelyn and Hope. Get up. I want to ask you a question."

"Why do I have to get up for you to ask me a question? And, before you ask, the answer is; I don't have it, no, or I don't know."

"Very funny, Butt-head. I've come to ask you a serious qucstion and you're playing. Now, listen to this. When are you planning to marry Jocelyn?"

Shaking his head, Derrick twisted his face and asked, "What?"

"When are you planning to marry Jocelyn?"

Taking a deep breath, Derrick asked, "Who told you I was marrying Jocelyn?"

"A birdie. You've been with Jocelyn longer than you've been with anybody in years. I know you wouldn't marry anyone but Jocelyn. With the exception being the nut woman who left One and Two at the hospital. And, you would have married her, if she had kept her skirt on a few more minutes. Besides that, I know you, Derrick. You love Jocelyn. And, don't bother denying it. I hate it when you lie. So, all I want to know is when."

"Okay. Why?"

Mumbling, David said, "Because I want us to do it together."

Confused, Derrick asked, "You want us to do what together?"

"Get married."

Shaking his head, Derrick pulled the cover back and got out of bed saying, "Oh, no. No. No. No. I get into trouble by myself. You get into trouble by yourself. Forget it, David. You need to get married right now. I don't have to."

David followed his naked brother into the bathroom whining, "Aw c'mon, Derrick. I would do it for you."

"Get the hell out of here, David. You wouldn't double date with me. No."

Ignoring Derrick, David kept begging while his brother relieved himself, brushed his teeth and got into the shower. David told Derrick he just couldn't get married by himself. He didn't really know why. But, if Derrick did it too, he thought he could do it.

Derrick slid the shower door open a little and said, "Let me get this straight. If I agree to do it with you, you think you can do it. What happens if you can't, David? Do I get to marry Hope and Jocelyn?"

"We're not Mormons and that's illegal, Derrick. Aw c'mon. You're going to marry Jocelyn soon anyway. Why not do it in a double ceremony? Mom would love it."

Through the stall door, Derrick yelled, "No! Get out of here, David!"

David was sitting on the hamper when Derrick stepped out of the shower. He looked at his older brother and said, "You know, I just thought you were insane when we were growing up. All of those times you talked me into bringing your back-up girlfriends to this party or that game. With me being the one who always wound up being blamed for everything that went wrong. But, now I know you're insane."

"I know you're not still crying about any of that, Derrick. You got to sleep with three of those four back-up girlfriends. I didn't hear any complaints then, little brother. If memory serves me well, you loved consoling my old girlfriends.

"Besides, I'm not asking you to marry Hope. I'm just asking you to be there with me."

"I can be your best man, David."

"I don't want you to be my best man. I want you to get married, too."

"Why?"

With a thick white towel wrapped around his waist, Derrick stood shaving in the mirror. David looked at his brother and tried to think of an answer Derrick would swallow. There was none. So, he decided to try the truth. Or, as close to it as David could get with a straight face.

"I want the games to be over for both of us at the same time."

"Oh bullshit, this is more of David's misery needing company."

"Are you saying you'll be miserable married to Jocelyn, Derrick?"

"No. I don't think I would be miserable. I'll get married to her when I'm ready. Do you think you're going to be miserable being married to Hope?"

"After this Cassandra crap? Are you kidding? I haven't slept well since Hope came home."

"Why? Is she threatening to kill you in your sleep?"

"No. She's mean enough when I'm awake to let me know she could kill me in my sleep. If she could handle ruining the baby's life before it was born, she would too. I tried to touch her in bed one night and she stuck me with something sharp. I still don't know what it was."

Derrick howled with laughter. Hope was torturing his brother and he loved it. Derrick knew Hope wouldn't really hurt him. She loved David's sick ass. His games. Letting Cassandra pretend to be her friend was the straw. If Hope wasn't pregnant David would be regretting his little transgression even more. Hope would parade a line of guys past David that would drive him insane. Every last one would be one of his best friends, or his worse enemies. And, Hope knew them all.

Still laughing, Derrick asked, "Are you getting married so you can touch Hope again?"

"Well, yeah, that too. But, that's not the only reason. I can't have my kid coming here without a legitimate father."

"Do you love Hope, David?"

Grimacing, David said, "You know I love Hope, Derrick. Why does everybody insist I say it every ten minutes? Do you tell Jocelyn you love her every day?"

"Yes, I do, even when I'm not talking to her. I write it down and send it to her."

"Oh, you're sickening, Derrick. Will you do it, or not?"

"I don't think so, David."

Giving Derrick that sly look he was famous for, David asked, "Will you do it if Jocelyn wants to?"

Derrick's head snapped in David's direction when he said, "Don't you dare do that."

## *CHAPTER TWENTY-NINE*

David did not have to broach the subject of a double wedding with Jocelyn. He had already masterfully drilled the idea into Hope's psych for a few days, pointed her in Jocelyn's direction and let Hope do what he knew she would. Jocelyn merely smiled and replied, "Derrick hasn't asked me to marry him, Hope. I don't know how to answer a question like that."

Slowly rolling her exotic brown eyes and giving her teeth a quick loud suck, Hope looked at Derrick and asked, "What's taking you so long to propose? Waiting for a Cassandra moment?"

Jocelyn laughed and said, "I don't think he's waiting for her, Hope. She's been through here already."

Scanning the three with a frown of distaste, Derrick replied with sarcasm, "Everybody's going to be leaving soon. Right?"

"Not me, sweetheart. I'm not with them," Jocelyn said from her position on his lap.

Jocelyn's robe fell open exposing her bare thigh. Derrick followed David's brazenly interested gaze as it wandered the length of Jocelyn's bare foot and long and shapely leg. His expression was one of lustful approval and anticipation.

Angry with David again, Derrick said sharply, "That's why you stay in so much trouble, David! Nothing gets past you!"

Patting Jocelyn's back, Derrick said, "You, go upstairs and get dressed. Why aren't you dressed anyway?"

"How was I supposed to get dressed? I had Mia and Miranda by myself all morning. I was lucky to get a shower."

Not waiting for Derrick's response, Jocelyn popped up and stomped up the stairs. The expression on her face wasn't pleasant. Glaring at David, Derrick said, "Now, look what you've done. She just started talking to me. She'll probably be going out with good old Greg again this week."

Perplexed, David asked, "Who the hell is good old Greg?"

Derrick didn't answer. He got up and followed Jocelyn up the stairs. In his bedroom, he found her tossing things around in a drawer and talking to herself. Derrick closed the bedroom door and as an afterthought, he turned and locked it.

The click made Jocelyn look around and she asked angrily, "What do you want now, Derrick? I'm getting dressed, like I was told."

"Your robe fell open and David was staring at your legs. That's why I said that. I'm sorry if it sounded like I was telling you what to do. But, I was. And, I meant it."

Jocelyn's frown said it all. She had no idea what was with Derrick today. He was sorry if it sounded that way, but he meant it. How does one reply to that? Talking to herself again, Jocelyn said, "Just don't bother. Get dressed and forget he said anything at all. Or, get dressed and go home. That way you won't have to try to decipher anymore of Derrick Dawes' scrambled messages."

Derrick walked over to where Jocelyn was leaning over the drawer and embraced her. He massaged her stomach. The heat and motion of his hands caused a silky stirring in Jocelyn's abdomen. Biting her lower lip and closing her eyes, Jocelyn slapped his hand. That didn't stop Derrick. Bending over Jocelyn, he squeezed her tightly and kissed the top of her head.

Weakly, Jocelyn complained, "Stop, Derrick. I'm doing as I was told and you're distracting me."

"Yeah, I know. You haven't kissed me today. Does that mean you don't love me anymore?"

"No. It means private, intimate moments are at a minimum in this house. I can't even expose a limb around here."

Nibbling Jocelyn's ear, Derrick whispered, "You can expose anything you'd like now, sweetheart. I locked the door."

The room temperature skyrocketed. Derrick's hot, wet kisses in Jocelyn's ear and down her neck began. His hands ignited tiny exciting fires beneath her robe. Letting her head dangle back onto his chest, Jocelyn parted her lips and received Derrick's kiss up-side down.

That was one of many defining moments for Jocelyn. There was only one explanation for Jocelyn's acceptance of Derrick's irrational, rude, insensitive and stubborn behavior. She truly loved Derrick Dawes. He could not talk to her if he didn't want to, boss her around, run her dates off and make love to her anytime he felt like it. And, she didn't give a damn what anybody had to say about it.

And make love they did. Derrick undressed and sat on the side of the already disheveled bed. Jocelyn's robe slid to the floor, as she straddled and lowered herself onto his lap. They both struggled to keep the noise down, but Jocelyn couldn't suppress an occasional high-pitched squeal or two. Derrick leaned back on his elbows, moaned, panted and called Jocelyn's name from time to time. He loved the way Jocelyn always let him start things and then took over. Sexually, she was as aggressive as Derrick and she didn't care if he knew that either.

Neither Derrick nor Jocelyn heard Miranda's constant calls from the bottom of the stairs. David picked up Mia and Miranda and carried them both down to the recreation room. Not knowing the Barney trick, David had to play with them. Of course, he didn't mind. They seldom got upset stomachs anymore when Uncle David flipped them up-side down.

After bathing again, dressing and making the bed, Derrick and Jocelyn joined the group in the recreation room. With her sweat soaked hair pulled up into a ponytail, Jocelyn wore a pair of jeans she had left in Derrick's closet and one of his sweatshirts. Derrick simply redressed in his sweats.

Mia and Miranda ran and squealed at the sight of them. Mia climbed Derrick and clutched his neck. That meant she had no intentions of letting him out of her sight anytime soon. He hadn't given her enough individual attention for the day.

Miranda tugged at Jocelyn's shirt, pointed at David and said, "Unkie Dabid say no, Dosh. No." She shook her head from side to side to emphasize the word.

Picking up the obviously distressed child, Jocelyn asked, "Why did you say no, Uncle David?"

Not taking his eyes off of the video game he was playing, David said, "She wanted to come upstairs with you and Derrick. I didn't think that was such a good idea."

Derrick mumbled, "He finally got one right."

Jocelyn stroked Miranda's curls and said, "It's okay, sweetheart. We're here now. And, we're here to stay for a while."

Looking at Derrick, Jocelyn asked, "What are we eating, Derrick? I'm starving."

Abandoning his plan to go get a haircut, Derrick asked if everyone wanted Chinese. Hope said, "Sure. As long as I can have a hot dog first."

"What's a hot dog got to do with anything?" Derrick asked with a twisted frown.

David said, "She eats a hot dog with everything, Derrick. And, don't ask any more questions about Hope's eating habits. I'm sure there will be some. Just don't ask."

Pointing up, Derrick said, "There's plenty hot dogs in the freezer, Hope. As a matter of fact, I'll put one on for you and the girls."

"Two for me, Derrick," Hope offered quickly.

With Mia and Miranda at his heels, Derrick went up to the kitchen. He called in a delivery order at the Chinese restaurant in the Mall and put on hot dogs. Immediately after hanging up the telephone rang. Derrick picked it up and the moment he heard Roger's voice, he thought the worse.

Totally disregarding customary amenities, Derrick asked, "What's she done, Roger?"

"Nothing that I know of, Derrick. You'll know before me. She has no idea I'm your attorney. They'll notify you. I just wanted to make sure you were keeping your nose clean. No new bones in your closets. No aberrant behavior patterns developing. Your image is all you've got going in this. If she has any real dirt on you, it's all over."

"What about her dirt?"

"Mothers take on a Mary personae in the eyes of the court. You know, Jesus' mother. You don't throw dirt on the mother of Jesus, Derrick."

"Oh, but they can throw it on Jesus?"

"If you recall, they did more than that to poor Jesus. Nailed him without a stiff drink or a decent blindfold. Are the babies in good health?"

"Other than an occasional hickey on their heads, they're fine."

"How do they get hickeys?"

"Flipping and jumping off of things they shouldn't, Roger. You don't have any children, do you?"

"Yes. I have three girls. If they ever had a hickey, I was too tired to notice. Anyway, try to keep the hickeys to a minimum too. Call me the minute you're served. And, there's one thing I have to ask you again. Are you sure this Angelique Kelly is the mother?"

"As sure as I can be. Why?"

"Some things aren't jelling for me. She was separated from her husband during the time of the pregnancy. But, no one she worked with noticed any weight gain. There is absolutely no record of any prenatal care. Here, or in Denver. I checked in her real name and the one she gave at the hospital. But she was on vacation for six weeks when the girls were born. Where she went for those six weeks is also a major mystery–giving her ample opportunity to deliver them and recuperate."

"Maybe she hid the weight, Roger. Women are good at doing that."

"Do you know what pregnant women look like, Man? They couldn't hide that, if they wanted to. Twins? Never.

There's something else you should be prepared for. Her husband, Aaron, looks a great deal like you. I thought he was David in the photograph I saw of him. Did you have the DNA tests done?"

"Yes."

"Well, what were the results?"

"I don't know. I didn't read it."

"What are you waiting for?"

Looking at One and Two fighting over his pant leg and then touching each other's hair, Derrick said, "I'm waiting to see if it's really necessary. Other than this mess, it doesn't matter what it says."

"Okay, Derrick. There's one other little piece of information that may, or may not, fall in your favor. Mr. and Mrs. Aaron Kelly were trying to conceive a couple years ago and failed. They were looking into the problem with a fertility doctor named Lamar Jessup. His secretary told me, under wraps, that the problem was Aaron's. They thought it was cleared up, but Angelique never conceived. Just be prepared for anything, Derrick."

"I will."

Giving One and Two another look of pure adoration, Derrick said softly, "So, good old Aaron was shooting blanks. You're mine. I don't have to read the results."

From behind him, Jocelyn asked, "Who is good old Aaron? And, what kind of blanks did he shoot?"

"Aaron is Angelique's husband. He's had a fertility problem. Roger says for me to be prepared for anything."

"If you really want to know if they're your babies, Derrick, all you have to do is read the results."

"I don't want to read the results, Jocelyn. They're mine now. And, that's that."

"Excuse me, Mr. Dawes. Did you order dinner?"

"Yes. Did those two pounce on you about that double wedding stuff?"

"Yes and no. Heavy hinting should cover it."

"What do you really think about it, Jocelyn?"

"Like I said, Derrick. You haven't asked me yet."

"You know I intend to though. Don't you?"

"Before last night, I didn't know if you intended to speak to me again. Marrying me wasn't on the table."

"Waving his hand in impatience, Derrick said, "Yeah. But, before then, didn't you know I intended to ask you?"

"No."

"Well, will you?"

"Will I what?"

Angrily, Derrick snapped, "Marry me, Jocelyn."

"Oh, this is a proposal?"

"Yes."

Blowing on the piece of hot dog she'd stolen from the pot, Jocelyn said nonchalantly, "I guess the answer is yes then, Derrick. Are we doing it with David and Hope?"

Mumbling, Derrick said, "Only if we have to."

"No, we don't have to. But in case you're interested, they're doing it the Wednesday evening before Thanksgiving."

Dumbstruck, Derrick shouted, "That's next week! We don't have a license! We can't do it with them!"

"We can apply for one on Monday. It only takes a day for them to process the paperwork. Dr. Willows can do our blood tests. He loves drawing your blood, Derrick."

Looking at Jocelyn seriously, Derrick asked, "Do you really want to do it with them?"

Smiling, Jocelyn said, "It would be different. As long as we don't have to spend the night with them, I don't mind at all."

Giving it a little thought, Derrick said, "We can do it on one condition."

"What's that?"

"We won't tell David we're doing it. I want him to think he's facing the henchman alone."

Jocelyn yelled, "The henchman?! If that's the way you feel about it, forget it!"

Derrick tried to walk over to Jocelyn, but with One and Two holding onto his legs, he couldn't move. He motioned with his finger for her to come to him. Pouting and rolling her eyes, Jocelyn complied.

When she was close enough, Derrick wrapped his arms around her. One and Two wrapped an arm each around her legs. Looking directly into Jocelyn's eyes, Derrick said, "I'd face ten henchmen empty-handed for you, Jocelyn. I love you."

Lowering his lips onto hers, Derrick and Jocelyn forgot all about the two little girls hugging their legs. Never referring to themselves as me, Mia pulled at Derrick's pants and said, "Kiss One, Daddy." Miranda did likewise saying, "Kiss Two, Daddy."

With Derrick's tongue still in her mouth, Jocelyn giggled and muttered, "Yeah. And, then take them to the bathroom before you have to change their pull-ups, Daddy."

## *CHAPTER THIRTY*

Having to give up more blood did not endear the idea of marriage to Derrick. He had lost track of why he had given up so much blood since he met Jocelyn. After all, this was the third time in less than a year. Anger made Derrick's mouth twitch in his hypodermic psycho haze. As a matter of fact, he started an argument that threatened to completely cancel the tentative wedding plans.

After being subjected to another round of what he referred to as mandatory therapeutic vampirism, Derrick pouted and rolled his sleeve down. Jocelyn shook her head and smiled at her big handsome baby. With Derrick's vial labeled, she happily extended her arm for Dr. Willow to draw her blood.

Just as Dr. Willow removed the needle from Jocelyn's vein, Derrick asked sarcastically, "Since I never got to use the last blood test, if the marriage doesn't work, will I get any of this back?"

Startled stiff by Derrick's statement, Jocelyn stared at him silently for a few seconds. Surely, he intended to laugh and apologize. He had to know what he said was minimally inappropriate and ultimately incorrect. Derrick sat with his arms crossed and the scowl he always had on his face when he hadn't slept long enough. He gave no chuckle or an apology.

With genuine anger, Jocelyn glared at Derrick and spewed, "Give it back to him right now, Dr. Willow!"

"Why are you yelling like that, Jocelyn? I was just joking. Sort of." Derrick asked, shocked and puzzled by her reaction.

Dangerous flames glinted in her eyes, when Jocelyn screeched, "What?! Is your memory really that short, Derrick?! Is that why you didn't know who Mia and Miranda's mother was?!"

Allowing some of his own anxiety to hit the air, Derrick yelled back, "What are you talking about now, Jocelyn?! What has one thing got to do with the other?!"

Silently and protectively, Dr. Willow took the precious vials out of harm's way. He knew a case of wedding jitters when he saw it. If given the opportunity, Jocelyn would throw the vials against the wall, or pour their contents down the drain. Dr. Willow would have to draw them all over again, after the storm. Not today. They only had enough time for the fight.

Racked with laughter, Dr. Willow fell against the wall in the foyer when Jocelyn said, "It's the same thing, Derrick! Do you know where babies come from?! Do I need to explain it to you?!"

Not liking the direction of this discussion, Derrick lowered his voice when he said with syrupy sarcasm, "No, you don't have to explain anything to me. I just don't see what One and Two have to do with any of this."

With one arched eyebrow raised and arms crossed, Jocelyn asked, "What was the last blood test for, Derrick?"

Without hesitation, he recited automatically, "Communicable diseases. So we could have unprotected sex."

"And, have we?"

Absolutely confident of his answer, Derrick responded crisp and clearly, "No."

Screaming spastically, Jocelyn said, "Derrick Dawes, either you're a really good liar, or you're the biggest shit-head this side of the sun! What have you been doing all weekend?! Did you call that protected?! Would you like to share the prayer you used with me?! Maybe it only works if both the woman and man say it! Maybe that's what happened with Mia and Miranda! You said it all by yourself!"

Giving the time spent with Jocelyn over the weekend serious thought, Derrick moaned miserably and ran his hand over his face. For the life of him, Derrick couldn't remember reaching toward his nightstand once. "That's not what happened with them. I didn't use anything this weekend though, did I? Did you?" Derrick frowned and mumbled.

"Now is a good time to ask, Derrick. The answer is no. I wasn't prepared to be swept off my feet, but you probably don't remember not talking to me for over a month either. So, if I'm pregnant, does that mean we have to go through the entire paternity thing again? It might be good old Greg's."

Feeling like a complete idiot, Derrick gave a twisted smirk. Still not thinking clearly of the consequences of what he was saying, Derrick sighed and said, "I've let David push me into another spot I'm not sure of."

Truly disappointed to hear him say that, Jocelyn said softly, "Let's just forget it then, Derrick. I don't want to do anything you're not sure of. It's a lifelong commitment for me. I've already been disappointed once. To go into it with someone who feels like they're being pressured is a waste."

Feeling Jocelyn move away from him emotionally snapped Derrick back to reality. He stood and crossed the room in one giant step. Sliding his arms around her waist, Derrick pulled a rigid unresponsive Jocelyn close to him. He stroked her back, nuzzled and kissed the top of her head.

In the stillness of the brightly lit, gaily decorated examination room, Jocelyn listened to Derrick's heartbeat. She closed her eyes and let the strong, steady rhythm lull her. The deep-seated peace and security Jocelyn found in Derrick's heartbeat could only be found in someone you loved absolutely. It flourishes and grows in the rich hallowed field of destiny's ordained love.

In Sonya's words, "True love runs deep. It possesses irresistible beauty, caresses the tormented sounds of hell and makes you think they're heaven's harps. It smoothes the unpaved roads of life, makes Spam taste good and the contents unimportant. If it's done right."

That ever- elusive soul mate for Jocelyn, meant Derrick. Tears filled her tightly closed eyes and spilled silently onto her cheeks. If Jocelyn had not loved and lost Justine, she never would have recognized how much more she loved Derrick. To hear him say he was being pressured to marry her, by David of all people, was heart-wrenching.

So absorbed in her own thoughts, Jocelyn barely heard Derrick say, "I'm sorry I said that, Jocelyn. That's not what I meant at all. You know I love you, don't you, sweetheart?"

Resting her forehead on his chest, Jocelyn said, "I can't tell you what I know when it comes to you, Derrick. You change more than any man I've ever known. If you didn't want to get married, you shouldn't have asked. Or, asked and offered a date in the future. I didn't do anything to make you think I wanted, or needed, to be married right this minute. I haven't complained about not having enough time, or anything else. Truthfully, we didn't give this any real thought. Let's just start over and discuss it later."

"We're not going back, Jocelyn. We're getting married sometime this week and that's that. We can do it with, or without David and Hope. You tell me which way you want it."

Looking up at Derrick with eyes brimming in tears, Jocelyn said, "As long as I end up with you, I really don't have a preference, Derrick. I love you just that much."

Tightening his grip on Jocelyn, Derrick said, "You know I feel the same way, as long as I end up with you. So, you want to torture David or not?"

Smiling mischievously, Jocelyn said, "You won't be happy, if you don't. We'll torture David."

With the completed license application at Dr. Willow's office, all Derrick had to worry about was a ring. Because Jocelyn had not been properly proposed to and given an engagement ring, Sonya felt her wedding band should be elaborate. Derrick said she wouldn't be able to work with it. Sonya's remedy for that problem was, "Oh, you can afford to throw in an everyday, go to work wedding band, Derrick. But, when I see the child on Sundays, I'd like to see what you thought of her reflecting chandelier lights. I know you're not going to let David show you up on this one. I'm not worried about it."

Derrick decided her wedding band should be diamonds and sapphires. He thought Jocelyn would like the fact that he remembered her birthstone. The wide band of pave' sapphires, lounging between two carats of channel set diamond baguettes should reflect enough chandelier light for Sonya. It had cost so much, Derrick considered suggesting his mother remove some of the bulbs in her chandelier. A thin gold band Jocelyn could wear everyday came with it.

After receiving a formal dress down from Sonya, David was told there would be no marriage ceremony performed on Wednesday. They could do it on Thanksgiving Day, before dinner, of course, so that all immediate family members could be present. If both of their sons were getting married, Sonya wanted family and pictures. Thanksgiving dinner would serve as the reception meal. Ethan agreed and mumbled loudly, "Now, if only I can find someone to do it at home, over an already scheduled meal with Deandra."

Jocelyn managed to do the things she wanted to do for her wedding day and stay reasonably calm. Of course, she insisted Dr. Kane and his receptionist, Olivia, attend. They both promised they would come for the ceremony and take the newlyweds out to dinner before the New Year came in.

Jocelyn pondered calling her mother and dismissed the idea twice. The two women had very little in common and saw eye to eye on absolutely nothing. They spoke in civil distant tones only on major holidays. When Justine died, no consoling conversation or touch passed between them. Just a constant string of, "I told you he was irresponsible and not worth the marriage license," stares. Like their wedding, no one in her family, except her grandmother, had attended

Justine's funeral services. Now that her grandmother was gone, Jocelyn had no family she cared to share with.

The fact that Justine left Jocelyn the substantial sum of two hundred and fifty thousand dollars in life insurance didn't even lighten her mother's judgment of him. According to Mrs. Preston, he owed Jocelyn that much for squandering her time and virginity.

At Derrick's house on Monday evening, Jocelyn asked, "Should I call my mother? Maybe tell her I'm getting married? I know it's too late for an actual invitation. She probably won't want to attend anyway. Think I'm marrying another waste of human flesh."

Shaking his head slowly, Derrick responded, "My life wouldn't be worth living if I got married without telling Sonya and Ethan. So, I can't help you with that decision."

Slightly irritated, without understanding why, Jocelyn said bitingly, "Well, I don't have the kind of relationship with my mother that you have with yours. Sonya is a mother. My mother is a benefactor. She pays for everything. Offers absolutely no emotional input. Then, moans and groans her complaints for the remainder of your life."

Giving a weak little laugh, Derrick said, "Your mother can't possibly have a complaint about you, Jocelyn. You've done remarkably well with your life. There are some things no one has any control over. No matter what the so-called experts write in books."

"That's easy for you to say, sweetheart. You love me the way I am."

Lovingly, Derrick squeezed Jocelyn and massaged her sides, as he said, "Sure do. And, I can't imagine what more anyone else could have wanted from you either."

"For openers, I could have been my father's child. Since I'm not, I was shipped south, to be hidden in the woods with my grandmother and every other unfortunate cousin I had."

Not knowing if he wanted to step into this, but feeling Jocelyn wanted him to, Derrick asked, "Are you saying your father isn't your father, Jocelyn? Seriously?"

"Yes. My real father is East Indian. Not even an American. When I was born with a strange complexion, people adjusted. Hell, Black babies come in all kinds of colors. After all, I was sort of brown. Just not a shade they were familiar with. It wasn't until they realized my way too black hair was never going to curl that the questions started flying around.

"My mother's in-laws started whispering that there was a white man in the mix. That's when my mother shipped me to her mother. Her husband was always very nice to me. He saw that I was well taken care of and educated. Boxes and boxes of anything I may have needed arrived every other month like clockwork. Unlike the other children stored at my grandmother's house, if I got sick, I was taken to a doctor. They went to clinics. I went to a dentist twice a year. If the State didn't provide it, they didn't get it.

"This didn't set well with my cousins. They gave me hell every time my grandmother turned her back. The fact that Grandma made me work right along with everybody else and slapped my mouth if I said a word out of place like everybody else didn't appease them one bit. I won't even tell you what all they did to me, Derrick."

Derrick knew it must have been horrendous because there were tears in Jocelyn's eyes when she said, "Mia and Miranda are so lucky to have been born together. No matter what happens, they'll always have each other."

Trying to put the best spin on a bad situation, Derrick offered, "Maybe your mother did that to protect you from an even worse fate, sweetheart."

Cynically, Jocelyn laughed and said, "My mother did that to protect my mother. She has four other children I've never been good enough to eat a bologna sandwich with, Derrick. I don't know much of anything about any of them. I doubt if they know I exist at all.

"My mother and her husband stopped in to see me every now and then. They met and completely disapproved of Justine in a flash. The more my grandmother raved about him, the more they disapproved. He was way too fast and irresponsible for the little illegitimate girl. The truth was he was too poor. They intended for me to go to college, find a nice, respectable, rich guy and get out of their hair."

Suddenly, as if she hadn't realized she was talking, Jocelyn stopped and said, "No, I'm not taking myself on that trip. I'll just invite a couple friends, if your mother won't mind."

Lovingly stroking Jocelyn's back, Derrick said, "I'm sure she won't mind, sweetheart."

The weddings went off on Thanksgiving as planned—as planned by Derrick. David angrily accepted his younger brother's presence as his best man. Because Hope's sister stood in as her maid of honor Jocelyn was not missed by David.

Derrick watched his elder brother pout, stomp and sweat his way through the little ceremony in the den, and reveled in every familiar, "I could break your neck," glance David sent his way. Derrick handed over Hope's wedding ring, with a smile, as scripted. He was the first to kiss the bride and shake his brother's hand after the brief, somewhat chaste, ceremonial kiss.

When all of the congratulations died down, Derrick asked David to join him near the fireplace again. The exact spot they had stood in less than half an hour before. Because the minister was in his original spot, David thought this was going to be some spiritual thing Sonya demanded and he was unfamiliar with. The fact that the center of the room was cleared again and *The First Time Ever I Saw Your Face* played softly, didn't give David a clue, and his mother's quiet sobbing only elicited a confused frown from David. When Deandra escorted Mia and Miranda, who still had bouts of not walking too well, dressed in beautiful pink chiffon dresses with delicate flowers at the waist and hems, down the aisle, no bell rang for David.

Jocelyn's appearance in the doorway, dressed in a beautiful cream colored, beaded and sequined, off the shoulder dress and a matching halo adorning her lustrous black hair, brushed back and caressing her shoulders; didn't even rattle David's marbles. The elaborately ribboned pink and cream floral arrangement Jocelyn carried was breathtaking. David tipped his head in Derrick's direction and asked, "What are the flowers for?"

Grinning from ear to ear, Derrick said, "That's her bridal bouquet, David."

Still not up to speed, David said, "The wedding's over. And, the bridal bouquet was red, not pink and white."

Derrick gave his brother a quick "*You can't be that stupid*" glance and silently pressed Jocelyn's wedding ring into his hand.

Staring at the ring in his palm for what seemed like a very long time to Derrick, David suddenly asked loudly, "How much did this cost, Boy?! Do you know it glows in the dark?! Damn!"

The room erupted in laughter—everyone except Derrick. Jocelyn stopped momentarily to chuckle herself. David's mumbling through the entire ceremony distracted the bride and groom several times. He distracted the minister when he said, "I know why Cane slew Abel, Derrick. He tried to make his brother look bad every chance he got."

After a much more romantically intense kiss than the one shared by David and Hope, Deandra released the two highly agitated and fidgeting babies. One made it to Derrick without falling. Two took a spill and needed assistance. She pulled up her dress and showed Jocelyn her new boo boo.

Now that Jocelyn was a legal member of the family, Aunt Sylvia felt perfectly comfortable asking her, "What the hell are you, Jocelyn?"

Tired of a lifetime of answering that same stupid question, Jocelyn smiled demurely and said, "I'm Derrick's wife."

With quite a few brandies in them, Derrick and David got a big kick out of Jocelyn's response. Giving each other a high five, they nodded and said, "Damn good answer!"

Ethan ducked behind a wall and laughed at his sister's facial expression. She hated not being taken seriously more than anything in the world. And, Ethan had taught his sons to never take her seriously.

Not to be left out, Gran put in her prophetic two cents. Never able to talk about Jocelyn without touching her in the most intimate ways, Gran patted Jocelyn's breasts and said, "She's got plenty up here, Derrick." Then, touching Jocelyn's tiny waist and stroking her hips she said, "But this girl ain't got nothing on the bottom. She can't carry no baby in that little belly or them little hips."

Pop rallied and said, "What you talking about now, Tiny? That girl makes two of you in any way you want to look at her, and you carried four great big babies."

Shaking her head, Gran said, "Naw, my waist ain't never been that little."

Not liking the look of concern on Derrick and Jocelyn's faces, Sonya said cheerfully, "Be quiet, Tiny. Jocelyn can carry anything anybody else can carry."

Shaking her head in disagreement, Gran held her peace after that exchange. There was no more baby talk. It moved to something even more embarrassing. Sex. They teased David relentlessly about having to beg all night and then having to be careful if he got it. Then, Pop and Ethan told everybody Derrick would get the job done, but he had drank so much that he wouldn't remember, and he wouldn't wake up to refresh his memory tomorrow either. They howled with laughter. Jocelyn joined them because she knew Derrick wouldn't wake up before tomorrow evening, too.

At the conclusion of the evening, Ethan gave David and Derrick keys. His gift to them was the weekend in Bridal Suites, at opposite ends of the hall, at the Hilton Hotel. This meant the two happy, intoxicated brothers had to make it home, pack a bag and maneuver their way to town, without getting caught driving. Hope and Jocelyn shared a quick look of disgust and took the car keys from them.

## *CHAPTER THIRTY-ONE*

A little after noon on Friday Jocelyn tried to turn over, and as usual, Derrick impeded any genuine movement. She had to take a deep breath and push real hard to get him to move. Bumping into unfamiliar pieces of furniture in the lavish suite, she maneuvered her way to the bathroom. Jocelyn splashed water on her face and brushed her teeth in the largest, most elaborate face bowl she had ever seen.

Catching her naked reflection in the full-length bathroom wall mirror, Jocelyn flinched. Standing there, wearing only the diamond earrings, Derrick gave her for Christmas and the magnificent wedding ring he had given her the day before; Jocelyn ran her fingers through her mangled hair and studied her figure. For a woman who would be thirty on her next birthday, Jocelyn didn't think she looked bad at all. But, she hadn't endured a real test of time. Nothing living had passed through this vessel.

Jocelyn ran her hand over her flat stomach, took a deep breath and cinched her tiny waist. Just as she turned to examine her hips from a better angle, Derrick stumbled into the bathroom. His eyes barely open. He went straight to the commode. Jocelyn didn't think he even saw her. She decided to give her new husband the privacy that never seemed to phase him. Retrieving a robe from her case, Jocelyn put it on and jumped when she heard Derrick's raspy sleepy voice.

"Did I bring a toothbrush?"

Turning quickly, she said, "Sure did. It's in your bag. Need me to get it for you?"

Leaning in the bathroom doorway, naked as the day he was born; with the exception being his gleaming gold wedding band, Derrick gave Jocelyn a weary nod. He looked horrible, but Jocelyn was proud of him. He actually woke up before it was dark again. A fabulous meal, brandy, a good bottle of wine and a night of passion put Derrick into a coma every time.

Handing him the toothbrush, Jocelyn asked, "Would you like me to order breakfast, honey?"

In a whisper, Derrick asked, "Are you hungry?"

Jocelyn nodded.

"What time is it?"

"I don't know. But the sun hasn't gone down yet."

Waving pathetically and nodding his head, Derrick turned and said, "Okay. Order breakfast. Could you call and check on One and Two for me please?"

Knowing a discussion about the babies belonging to both of them now would fly over Derrick's brandied brain, she let that pass with a, "Sure."

Ethan answered Jocelyn's call. He couldn't believe Derrick was up before five. The boy was drunk as a skunk when he left the house. Ethan demanded Jocelyn put Derrick on the telephone. She laughed before saying, "I said he was awake, Ethan. I didn't say he could speak."

"Okay. I can buy that. Don't turn your back, Jocelyn; Derrick's not really awake. Tell him the girls are fine. They threw their usual tantrum when they realized he wasn't here but that's been hours ago."

As Ethan and Jocelyn chatted on the telephone, Derrick found his way back to the bed. He laid his head in Jocelyn's lap, stretched out and fell asleep again. A knock on the door ended the conversation with her father-in-law.

Shaking her big naked husband awake long enough to make him turn around in bed so she could cover him, Jocelyn answered the door. A grinning Hope stood there.

She peeked past Jocelyn to see the still sleeping Derrick and entered the room.

Walking over to the bed, Hope asked, "Had breakfast yet, sister-in-law?"

Struggling not to laugh, Jocelyn said, "Not yet. I've ordered it though."

Hope gave Derrick a poke with her finger. He didn't respond. She turned to Jocelyn and said, "Good. Want some company? My husband's in the same condition as yours."

The two women ate breakfast together, ordered lunch and ate it too. They watched the soaps and considered going down to the mezzanine to see if any of the shops were open.

The telephone rang at ten minutes to five. Jocelyn didn't move to answer it. She wanted to see if Derrick would. After the third ring he searched the bed with his hand, realized Jocelyn wasn't there and answered.

In a panic, David wanted to know if Derrick had seen Hope. Of course, Derrick told him he had not. David relaxed a little when Derrick told him Jocelyn was missing too. David concluded their conversation with, “I’ll be down there in a few minutes.”

Not knowing Jocelyn and Hope were both looking right at him, Derrick raised the sheet and started to get up. Jocelyn's voice stopped him. "I wouldn't do that if I were you, sweetheart. We have company."

Without actually seeing her, Derrick said, "Hi, Hope, your husband's on his way down here to get you. Jocelyn, did you ever order breakfast? I'm starving."

The two women looked at each other, shook their heads and laughed hysterically. Derrick frowned and asked, "What the hell did I say that was so funny?"

David's knock didn't even interrupt the laughter. He couldn't imagine what was going on anywhere. Derrick was still in bed, he had just dragged himself out of bed, and Jocelyn and Hope appeared to be having the time of their lives together. All David wanted to know was, "Are you all right, Hope?"

"I'm fine, David."

"Why didn't you wake me up and tell me where you were going?"

The spontaneous laughter began again. Dismissing both women, David turned his focus to his equally miserable looking brother and asked, "Did you eat anything, Derrick? I'm starving."

Derrick said, "Jocelyn, order me something to eat please."

Jocelyn shook her head and said, "I'm not calling down there again. I've already made two orders today. They'll think I'm up here on a Bolemic trip."

"You ate twice without me?"

"Yes, Derrick. I had a pregnant guest. When she says she's hungry, we eat."

Sitting, with his hands folded in his lap, Derrick looked at Hope and said, "Okay Fatso, it's your turn to order then."

Putting her hands on her hips, Hope asked, "Who are you calling Fatso, Brandyman? You and David can order your own food."

David snapped, "Where's the menu? I don't need anybody to do anything for me."

In mock sarcasm, Hope said, "That's not what you said last night, Big Boy."

Ignoring her, David sat in the wing chair and dialed room service. He ordered almost everything on the menu. And, when it arrived, David and Derrick devoured every crumb on both trays. They swatted Hope's hand twice for trying to steal.

The honeymoon weekend was relaxing and exhilarating. If Derrick had not noticed the longing in Jocelyn's eyes every time she looked at Hope, it would have been perfect. Jocelyn wanted to know what it felt like to carry a baby of her own desperately. Mia and Miranda had held yearning for motherhood at bay for her for a while. They just couldn't do anything with the need to actually do it herself.

Just as promised, Derrick vacationed the entire month of December and Jocelyn joined him. Most of their free time was spent really getting to know each other. Both had been on their own for so long that just being in the presence of another adult for an extended period of time was a challenge. One or the other asked everyday, "Are you ignoring me?" The response was always, "Oh. Are you talking to me?"

Derrick and Jocelyn went all out with the Christmas decorations for Mia and Miranda. Appreciation for every sparkling bauble and twinkling light showed in their silent awestruck head snapping. The precocious twins only pulled the tree down once.

It was agreed that Jocelyn would sponsor Christmas dinner for the Dawes family and Hope would host the New Years festivities. The holidays were glorious, especially for Jocelyn. For the first time in her life, she actually felt like she belonged to a family that loved her. Oh, her origins were still questioned from time to time by good old Aunt Sylvia, and her narrow hips still troubled Gran, but overall she was an accepted member of the Dawes family.

The holiday traffic at Derrick and Jocelyn's house never seemed to slack up. Every relative and friend filed through to congratulate the couple on their nuptials. Gifts for the newlyweds were plentiful. Christmas gifts for Mia and Miranda piled so high around the tree, Derrick thought about returning some of the stuff they got from Santa. Tyson even brought their gifts from Cynthia. She could not get back home in time for Christmas.

With Jocelyn protesting loudly, Derrick returned the packages sent by Angelique. It only made Angelique call two days after Christmas. Jocelyn answered and without hesitation gave the telephone to Derrick, stood back and watched the heated exchange.

Obviously agitated, Angelique asked, "Why did you send the girls' Christmas gifts back, Derrick?"

Flatly, Derrick responded, "They don't need anything, Angelique."

"It's Christmas, Derrick. Need has nothing to do with it. Their belated birthday gifts were in those boxes too. I really wish you would stop acting like a retard! It's not you, Derrick!"

"If you knew anything about me, Angelique, you would leave me and the girls alone. You didn't want to be bothered when they were born and I don't care to entertain your whims now! Let this be the last time I have to say this! They don't need one damn thing you're offering!"

Derrick slammed the receiver back into the cradle. Jocelyn waited for the entire telephone to slide down the wall. Somehow, it didn't. Knowing how protective and possessive Derrick was of Mia and Miranda, Jocelyn always wanted to say the right things to him about them. If there was a subject that could end their loving relationship, they were it.

After living with him as his wife for a month she realized Derrick would never relinquish primary care of those little girls to anyone willingly. Dead tired, he insisted on bathing and putting them to bed every night himself. Reading to them and answering all two million of their questions was his job alone. Occasionally, Derrick allowed Jocelyn to dress them and comb their hair. Jocelyn knew he loved her when he diligently started calling her Mommy in front of Mia and Miranda. They conceded by calling Jocelyn, "Mommy Dosh."

With the heated telephone call over, Jocelyn stroked Derrick's back and asked, "Want to talk about it?"

Snorting, Derrick said, "Not really."

"I think you should."

Turning to look down at Jocelyn and still upset, Derrick asked, "Why is she playing with Mia and Miranda's lives like this? They don't need things. They needed a mother who loved them. Not one who abandons them and changes her mind. Then, tries to weasel her way back into their lives with trinkets. I'm not having it, Jocelyn. If I have anything to say about it, Angelique will never set eyes on those two as long as I live."

Consolingly, Jocelyn responded, "That's just it, honey. You may not have the last word in this. Maybe if you tried not to piss her off, she would tire of the game and go away. Sending them gifts may be her way of making peace with herself. If you don't let her do at least that one little thing, she could cause real problems."

"I can't help the way I feel about it, Jocelyn. And, I could care less about Angelique's emotional or spiritual peace. She's the most selfish woman I've ever known."

"Why, Derrick? Because she did what men do every day all over the world?"

Turning his anger toward Jocelyn in earnest, Derrick asked, "So, what is this? The *If you can't be 'em join 'em* defense? I can't have what you have, so it justifies me stealing it from someone else who had absolutely nothing to do with any of it."

Confused, Jocelyn asked, "What's that again?"

Waving his hand, Derrick said, "Forget it, Jocelyn. No one will ever make what Angelique did right in my mind. If she had told me about the babies before they were born, I would have been upset. May have even suggested an abortion. But, she knew I would have helped. Been there for her. Angelique knows me better than anybody in the world, other than my own mother."

Not particularly caring to hear that some other woman knew him better than she did, but acquiescing to the possibility, Jocelyn said solemnly, "That's why she did what she did then, Derrick. She knew what the outcome would be for her girls. They would have a father they could depend on."

Believing his next statement, with every fiber of his chauvinistic being, Derrick said bitingly, "Those babies needed a mother who knew what she was doing. Not a father who was petrified for months he was going to do something that would kill them. If my mother hadn't been around, Jocelyn, One and Two would have been in really big trouble."

"You keep saying would have been and could have been, Derrick. Don't you think Angelique knew exactly what your circumstances were? Don't you think she knew Sonya would pinch hit for you? If she couldn't, then Gran would have. If she couldn't, Aunt Sylvia would have. You come from a family, Derrick. Do you know how rare that is? Yes, even for women.

"What makes you think women automatically know what to do with babies anyway? What makes you think they sleep easy knowing they haven't done something to kill the little creatures, too? And, for the first birth to be multiple, Derrick, you can't imagine what petrified is. You had one minute to adjust. She had to wallow with the fear for months, growing by leaps and bounds right along with those babies. By the time she gave birth, it was way more than she was ready to handle.

"If you can't forgive her, sweetheart, cut her a little slack. At least give her enough rope to lick her own wounds. After all, she gave you two of the prettiest little girls you're ever going to get."

Jocelyn had given Angelique an elaborate defense Derrick felt the woman was totally unworthy of. First of all, Angelique came from an even tighter family than Derrick's. Her mother told everyone Angelique's teenage sister's child was her own to protect them from gossip. They were more rigid in their standards than the Dawes clan, but rallied when forced.

Angelique was a grown woman. She knew what caring for babies entailed. And, she had a husband. Even if she thought Derrick was the father. According to Roger, Aaron wouldn't have known the difference anyway. Derrick couldn't imagine why Angelique had done this to One and Two. Cap that off with he didn't care to know anymore, and every time Angelique sent a package to his house for them, Derrick wrote undeliverable on it and gave it back to the postman.

## *CHAPTER THIRTY-TWO*

Nothing prepared the happily married Mr. and Mrs. Derrick Dawes for the dramatic highs and lows they would face in their first year together. Jocelyn missed her first menstrual cycle in February and confirmed her pregnancy two days before Hope gavc birth to a magnificent little boy in March.

To punish David, Hope threatened to name their new son Steven. That was the name of the guy she dated before David. With the entire family holding its breath, Hope actually named him David Ethan Dawes, IV. The real fight over what to call the little fellow began after that.

On April 29th, Derrick, Jocelyn and the girls were strolling through the Mall. They ate lunch at Burger King and let the girls play at Discovery Zone for an hour. Jocelyn felt a little uncomfortable in the car during the ride home. She attributed it to the food she had eaten. Eating and pregnancy hadn't mixed well for her.

At home, Jocelyn told Derrick she thought she needed to rest. He took the girls down to play in the recreation room while Jocelyn went up to take a nap. Derrick always had something to work on down there anyway. The girls had desks now, too. They pretended to draw like Daddy off and on for the remainder of the evening. Barney entertained them some too.

Derrick fed the girls dinner at six. He called up to Jocelyn and got no response. Thinking she was still asleep, Derrick held the girls hostage downstairs until he put them to bed at ten.

Entering their bedroom and issuing a great big sigh, Derrick noticed Jocelyn wasn't in bed. He heard what he thought was a whimper coming from the bathroom. Calling Jocelyn's name, Derrick followed the sound. He found her crumpled on the floor, crying uncontrollably.

After calling Sonya to come sit with the girls, Derrick took Jocelyn to the hospital to confirm what she already knew. Jocelyn had what they called a spontaneous miscarriage. There was no reason they would ever be able to detect. Physically, Jocelyn was fine. There was absolutely no reason why she should not be able to carry a fetus full term.

Jocelyn's depression that followed was hard on Mia and Miranda who didn't understand anything. Things perked up some when Derrick took Jocelyn to Barbados for a week in July and stayed that way until Jocelyn missed her cycle again in October. Everyone held their breath until Jocelyn miscarried again in December.

Christmas for the busy two-year-olds was sponsored by Sonya and Ethan because Derrick didn't want to put any more pressure on Jocelyn. At least that's what he said. The truth was, Derrick wasn't up to the festivities either.

The most difficult thing David ever had to do was tell Derrick that Hope was pregnant again in February. This child would be due in September. Derrick never bothered telling Jocelyn. She would see it for herself soon enough because they all still had dinner with Sonya and Ethan every Sunday. With Deandra off at college their presence seemed more important.

To Derrick's surprise, Jocelyn seemed genuinely happy to hear about Hope's new baby. As Hope grew, Jocelyn's fascination with the process grew with it. She wanted to know what Hope did every minute. What Jocelyn never told anyone was she actually thought there was something she was doing wrong, because she didn't know any better.

All Jocelyn found out from Hope was she did everything she always did. Nothing changed because she was pregnant. Jocelyn needed Hope to tell her that she stopped having sex with David, stopped eating in the kitchen, or gave up wearing purple on Sunday. Anything. Factual or superstitious.

In August, Jocelyn missed her menstrual cycle. She didn't bother Derrick with the news. If he noticed, he never said a word about it. August came and went with no problem, as did September. The third birthday party for Mia and Miranda was special, as usual, and Derrick returned their gifts from Angelique, as usual. Hope's second son was born on the twentieth and Jocelyn was the first in line to see him.

Not until October tenth did Jocelyn muster the nerve to go to the gynecologist. He smiled and told her she was officially something she had never been before—twelve to fourteen weeks along in her pregnancy. His only suggestion was that Jocelyn take it easy for a while. Maybe stay at home until she was in her final trimester. That way they would have a fighting chance to save the baby.

At home that night, Jocelyn asked Derrick if he would mind her taking a sabbatical without him. Of course, he wanted to know why. She told him she just felt tired and needed a little break. Dr. Kane was willing to give her as much time as she needed, and if it was all right with the good doctor who was Derrick to say no. The one who complained until Jocelyn swore her to secrecy and explained, was Sonya.

Finding Sonya and Jocelyn at the kitchen table every evening, with One and Two chasing each other around the room, was commonplace for Derrick after a week. Derrick wanted to put them in nursery school this year, but Sonya threw a fit to be envied. They would be in school for more than enough years. They could wait one more. At least, that's what Grammy Sonya thought.

Jocelyn had been a little reserved Thanksgiving. Not particularly unhappy. Just not wanting to go to Sonya's for dinner. Sure the problem was David and Hope's new baby, Omar, Derrick didn't push the issue. Sonya prepared a special dinner for Derrick and Jocelyn to share at home. Mia and Miranda were not excused from the normal family gathering.

Spending a day with their cousins, without Daddy, didn't upset them one bit anymore. They looked forward to it these days.

Thanksgiving was the first time Derrick felt that something was up. Jocelyn never uttered the phrase, "I'm pregnant" to Derrick. She was, however, changing physically right in front of his eyes with Derrick refusing to acknowledge those changes. David had to be the one to pose the question to Derrick that forced reality into his fog.

On the first Saturday afternoon in December, David and Derrick were assigned babysitting duties, while the women did some Christmas shopping. Derrick was just glad to see Jocelyn actually get out of the house for once. She rarely left the bedroom anymore.

The two men sat staring at the television silently. One and Two pushed David's shy little firstborn, known as Peepers, around on a Big Wheel. The little guy screeched with joy. One and Two were the only people Peepers was fearless of. He was so shy he wouldn't look anyone else in the eyes. Sonya insisted that was because David had tormented Derrick all of his life.

David leaned forward, picked up his glass of soda and asked, "So, when's the baby due?"

Nonchalantly, Derrick asked, "What baby?"

Ducking his head to get a better look at his brother, David said, "The one your wife's carrying, Idiot."

Defensively, Derrick asked, "Who told you my wife was carrying a baby?"

Without hesitation, David called Miranda. She came immediately and jumped up on her uncle's lap. David asked, "Where's the new baby, sweetheart?"

Looking at the bassinet, Miranda pointed and said, "Omar."

David shook his head and said, "Not Omar, Mandie. Where's your new baby?"

Giggling and covering her mouth with her hand, Miranda whispered loudly, "Mommy Josh's tummy. Don't tell Daddy."

David gave Derrick his I told you so stare. Derrick gave a nervous chuckle and said, "Two, you don't know what you're talking about. Who told you that? Uncle David?"

Shaking her head, Miranda answered seriously, "No, Daddy. Mommy did. The baby's in her tummy. He wiggles."

Nodding her head enthusiastically, Mia chimed in gleefully, "Yeah, he wiggles."

Shaken, Derrick asked, "Who wiggles?"

Both girls responded, "The baby!"

David couldn't resist asking, "Didn't you notice your wife was pregnant, Derrick?"

"No," Derrick lied.

"Really? What did you think happened to make her swell like that?"

"I don't know. It could have been anything. I'm not a doctor. She never told me she was pregnant."

"Did you ask?"

"No."

Shaking his head in disbelief, David said, "Well, now you know. You can take your head out of the hole you've had it in for the last four months."

Swallowing hard, Derrick asked, "Has she been carrying it four months, David?"

"Yeah, Fool. Two months longer than she's ever carried one before. The doctor says it looks extremely promising."

Looking truly pathetic, Derrick said, "He's said that before, David. What if Jocelyn loses this one too? Her sanity won't hold for many more miscarriages. Not to mention my own."

"Well, Derrick, if she carries him a couple more months, he has a fighting chance. I'm willing to bet on him."

Fidgeting, Derrick asked, "Why do you keep calling it a him?"

Looking at the girls, David sighed as if honestly bored and asked, "Mia and Miranda, what's the new baby, a boy or a girl?"

Together they screamed, "A boy!"

That night in bed, Derrick realized Jocelyn intentionally avoided him. Perhaps that was why he hadn't been paying as much attention as he should have. She didn't put on one of her beautiful nightgowns to come to bed. Instead, she went into the bathroom and emerged in Derrick's Steeler tee shirt. No wonder he never noticed. In that thing, Jocelyn looked like she always did. All he could see clearly were her arms and legs.

It wasn't until Jocelyn reached over her head, to put something on her ponytail, that Derrick saw how her stomach really did extend beyond her breasts. Still unsure how he felt about it, Derrick asked, "How was your shopping trip today?"

Easing down on the bed, Jocelyn said, "A little tiring, but progressive. With Sonya's help, we got most of the things we wanted for the children."

"Oh, Mom went with you guys today?"

Nodding innocently, Jocelyn said, "Yes, Derrick. Why are you asking me so many questions tonight? Your Mom goes to the Mall every Saturday and you know it."

Hoping Jocelyn would give up and tell him she was pregnant, Derrick just shrugged and lay down. When Jocelyn made herself comfortable, Derrick attempted to put his arm around her. She grimaced and complained, "Derrick, please. Your arms are way too heavy. I can't breathe."

Leaning on his elbow, Derrick asked, "Since when?"

Not looking back at him, Jocelyn answered a question with a question, "Since when, what?"

"Since when has my arm gotten so heavy it stops you from being able to breathe?"

"I don't know, Derrick. Can't you just put the other one under my neck? I'm much more comfortable that way."

"Since when?"

Again, she asked, "Since when, what?"

"Since you obviously don't want to tell me you're pregnant, why don't you try, 'Now that I'm stretching in the strangest places, your arm makes me uncomfortable.' That might work."

In a frightened whisper, Jocelyn said, "I didn't want you to get your hopes up again for nothing, Derrick."

"Are your hopes up, Jocelyn?"

"Yes and no."

"Why the no?"

"You know why, Derrick. I could wake up in the middle of the night and lose this baby for absolutely no reason too. Didn't Gran say my hips were too narrow?"

Unable to resist taking the jab, Derrick said, "Well, she hasn't seen them lately."

Unprepared for the cutting remark, Jocelyn gasped her surprise and froze momentarily. Then, she asked with tears gathering in her eyes, "Are you saying my hips are spreading all over the place, Derrick Dawes?"

Stifling a genuine laugh, Derrick could only shake his head in reply.

Not finding any humor in his remark, Jocelyn said snappily, "Now I know why Angelique didn't tell you she was pregnant. If my hips are wide, imagine how wide hers were with twins."

"Touche', Fatso. Get over here, with your wide hips and give me a kiss goodnight."

Rolling her eyes, Jocelyn asked, "Are you going to call me Fatso for the remainder of this pregnancy, Derrick?"

"Sure. What fun would it be, otherwise?"

Really happy he finally knew she was pregnant, Jocelyn sucked her teeth and turned over. She not only gave Derrick a kiss, she let him make love to her for the first time in weeks. The fact that they were both afraid for the baby made it a true exercise in self-control, but they enjoyed it just the same.

For the rest of the night Derrick asked one question after another every fifteen minutes. "Are you sure you're pregnant, Jocelyn?" "Are you sure everything is all right, Jocelyn?" "Are you sure it's all right for us to have sex?" "Should you have gone to the Mall today?" "Are you sure you feel all right?" "Are you sure it's a boy, Jocelyn?"

That's when Jocelyn knew she had made the right decision not to tell him too soon. Derrick would worry himself into an early grave at this pace.

## *CHAPTER THIRTY-THREE*

With Jocelyn's confirmation of the pregnancy, Derrick wanted to stay home with her everyday. After all, this was the first December Derrick had worked since they met. Jocelyn insisted Derrick hold as much vacation time as he could because she would need him at home when the baby was born in April.

Derrick pouted and went to work everyday. Knowing Sonya was at the house with Jocelyn was the motivating factor. He only called once every hour or so.

To distract him, Tyson forced Derrick to start talking about his own firm. Insisting the only way he would make the kind of money he needed for his expanding family was if he had a better position in a smaller concern. Derrick played along with him. After all, Tyson was not only Derrick's best friend he and Cynthia were Mia and Miranda's god-parents. A position they both took seriously. The well being of the Dawes family meant a lot to them. The four had discussed at length Mia and Miranda's educational options. Regardless what Sonya said, the following fall would find those young ladies in school.

The Saturday morning before Christmas began normally enough. Mia and Miranda opened the day by lying their heads on Jocelyn's stomach and waiting for the baby to move. They loved doing that–so did Derrick. But his fears made him refrain from doing it and he held the girls at bay too. Afterwards, Jocelyn eased downstairs and started breakfast while Derrick dressed the noisy twins.

The doorbell rang at nine-thirty and Jocelyn yelled from the kitchen, "I'll get it!"

Without looking to see who was at the door, Jocelyn opened it. Not having any idea who she was looking at, Jocelyn smiled and said, "Hello."

An extremely attractive and well dressed, biscuit colored woman with short wavy black hair, impeccably cut, stood thoroughly examining the now obviously pregnant Jocelyn. With a smile of her own, the woman said comfortably, "Well, hello. Is Derrick in?"

Stepping aside, Jocelyn said, "Sure. Come in. He'll be down in a minute. He's dressing Mia and Miranda."

It wasn't until Jocelyn noticed the packages stacked in the doorway that she had a hint who this beautiful woman was. To quiet her miserably churning mind, Jocelyn insisted it didn't have to be who she thought it was. The woman picked up the packages and walked in. She headed for the living room, as if she knew exactly where she was going. With Jocelyn standing in the doorway looking at her, the woman put the packages on the coffee table, removed her coat, took a seat on the sofa and smiled warmly up at Jocelyn.

Not knowing what to do, Jocelyn stayed put in the living room doorway. When the boisterous trio made their way down the stairs, Derrick asked, "Who was at the door, honey?"

Pointing, Jocelyn said weakly, "She was."

Thinking this was another impromptu Cassandra visit, Derrick walked into the living room with Mia and Miranda at his heels. The last thing Derrick wanted was Cassandra upsetting Jocelyn. Who Derrick actually saw in the living room rendered him speechless. Fury couldn't encompass the explosion in his mind.

Never actually looking at Derrick, Angelique studied the two positively divine little girls. They had Derrick's magnificent complexion and eyes. Beautiful, shoulder length, thick, black wavy braids and smiles to die for. Angelique couldn't believe there were actually two of the same.

Angelique didn't rally until Derrick asked none too nicely, for the second time, "What do you want?"

Looking up at the man she had loved more than life itself for years, Angelique didn't flinch. She smiled and said, "Hello, Derrick. How are you? Are these the lovely Mia and Miranda I've heard so much about?"

Before Derrick could answer, Mia and Miranda's identical heads happily bobbed up and down. Angelique pointed at the packages and said, "Well, these gifts are for you two. If I had known there would be another addition to the family, I would have brought another gift."

Derrick held onto Mia and Miranda. His mood was not one shade brighter than pitch black. He glared at Angelique with as much hatred as was humanly possible. Sensing the ugly exchange about to transpire, Jocelyn took Mia and Miranda's hands and insisted they start eating breakfast.

Alone in the room with Angelique, Derrick didn't mince words. He said emptily, "Get out of my house. Take that crap with you."

Looking at Derrick with misery in her eyes, Angelique asked, "Why are you treating me like this, Derrick? What have I done to you?"

"You know exactly what you did, damn it! Don't play with me, Angelique! My wife is pregnant and not well! Please don't play with me! Take that shit and get out of my house!" Derrick shouted feeling closer to hitting a woman than he could have ever imagined being.

Tears streamed down Angelique's face, as she pulled her coat back on. She ran her hand down the side of her hair, the way Derrick had seen her do a thousand times and picked up the packages. Turning toward him and struggling not to choke on her steaming tears, Angelique said, "I'm so sorry you never believed me when I said those were not my babies, Derrick. I wish they were. To have had you and them would have been all I ever dreamed of. Now, it seems you're adding even more joy to your life. I didn't know you were married, Derrick, nevertheless expecting another baby. You haven't shared a civil conversation with me since Christmas Eve four years ago. I've missed you. You were my best friend."

There was no response from Derrick. Angelique moved toward the door and saw Mia and Miranda's pretty little heads peeping out the kitchen doorway. She looked at them for a few seconds while she waited for Derrick to open the door. They returned her weak, tear-streaked smile and gave her a wave.

Desperate not to frighten Mia and Miranda, or push Jocelyn into an even more stressful situation, Derrick struggled with his own composure. Opening the door, he said, "Angelique, do us all a favor. Leave us alone. We're doing fine. That's what you wanted for the girls. Right? For me to take care of them, so they wouldn't put a damper on your life. If we were all you ever wanted, you sure as hell had a strange way of showing it. You didn't want Aaron to know what you did that Christmas Eve and you weren't sure if they were his or mine. So, rather than take the risk of them not being your husband's, you kept the pregnancy a secret from both of us and dumped the babies off on me. That's how it went. Isn't it, Angelique?"

Staring at Derrick, as if this was the first time she had ever seen him, Angeliquc said vaguely, "If you say that's what happened, Derrick, that's what happened. I'm going now. Good-bye."

Slamming the door behind her, Derrick yelled, "Good-bye!"

No one in the Dawes household mentioned that exchange. Derrick kept an eye on Jocelyn through the holidays. She seemed to handle Angelique's visit with her usual non-threatened calmness. Jocelyn only had one thing to say on the subject, "I don't believe she's really their mother, Derrick."

The New Year came in without a hitch. Everyone had a great time and Jocelyn's pregnancy was holding. On the morning of January third, there was a knock and a ringing of the bell at Derrick's house. Because Derrick had returned to work and Jocelyn was still asleep, Sonya answered. The stiff, non-descript man at the door asked for Derrick Dawes. When Sonya told him he wasn't at home, the man turned and left without saying another word. At his office, later that afternoon, Derrick was served his subpoena for a custody hearing scheduled for January fifteenth.

## *CHAPTER THIRTY-FOUR*

Tyson found a motionless Derrick, sitting at his desk with a folded sky blue backed document in his hand. Leaning over Derrick's shoulder to read the black writing, Tyson visibly flinched when he saw the word, "Subpoena." Keeping his eyes on Derrick, Tyson slid the packet from Derrick's loose grip. After giving the papers a cursory reading, Tyson dialed Roger's office. Roger told him to fax a copy to him immediately.

After doing as Roger instructed, Tyson returned and said to the stillest live man he had ever seen, "Big D, I've already called Roger. He's working on it. Now, if you don't start moving, I'm calling your mom. I don't know what else to do."

Without any indication he heard or understood one word Tyson said, and devoid of the slightest human emotion, Derrick said, "There's nothing anyone can do. This is where she walks back in and takes the girls off into the sunset. No questions asked."

Truly agitated by his friend's lifeless reaction, Tyson yelled, "What the hell do you mean, no questions asked?! Fuck that! I've got a whole lot of questions for the slut! Starting with, 'Where the hell do you get off pulling some lame shit like this?!'"

"You don't understand, Tyson. The courts don't give a damn about a man's rights when it comes to custody. She'll get top dibs on the whole ball of wax with no regard for what she's done. They'll give One and Two to her as if they were born yesterday to a mother who loved the air they breathed."

Waving his hands, Tyson ranted, "Bullshit! You've taken care of those girls for over three years without so much as a postcard from anybody! She can't just walk in and take them! Not if I have anything to say about it! This is still America, buddy! She won't get them if I have to burn her house down to keep her from having anywhere to take them! One dirty turn deserves another!"

Derrick gave the deepest sigh Tyson had ever heard and said, "Yeah. You're going all the way to Denver to burn down her house. Then, I'll have to get your dumb ass out of jail and hand over my daughters in a smoky field."

Smiling, Tyson bellowed, "That's what friends are for, Big D! Bail money!"

Disregarding Tyson, it was a weary Derrick asking, "What am I going to do now? I can't take this home. Jocelyn's been doing so well with this pregnancy. If she loses this baby because of Angelique, I think I might kill the woman."

Before Tyson formulated an answer, Derrick's telephone rang. It was Sonya. Something was wrong with Jocelyn. She was taking her to the hospital. Derrick and Tyson left the office without saying anything to anyone.

At the hospital, Sonya, Mia and Miranda sat in the waiting room, while the doctors looked at Jocelyn. They wouldn't commit to anything until her gynecologist came down. When Derrick walked into the cubicle where Jocelyn was, he was relieved to see she wasn't in any obvious distress. As a matter of fact she smiled at him and said, "Hi, honey. What are you doing here?"

Bending to kiss her, Derrick gave a limp smile and said, "Oh, I don't know. I get a call that my fat wife is going to the hospital. I lose it and run right down here. What an idiot I am."

Returning Derrick's kiss, Jocelyn said, "You sure are. I'm fine. Or, should I say we're fine?"

Stroking Jocelyn's abdomen lovingly, Derrick said, "Both."

Dr. Swanson stepped into the cubicle, with a big smile of his own. He extended his hand and said, "Hello, Mr.

Dawes. I heard you were here. Perhaps we could talk in the foyer. Mrs. Dawes already knows what's going on."

Fear gripped Derrick's chest so tightly he couldn't respond verbally. He merely nodded and followed the doctor. If this man said there was something wrong with his wife and baby that they couldn't do anything about, Derrick thought he would surely lose his mind.

Seeing Derrick's rigid posture, Dr. Swanson said, "Relax, Mr. Dawes. Have a seat. It's all going to be all right. Really."

Merely following instructions, Derrick sat and waited for the doctor to speak again. He didn't make him wait.

Speaking slowly, Dr. Swanson said, "Your wife is fine. Your baby is fine. There just seems to be a problem with her uterus contracting prematurely. We gave her something to stop it. There is no more spotting.

“For everyone's peace of mind, I'd like to admit her for observation for a few days. If the contractions don't start again, she can go home on bed rest. I know how much this baby means to you and Jocelyn. I've been her doctor for about six years now. I know about the miscarriages. This is similar, but she's much further along. These contractions are not strong enough to cause any real damage and I think we have it under control. If you don't panic, Mr. Dawes, she won't. Okay?"

Nodding his agreement, Derrick dropped his head into his hands and gave another great sigh. That's when Derrick realized he had a splitting headache. He asked the doctor if they could spare some aspirin for a desperate man. Dr. Swanson got the aspirin and water personally.

When Derrick walked back into Jocelyn's cubicle he looked a little better. His smile had a few more teeth in it. And, he made a joke.

"Hey, Fatso. Looks like you've won a fully monitored holiday. Feel better now?"

Jocelyn couldn't resist saying, "I'll stay if you make me one promise."

"What's that?"

"You won't call Cassandra over to do a striptease and a little lap dance."

Derrick snapped his fingers and said, "Damn! If I can't do that, then you may as well bring those old noisy monitors home to entertain me."

Jocelyn's misadventure served two purposes. One was to insure Jocelyn and the baby's health. The other provided Derrick with the time needed to get his bearings, without upsetting Jocelyn more than necessary. Now, the fact that big mouth Tyson had shared the subpoena news with Sonya didn't help. Derrick had to listen to her tirade for hours, too.

Because Jocelyn didn't come home with them, Mia and Miranda gave Derrick a really hard time about going to bed. They wanted to know where Mommy Josh was. His answers never satisfied them. Jocelyn called at ten and talked to both girls on the telephone. Then, they drifted off to sleep in bed with Daddy.

Derrick watched his two sleeping demons and sizzling tears of frustration blazed their way out of his eyes. The thought of losing One and Two caused a searing pain in his chest that made breathing nearly impossible. He had been looking over these two all of their little lives. Derrick couldn't even list all of the things he'd learned about living and loving from them. How much humans really needed other humans was at the top of the list though.

He stroked their perfect little heads and remembered the first time he had ever done that. How afraid of them he was. He tried desperately to recall the first time he realized how much he loved them and couldn't. Derrick couldn't remember not loving them. Now, because he wasn't willing to be diplomatic or play footsies with their mother, she was taking them away from him.

Roger spoke to Derrick for the first time since Tyson's call in his office the following afternoon. He opened with the fact that Angelique had a pretty good lawyer. They were demanding all of the same information from Derrick that Roger intended to demand from them. What Roger wasn't prepared for was Angelique denying Derrick was the father. The Petitions were filed on behalf of Aaron and Angelique Kelly.

Derrick asked, "So, what does that mean, Roger?"

"That means the judge will wonder what's going on. A mother denying paternity of record, a father refusing custody, temporary or otherwise, to a mother who gave birth under highly suspicious circumstances and using a fictitious name. What we'd all better hope is that the judge is in a good mood."

"If he's not, what will he do, Roger?"

"Make Mia and Miranda temporary wards of the State until the fog clears. Would you be willing to consent to giving her temporary custody, to keep the girls out of the State's hands, Derrick?"

Miserably, Derrick said, "They won't understand what's going on, Roger. They've never been away from me and my family. Without any of us what will they think?"

"I understand the turmoil you're in, Buddy. But, the bottom line is this; they spend a few weeks with their mother, or with people who potentially could care less. Possibly each in a different home."

In a fighting mood again, Derrick snapped angrily, "What if it's more than a few weeks?! What happens if she takes them back to Colorado?! Will I have to move the battle out there?!"

"I've already filed a Jurisdiction Request, Derrick. Would you like to give me those DNA test results now? She's saying you're not the father."

A dark frown covered Derrick's face. He spoke slowly when he said, "I don't know where they are, Roger. I never opened them."

Losing his composure, Roger yelled, "You mean you never read the damn things either?! What's wrong with you, Derrick?! Do you know what she can do to us in the time it could take to duplicate that damn test?!"

Stilling himself, Roger said urgently, "Find the papers, Derrick. Get a copy of the results. Or, run down to the hospital and do it over now. We cannot walk into that courtroom not knowing what we're talking about. They'll snatch Mia and Miranda from you before I set my briefcase down. It's just that simple. Somebody better be able to prove something to the judge."

Derrick called his mother and asked, "Mom, do you know what I did with those DNA test results?"

"No, Derrick. You never let me see them. Remember? Why?"

"She's saying I'm not their father."

Wanting to squeeze the absolute life out of something, Sonya gritted her teeth and clutched the telephone receiver to her leg until the desire passed. She heard an excited Derrick calling her name frantically when she picked it up again. Through clenched teeth, Sonya asked Derrick, "Did you say she's saying you're not their father?"

"Yes, Mom."

"Who is she saying their father is?"

"Her husband."

Loud enough for the neighbors to hear her, Sonya asked, "If the slut had a husband, why did she leave those babies at that damn hospital and say they were yours?! Where does she live, Derrick?! I want to talk to Angelique myself! We don't need a judge! This story started in the hospital and I can see that it ends there!"

Hating it all, Derrick simply said, "Mom, please. If you don't know what I did with the papers, I'll just have to ask Jocelyn. I didn't want to bother her with any of this."

Spirited to an even higher anger level, Sonya screamed, "Don't you dare call that hospital and bother Jocelyn with this mess! She'll lose that baby for sure! I'll look for the damned papers! Where was the last place you remember seeing them?!"

"Truthfully, Mom, I don't remember ever touching them after I left Dr. Kane's office. They must still be in one of those diaper bags."

In a chant, Sonya said, "Diaper bags, diaper bags. I gave so much of that stuff away after Mia and Miranda outgrew it, I'll have to look, Derrick. But, don't you tell Jocelyn one word about the girls and that stupid woman."

After being told that copies of the information he requested could not be retrieved for six weeks with or without a court order, Derrick refused to risk the wait. He took the girls back to Dr. Kane. Of course, Dr. Kane had no problem duplicating the test. But, he could not promise to have the results back before the January 15th court date. It took Sonya two days to remember whom she had given those diaper bags to and a week for the recipient to remember what she had done with the envelope she found in it.

Sonya ripped the envelope open as soon as it touched her hand. The contents only puzzled her. As far as she could see they didn't say anything either. There was no straightforward yes or no. The paper said, "At this stage of development, without sufficient maternal data, Derrick Dawes can not be excluded as the father of Mia Dawes."

After asking if Jocelyn would be all right while she ran an errand, Sonya packed up Mia and Miranda and took the DNA results to Roger herself. She waited for him to explain. Roger told Sonya the results meant just what they said. When the test was done, it was impossible to say conclusively that Derrick was their father. But, it leaned far enough in his favor to not be totally excluded. According to Roger, it was good enough to get child support, or send a man to death row.

How Derrick managed to keep it all from Jocelyn was the true mystery. She knew something was wrong, but she assumed Derrick was just worried about her and the baby. What puzzled Jocelyn was Derrick's insistence that the girls play in his bedroom when Jocelyn wasn't up to going down to the wreck room. He usually hated the way they destroyed his bedroom. They either demanded they watch Barney or Sesame Street on television, or they kept up so much noise, Derrick couldn't hear whatever it was he wanted to watch.

On the evening of January fourteenth, the Dawes telephone rang. Jocelyn reclined in bed with her husband's head in her lap. The remainder of the family milled around the room, making as much noise as they possibly could. Jocelyn barely heard whom the caller was asking to speak to. Eventually, she handed the telephone to Derrick.

Laughing at Mia and Miranda dancing to a rap video on television, Derrick gasped and said cheerfully, "Hello."

With all of the noise, Derrick still recognized Angelique's voice when she said, "Let's share the girls and forget this court business, Derrick."

Derrick held the receiver in his hand without responding. Speaking a little louder, Angelique called out, "Derrick. Derrick. Did you hear what I said?"

Softly, Derrick said, "Yeah."

The next thing Angelique heard was the click of Jocelyn hanging up the telephone. Never taking her eyes off of the two hard dancing little girls, Jocelyn asked, "Who was that, sweetheart?"

Not knowing whether Jocelyn recognized Angelique's voice or not, he didn't lie. "Angelique."

Jocelyn's head swiveled slowly in his direction. She patted Derrick's head so he would raise up enough for her to see his eyes when she asked, "What does she want?"

Never saying a word, Derrick simply looked at Mia and Miranda.

# *CHAPTER THIRTY-FIVE*

Leaving for the courthouse the following morning as if he were going to work was the plan. Derrick refused to tell Jocelyn anything he didn't have to. Now, if only Sonya could keep her cool until Derrick called from the office. She wanted to go with him and kill Angelique with her bare hands.

Derrick had his hands filled trying to keep David and Ethan from killing quite a few people in the courthouse. Angelique and Aaron Kelly were in more peril than they could have ever imagined. Ethan swore that if their lawyer told one lie, he would not be able to squeeze another lie past his collapsed windpipe ever again. Roger convinced David and Ethan that if they aggravated the judge, it could go ugly for Derrick and the girls.

Hearing Roger argue his case gave Derrick a new respect for the man as a lawyer. Every time Angelique and Aaron's lawyer thought he had the case sewn up with psychiatric reports on Angelique and a lot of case quotes on Aaron's rights as the natural father of the children, Roger countered with something to undo it. He made it abundantly clear that while the DNA tests done when the girls were infants were not conclusive they were not exclusive of his client. And, that those tests were at this very moment being updated. There was also the small issue of Angelique being unable to retrieve a copy of the children's birth certificates because she couldn't recall the name of the mother listed.

The argument of "Natural Parentage," both maternal and paternal, was greatly questioned by Roger.

Mrs. Monet, whom Derrick had not spoken to since he inherited the girls, testified that these babies were indeed abandoned by their mother. That Derrick Dawes had been indicated as the father on all official hospital documents, and upon notification, he stepped up and took responsibility for the infants. Mrs. Monet specifically indicated that while he was taken completely by surprise there was absolutely no need for the authorities to be contacted.

The judge gave the participants a good long looking over before he said anything at all. Then, while tapping the tip of his nose, he asked, "Mr. Dawes, do you still have custody of these two young ladies?"

Derrick answered immediately, "Yes, Sir."

Giving a nod and a smirk, the judge said, "Mrs. Kelly, I have no idea what possessed you to do something like this. And, if I were not bound by law to entertain your Requests, I would throw this pile of papers out the window. No one knows how weary we get of settling these imbecilic Requests. If a person abandons, they should stay that way. These are not socks. The lives of these two little girls should have been decided by the two people who were supposed to love them most in the world. Not a man who doesn't have a clue what's going on.

"Anyway, keeping the best interest of Mia and Miranda Dawes uppermost in my mind, while adhering to the letter of the law, here's how it's going to go, children. I'm scheduling another court date for March fifteenth. Between now and then, I want several things, an absolutely positive DNA test from either one of you. Mr. Dawes, this court must insist that you make Mia and Miranda available for testing with Mr. and Mrs. Kelly. I want proof of residence in this state for temporary custodial consideration from everyone. And, admitting that I have no idea what I'm doing, I'm asking all parties concerned if they will voluntarily agree to a visitation agreement today. If not, Mia and Miranda Dawes will be remanded to the custody of Human Services, until such time as this court has determined biological parentage."

Angelique and Aaron agreed immediately. Derrick sat thinking about it for a few moments. The judge had said they would only have to visit with them. What did visitation mean in this environment? Hating the idea of it, but not wanting to alienate a judge who seemed to be on his side, Derrick reluctantly nodded his agreement.

The judge smiled and said, "Good. Mr. and Mrs. Kelly, you have this court's permission to visit Mia and Miranda Dawes, in the offices of Mr. Dawes' attorney, Roger Kingsley, every Saturday from now until March fifteenth. Since you are already in town, let this Saturday represent your initial visit. Mr. Dawes, please have the girls in Mr. Kingsley's office at nine-thirty on Saturday morning. You can pick them up at three o'clock."

Looking at the two lawyers, the judge asked, "Are there any more Motions, Requests or Petitions I need to read over in the meantime, gentlemen?"

Barely able to contain his glee, Roger grinned and said loudly, "No, your Honor."

Happy as hell he didn't have to turn the girls over right away, Derrick couldn't understand Roger's absolute joy. He acted as if the judge had really thrown those papers out the window. What if the DNA tests came back saying Angelique and Aaron were really Mia and Miranda's parents?

Giving Aaron a good look for the first time, Derrick had to admit, there were definite similarities between them. His coloring wasn't a perfect match, but it was close enough for family. He could also see how their sizes might force a point of correlation. Aaron didn't have Sonya's mother's widow's peak though.

Outside the courtroom, the beautiful Angelique didn't look as confident about her decision. Derrick couldn't tell whether that was because David and Ethan had their killing faces on or not. Ethan refused to stay completely silent. Just loud enough for anyone who wanted to start something to hear, he said, "If my wife slept with another man and tried to pawn off babies all over town, I'd plant something in her ass she wouldn't be able to get rid of so easily." Aaron heard him and wisely chose to ignore the remark.

There was no need for any conversation between Derrick, Angelique and Aaron. Wiser still, Roger hustled his hostile group down the hall as fast as he could. Round one ended in the best way it possibly could. Angelique and Aaron didn't get immediate custody. They didn't even get unsupervised visitation.

Now, if the DNA results came back saying Derrick was minimally, the father, Roger felt confident the judge would not take the girls from him completely. Knowing Angelique had them for one minute would never satisfy Derrick and Roger understood why. But, as far as Roger was concerned he had done his job very well today.

## *CHAPTER THIRTY-SIX*

Making Sonya understand what transpired in the courtroom was nothing compared to making Jocelyn understand where the girls would be going every Saturday from nine to three. If Derrick said Mia and Miranda were at David and Hope's, Jocelyn would call them there. Or, demand that Hope bring the boys to their house. If he said Mia and Miranda were at Sonya and Ethan's knowing how much they enjoyed telephone calls, Jocelyn would call them there constantly. If Derrick said he was taking them somewhere for the day, with Jocelyn moving so close to her delivery date, she would start crying about him leaving her alone. Sonya sufficed during the week, but weekends were out.

So, when Jocelyn asked, "What's going on for real, Derrick? I know you're not used to sharing, but please tell me. I promise I won't get upset."

Whining and rambling, Derrick asked, "Are you sure, Jocelyn? It's getting to be a lot of nerve wrecking crap flying around this house. People threatening me. Babies coming. Babies going. My parents screaming and cursing in one ear. My friends screaming and cursing in my other ear. Tyson's threatening arson. David's threatening murder. If your nerves don't give out, Jocelyn, mine will."

Frowning, Jocelyn shifted in the bed and asked, "What are you talking about? What babies? Coming and going where?"

If Jocelyn didn't want to know before, she definitely wanted to know now. So, Derrick shared it with her. He gave her the entire story. Telephone calls, subpoenas, court dates, judge's decisions, all of it.

After hearing the entire story, Jocelyn stroked her immense stomach and said relatively calmly, "Let her have her visits with the girls, Derrick. She's not their mother."

"How can you be so certain she's not their mother, Jocelyn? I'm not."

"I don't know. There was nothing familiar about her when she dropped by. If she were Mia and Miranda's mother, I think I would have recognized her. They look like you for the most part, but there's someone else in there too. And, it's not your precious Angelique."

"Oh, now she's my precious Angelique? What next?"

"Don't get defensive now, Derrick. I think somewhere in your psych you want Angelique to be the mother. The similarities begin and end at the hair. She just isn't. That's all I'm saying."

"Well, I certainly hope you're right, Jocelyn. That's the only way I won't have to, at minimum, share One and Two with her. But, if she's not their mother, why would she go to this much trouble? And, who the hell is?"

"Besides the fact that I heard her deny they were her babies, honey, I think she's just hurt and angry with you for insisting she would stoop so low as to do this to you. Now, I could be wrong, but I believed her when she said she loved you and wished those were her children. I think she's doing it because of what you're building with me. When she saw me, you and the girls, it was more than she could handle. This was supposed to be her life, Derrick. How dare you let her love for you slip away, turn around and give the life she dreamed of to someone else? Are you listening to me?"

Nodding slowly, Derrick said, "Sure."

If worrying about Jocelyn's well-being wasn't enough, the trauma Angelique and Aaron caused Mia and Miranda catapulted Derrick into a place where he wanted to kill or be killed. On Saturday morning, as instructed, Derrick took Mia and Miranda to Roger's office. He patiently explained to the twins that they would be visiting with the nice lady who brought them the packages for Christmas and took them back. Derrick promised One and Two she would give the gifts to them now. They nodded happily. Of course, Derrick never said he would be leaving them alone with the strange lady. For all three-year-olds, everything sounds okay. Actually doing it is something else.

In Roger's office, Derrick gritted his teeth and introduced Mia and Miranda to Angelique and Aaron. He mentioned no relations and fully expected them to follow suit. Just staying in a room with them for five minutes was about as much as Mia and Miranda were really ready to deal with. Their miniature minds were saying, "Just give us the stuff you repossessed and beat it, lady. We have to get home and play with our own stuff."

The couple seemed truly taken with the two little girls. Angelique did most of the talking. She was impressed with the way Mia and Miranda held cohesive intelligible conversation at three years old. Remarking on how beautiful Mia and Miranda were, Aaron didn't appear as convinced they were his children as he had in court. Derrick and Roger noted his expression and aloofness.

Moving toward the door slowly, Derrick whispered, "Keep an eye on my girls, Roger. Please."

Waving and nodding, Roger moved closer to Mia and Miranda, so they wouldn't see Derrick slip from the room. The ploy worked for three minutes. Mia turned around and didn't see her father. She jumped down from the sofa and completely immersed herself in a search of the premises. Seldom having to call Derrick, Mia whined, "Daddy." Immediately Miranda's antennae went up. Scanning the room with nothing less than approaching panic, she joined Mia in the chant of, "Daddy."

Not completely unfamiliar with children, Angelique quickly distracted them again and began a little sing-a-long. As the children clapped and sang Barney songs, Angelique mentioned the scheduled DNA appointment they had at ten o'clock. Roger didn't like this. Something should have been said before Derrick left the office. Somehow, Roger thought Angelique knew that. This meant Roger would have to accompany them to the hospital, without Derrick's knowledge or consent. Anything illegal, or potentially illegal always set Roger's teeth on edge. This was no exception. But, the judge said it had to be done.

To Roger's surprise, Angelique and Aaron's car was equipped with car seats for the girls. This meant Roger would have to follow them in his car. Roger's teeth continued telling him one thing and his brain something else. Listening to his brain, Roger allowed Angelique to strap the girls in her car and drive them to the hospital. He followed and the ride was uneventful.

In the hospital, they were directed to Hematology. Roger followed the group up to the department doors. He allowed them to go in without him. His teeth were telling him to call Derrick and let him know where the girls were, and what was happening to them. Roger found a bank of telephones at the opposite end of the hall. Unfortunately, there was a bend in the hall and he wouldn't be able to actually keep an eye on the Hematology doors. Knowing they couldn't do whatever they had to do in a matter of minutes, Roger dashed down the hall and made the call to Derrick.

Because Derrick went to the recreation room first, Jocelyn had a small problem making him hear her calling him. Every time she pushed down on her diaphragm to speak loudly, the pressure in her abdomen was excruciating. Giving up, Jocelyn threw Derrick's giant sneaker down the stairs. He heard that, thought his wife was falling down the stairs and came running.

From the top of the stairs, Jocelyn said disgustedly, "Telephone, Derrick. It's Roger."

Picking up the receiver in the kitchen, Derrick said, "Hello."

In an excited rush, Roger snapped, "What took you so long to come to the telephone?! They brought Mia and Miranda to the hospital to get their DNA tests taken. I had to come behind them because there was no room in their car with those damned car seats the kids have to sit in. They're in the lab now."

Not liking the sound of what Roger said, Derrick asked with blatant suspicion, "Car seats? They had car seats, Roger? Why would they buy car seats, when they're only supposed to have visitation in your office?"

"Yeah. I thought that was a little strange too, Derrick, but they have them."

Shockwaves rattled Derrick's tongue. He couldn't say what he wanted fast enough. "Get back there and see if they've left that damned hospital with One and Two, Roger! Don't hang up!"

Leaving the telephone receiver dangling, Roger ran back to Hematology. He asked the receptionist if Mr. and Mrs. Kelly and the children were still back there. After giving Roger a suspicious once over, she said, "Oh, it only took a few minutes to draw the blood and do the swabs. They left about two minutes ago. The two little girls didn't enjoy the experience. They screamed their heads off. As a matter of fact, they were still crying when they left."

Balling his fists and stomping his foot, Roger snapped, "Damn it! Call downstairs and see if you can stop them from leaving."

Nonchalantly, the receptionist looked at the distressed attorney and asked, "Why?"

"Because those aren't their children!"

Quickly scanning her list, she assured herself it said, "Aaron, Angelique, Mia and Miranda Kelly." As far as she was concerned, those were their children and she wasn't getting into any funny business. The blue-eyed, blonde-haired cutie gave Roger a dimpled smirk and turned her back to him in silence.

Forgetting Derrick, Roger dashed down the three flights of stairs to the hospital lobby. He saw the Kelly's car pull out into traffic. Angelique and thc girls were in it. Throwing his hands in the air, Roger exclaimed loudly, "What the hell is she doing?!"

Aaron waltzed into the lobby carrying two containers of orange juice and a package of cookies. Roger couldn't resist walking over and asking him, "Who are those for?"

Looking around the lobby with a peculiar frown on his handsome face, Aaron said, "The girls. Where are they? I left the three of them sitting right over there."

Pointing out the window in disgust, Roger said, "Your wife just pulled out of the parking lot with the girls, Mr. Kelly. Do you have any idea where she's taking them?"

Not believing Roger, Aaron didn't answer. He continued to search the lobby for his wife and the two little girls. Aaron walked over to the receptionist and asked if she knew which way they went. Her response verified what Roger had said. "They headed toward the parking lot, Sir."

Aaron spun around to say something to Roger, but he had disappeared too. However, Aaron saw him headed toward the bank of telephones on the back wall. Wasting no time, Aaron caught up with him and asked, "What are you going to do now, Mr. Kingsley?"

Without stopping, Roger replied, "First, I'm calling the police. Then, I'm calling Derrick."

Panic blazed in Aaron's eyes when asked, "What are you calling the police for? She's not going anywhere with the children. She's probably trying to console them. They were very upset about the needles. Please don't call the police."

Waving him off, Roger dialed 911 and reported two missing little girls. He gave them Angelique, Mia and Miranda's descriptions, one of the car and its license plate number. Roger was glad his teeth told him to memorize it. Then, as promised, he dialed Derrick's number. A frantic Jocelyn answered on the first ring.

"What's going on, Roger? Derrick left here like a bat out of hell. Are the girls all right? That woman hasn't done anything to them, has she, Roger?"

Barely audible, Roger replied, "She left the hospital with them, Jocelyn."

Literally screaming, Jocelyn asked, "What hospital?! What were they doing in a hospital?!"

Pleading, Roger said, "Jocelyn, calm down. I've already called the police. They'll stop them somewhere and bring them back to the hospital. I'm staying right here until they do. She has to come back, Jocelyn. She left her husband here too."

While Roger answered all of Jocelyn's questions, Aaron called their lawyer and Angelique's mother. He had no idea where Angelique was going with those two little girls, and this was beginning to look like someone might be charged with kidnapping. If those were their children, Aaron felt that the courts should handle everything. Angelique was only turning this into a miserable mountain of legal problems that would take forever to resolve and cost a fortune.

Aaron still hadn't been able to digest when Angelique gave birth to Mia and Miranda, or why she had abandoned them in the first place. The Kellys had their share of problems, but none deep enough to hide a pregnancy in. At least as far as Aaron was concerned, he never knew anything about Mia and Miranda before they left for the airport two days ago. When he walked into the lawyer's office, all of the papers had been filed. Angelique gave vague answers to all of his questions. None of this was making any sense to Aaron.

He wasn't fond of Angelique's mother, but they needed someone else who might have a clue about what was going on. When Aaron shared what he knew with Mrs. Thomas, and asked if she would come down, in case they needed her, she treated Aaron as if he had lost his mind. Abandoning his pleading stance, Aaron gave Mrs. Thomas his version of an ultimatum.

"If you don't come down, Mrs. Thomas, your daughter will be charged with kidnapping all alone. If they lock her up, you bail her out and drag a story that makes sense out of her. I'm leaving, Mrs. Thomas. I don't know what's going on and I don't like the way this feels." She agreed to come down.

Aaron hung up the telephone and turned to face the angriest man he had ever seen in his life. Derrick's blood boiled. He was at his rope's end with this situation.

With Roger pleading with him not to do anything he would regret, Derrick grabbed a fist-full of Aaron's overcoat and banged him into the wall four times. Each bang was a little harder than the preceding one. Telephone receiver's hit the wall and wobbled noisily. Derrick spat ferociously into Aaron's face, "Where are my children?"

Attempting to wring Derrick's hands from his coat, Aaron shouted, with his own anger bubbling up, "I don't know! Get your hands off me!"

The two big men stood eye to eye for a few seconds. Glaring. Derrick tightened his grip on Aaron's coat. The condensation forming on Derrick's nose told the story. He was building up a head of steam that no conversation could relieve. Not knowing any more than he did, Aaron could never have aspired to the level of anger Derrick achieved.

Aaron saw something in Derrick's eyes that paralyzed him—rage . . .fury . . . insanity, all of them at once. He refused to drop or expand his vision. That's why Aaron never saw the punch that plunged him into a cavern of darkness. It was a good thing too, because he never saw the powerful rain of devastating blows that followed either.

With Roger and two security guards dragging him, Derrick wouldn't relinquish his hold on Aaron. If he had grabbed Aaron's neck, there would have been a dead man in the hospital lobby.

Two policemen came running to help Roger and the guards rip Aaron from Derrick's hold. The emergency medical staff stepped in to help Aaron immediately. His head had snapped so viciously when Derrick hit him, they braced his neck before placing his unconscious body on a stretcher. After a horrendous scuffle, what had by then expanded to two guards and four officers, they managed to cuff Derrick's hands behind his back. One officer held onto Derrick, while one of the others asked the guard what was going on. Of course, they had no idea. Roger attempted to explain.

Following the normal pattern of Dawes emergency relay calling, a hysterical Jocelyn called Sonya. Sonya called David, snatched up Ethan and headed for the hospital. David called Gran and moved briskly to his brother's aid. Gran called Sylvia, snatched up Pop and did likewise. The same excited phrase was passed before the caller hung up. "That silly woman disappeared with Mia and Miranda. Meet us at the hospital." No one wasted time asking, "Why the hospital?"

David arrived first. He came unglued at the sight of his brother pacing frantically back and forth, with his hands cuffed behind his back. The officer assigned to keep an eye on Derrick had given up the foot race. His head simply followed Derrick back and forth. David's boisterous demand for information announced his arrival. "What the hell is he handcuffed for?!"

The policeman's response to that was to whip out another pair of cuffs and his nightstick. Roger dashed to intervene. He quickly explained to David that Derrick had an altercation with Aaron. They would uncuff him if Aaron was all right and didn't want to press charges. If he did, then they would have to follow Derrick down to the precinct and bail him out.

Unimpressed, David looked at the policeman and said, "He should've knocked him on his ass! If they stand him up, I'll do it again! Where the hell are my nieces?!"

The policeman assigned to watch Derrick responded, "We don't know. But, everyone's looking for them. Why don't you just calm down and not make this any worse than it already is?"

Without hesitation, David asked in an excited rush, "Did anyone check the airport? Angelique lives in Denver. She's probably trying to take the girls home with her."

Sonya and Ethan came running in next. Sonya took one look at Derrick and yelled, "Why the hell is my son handcuffed?! His children are missing!"

Roger repeated his earlier act of interception. Sonya brushed him off and went to check Derrick's wrists. She'd heard the awful stories about tight handcuffs. If they thought they were going to cripple her child in front of her face they could just get their pistols ready to shoot her.

Wanting real information, Ethan and Roger spoke with the policeman in more civil tones. The officer had already spoken to the dispatcher about the airport possibilities and told her to alert the State Troopers. Maybe Angelique preferred to transport the girls by car.

At noon, Jocelyn wobbled slowly along the walkway. With the exception being the miserable handcuffed Derrick, the Dawes family saw her through the windows and gave a collective groan. All they needed was for her to go into labor. Then, Derrick would be facing the possible loss of all of his children at one time. He hadn't sat, stood still, or said one word since they cuffed him. As always, the torturous situation drove Derrick into himself.

No one recognized the man who held the door for Jocelyn. He was Aaron and Angelique's attorney. Dressed in sweats, Roger didn't even know who he was until he cleared the lobby and asked for Mr. Kelly. David met a seemingly composed Jocelyn. He explained the handcuffs Derrick was wearing before Jocelyn had an opportunity to ask. After that, she wanted to know how badly Derrick had hurt Aaron. David smirked and said, "His head may dangle at an angle for a while, but he'll live."

Roger and the attorney made their way to the bank of telephones for a little privacy. Feeling a great deal of responsibility for what was happening, Roger wasn't in the mood for prolonged diplomacy. He simply made it clear that if Aaron made a big deal of the assault, they would make a bigger deal of the blatant disregard of a Court Order. Because Aaron Kelly is named on said Order, he automatically bears the burden with his wife. If the children were not returned before the scheduled visitation time expired, they would make a really big deal of the kidnapping. And, if Derrick's wife loses the baby she's carrying, absolutely nothing would stop them from bringing every charge possible against both of his clients—criminal and civil. Leaving the attorney standing at the telephones without waiting for his response, Roger joined David, Jocelyn and the pacing Derrick.

## *CHAPTER THIRTY-SEVEN*

Jocelyn sat on a chair near Derrick and rubbed her stomach. Occasionally, a strained expression would distort her beautiful face, but she never said one word. Seeing this happen twice, Derrick stopped his frantic pacing and walked over to the officer assigned to making sure he didn't make a break for it. After explaining what he feared might be happening with his wife, Derrick asked him to remove the cuffs. Giving Jocelyn a brief inspection, the officer relented and released his prisoner.

Derrick told David to move and sat next to his wife. He automatically embraced her and stroked the expanse of her stomach. While Derrick couldn't imagine Jocelyn getting any bigger than she was at that moment, he knew she had to carry the baby at least six more weeks. The baby turned easily under the familiar pressure of his father's hand. That was just enough to assure Derrick that the little fellow was still all right in there.

Jocelyn gave Derrick a smile, lovingly covered the hand on her stomach with her own and said softly, "It's going to be all right, honey. They're going to bring Mia and Miranda back. Wherever they are, those girls are demanding an appearance by their daddy, and none to nicely by now either. Try not to worry so much."

Fear wouldn't allow Derrick to embrace that idea. If it didn't turn out that way, it would be best if he hadn't. Oh, he had been praying fervently. God just hadn't allowed his mind to relax long enough to weave any hopeful scenarios. Not trusting his voice, Derrick nodded solemnly and kissed the top of Jocelyn's head.

They all sat in that lobby and waited in the thickest of silences. A sigh made all heads swivel in its direction. Having seen similar scenes play out with families waiting for word of a loved one, the officers made several coffee and donut runs. They stayed in contact with the dispatcher and relayed the lack of reports to them.

At 1:45, Mrs. Thomas, Angelique's mother strolled into the lobby. She had known the Dawes family since Derrick and Angelique attended college together. Mrs. Thomas had always hoped Derrick would be her son-in-law. In her critical estimation, he was an excellent catch, a wonderful young man. Angelique and Derrick seemed so much in love with each other back then, she couldn't imagine what this mess was all about.

Sonya approached Mrs. Thomas and said abruptly, "Hello, Rochelle. Where is Angelique?"

Defensively, Mrs. Thomas replied, "Hello, Sonya. I haven't got the slightest idea where she is. What's all this about children? Angelique doesn't have any children. Her husband is sterile. Or, at least that was the last report I heard. Where is that idiot anyway? If he called me and left anyway, I'll kill him."

"Your daughter made a little trip down here a few Christmases ago. She spent the night with Derrick. Now, it seems the two have a set of twins that Angelique decided she didn't want at the time. So, she left them in this very hospital, with Derrick's name and address. He's been struggling with those babies ever since.

"They belong to him! I don't know where she gets off thinking she can just sashay her special ass back into the picture and take them! Now, if you have any idea where she is, I suggest you tell it to the officers! Maybe some of the trouble can be avoided! But, if anything happens to my kittens, you're going to be down one daughter! As God is my witness, I will kill your kid, Rochelle!"

In defense of her own child, Rochelle yelled back, "Why would Angelique steal or hurt your kittens, Sonya?! And, they're not her children! She didn't leave them anywhere! My daughter doesn't have any children! I think I would know if she did!"

Not backing down from her stance one pitch, Sonya said fiercely, "You're damned skippy she doesn't have any! And if she comes up for air without the two she left here with this morning, she never will! That's all I have to say to you, since you don't know anything!"

Ethan tried to calm Sonya. Her granddaughters were missing and she wanted to hurt somebody. In Sonya's mind, Rochelle could take the weight for her daughter.

Mrs. Thomas walked over to Derrick and Jocelyn. She didn't know Derrick had married either. Looking at the desperate expression on Derrick's face, she said, "I don't know what's going on, Derrick. Are you all absolutely sure Angelique took the children?"

"Yes, Ma'am. The Court Order said she could visit One and Two every Saturday at my lawyer's office until some things were cleared up. Angelique has taken it upon herself to walk away with them, the same way she walked away before. Without a word, or a trace. Leaving me to hold the bag, or the grief."

Searching for some reason for Angelique's behavior, Mrs. Thomas offered, "Why this is absolutely ridiculous. You hurt Angelique when you refused to marry her, Derrick. She's never gotten over it. That man she married just reminds her of you. She doesn't love him and he can't give her the one thing she wants desperately . . . a family. If she's done any of this, you'll have to take part of the responsibility for her behavior."

Waving his hand and giving a long exhausted sigh, Derrick said, "That's only partially true, Mrs. Thomas. Angelique left me because she couldn't have what she wanted, when she wanted it. Well, that's life. Throwing another man in my face wouldn't make me do what she wanted, so she married him. If it hasn't worked out for her, those were her choices. I loved your daughter. Would have married her eventually. When I felt I was in the right frame of mind and financial situation to give her the kind of husband every woman deserves. But, none of that gave her license to do this. She's playing with the lives of two innocent children."

The sudden movement of all of the officers at once made Derrick stop speaking to see what was going on. They all gathered in a huddle outside the sliding glass doors and spoke in their trademark conspiratorial tones. One broke away from the group, came in and asked David to step outside. Ethan forced Sonya to sit down with Gran and Pop and followed David.

There was a lot of commotion going on out there. Roger told Derrick to stay where he was. He had to go make sure David wouldn't do anything to make this situation any worse than it already was.

Jocelyn's tiny flinch distracted Derrick. He asked nervously, "Are you all right, Jocelyn? Please don't say yes if you don't mean it. I couldn't bear anything else going wrong today that I can't do anything about."

Sounding convincing, Jocelyn said, "I'm fine. I get a twinge every now and then. But, I get them at home when nothing's happening too."

Whatever was going on outside, the officers would only allow David to go see. Roger held his hand up to quell the fears of the waiting crowd. Seeing something, Roger's palm with all five fingers extended, changed to one finger. Roger held that finger up for what felt like hours to Derrick. If Jocelyn hadn't been clutching his arms so tightly, he would have gone outside himself. She relayed her fear physically.

Ethan and Roger's heads began to nod up and down at the same time. The expressions on their faces ran the emotional gamut, from wrenched relief to radiant smiles. Roger's one finger went back to an open palm as he leaned on the window for support. Suddenly, his legs felt like rubber on a sizzling hot day. The man had never been so afraid of anything for that length of time in his entire life.

Finally, David cleared the window with Mia and Miranda balanced on his forearms, desperately clinging to his neck. For the first time ever, they wouldn't give up David for Ethan. Never having been in the company of so many strangers in their little lives, they were frightened near to death. The identical sets of terror-filled, swollen, caramel eyes spoke volumes. "We're not letting Uncle David go. We don't know what's in the air between him and Gramp. Might be another hole with a strange lady and no Daddy in it."

A loud, head slapping chorus of, "Thank You, Jesus!" went up. Sonya and Gran openly wept with relief. Derrick's head dropped and his eyes closed. Giving a great sigh of thanks, he bit his lip and rose from the seat. Remembering Jocelyn he turned to look at his wife who was struggling with allowing relief to express itself. She waved him on.

When Derrick stepped outside the sliding doors, the two little tear-stained faces broke into huge, pathetic smiles and up went the most heart-wrenching relieved chorus of, "Daddy!"

# *CHAPTER THIRTY-EIGHT*

After two hours of legal wrangling at the hospital, Aaron agreed not to press any charges against Derrick for the sound beating he had received at the hands of the angry man. The officers informed Roger that while what Angelique had done was in conflict with a standing court order, technically she had not committed a kidnapping. They had approached her car in a traffic jam heading toward the interstate. Not actually on the interstate and clearly not outside the city limits. The twins, strapped securely in the back seat of Angelique's car, could be heard screaming a hundred yards in every direction. The police stopped counting after the tenth report of children in distress from car phones.

Weighing the options, Roger deducted that since Angelique was found and the girls returned before the visitation time expired, the judge probably wouldn't do anything more than yell at her. He could hear Angelique's attorney whining on and on about the distraught mother losing control after seeing her children for the first time in more than three years. The girls were not physically injured and the psychological damage would be dismissed as reasonable in an effort to restore a family unit.

Derrick refused to agree to forget about the broken visitation agreement. He was adamant about not ever bringing, or leaving, Mia and Miranda in Angelique's presence again. If jail was where he had to go for enforcing that stipulation, so be it. The entire Dawes family agreed wholeheartedly. There would be no more visitations until everything was cleared up.

Angelique's attorney's parting remarks to Roger were, "If your client refuses to bring the girls to your office one week from now, I'll be forced to file a Complaint of Non-Compliance. Just because the first visit didn't flow to his specifications doesn't give him the right to alter or dissolve that Agreement."

Roger turned to Derrick and asked, "Are you entertaining this at all?"

Derrick replied with angry defiance, "Hell, no!"

Roger turned back toward the departing group, shrugged his shoulders and said, "File away, Counselor. We'll see you in court."

The attorney led the Kellys from the lobby, with Aaron's neck still in the brace, and amidst Angelique's pleas of, "But they're my children, too. Derrick can't do that. The judge won't let him."

At home, a concerned Derrick noticed Jocelyn looking both tired and slightly drawn. There were dark circles gathering beneath her eyes. She insisted she was finc, no matter how many times he asked though. Derrick insisted she go straight to bed anyway.

Derrick spinning around in the kitchen with Mia and Miranda in his arms, trying to orchestrate the preparation of a meal was better than a Red Skeleton skit. Of course, he eventually realized it couldn't be done, abandoned the attempt and ordered a delivered meal by telephone. So he could keep an eye on his wife and hold both girls, dinner was eaten in Derrick's bedroom.

Derrick longed to return to the days of the unpredictable newborns and the man who had no idea what to do with them. He and Jocelyn learned a valuable lesson from the two terrorized little girls. Traumatized three-year-olds traumatize others.

After an evening of holding and reassuring, the furthest Mia and Miranda would wander from Derrick was the foot of the bed. The fear in their eyes even rejected Jocelyn. All women, from that day on, would be suspect in the eyes of Mia and Miranda. They spent time with Jocelyn and Sonya in fretful reluctance. Waking from a nap to anyone other than Derrick frightened them into fits of ear piercing screams for long periods of time. Crying was something they had abandoned years before and adopted again.

Mia and Miranda slept with Derrick and Jocelyn for three nights after that incident. Needless to say, Derrick was a nervous wreck. He had women jumping for different reasons, on both sides of him all night. Getting the girls back into their own room on Tuesday night was a major accomplishment for him. The fact that they insisted on being in the same bed was troubling, but Derrick could live with it.

The distance Angelique caused between Sonya and her kittens was not appreciated at all. Given the opportunity, Sonya would have gladly shown Angelique just how much. With wide fearful eyes, Mia and Miranda clung to Sonya after fits of crying for Derrick. Sometimes Sonya cried right along with them while she tried to console them. Ethan had better luck with the girls. Feeling more secure, they played in his presence as if nothing had happened. David got a similar response from them. Hope could not pry or cajole a kiss from either twin.

Feeling completely left out in the cold, Jocelyn held her peace. After all, she had her own problems brewing. The contractions in her abdomen got stronger everyday. They never came closer than thirty minutes apart, but the growing intensity was impossible to ignore. To keep Derrick from worrying anymore, she decided not to say anything to him about it until the pain was too much, came every five minutes, or her water broke. Jocelyn had discussed it all with her physician and he agreed with her decision to grin and bear it as long as possible.

At work on Wednesday afternoon, Derrick sat at his desk staring into space. Stillness was a rare commodity in his world these days. So, when his telephone rang, not wanting his brief stolen moment of solace disturbed, Derrick made no move to answer. He never noticed when it stopped ringing.

A few moments later, Tyson stuck his head in Derrick's door and said, "Hey, Big D, Roger's trying to get you on the horn. I'm sending him back. Pick it up."

Giving a great sigh, Derrick swiveled in the direction of the telephone and waited for the ring. Picking up the receiver, Derrick asked emotionlessly, "What's the verdict, Barrister?"

Loudly clearing his throat, Roger replied as if he were reading from a script, "I spoke to the judge this morning. While he understands how you feel, he has to insist that the Order be adhered to. The fact that Angelique lost it during her first visitation can be explained away by tons of psychiatric bullshit reasons. He has to give her another chance, or they will cause the judge an unnecessary headache."

"How?"

"Oh, he can be made to explain his decision to any number of different organizations. Women's groups will picket the courthouse and sit in on all of his hearings. Make his life one big ball of misery. And, that's just the beginning of the nightmare. Knowing he's right is the only way he'll face that squad."

"If I refuse to put the girls through it again?"

"You won't be helping them. The judge will be forced to have you thrown into jail. That means the girls will either go to Angelique until this situation is cleared up, or into foster care. The judge has given you permission to stay in my office during the visit. You just can't interfere with it. That's the best I can do for you right now, Buddy. I suggest you take it, Derrick."

"You do? Can I say to you that I don't know if any of this is worth it? One and Two don't sleep all night anymore. After picking through their meals, they have bouts of diarrhea and nausea everyday. From the moment I clear the door, they scream if they look up and don't see me. My wife and mother can't do anything for them at all. They cry because the girls are afraid and they can't console them. In another moment of selfishness, Angelique has changed my life irrevocably. Roger, are you absolutely sure there is no way we can circumvent all of this?"

Slowly, Roger replied simply, "No, Derrick. The only way out of this completely, is if by some miraculous stroke of fate, Angelique turns out not to be their mother. I know you never gave this a thought, but in all fairness I have to prepare you for every possible scenario. If the girls are not biologically yours or Angelique's they'll remove them from your custody, Derrick."

In the most defeated voice Roger ever heard, Derrick said, "I'll see you on Saturday morning then."

Tyson stood in Derrick's doorway. He hadn't heard most of what was said because Cynthia had called right after Roger. Tyson tried to get rid of her without telling her everything that was going on. Why worry her? After all, what could she do about it?

Before Tyson could ask any questions, Derrick's telephone rang again. It was Jocelyn. Tyson could tell by the way Derrick forced himself to perk up his tone. He backed out of Derrick's office without asking a lot of questions he knew Derrick didn't feel like answering anyway.

## *CHAPTER THIRTY-NINE*

Somehow, the Dawes family survived the work week. The Friday night following the traumatic visit with the Kellys brought with it all kinds of unique problems. First, Derrick tried explaining to the emotionally scarred twins that they had to go to Roger's office and see Angelique again. One and Two exchanged glances, frowned miserably and shook their heads. Whatever Daddy was talking about, they didn't agree. Derrick promised over and over again that he would not leave them. He promised to take them to Delivery Zone to play with the children and to see Lion King for the fifth time. The response the twins gave was, "Don't wanna go, Daddy."

Hearing Angelique's name only did one thing for One and Two–it robbed them of a good night's sleep. Every time they dozed off, one or the other woke looking for that lady and in time woke the other. They spent another fitful night in the room with Derrick and Jocelyn.

At nine that evening, Derrick saw Jocelyn take a deep breath, bite down on her bottom lip and let her head dangle backwards for a few moments. There was perspiration and a strained expression on her face when she came up for air again. Her hand soothingly stroked her abdomen.

Refusing to lend weight to the panic he felt, Derrick lightly stroked his wife's arm and calmly asked, "What was that about, Jocelyn?"

Taking another deep breath, Jocelyn asked absentmindedly, "What was what about?"

Already irritated by the broken sleep pattern of the twins, Derrick snapped bitingly, "Don't play games with me, Jocelyn. Something's hurting you and you're fighting it. Should I be taking you to the hospital now? Maybe calling my mother to come over to stay with the girls?"

Slowly massaging her temples, Jocelyn said, "Calm down, please. We've got a few weeks to go before we make that trip, Derrick. I get a contraction every now and then. Been getting them from the first day I got pregnant. I'm fine."

Derrick saw Jocelyn go through that same routine once more before he drifted off to sleep. During the night she jabbed him in the ribs with her elbow at least once more when it happened. Still, when Derrick asked, Jocelyn insisted she was fine.

At seven, on Saturday morning, Derrick got up. He bathed and dressed himself, One and Two. All three were grumpy as hell. One angrily swatted the brush across the room as Derrick tried to brush her hair. She didn't want to be bothered. Shrugging his shoulders in defeat, Derrick moved on to her sister. Two whined loudly, twisted and dodged the brush. Derrick finally gave up. There was nothing wrong with their hair anyway. Jocelyn had put the braided ponytails in while they slept during the night. Sonya insisted that, at the very least, all humans should brush their hair every morning

When they went down to the kitchen, Sonya had already prepared breakfast for them. She smiled weakly and said as cheerfully as possible, "Good morning. How are Grammy's kittens doing this morning?"

Two shook her head miserably and whined, "Don't wanna go see the lady, Grammy."

One pouted, rolled her beautiful caramel eyes at Derrick and repeated stubbornly, "Don't wanna go see the lady, Grammy."

Sonya fought the tears in her eyes and said, "I know, Sweeties. You just go this time and be good girls for Daddy. He won't let the lady take you in the car this time. Will you, Daddy?"

Derrick shook his head and said with great emphasis, "No way. I'm not leaving them with that lady for one minute."

Then, Derrick turned to his mother and said, "Mom, please keep an eye on Jocelyn today. I think something's wrong and she's not saying anything. If you have to get her to the hospital, just take her and call me. I'll meet you there."

Knowing the last thing Derrick needed to worry about this morning was the possibility of something happening to his wife and unborn son, Sonya said with confidence, "Five weeks early might not be too bad, Derrick. They save babies much younger than that now. Don't you worry about Jocelyn and the baby today, I'll take care of them. You take care of my kittens and don't let that crazy heffa run off with them this week. I can't take another day like last Saturday."

For the first time in their lives, Mia and Miranda were not pleased with Daddy at all. They didn't give him one smile. Kisses and hugs were out of the question. Both girls refused to come when Derrick called them. They didn't lift an arm to help getting into their jackets either. Every time Derrick made eye contact with one of them they turned away. It was their way of saying, "You've betrayed us, Dad." They didn't need to go through the routine, Dad already felt like Benedict Arnold straight through to the core of his existence.

The girls sat in their car seats and never made a sound. In the parking lot of Roger's office, Derrick released One, picked her up and stood her outside the car. When he backed away to close the door, he realized One had sat down on the ground and crossed her arms. Reaching for her hand, Derrick lifted One to her feet. There was only one problem. As his mother would say it, "All of the starch had gone out of the child." One's legs wouldn't support her.

Seeing One was refusing to stand, Derrick picked her up, closed the door and walked around to get Two. Derrick had to put One down to get Two out of her car seat. When he lowered her, One's lifeless legs automatically began to collapse. Derrick couldn't let her sit on the ground. There was oil down there. So, he sat her in the door-well of the car. One tried to slide down from there too.

Holding One up in the door-well with his leg, Derrick released Two. Before he could pick her up, tears began to flow and Two said in a retched three-year-old rush, "Don't wanna go, Daddy. Not like lady. Not Mommy. Not ride wif her."

With his own heart breaking at the thought of forcing his babies to do something none of them wanted, Derrick picked Two up and rocked her. Stroking her head, as she cried into his shoulder, Derrick said miserably, "Sweetheart, if Daddy could think of any way to take you home and not have to do this, he would do it. We have to go in, Two. I won't leave you today, sweetheart. Daddy's going to sit right there with you. I promise. Okay?"

No, it wasn't okay. Both girls screamed and tried to push their way out of Derrick's arms, as they cleared the deserted lobby of Roger's office building and entered the elevator. The Dawes family was five minutes late and Angelique had no intentions of letting Derrick think she hadn't noticed.

An obvious bundle of exposed raw nerves, Angelique jumped up the moment Derrick managed to get the office door open. The fact that the girls were hysterical and inconsolable did not interest Angelique. She yelled over their screams, "Why are you late, Derrick?! If I can get here from Denver on time, why can't you do the same?!"

Looking Angelique up and down as if she were a foul smelling piece of road kill, Derrick dismissed her with a smirk. He sat down and tried to calm his girls. One and Two clung to Derrick's neck and jacket collar. After fifteen minutes of crying and clutching their father, One and Two quieted. Loosening their grip on Derrick was still out of the question though.

Standing on Derrick's legs, holding his collar firmly, One and Two dared to look in Angelique's direction. From where she sat across the room, Angelique smiled and waved at them.

Again, they buried their terrified faces in Derrick's neck. To help break the ice, Derrick asked, "Where's Aaron?"

Stiffly, Angelique replied, "He's not here."

"I can see that. Where is he? Didn't he want to see his children this weekend?"

"Don't start, Derrick. He had business to take care of this weekend. You just be glad it doesn't entail suing you for damages. He'll be in that damned neck brace for weeks."

In an obviously facetious tone of voice, Derrick said, "Oh yeah, I'm the lucky one all right. At least, whenever it involves you."

"What's that supposed to mean?"

"Every time you enter my life and exit, I'm faced with some possible legal action or another. Three years ago, it was child abandonment. Now, it's assault. What next, Angelique?"

Giving Derrick the most hateful stare he had ever seen and not given a damn about, Angelique said rigidly, "Yes. And, you were not exactly shrinking from the thought of pressing kidnapping charges against me either, Lover Boy. Anyway, I think this meeting would go much smoother if you left the girls here with me and you went into the other room."

Laughing, Derrick said, "Look at them, Angelique. They're scared to death of you. If I try to leave, they'll scream so loud, you won't hear anything for the next month. Do you really think you could sit in this room with them alone?"

Ignoring Derrick, Angelique stormed over and attempted to take Two from his lap. The little girl's screech rattled the door and all of the windows. Two dug her nails into her father and refused to let go. Immediately coming to her sister's aid, One hit Angelique. When that didn't make her let Two go, One bit down on Angelique's wrist with furious tenacity. One eventually released Angelique from her grip when Derrick squeezed her jaw.

Frustrated now, and in pain, Angelique raised her hand as if she planned to strike One. Derrick grabbed it in mid-air, gave it a not so gentle twist and spat angrily, "What the hell do you think you're doing? Hit her and your husband won't be the only one in a neck brace, Angelique."

Running her hand through her short hair, Angelique yelled, "I can't believe I ever loved you, Derrick Dawes! How could you turn those children against me?! What have I done to deserve to be treated this way?! Nothing! You started this, not me!"

Breaking down into a torrent of tears, Angelique sat. Derrick, One and Two stared at her. One finally said, "Lady crying, Daddy."

Unimpressed, Derrick said, "Yes, I see the lady's crying, One. She'll be all right."

Angelique continued to cry. One and Two sat comfortably cradled in Derrick's lap. They looked up at their father and over at the crying lady for better than five minutes. Two broke the ice this time by saying, "Don't cry, Lady."

Angelique sniffed and said, "Okay."

Not really meaning it, One looked at her feet and said, "Sorry, Lady."

"Thank you, Miranda."

Giving Angelique her how stupid can you be look, One said, "Not Manda. Mia."

"I'm sorry, Mia. Thank you."

Sniffing again, Angelique asked, "How do you tell them apart, Derrick? They're truly identical. I can't find one real difference."

"Honestly, I don't know how I know them apart. If I think about it, I guess the truth is I just know them. One, I mean Mia, is the one who seems to be most standoffish to strangers. She's the protector of the two. Smiles much less than her sister. Doesn't ask for attention. She demands it. Miranda is friendlier to everyone. More sensitive. Affectionate. More likely to express what the two are thinking."

"If they're not facing you, can you tell which one is which?"

"Yes."

"How?"

"I just know them, Angelique. They're exactly alike for all intents and purposes. No height or weight differences. Their hair is exactly the same color, length and texture. They don't have any distinguishing birthmarks worth mentioning. My knowing may be instinctive."

Stopping and giving Angelique a sarcastic glance, Derrick continued, "When you take care of someone's every need, day and night, day after day, year after year; you simply know them."

Disregarding his antagonistic tone, Angelique asked, "Can your wife tell them apart as easily as you, Derrick?"

"Yes."

"They love her?"

"Yes."

"They think of her as their mother?"

"Yes."

"If the judge says we have to share custody, do you think they'll ever be able to think of me as their mother?"

"I can't answer that, Angelique." Stopping momentarily, Derrick gave Angelique an innocent sigh and smile. Then, he asked, "Are you saying there's a possibility they may not be Aaron's, Angelique?"

Running her hand through her hair again, Angelique said, "I'm not saying anything, Derrick. I just posed a hypothetical."

Hoping Angelique was finally coming to her senses, Derrick said, "This is very detrimental to the girls, Angelique. If we have to share them, we'll have to give them a chance to get to know you. You can't expect them to accept a complete stranger as their mother overnight. They're three-and-a-half. If you love them at all, Angelique, you've got to give them a chance. Don't confuse them anymore than they already are." Pausing for a moment, Derrick swallowed hard and said, as if it were the most difficult word he ever uttered, "Please?"

Angelique didn't respond. She just stared at the two little identical faces looking back at her and began to cry again. Both girls took turns saying, "Don't cry, Lady."

At eleven, Two whispered to Derrick that she had to go to the bathroom. He relayed this message to Angelique and asked if she would mind him taking her. To his surprise, Angelique said, "We'll all go together. They have to get used to my presence, Derrick. After all, I'm their mother. Right?"

If Derrick heard Angelique, he never responded by word or gesture. Instead, he folded the girls' jackets and prepared to make the trip to the bathroom.

Pointing at Angelique, Two asked in confusion, "Mommy?"

One said emphatically, "Not Mommy."

Looking directly into Derrick's eyes, Angelique said, "Tell them who I am, Derrick."

Refusing to budge on the subject, Derrick said, "Not today, Angelique. They're not ready."

"I'll make you sorry for that."

Smiling cynically, Derrick said, "Throw it up on the pile of other things you've made me sorry for, Angelique."

One and Two actually walked to the bathroom. Angelique was truly surprised to see that Derrick had no reservations about entering a lady's room. Waiting for her father to cover the seat, One hopped up on the commode with little assistance from her father and did what she had to. With her clothes neatly tucked back in and her hands washed, One was ready for her return trip. Still not ready to risk Angelique running off with them again, both girls grabbed Derrick's hands.

Back in Roger's office, One and Two played with the toys Angelique had bought them on the floor at Derrick's feet. Derrick explained what everything was and told them the correct colors. Angelique watched them. Her real interest lay in Derrick though. She couldn't resist asking, "What's your wife's name again, Derrick?"

Looking up slowly, Derrick said in a cautioning tone, "Jocelyn."

Appearing vulnerable for the first time, Angelique said, "Right. Tell me what Jocelyn has that I don't."

Frowning and throwing his hands in the air, Derrick asked, "Why do women always ask that dumb question? How are we supposed to answer it? She has an extra neck near her navel? What?"

For the first time that morning, Angelique laughed. She had forgotten what a quick wit Derrick could be, when he was being congenial. The more Derrick and Angelique conversed, the more relaxed One and Two were. Not to be thrown off of the subject, Angelique asked more specifically, "What was it about Jocelyn that made you know you loved her more than you loved me, Derrick?"

Smirking, Derrick asked, "What makes you think I love Jocelyn more than I loved you?"

In a painful, breathless whisper, Angelique replied, "You married her, Derrick."

Holding his finger up, Derrick said, "You married Aaron five years ago, Angelique. How did you know you loved him more than you loved me?"

Angelique answered simply, "I didn't love him at all, Derrick. He was just as close to you as I could find. He only looks like you though. I thought I could teach him to act more like you, I guess. I don't know what I was thinking. I do know I made a mess."

"So, why are you dragging the girls into the mess? What did they do to deserve to be muddied?"

Clearing her throat, Angelique said, "Let's not discuss the girls right now, Derrick. Tell me how you knew you loved Jocelyn. Enough to marry her."

Without giving it any thought, Derrick said, "Jocelyn is the most loving woman I've ever known. She doesn't emasculate me for things she can't possibly understand. She's patient, unselfish, confident, never jealous, seldom demanding, affectionate and passionate. She actually let me propose to her in my own time and in my own awkward way."

Sarcastically, Angelique said, "Wow. The only thing missing was beautiful."

"I didn't have to say that. You've seen her. You know she's beautiful."

"Are you trying to tell me Saint Jocelyn didn't get upset when you inherited Mia and Miranda?"

All of the talk of Jocelyn made One and Two start looking for her. Two patted Derrick's hand and ask, "Where is Mommy Josh, Daddy?"

"She's at home, Two. We'll see her in a little while. Okay?"

Looking over her shoulder at Angelique, a relieved Two said softly, "Okay. Mommy's home."

Continuing the conversation, Derrick said, "I already had One and Two when I met Jocelyn. She was their nurse."

"She probably doesn't think very highly of the woman who left them on you like that."

"Believe it or not, Jocelyn and my mother actually tried to explain why you might have done it. They did such a good job, I had trouble discerning whether they thought of you as a pioneer or just another worthless woman."

Realizing she was wasting her time trying to find the nick in Jocelyn's armor, Angelique dove for the root of her ponderings. "When you see me, Derrick, do you feel any of what we had before all of this madness? When you see me, what do you see?"

Smiling, Derrick said, "I see a beautiful, but confused woman. I'm not in love with you anymore, Angelique. And, after what you've done to One and Two, I could never be in love with you again."

Sadly, Angelique asked, "Not even if they forgive me for it?"

"They very well may forgive you someday, Angelique, only because they were too young to remember. But, the damages are unseen and immeasurable. I can only hope the love I've tried to give them made up for some of it. No one can duplicate or replace the love of a mother. I say that because I can't imagine anyone being Sonya for me, except Sonya. She knows more about me than I do. She would die for me on a moment's notice and I would do the same for her. As much as I love One, Two and Jocelyn, it still doesn't compare to the way I feel about my mother. I can't explain it to you."

"The way you know Mia and Miranda, it's plain to see they haven't missed out on much by not having their flesh and blood mother. I can tell, Derrick."

Just as Derrick was about to change the subject to lunch, the office door burst open and in marched Ethan and David. Before Derrick could formulate a reason for their sudden appearance, Ethan said, "Go home, Derrick. We'll stay here with Mia and Miranda. They'll be fine. Don't worry."

Knowing something was wrong with Jocelyn, Derrick moved toward the door quickly. One and Two moved with him. David scooped them up and spun them. As usual, they started laughing. By the time David stopped spinning, they were too dizzy to discern whether Derrick was present or not. Derrick slipped soundlessly from the room.

Angelique interrupted by snapping angrily, "The judge said Derrick could be in the office during our visit. Not Derrick's family."

Sternly, Ethan responded, "I'm not in the mood for your nonsense today, young lady. You just sit down and shut up, or play with the girls. Derrick has to go home and the law says those girls have to stay here. It's me, David, Mia, Miranda and you or nothing. If you don't like it, call your lawyer and we'll sort it out on Monday. I don't like what you've done and I really don't care what else you do."

Looking around the room, Ethan asked, "Where's that sorry husband of yours? I may as well tell him what I think of him too, while I'm in the mood to talk.

## *CHAPTER FORTY*

Knowing Jocelyn had been experiencing contractions all night had provided Derrick with just enough information to keep him from panicking. However, he did not understand why Sonya had not just called the doctor and taken Jocelyn to the hospital, but he wouldn't press the panic button for that either. David and Ethan's presence had obscured Derrick's disappearing act long enough for him to not be further frustrated by One and Two's pending disappointment. Truthfully, the older the girls got, the more they preferred Uncle David anyway. He was just chocked full of noisy foolishness.

After the twenty-minute drive from Roger's office, it was a relatively composed Derrick Dawes who inserted his key into his front door lock. Just as Derrick turned toward the stairs, two of the most frightening sounds he had ever heard stopped him dead in his tracks. A high-pitched, extremely loud and strangled scream shredded the silence. A thick, wood shattering thud followed immediately. What Derrick heard next made him take the stairs three at a time.

Obviously distressed, Sonya yelled in quick tearful succession, "Jesus, Jocelyn! Jesus! What do you think you're doing?! Jesus!"

Running into the bedroom, the only thing Derrick noticed was the dangling telephone cord on his night table. The sight in the bathroom literally made him stop breathing. His mother kneeling in a steadily growing pool of water with the faintest pink discoloration and in her arms laid a panting, heavily perspiring, frantically clutching, obviously suffering, weeping and pleading Jocelyn. Derrick heard Jocelyn say, "Please don't let them kill my baby, Sonya. If I could just carry him a little while longer, he'll be all right. Please don't make me go to the hospital. It's too soon. He'll die."

Stroking Jocelyn's soaking wet hair, Sonya wept and tried to comfort her frightened daughter-in-law. Sonya didn't even know Derrick was standing right behind her when she said, "Don't worry, Jocelyn. They'll take care of that little fella at the hospital. He's going to be fine. You shouldn't have locked yourself in here this long though, honey."

Derrick finally found the courage to move again. He stepped into his mother's view. Without preliminaries, Sonya said impatiently, "Get down here and check to see if that baby is on his way out, Derrick."

Feeling more frightened, dumbfounded and impotent than he had ever felt in his life, Derrick yelped, "What?!"

Screaming, Sonya repeated, "Get down here, Derrick! Check to see if the baby is on his way out! There's blood in this water! You don't want him to suffocate, do you?!"

Like a child being thrown into a pool of water for the very first time, Derrick was paralyzed by timeless fear. It had to be a major dose of man's original fear because all Derrick felt was an ancient arctic cold that locked him in a frozen, airless abyss Derrick could not force himself to move around in.

Sonya screamed again, "Move, Derrick!"

Gritting his teeth so tightly they made a loud grinding sound, Derrick stiffly moved toward Jocelyn's feet. Issuing a silent plea to God for courage, Derrick dropped to his knees in the pool of unbelievably warm water. Touching Jocelyn's knees as if the slightest pressure would break them, Derrick gave them a gentle push. What he saw made him wish he were back in Roger's office fighting with Angelique.

Struggling to keep the panic out of his voice and with his lips barely moving, Derrick said softly, "Mom, I think that's his head."

Openly weeping and obviously frightened to death, Jocelyn asked miserably, "Is his face out? Don't let his airway get blocked, Derrick."

Before Derrick could say he only saw the top of the baby's head, Jocelyn's face contorted in a painful grimace and she let out another joint jarring scream, like the one he had heard downstairs. Then, Derrick saw the most amazing thing he would ever see in his life. His son's head slid into the world and moved as if he were terribly uncomfortable. Derrick's hands automatically moved to make sure the little head didn't make contact with the floor. Just as automatically, Derrick wanted to let it drop when a frustrated, muffled cry emanated from the not even half person. The head kept its noise going for all to hear.

As if Derrick and Sonya were in another room, Jocelyn yelled, "He's crying, honey! Listen, Sonya! He's crying!"

At her wits end with Jocelyn and Derrick, Sonya wept and nodded. Choking on every emotional syllable, Sonya asked, "Are you holding his head up, Derrick?"

Clearly feeling some relief and encouragement, Jocelyn shouted, "Clean his mouth out, Derrick. He sounds like there's something in it."

"How am I supposed to do that?"

"Just run your finger through his mouth. Sweep it out with your finger."

Holding the miniature, slimy, pale head in the palm of one hand, Derrick attempted to get his little finger into the baby's mouth. Of course, the infant knew Derrick was going to do that and shut it. Bending down to get a closer look at the tiny head, it appeared to Derrick the baby had fallen asleep. Determined, and concentrating on how to get his finger into the baby's mouth, Derrick asked, "How long before the rest of this little dude gets out?"

The unfamiliar excited ringing of the doorbell and Jocelyn's simultaneous scream and agonized groan answered that question for Derrick. Frightened again by it all, and looking around for God only knows what, Derrick almost let the baby's body slide onto the floor. The tiny fat fellow's bottom lip pouted and quivered violently before he let out his loud complaint.

Seeing Derrick jostle the baby's slick body like a wet football, a completely rattled Sonya snapped, "Wrap that boy in a towel and lay him on his mother, Derrick! I have to go let the paramedics in!" Then, as a quick afterthought, she asked, "It is a boy, isn't it, Derrick?"

Derrick wanted to complain about having to pass his son off before he even got to get a good look at him. Then, he noticed the baby was still tethered to his mother by something so bizarre looking, Derrick didn't even want to think about having to touch it. Quickly reaching for towels to wrap the screaming and squirming baby, Derrick said, "You bet it's a boy, Mom."

The last thing Sonya heard the frantic Jocelyn ask Derrick was, "Is he all right? Is he all there?" Sonya simply thanked God for His graciousness and dashed down to let the paramedics in.

The moment Derrick lay the wailing infant in Jocelyn's arms he saw something he never thought he would ever see. The beam in her eye passed from father to son and would remain that way for weeks to come. Jocelyn's greatest prayer had been answered and she had every intention of treasuring it. She somehow forgot the infant wasn't just her blessing.

In a matter of moments the paramedics had taken over. The umbilical cord was cut and the baby pronounced as healthy as a premature home born baby could be. The constant, strong bellowing told them there was absolutely nothing wrong with his lungs. They congratulated Dad on a delivery well done, and after wrapping the baby warmly, they began the trip to the hospital. Derrick quickly changed his soaked jeans and followed the ambulance.

Two hours later, no one would have ever guessed how the little fellow had made his entrance. He lay in his mother's adoring arms in her hospital room, with his father sitting in a chair trying to get a good look at him. Jocelyn kept saying, "You look like your father, but that's okay." Derrick didn't know exactly how to interpret that.

The entire Dawes family arrived after dinner. Mia and Miranda ran to Derrick and climbed up on his lap. In truly dedicated three-year-old attempts to see their new baby brother, they dangled dangerously over the bed. Jocelyn pulled the cover back for them, but she refused to expose her precious bundle to the possible gymnastics of Mia and Miranda. Everyone noticed her reticence. Knowing how long and hard it was for Jocelyn to have the little fellow, no one made a big deal of it. They just all thanked God it was over and the baby was fine.

Inspecting his nephew, David asked, "Okay, what's his name?"

Speaking up for the first time since everyone's arrival, Jocelyn said sarcastically, "Don't be ridiculous. You know what his name is, David."

"How am I supposed to know what his name is, Smarty Jocelyn?"

Rolling her eyes at David and giving her new son another glance of undiluted love, she said, "He'll have his father's name, if you don't mind."

Unable to ever let Jocelyn have the last smart word, David said, "His father doesn't even have his own name. His father's name is Derrick Ian Dawes, II. He's named after Pop's oldest brother, Jocelyn. So, you're holding Derrick Ian Dawes, III."

Feeling stupid, Jocelyn asked Derrick, "Why didn't I know you were a second?"

Trying to keep the girls from falling on Jocelyn and the baby, Derrick said, "I don't know, Jocelyn. It's on our marriage license."

Frowning, Jocelyn asked incredulously, "Is it really?"

David answered, "Sure is. You were so glad to get the man, you didn't read the fine print."

Rolling her eyes, Jocelyn said bitingly, "Shut up, David. So, his name is Derrick Ian Dawes, III. And, I guess we'll have to call him Ian. I like that. Ian."

Not to give Jocelyn the last word, David asked, "Is that all right with you, Derrick?"

Absentmindedly, Derrick asked, "Is what all right with me?"

"His name, Dumbo?"

Blinking and juggling the two fidgeting girls, Derrick said shortly, "If he's named after me, why wouldn't it be all right with me, David? Isn't your son named after you? Stop trying to start a fight. How did the rest of One and Two's visit go?"

David gave a truly nasty snarl and said bitterly, "Oh, it went. She didn't seem too happy to hear that you were probably on the way to the hospital to await the birth of your son though. Angelique broke down in tears when she tried to pick up Mia and the kid screamed Daddy so loud the fillings probably fell out of her teeth. I can't imagine how she stood being locked in the car with both of them doing that. Dad deemed the entire episode a disaster and demanded it be terminated. We packed up Mia and Miranda and made a mad dash for the elevators. Angelique never made a sound. Just stood watching like a deer in headlights."

The week following the birth of Ian was a strange one for the Dawes family. Derrick had his hands filled to capacity with the whims of women. His usual retreat into himself was not achievable. With an incapacitated wife, two toddlers and an infant, there was way too much to be done.

## *CHAPTER FORTY-ONE*

It was a frazzled Derrick Dawes who was forced to take a few weeks of vacation time to care for his family. While Derrick didn't mind doing any of it, his wife seemed to have lost sight of the fact that she had two other children and a husband who might be interested in the newest addition to their family. Derrick understood that Ian was premature and required constant monitoring, but he thought Jocelyn had gone overboard in her zealous protection of her new son. Mia and Miranda coveted their wounded expressions and refused to enter their parents' bedroom. The obvious abandonment of Jocelyn only made the twins cling more desperately to their Derrick.

Ian was two weeks old before Jocelyn realized the girls never entered their bedroom anymore. Because Derrick prepared all of her meals and served her in the bedroom, the only time Jocelyn could recall being in their presence was when they all spent time in the recreation room. With the fear of losing Ian growing more of a distant memory everyday, Jocelyn began to ask questions.

"Derrick, where are the girls?"

"In their room, playing."

"Why haven't they been playing in here lately?"

Derrick gave Jocelyn a strange look and said, "They know where they're not wanted, Jocelyn. You're lucky I'm older than they are and so expected to possess the fortitude to endure this chilling experience."

Risking waking the sleeping infant, Jocelyn yelled, "What are you talking about, Derrick?! What chilling experience?!"

"The great Jocelyn and Ian love affair. We haven't been so much as allowed to peer into his bassinet and get a good look at His Highness without being berated about our nearness threatening his existence. I know if I sneeze once in this room I'll be banished until I can produce a formal document saying I'm germ free. Personally, I envy One and Two their ability to retreat to another room."

"Have I been that obvious, Derrick?"

"You didn't notice we were all gone on Saturday for another visit with Angelique. My mother said you never asked where we were."

Feeling completely selfish, a single tear slid from her eye as Jocelyn asked solemnly, "How did the visit go, Derrick?"

"As well as can be expected when you have two little girls being forced to spend time with a woman they don't like and fear greatly. If she moves to touch them they scream and run. The worse thing Angelique could have ever done was take them without getting to know them first."

Wiping at the tears falling onto her cheeks, Jocelyn asked, "What is Roger saying about the custody hearing?"

"The last time I spoke with him, he sounded like the cat who ate the canary. He just keeps saying it's in the bag. Whatever that means."

"Are the DNA test results in yet?"

"My sealed results were delivered to Roger two days ago. I gave him permission to open them without me. When I asked what they said he just laughed and said something about this being the most bizarre crap he had ever seen in his life. I don't think Angelique and Aaron's DNA results have been completed yet."

"She's not their mother, Derrick. She told you that herself. I don't know why you don't believe her."

"If she's not their mother, why is she filing for custody, she has to know the tests will blow her cover."

"This is the absolute last time I'm telling you this, she's hurt. This little charade has allowed her to spend time with you and the girls, Derrick. There's no way a woman who loves you the way Angelique does would not take full advantage of a pregnancy. She would have reeled you in, not abandoned the babies to you. The woman who left Mia and Miranda was overwhelmed with her pregnancy and the prospect of you rejecting her. Does that sound like Angelique to you?"

"No. But, if Angelique's not their mother, who is, Jocelyn?"

"I can't answer that question for you, Derrick."

"Okay, when Ian wakes up can I hold him?"

Reminded of what had started this conversation, Jocelyn dropped her eyes and answered, "Of course you can hold him, Derrick. He's just as much yours as he is mine."

"Good to know you've finally acknowledged that. Can Mia and Miranda hold him too?"

Honestly shaken by the prospect, Jocelyn stammered, "They're not big enough to hold him yet, Derrick. He's so tiny."

Smirking, he said, "Well, I'll wait until they can hold him too. I'm all they have right now and the last thing I want them thinking is that I've abandoned them for Ian. Besides, he doesn't even know I exist yet."

A freshly agitated Jocelyn rose from the bed and headed for the bathroom while asking, "Why don't you go downstairs and get the whole box of salt to throw in the wound, Derrick?"

As if by signal, the moment the bathroom door closed, Ian began to complain. Derrick scooted over to Jocelyn's side of the bed to see if there was anything he could do to comfort him until his mother returned. The last thing he thought he would have to do was pick him up.

With Derrick only talking to him, Ian whined and wiggled. Derrick patted his son's back and Ian let out a terrible cry. Expecting Jocelyn to come running for him, Derrick retreated and decided to give rocking the bassinet a try. That wasn't well received by the wailing infant either. Derrick had to pick him up. It took a few moments for Ian to quiet, as Derrick rocked him in his arms. Silently, two little sets of hands climbed Derrick's back. Mia and Miranda leaned on their father and peered shyly at the baby over his shoulder.

Seeing this as his opportunity to introduce Ian to his sisters, Derrick asked, "One and Two, you want to hold your brother?"

With excited eyes the size of saucers, One nodded, "yes" and Two shook her head, "no."

One eagerly plopped down next to Derrick and waited for the delivery of Ian. She had held Omar when he came home from the hospital and she couldn't wait to hold Ian. Derrick slipped Ian over to One's lap and she cradled his head the way Grammy told her to do with Omar. One gazed at her new brother lovingly and planted a big kiss on his tiny forehead. He wiggled and gave a little grunt. The smile One gave Derrick was worth any amount of Jocelyn's disapproval. Two eventually took her place on the other side of her father and waited patiently to timidly take her brother into her arms and give him her first kiss, too.

When Jocelyn returned, Ian lay in Two's lap with One standing in front of them. Ian looked from one sister to the other as if he were trying to figure out what was going on. He held on tight to One's finger the entire time. As One and Two sang their favorite Barney song for their baby brother, Jocelyn took a seat in the wing chair and wept silently. Seeing Ian in someone else's arms suddenly made him more real to his mother than he had been previously. He wasn't a wish or a dream anymore. Derrick Ian Dawes, III was flesh and blood and destined to be spoiled rotten by all of the people who loved him just as much as his mother.

# *CHAPTER FORTY-TWO*

The third Saturday visit for the twins and the Kellys loomed large on Derrick's horizon the Friday night before. No amount of talking made One and Two understand why they had to go visit the lady and Ian didn't have to. As a matter of fact, they couldn't understand why Peepers and Omar didn't join them for the visits either. They all visited Grammy, Gramp, Gran and Pop together. For the life of them they could not fathom what was so special about this lady that none of the boys had to go to Roger's office to visit with her. Derrick was at the actual end of his rope when Two asked, "Can Uncle David go with us, Daddy?"

On Saturday morning, Jocelyn prepared breakfast for the three long-faced Dawes family members and kept her comments to herself. Derrick appreciated the silence. Ian sat propped up in his chair on the kitchen table looking from one face to the other quietly. The ringing telephone interrupted Derrick's precious silence and he moaned out loud at the prospect of having to answer it. Jocelyn let the telephone ring three times before she moved to answer it.

Derrick heard her say Roger's name and watched her hand him the telephone. Before Roger could say a word, Derrick asked, "What couldn't wait until I got there, Roger?"

"That's no way to greet a brother, Derrick."

Sarcastically, Derrick sniffed and said, "Yeah, right. Could you tell a brother what couldn't wait until he got there?"

"You don't have to come unless you just want to look at my handsome face. Of course, you may want to hug and kiss me, but a brother can't have all of that."

"Okay, Roger. Now, you want to tell me what's going on from the top, or do I have to come down there to drag it out of you?"

Musing, Roger said, "Well, from the top . . . like I said, you don't have to come down here at all. It's all over, Derrick. Mia and Miranda belong to you lock, stock, tuitions and weddings. Their mother has proven to the judge's satisfaction that she is in-fact their mother. Her DNA matches the twins without any room for error. She has given you complete custody of the girls on two conditions."

Not believing one word Roger was saying, Derrick asked haltingly, "What two conditions?"

"First, that you promise to contact her through me if you ever feel the girls are too much for you to handle."

Interrupting Roger, Derrick asked sharply, "When is that supposed to happen? If I survived the pampers, temperatures, tantrums and sleepless nights when will they be too much?"

"Don't speak too quickly, Derrick. I hear puberty is the real test of parenthood. Anyway, would you like to know the other condition?"

"Sure, why not? It's probably every bit as ridiculous as the first."

"You have to abandon all efforts to find out who she is. If the girls want to know later on, they can contact her through me."

Dumbfounded, Derrick asked, "What are you talking about, Roger? I already know who she is. She's Angelique Kelly. Right? Right, Roger?"

"No, she's not Angelique Kelly, Derrick."

Pouncing out of his chair and pacing the kitchen floor, Derrick yelled, "What?! Well, who is she?!"

"Are you turning down the offer, Derrick?"

Panicked, Derrick rambled, "No! Of course not! I just want to know who she is, Roger! Don't I have the right to know?!"

"Under these circumstances, no you do not have the right to know. Now, if you insist I tell you who she is, I have to go back to her and tell her that. She can then file all of the same Motions Angelique filed and this time will be different, Derrick. This woman is definitely their mother. The games are officially over now."

Still quite unsettled, Derrick asked pathetically, "Aren't I at least entitled to know why she abandoned them, Roger?"

"Only if she feels inclined to share her story with you, Derrick. Can't you just take Mia and Miranda and ride off into the sunset without making this woman explain? She cared enough to save the girls from being dragged off by one of your old fruity flames. She didn't have to do that, Derrick. She has risked exposure by doing so. If the girls are not going to be with you, she wants them back."

"I'm having a problem deciding who you're representing at this point, Roger. How did she know the girls needed rescuing from Angelique? How did she know to contact you? How did she get the DNA test done without Mia and Miranda?"

"I'll answer what I can without infringing on her demands. All she did was contact me. I asked Dr. Kane if he could arrange for her samples to be compared with your samples. He did it for Jocelyn. The strain of carrying her own baby and the possibility of losing two she already loved dearly was taking a grand toll on her."

"Dr. Kane? That was weeks ago. You've known who she was all of this time and you let me put the girls through all of that torture for nothing?! Does Dr. Kane know who she is, Roger?!"

"No one knows who she is, except me, Derrick. If you ever find out, guess who she's going to blame it on? With the agreement broken, guess what she's going to do after that? Let her have her privacy, Derrick. You have a magnificent wife, three gorgeous children, a great job and life in abundance before you. She's serious. Take the offer and move on."

That was the first time since the telephone rang that Derrick turned toward his family. Every eye was on him. Derrick looked at Mia and Miranda and knew what the answer was to their mother's demands. Derrick's gaze touched Jocelyn, came to rest on Ian and his final question formed in his mind.

Turning his back on his family again, Derrick nervously cleared his throat and asked, "Roger, what were the results of my DNA test?"

## *CHAPTER FORTY-THREE*

Derrick and Jocelyn Dawes made settlement on their spacious, four-bedroom, split level home on Mia and Miranda's fourth birthday. They would be moving in the next day and the party was planned for the following Saturday. Derrick and Jocelyn looked so forward to being in a larger home so that they might enjoy a modicum of privacy. With Ian in their bedroom for the past five months, life had not taken on any semblance of normalcy as far as they were concerned.

However, the greatest obstacle they had to overcome in those five months was answering the never-ending questions of Mia and Miranda about their mother. Listening to Derrick on the telephone that day had spurred the questions. First, they wanted to know if they had been in Jocelyn's belly. Then, they wanted to know if they had been in Grammy's belly. Finally, they wanted to know if they had been in that lady's belly at Roger's office. Hoping to stop the questions, Derrick told them the truth. "I have absolutely no idea whose belly you guys were in. I inherited you." That made them giggle every time they thought about it and Derrick repeated it every time they asked. The fact that Mia and Miranda had no idea what inherited meant didn't matter.

All moved in and partially unpacked, Mia and Miranda's birthday party guests began to arrive on Saturday afternoon. The theme of the party was Barney, of course. Barney himself was expected to arrive to entertain the children between three and five o'clock. Sonya and Jocelyn had outdone themselves with the decorations in the yard. Bright purple and green streamers were attached to poles with huge bows, giving the yard a tented effect. Balloons were gathered in bunches and tied to purple and green baskets filled with party favor bags for the children. The tables were set in all of Barney's glory and the cake was Jocelyn's favorite character, Baby Bop.

The children ran through the yard chasing each other, squirting water and screaming. Omar and Ian were safely tucked away in the playpen. Jocelyn and Hope had to make sure Omar didn't poke one of Ian's eyes out while he inspected his new cousin. Ian seemed happy to simply have Omar in the playpen with him no matter what happened. The two had a fine time crumbling everything anyone offered them. The playpen was a mess.

When Barney appeared at three, Omar wanted out of the playpen. Hope gathered him and Jocelyn did likewise with Ian and moved closer to the festivities. Both babies were familiar with all of the Barney songs. Omar happily attempted to sing along while Ian bounced.

All of the children's eyes twinkled brightly at the sight of Barney. It wasn't until they went to sing Happy Birthday to Mia and Miranda that anyone noticed that Miranda was not among the children. Jocelyn spun around in a circle with Ian on her hip looking for her. Calling to Derrick she asked, "Where's Miranda?"

"She's not over there with you?"

"No, Derrick. Look in the house."

Knowing she was somewhere nearby, Derrick simply started to look for her. David volunteered to scan the yard while Derrick went into the house. Both brothers met again at the front door and neither had Miranda. After five minutes of searching for Miranda, the mood of the party began to change. Mia looked for her sister, calling her name the entire time and getting no answer began to whine. Derrick scooped her up and began to search in earnest.

Ten minutes passed and no one had found Miranda. The late arrival of the twins' godparents, Tyson and Cynthia, went without notice. Tyson asked one of Derrick's cousins, "Who is everyone looking for?"

"Miranda. We can't find her."

Without another word, the two joined the search. Since Derrick's property was covered by family and guests, Tyson and Cynthia moved on to the neighbor's yard. They both called and searched frantically for the missing child. No bush was too nice to disturb and no stone was left unturned. Cynthia banged trashcan lids loudly as she inspected their contents. Tyson thought he heard a child crying and told Cynthia to be quiet for a minute. Following the muffled sound, they came to a set of double green cellar doors that lay close to the ground and butted against the huge white house.

On his knees, Tyson called, "Miranda, honey, are you down there?"

He heard her wail, "Daddy! Mia! Mommy Josh! It's dark!"

Getting to his feet quickly, Tyson pulled on the door. It was locked from the inside and wasn't budging. Tyson turned to a petrified looking Cynthia and snapped, "Get on your knees and talk to her. Try to calm her down until I get Derrick over here." Before she could respond, Tyson darted for Derrick's yard on the other side of the high wooden fence.

Seeming frightened near to death, a stiff Cynthia knelt close to the cellar door and ran her hands over it as if looking for a magic latch. Hearing Miranda's pathetic whimpering made Cynthia's search more desperate. She found a tiny opening in the door just big enough to get two of her fingers through. In a tense whisper, Cynthia called, "Miranda, honey, look up. See the little hole, sweetie. Don't cry, I'm up here at the little hole."

Miranda whined, "Who are you?"

"It's Cynthia. I'm your godmother. Remember?"

"Uh huh. Tell Daddy it's dark in here. I'm scared."

Adopting Mia's pet name for her twin long ago, Cynthia said, "Don't be scared, Manda. I'm right here with you. Daddy's coming and he'll get you out of there real soon. I'll stick my finger through the hole so you can hold it, okay?"

Desperate for any confirmation that the people she heard were real, Miranda nodded and said, "Okay."

Comforted by the touch of Cynthia's fingers, Miranda asked, "Did Daddy tell you to come get me, Cynthia?"

"No, Manda. Everyone is looking for you at the party. Daddy's frantic. How did you get down there anyway?"

"Lauren told me to hide down here and she closed the door. She left me, Cynthia. Mia didn't come with me."

Sounding slightly tense, Cynthia asked, "Does Mia know you're down there, Manda?"

"No. Did God send you to get me, Cynthia?"

"Yes. No. I mean maybe. I don't know, Manda. I'm just glad I'm here."

Miranda quieted for a few seconds and asked, "Did me and Mia sleep in your tummy, Cynthia?"

Staring at the cellar door as if it had suddenly turned to flames, Cynthia answered, "No, Manda. Jocelyn is your mother. Why do you think I carried you in my tummy?"

"Because Mommy Josh didn't. Daddy didn't. Grammy didn't. Aunt Hope didn't."

As Miranda continued her list of who had not carried them in their tummy, she held onto Cynthia's fingers tightly. Derrick and every guest from the party appeared in his neighbor's yard. David went to knock. With Tyson saying the cellar door was locked, David thought it appropriate to at least ask them to open it before they tore it to smithereens. Unfortunately, there was no reply to David's thunderous knocking.

Reaching the cellar door with Cynthia leaning on it, Derrick asked in frightened succession, "Is she all right? Is she hurt? Is anyone else down there with her?"

Looking up at Derrick like a frightened squirrel, Cynthia answered, "She seems to be all right. She hasn't mentioned anything hurting and not a word about anyone being down there with her."

Hearing Miranda's voice, Mia scooted down from Derrick's arms and lay on the doors calling her sister's name. Speaking into the cellar door, Cynthia said, "Manda, let my finger go. Mia will put her finger there for you. Would you like that better?"

Miranda wailed, "No, Cynthia! Please don't leave me!"

Stroking the door as if actually comforting Miranda, Cynthia mumbled, "It's okay, sweetie. I'm not going anywhere until they get you out of there." Turning to Derrick, she hissed angrily, "Get her out of there and I don't give a damn how you do it. Just do it now."

Reaching for the handle, Derrick pulled on the door as hard as he could. It didn't budge. Using both hands he tugged at it again. There was a great moan of wood and metal, but the door didn't budge. Dropping down to inspect the door more closely, Derrick saw that the doors were not overlapped in any way and the door should not be so hard to pull open. However, the doors were so neatly crafted that it was impossible to see through them, and there had to be some type of automatic lock inside. Just as Derrick began to look around for something to pry the door with, David handed him a crowbar he had retrieved from the trunk of his car.

Propping the crowbar tip in the opening of the door, Derrick leaned on it and heard the door begin to complain. To his amazement, only one board broke free under the pressure. David and Derrick bumped heads trying to see what was holding the door shut. They both yelled, "It's a steel slide lock that can only be opened from down there!"

After rubbing his head, Derrick pried that door apart board by board until he had an opening wide enough to get his daughter out without her getting scratched. Miranda refused to relinquish Cynthia's finger before she saw Derrick's entire arm clear that opening. Climbing out of the cellar and into Derrick's arms, Miranda clung to her father and searched the surrounding faces for her sister. Seeing her panic, Cynthia picked up Mia so Miranda could see her easily and everyone headed back toward

Derrick's house. They all knew he would have to answer a lot of questions about that cellar door, but Derrick didn't care.

Back at the house, Cynthia sat on the sofa with Mia and Miranda while the twins acclimated themselves again. Derrick came and went frequently. Jocelyn sat staring at the threesome with Ian on her lap. Ready to return to the party, Mia and Miranda left the ladies and Ian in the living room.

Alone in the room with Cynthia, Jocelyn asked softly, "Why did you leave them, Cynthia?"

Looking up at Jocelyn curiously, Cynthia asked, "Why did I leave who?"

"Why did you leave Mia and Miranda at the hospital?"

"Am I being accused of being their mother again?"

"Yes, because you are their mother. I can see it clearly when the three of you are together. Physically they have your hair, the shape of your face and nose, but most of all, Miranda has your bearing of uncertainty. Why did you leave them? What were you so afraid of?"

"They don't look like me, Jocelyn. They look like Derrick and whoever their mother is."

Giving Cynthia a cynical smirk, Jocelyn said, "Your secret is safe with me. I just want to know why. Not because I want to judge you, Cynthia. More than anything, I want to understand."

Looking down at her hands, Cynthia muttered softly, "Derrick will hate me if you tell him, Jocelyn. I can't say I could blame him for it either. I was wrong to do this to him. He'll forbid me seeing the girls, too. Then I'll be forced to consider torturing Derrick and the girls even more to satisfy my own selfish needs. I know I don't deserve the title of mother, Jocelyn, I just want to be a small part of their lives."

Gathering her son in her arms, Jocelyn crossed the room and sat next to Cynthia. Stroking the distraught woman's shoulder, Jocelyn said, "Your secret is safe with me, Cynthia. The last people in this world I would hurt include Derrick, Mia and Miranda. Just tell me why."

As if her thoughts were coming from some distant place, Cynthia responded, "I was afraid of everything you have right now, because I wasn't getting it in the proper order. Oh, yes I was a college graduate. And, I had a respectable position to take care of myself, until Mr. Right came along and assumed the responsibility. I dated this potential prospect and that one. They all met the criteria set by my mother. There was only one problem—I didn't like any of them.

"Anyway, the year before I conceived the twins, I was pregnant by a man my mother thought was simply marvelous. I agreed with her until I told him I was carrying his baby. Jocelyn, he flicked that five hundred dollars at me for an abortion so fast, I think I still have the paper cuts from it.

"After that little episode I went back to dating men I thought my mother would approve of. The day I met Derrick, I didn't care what my mother thought anymore. Of course, she would have approved of him. What's there not to approve of? I went out with him to dinner once and we had a nice time. Two weeks later he asked me if I would like to be his New Year's Eve date. That's the most special night of the year and he wanted to spend it with me. I couldn't believe how lucky I was.

"Derrick and I had a fabulous time that night. Actually, I stayed with him two nights. I adored him, Jocelyn. So, I know I don't have to share my disappointment at not hearing from him again.

"I was devastated when I realized I was pregnant in March. Another abortion was out of the question. I couldn't do that to my baby or myself again. I also knew I could never share the pregnancy with my mother. Without a husband in tow, she would have disowned me ten times before the words dried on my lips. If she so much as thought I didn't know who the father was, I would have been forbidden to call her name as long as my feet rested on top of this planet.

"Being the only child of a mother who was abandoned by its father is no easy task. The disappointment in her eyes the moment I told her the same was happening to me would have been more than I could bear. 'Cynthia, please don't fall into the same trap I fell into.' If I've heard it once, I've heard it a million times. My mother had worked so hard to give me every opportunity she had missed out on. I owe her so much more than a bunch of illegitimate grandchildren.

"Don't take this all the wrong way, Jocelyn. I'm not blaming my mother for leaving the girls. She was merely one of the spokes in the wheel. One of the others was, I really did not know who the babies' father was. I hadn't had unprotected sex since I had the abortion the year before. I couldn't make myself stand in front of Derrick, or any other brother and tell him I'm carrying your child and not have any proof. If it was not his I would have looked like the biggest slut in town.

"I didn't know I was carrying twins until my ultra-sound was done in my fifth month. Double trouble. It was too late for an abortion, and I was scared to death. Derrick wasn't the only one who could have been their father and I knew the odds were against it being him. There was one guy I dated a few weeks prior to New Year's Eve. I had been with him for Christmas and once in early January. When Mia and Miranda were born so early in September, I really doubted they were Derrick's."

Looking Jocelyn in the eyes, a tormented Cynthia asked, "Is Derrick their father, Jocelyn? Roger couldn't tell me without getting his permission."

Giving Cynthia the weakest of smiles, Jocelyn answered, "If Derrick can't know that you're their mother, why should I tell you if he's their father. If he's not, you could simply ask for the girls back on those grounds."

Feeling unforgiven for what she had done, tears welled up in Cynthia's eyes and leisurely flowed down her face. With her hand over her mouth, she muttered miserably, "I just didn't know what else to do. I couldn't kill them. I couldn't relinquish them to total strangers and never know anything about them. And, I couldn't keep them. I had to choose between Derrick and the other guy. At least the girls would be with family. If not family, someone I thought would see that they were well taken care of.

Someone I could drop in on every once in a while to pacify my fears."

“Who is the person you named as mother on their birth certificates, Cynthia?”

Dropping her head in shame, Cynthia whispered, “My mother. Her maiden name is Paula Anderson.”

"Don't you think your mother would have gotten over her disappointment when she saw Mia and Miranda?"

"No, Jocelyn."

"You never gave her the opportunity."

"My mother would have been disappointed in me and my father until the day she died, Jocelyn. She would have reminded me that the two people she had loved most in this world had both let her down every chance she got. You don't know my mother."

Revealing a millimeter of her own pain, Jocelyn said, "Yes, I do know your mother. She sounds like she could be my mother's sister. No matter what you do, you will never live up to their expectations."

Openly weeping, Cynthia pleaded, "I know I never will. To make me afraid of babies, I was never taught anything about them. If I had brought Mia and Miranda home with me, I would have made the biggest mess and probably lost them to the system. Tell me I did the right thing by leaving them with Derrick, Jocelyn. Please."

Giving Cynthia’s request serious thought, Jocelyn paused, looked into the pathetically tormented eyes of the mother of her greatly loved Mia and Miranda, and said sympathetically, "You did the right thing, Cynthia. Derrick is their father."

## *CHAPTER FORTY-FOUR*

Life changed more drastically for the Dawes family that year than it had previously. There were new members, confirmed old members, new homes and new schedules. Mia and Miranda had begun school in September. Sonya had no babies to take care of because Hope's family sat with Peepers and Omar while she and David worked, and Jocelyn would not be returning to work until January of the New Year.

The thought of leaving Ian had nearly destroyed his mother emotionally. When the little fellow started walking and following his sisters everywhere, Derrick put his foot down. Jocelyn would not sit at home and turn his son into a Mama's boy. Derrick was more comfortable letting his grandmother do that to him.

As far as Derrick was concerned, there was only one unresolved issue left on his plate at the close of the year. Who was Mia and Miranda's mother? With the Agreement signed, sealed, and filed with the court, there was no doubt in Derrick's mind many years would close without his knowing the answer to that question. He often smiled at the thought of how she had lit his fire by abandoning the babies and banked it by assuring him no one would ever be able to take them away from him. However, not knowing who she was haunted Derrick even more because he would always wonder if he could have loved her as much as he loved Jocelyn, and given Mia and Miranda the family they deserved. God knows Derrick loved those two little girls and he could not fathom not loving their mother. To be able to thank her for them would have been nice, too. Derrick sincerely hoped life would be kind to her.

But, Derrick knew he couldn't have asked for a more perfect life than the one he shared with Jocelyn. Somehow, she had created a home filled with children that gave Derrick the most fulfilled and peaceful feeling he could have ever imagined. Silence, his old favorite, had only given him peace. But there was something positive to be said about recognizing the arms you wake up in every morning. He thought he would be bored by it, instead he was completely comforted by it. And, knowing he had played a part in giving Jocelyn the family she felt life would never grace her with gave Derrick great satisfaction.

On New Year's Eve, as Derrick lie in bed waiting for Jocelyn to emerge from the bathroom, Angelique fleetingly crossed his mind. Even though Roger insisted it wasn't true, Derrick still thought of her as Mia and Miranda's mother from time to time. Maybe Jocelyn was right, and he only wished they were Angelique's because he had once loved her. Knowing they were not conceived in a mutual love the way Ian was troubled Derrick deeply. The judge had been lenient with Angelique and Aaron for filing fraudulent claims. They were heavily fined and given probation. And, after the urge to strangle Angelique with his bare hands passed, Derrick had to admit he hoped life found a way to grant her heart's desires too.

Derrick's bottle of Bordeaux rested in the fluted lead crystal cooler next to Jocelyn's Chablis. The glasses were surrounded by all kinds of snacks; rows of steamed shrimp with neat lemon slices, sliced apricots and kiwi, strawberries tipped with chocolate and a bowl of whipped cream. Because there was no fireplace in this bedroom, colorful aromatic candles were all over the room. The sweet jazz was piped throughout all of the bedrooms because the children slept it to it, too.

Jocelyn finally entered the bedroom wearing a beautifully beaded, short, black nightgown that highlighted her mind-boggling breasts, accentuated her tiny waist and put her magnificent legs on display. Her glossy black hair was brushed smooth and caressed her shoulders perfectly. Her wedding ring played its own majestic melody with the candlelight and her smile created just the right amount of heat for her nearly naked husband.

As Jocelyn prepared plates for them, she smiled sweetly over her shoulder and asked, "Would you mind opening the wine, Derrick?"

Scooting off of the bed in his black briefs, Derrick stood next to his wife and opened the two bottles of wine. He filled their glasses, placed Chablis on her tray and Bordeaux on his. They each carried their own tray back to bed and placed them on the night tables. Propped up in bed by many pillows, Jocelyn and Derrick fed each other and licked whipped cream from each other's fingers and lips. They both sipped from their wine glasses and shared their flavors in a luscious deep and lingering kiss. Derrick massaged Jocelyn's waist with one hand and slid her strap down with the other. When Derrick's tongue lightly touched Jocelyn's nipple, she gave a soft hum, her eyes closed and her head drifted back slowly as his mouth smoothly engulfed it. Exploring the valley between her breasts with his nose, Derrick asked, "Are you ready to scale that wall and jump tonight, Jocelyn?"

Remembering that as the opening line from their first sexual encounter, Jocelyn replied, "As long as it's your wall, sweetheart, I'll be scaling and jumping all night."

Smiling at his wife's courageous reply, Derrick said, "Okay, start climbing, Hot Stuff. Just remember if you survive the fall you've done good."

Straddling Derrick's lap, Jocelyn nodded slowly, "Oooh, and you know how much I enjoy a good fall."

***THE END***

# THE AUTHOR

**Bernadette Y. Connor** was born and raised in North Philadelphia. While still in high school, she embarked on a musical career and was well known on the east coast as an accomplished vocalist. A graduate of a vocational school, Ms. Connor became a communications technician for AT&T, climbing telephone poles in an era when such an activity was a rarity for a woman – and, according to her co-workers, accomplishing it with perfectly-manicured nails and never a hair out of place! A divorced mother, she managed to purchase a house while her children were still young and see that they all excelled from kindergarten through college. It was this kind of determination, coupled with a compulsion to express herself, which led to her decision to achieve recognition through writing. The completion of four novels and the perfection of her craft were primarily accomplished in the wee hours of the morning while her children slept.

**ENJOYED INHERITED!**

**TRY OTHER BOOKS BY**
**BERNADETTE Y. CONNOR**

**DAMAGED!**

**ISBN 09715838-3-8**

**THE PARCEL EXPRESS**
**MURDERS**

**ISBN 09715838-1-1**